THE
EMPRESS
OF
TEMPERA

ALEX DOLAN

DIVERSIONBOOKS

Also by Alex Dolan

The Euthanist

Diversion Books
A Division of Diversion Publishing Corp.
443 Park Avenue South, Suite 1008
New York, New York 10016
www.DiversionBooks.com

For more information, email info@diversionbooks.com

First Diversion Books edition September 2016.
Print ISBN: 978-1-68230-297-2
eBook ISBN: 978-1-68230-296-5

To my parents, Philip and Virginia Dolan,
for giving me a lifelong love of the arts,
and to Sabrina, for giving me a lifelong love.

CHAPTER 1

Paire Anjou dreamed of killing Katie Novis. She sometimes imagined a bomb annihilating Katie in conflagrant florets, but in the end the world ushered her out with a quiet shuffle of papers.

Katie was a mousy girl from a family of criminals. Ripe for ruination. Ridicule had made her meek, and an easy target for bullies. On the nature channel, Katie would have been the wildebeest in the rear that couldn't haul ass fast enough. Paire Anjou couldn't stand her weakness.

Everyone in Abenaki, Maine, knew about the Novises. Families buzzed about them at their kitchen tables. They swapped gossip in churches and dog parks. In Abenaki, the Novis trial was more delicious than O.J.'s.

Lake and Cissy Novis had tarnished their daughter Katie's name while she was still an infant. Local Mainers developed hardened opinions of the girl before she learned to talk. By the time Katie reached high school, gossip clung to her like a remora. The few who dared befriend her were still ashamed to be seen with her in public, possibly worried that the same pestilence that had laid her family to waste would somehow glom onto them.

Katie hated her family name, and thus Paire did as well. Hearing the name, *Novis*, made Katie feel small, which wasn't far from the truth, because physically, she had been petite. At twelve a cornstalk, and by fourteen a cornstalk with boobs.

Today, Paire smudged Katie Novis from existence. She as good as buried her in an unmarked plot. And she did it all from inside a courtroom.

The judge was an old man with a frosted, groomed beard

and Benjamin Franklin bifocals. He didn't smile easily, and his rudimentary questions sounded more like accusations.

When he asked Katie Novis why she wished to change her name, Paire Anjou replied, "I'm an artist." It was the simplest explanation.

The judge stewed over the new name. He made her spell it, perhaps wondering if she was pranking the court system, and had somehow made it past gatekeepers who were supposed to ferret out this sort of bullshit. But he approved it just the same. In less than ten minutes, Paire received a notarized copy of a document printed with her new name. She hadn't been this happy in years. Maybe ever.

Drunk from endorphins, Paire bounce-stepped across the park as if she'd beaten cancer. Officially—even legally—she had disappeared Katie Novis. In the hardly notable void that Katie had left, she'd created a new girl. Paire Anjou. This was her transformation. The butterfly burst from the cocoon in a patchwork of tropical greens and yellows, drawing stares from strangers as her chin tilted toward the toothy horizon of flat rooftops along the perimeter of Union Square.

It was April, and stray cherry trees blossomed in the park. They would drip pink shags and shed themselves bare a few weeks from now. Paire was comfortable in her dress, and remembered that weather this warm wouldn't hit Maine for another month. Here in New York she felt a sense of grandeur, both in her new name and in the city itself, where after years of eyeballing photos of Manhattan, even the gum-stained sidewalks took on an air of celebrity. Her imagination sparkled at the possibilities.

Paire acted like a tourist, but she might as well have been one, because she'd lived in New York for only about two years. Closing in on the end of her second school year. None of this felt like home yet, but that was good. Home was where people javelined Katie Novis with insults, or stuffed dead lobsters into her locker to shame her.

Manhattanites didn't know about Katie Novis. Paire had adopted her new name since she'd entered the Manhattan School of Art and Design, known as MSAD to the student body. In New

York, Paire could lose herself in the endless crop of people. Every morning a new batch of faces. They smiled at Paire because she was pretty. They admired her petite pixie figure, slim all around except for flipper hands and feet, and grapefruit breasts. She wasn't *too skinny* here. Her nose wasn't *hooked*. In Abenaki she'd learned to round her shoulders to diminish her chest. In New York she pinched together her shoulder blades to push it out. In the city, she felt both cherished and anonymous.

During her time here, Paire had changed the way she dressed, from skin-sheltering black tees and jeans to wild, form-fitting dresses that let her gams loose. Today she wore a body-hugging dress, chosen because the green in the fabric matched her favorite painting of all time, *Portrait of a Young Girl in a Green Dress*, from her favorite artist, deco painter Tamara de Lempicka. Within a few months of matriculation at MSAD, she had dyed her hair a deep burgundy and styled it in robust curls, resembling a 1940s pinup girl. She'd taught herself how to smile, something Katie rarely did in Maine. This sounds like an overstatement, but in truth, she'd had to practice in a mirror until she could roll her lips appropriately, so she didn't expose her teeth like a bonobo. Instead of the lemon-puckers she was used to in Abenaki, people smiled back. Born again as a stranger among all of these friendly foreigners, she finally felt normal.

Paire guarded her old name like it was a nuclear launch code. No one here could know about Katie Novis. She never said her name aloud. A professor had called roll under her old name before she'd swapped it out, and Paire simply ignored her as the woman repeated the name over and over again in a reverberant lecture hall.

The history of Katie Novis was hard to find, but the intrepid web researcher could root it out. If someone searched for her, they might uncover a few tabloid-quality articles from her parents' trial. The articles were all published before the internet blew up, but sometimes enthusiasts scanned the print versions and posted them on true crime blogs.

For the most part, she had been able to keep that name off

tongues in New York. But when she signed her lease, she had to use her old name. Until one month ago, she'd lived in Park Slope with a couple named Hayden and Emily. They were in their mid-twenties and both worked in digital advertising. They had been roommates in a two-bedroom for two years, until they got drunk and slept together. As a couple they only occupied a single bedroom, and they rented the other out, usually to students like Paire who would tolerate a breadbox just for the privilege of bedding down in the greater metro. Eventually, the two were curious enough to Google their sublessee. During a dispute over who was leaving the cordless phone off the charger and draining the battery, Hayden had blurted it out: "*Lobster Baby.*"

Paire had moved out that evening.

For three nights she stayed at a bedbuggy hostel, until Derek Rosewood invited her to move into his apartment. They'd only been dating nine months, but it was her longest romantic relationship. Paire didn't know how deeply connected she felt to Rosewood but she jumped at the chance. This was another opportunity in a chain of new experiences. She had a boyfriend who was impressed with her, enough to invite her to live with him.

This meant having someone to dote on. So after she finished disposing of Katie Novis, she showed her devotion to Derek Rosewood by heading to the Fern Gallery, which was getting ready to showcase his new exhibit.

Rosewood was an artist, like her. But bigger, like she wanted to be.

Moreover, he understood why Paire would want to change her identity. He stressed how important personal freedom was for an artist. "Creativity springs from individuality, and individuality springs from independence," he'd told her. "In the end, autonomy is your most valuable possession." She felt like he knew what made her gears turn. Maybe that was what made him special.

She walked down Eighteenth. From down the block, she saw a man, just a speck at that distance, looking through the window of the Fern Gallery at the artwork inside. All alone on a quiet street full of residential brownstones. Other than the Fern, there was nothing to warrant gawking, unless someone decided to change clothes without the blinds drawn.

From the end of the block, she snapped a photo of him with her phone.

The Fern Gallery had about the same size and reputation of the thicket of art spaces in Chelsea, but it sat as a remote outpost in the Flatiron District, fairly close to MSAD. While no street in New York was ever barren, this stretch of Eighteenth didn't attract the cattle crowds that were half a block away on Seventh Avenue. This made the gallery seem more exclusive, and less like a tourist attraction. Because it was so close to the school, the gallery occasionally curated shows that might be popular among the students. A buzzworthy installation of Derek Rosewood made sense. Rosewood was supposed to be there to help with the installation, and Paire was curious to see which piece the gallery would hang in the front window.

Derek Rosewood was best known as a guerrilla artist. Paire had seen his work a decade ago without realizing it was his. He had risen to fame largely through a graffiti experiment called the *WANTED* campaign. Throughout major American cities, the campaign slapped stickers on lampposts, street signs, bathroom stalls, subway turnstiles, and any vacant public space where a two-by-two-inch sticker might affix. The sticker depicted a mug shot of actor Paul Reubens, better known as Pee-wee Herman, after he had been arrested for masturbating in a movie theater in 1991. Reubens was stylized in a black-and-white graphic, making his expression seem even more forlorn than the actual police mug shot. Above the photo, the sample caption read *WANTED*, the block letters reminiscent of Barbara Kruger's sans serif mock advertising type. Before she'd even met Rosewood, Paire found one of these in a coffeehouse in Portland. Later, they spread to Abenaki. A student had pasted one to Katie Novis's locker, where it sat askew like a lost starfish for most of her senior year, its relation to the taboo topic of masturbation no doubt intended to be its own insult.

The Guantanamo Bay detention camp had inspired Rosewood's *WANTED* campaign. The prison was established in 2002, and the artist's sticker campaign started a few months later. Rosewood wanted to spar with the government about how easy it was to vilify public figures. The night she first met Rosewood, he got tipsy and, to impress her, spoke as if he were giving an interview. He said, "We live in a country where people can fall under suspicion and disappear. This isn't Soviet Russia. It's right here, happening right under our noses. I wanted to remind people how easy it can be to have the world turn against you, like it did for Reubens. And I wanted to make people laugh. Humor gives people the courage to deal with their fears." He added, "I've got nothing against Paul Reubens. Pee-wee Herman gave me my boyhood."

She liked Rosewood, and wanted to impress him back by being thoughtful. "Are you trying to send a message or provoke discussion?"

"I want people to think for themselves, not tell them what to think."

As Paire closed in on the Fern, the man outside the gallery grew into a trim hunchback silhouette. He hadn't moved since Paire had first seen him. His rigidity interested her, and she took another photo of him as she walked closer, confident that he wouldn't catch her stealing his image. A timeless quality wafted from him, as if he were ancient steel that had been forged and aged in the elements. Like he'd always been on this sidewalk. Drawn by whatever was on the other side of that window.

For days, Paire had been aching to know what piece they were going to put in that window. Rosewood and the gallery had simmered through a disagreement on what the window should display. "They'll take it wrong. They always do," he'd said after he bickered with them on the phone.

The Fern Gallery wanted to hang a piece called *HERO*. He had completed the piece in January 2007, just after Saddam Hussein had been executed. Rendered on the silkscreen with his typical propaganda poster aesthetic, the graphic showed Perseus holding up a crudely severed gorgon head. Except instead of Medusa's, it was Hussein's. Same type treatment as always. Unlike the *WANTED* campaign, this particular piece had a clear message. The artist wished to shame any ghoulish Madame Defarges who took glee from the dictator's hanging. Of course, that last bit was Paire's analogy. Rosewood had never read Dickens.

Rosewood was sure his intent was obvious, but people misinterpreted the piece. For *HERO*, rednecks and war-whoopers appropriated the image as jingoistic icon. *HERO* bumper stickers rode the backs of trucks next to hunting racks and Confederate flags. A conservative news network purchased rights to the image, and showed it before a segment that covered American military actions in Iraq and Afghanistan. While Rosewood never divulged his sentiments on the record, he was ashamed of how his vision had been reinterpreted.

As she approached, Paire got a better look at the old man hunched by the glass. He was frail, with wispy white hair and sunken cheeks. He wore a charcoal suit that looked clean but had probably fit him better ten years ago, and now hung loosely around the arms and shoulders. When he finally moved, he rubbed his mouth slowly, possibly trying to comprehend the meaning of the art in the window. If they'd ended up hanging *HERO* in the window, possibly he was just shocked by the severed head. The way his jaw hinged, Paire thought he might be crazy—there were certainly enough crazy folks in the city. But he definitely wasn't homeless. His suit had been pressed, his wing tips polished. She hesitated before taking the next shot, this time without focusing, and she felt slightly guilty afterward. Something was wrong with him—she could tell that much even from this distance.

Instead of *HERO*, Rosewood had wanted to install a new piece called *TRUTH HURTS*. It was a graphic portrait of Edward Snowden, the former NSA computer pro who had spilled surveillance tidbits to the press. The press were still talking about Snowden, so Rosewood thought it would be timely. It would ignite the sort of discussion he wanted to create. Rosewood didn't have a message he was pushing with this one, so there would be no misinterpretation of the artist's intent. "Even though, between you and me, I side with Snowden," he'd confessed to Paire from the next pillow. "In another country, at another time, I'd be the one the government would throw under the bus."

The old man took a shuffling step toward the window, close enough to breathe on it. His face quivered, but Paire couldn't read his expression. It might have been sadness or anger. Whatever it was, he seemed volatile. Were this a younger man, Paire might have thought he was dangerous. But he was so delicate and moved so slowly, she kept moving toward him. She noticed how loud her heels pounded on the pavement, and she lightened her footsteps so she wouldn't jar the man from his reverie. He placed a palm on the window, the way prison guests might try to console inmates during visiting hours.

Paire wondered if *TRUTH HURTS* hung in the window. She couldn't see from this angle. The way the old man stared, she wondered if he might be fighting to recognize the man in the piece. Snowden was a common-looking white man with a trimmed goatee and the semi-rimless spectacles one saw on every other tech professional in New York. In fact, her ex-roommate Hayden wore glasses like that. The *TRUTH HURTS* canvas was big, bigger than *HERO*. When it stood against Rosewood's studio wall, it rose to Paire's nipples. Borrowing some of Warhol's palette, the portrait pigmented Snowden in lavender and gold, giving him the superstar treatment. Given the style, Paire wondered if the man might vaguely recognize the face, but not be able to place it.

Paire wondered if this man might work for the Fern Gallery. Maybe he was some kind of curator emeritus they brought on to make sure the installation had the appropriate feng shui, or at least that the corners weren't sagging. Now within speaking distance, Paire opened her mouth, ready to say something to him. She might have called out a friendly hello, since she was headed to his gallery anyway. But the man's face changed. His eyes fixed on the glass, the wrinkles around them deepened, and his face collapsed around a deep frown. A half a block away, his squinting had struck her as curiosity. This close, it was clear that the old man was fighting back emotion. He started crying. His small hunched back folded, and he cradled his face in one hand while the other braced himself against the window.

She had never been so affected by Rosewood's campy graphics, nor had she ever seen anyone who wept for them. If *HERO* hung in the window, she supposed Saddam Hussein's head could have stirred up some emotion. Maybe this was a veteran. He was too old for Desert Storm, even for Vietnam. Maybe he'd served in Korea. Saddam Hussein might have been enough of a trigger to remind him of his combat days, and how he couldn't escape the violence, even when passing by an art gallery. She wanted to comfort him. However, she'd learned the hard way that running up to someone on the street in New York was always treated as a potential threat, even when it was someone like Paire, who weighed just north of one hundred pounds. Because of her own background in Maine, she tended to mirror the emotions of those who were traumatized. She saw someone sad, and her own heart sank.

Paire drew close enough to hear him. Making the only sounds on the street, he moaned, giving the faintest indications of a tremulous voice pitched lower than she expected for a man his size. She could see now that he hadn't shaved in a few days. White hairs faintly barnacled his chin. He smeared his nostrils on his suit sleeve. What struck her the most was that this man didn't notice her, as close as she was. In New York, people tended to notice Paire. Maybe it was the peacock colors—the clothes, the hair, the cleavage. Regardless, the old man ignored her. When he took his face out of his hand, he just stared back through the window.

Though she was only a few paces away, the sun glared off the window so she couldn't see inside the gallery. Rosewood and crew might have been inside right now, staring out at them. A reverse exhibit. This close, she could smell a mothball scent, and a subtle body stink. She wondered how long he'd been out here, marveling at this window. She considered that whoever he was, crazy or not, he might be unsafe to approach. Yet she approached anyway. Years of being picked on gave her empathy for strangers. She wanted to provide the comfort no one had offered her when she was dirty little scrap Katie Novis.

A pair of eyeglasses lay at his feet. Presumably, he'd dropped them. They were old and broken like the rest of him. One of the lenses had chipped. Paire stooped and scooped up his glasses, then offered them back to him. "Here you go." The sound of her voice startled him, and he lethargically turned his head. She gave him one of her practiced smiles and repeated, "Here you go."

A hand with dirt-etched nails took the glasses. She wondered how much he could see without them. If whatever was behind the glass might have been a blur to him now, just recognizable by colors and contours.

A deep whisper came out. "Thank you." He seemed as fragile as spun sugar as he pocketed the glasses, and his hands disappeared into his pockets. Understanding from the way his focus floated in the air around her that the man couldn't see clearly, Paire inspected him more closely. A dirty man in a nice suit. She could tell the cut and fabric were expensive, even if the garment itself had aged. His eyes trailed back to the window, and his nostrils flared as he exhaled a moist, tragic gust.

Then he moved quick. His hands came out of his pockets, and he pounded his chest once, the way men pound their ribs to dislodge phlegm. He wheezed. After his hand dropped to his side, Paire saw the stain on his shirt. Blossoming red. Something fell from his hand. Paire only registered it when the object rattled on the sidewalk. A long, elegant silver letter opener. Minute letters monogrammed the handle, most of it slicked red.

The man wheezed in tubercular coughs, but he turned back to the window, again bracing himself against the glass. His hand smeared blood on the pane. He stared at his reflection as his chest flowered a gush of deep, rich blood. A thick river spread down his shirt, over his sterling buckle and through the trousers. He'd scored an artery.

Paire calcified, as rigidly rooted as the man had been, as if some magnet beneath the sidewalk pinned them both to their spots. The man held himself up for only a few seconds, then collapsed. She screamed.

When he dropped, she knelt beside him and pressed on his chest. Rather than giving him chest compressions, she placed fingers at the entrance wound, trying to dam up the dike. Blood flowed through her fingers. When she applied pressure, some of it sprayed on her dress. For a few moments, the man stayed with her, his eyes open long enough for him to shoot her a look that questioned her audacity. Distantly, Paire heard someone scream, from a block away or perhaps through a window.

He expired under her hands in moments. When his eyes fogged in death, she looked up and away. Her hands were shaking, and the man's gore ran up her forearms. She looked at the window, where his bloody handprint had smeared the glass. Behind it, Paire finally saw what hung in the window. Neither *HERO* nor *TRUTH HURTS*. It was Her.

The Empress. Painted on a canvas almost as tall as Paire, the woman was nearly life-sized. Maybe a few years older than she, dressed in a single garment, a red ornamental kimono with lilies climbing up the front in a sinuous pattern. She was seated on a chair, her legs spread beneath the silk. The wardrobe hinted that this was an ancient woman, long dead, but she'd been rendered by a modern painter. Her expression was self-aware, defiant. Modern. And her ethnicity wasn't clear. The woman might have been Japanese, maybe Chinese, doubtfully Korean, but her eyes were wider than Asian, with deep brown irises and black moon pupils, so large they almost obscured the whites. Subtle brushstrokes had given her smooth skin a hint of lifelike blush. Her bare hands and feet suggested a light body like Paire's, with long fingers and seductive arches.

She heard the approach of footfalls and clamor of voices, but her mind was a soup and she heard it all through liquid. Unaware of her actions, Paire rose in a waking sleep and pressed her own red hand on the glass, matching the old man's right handprint with her left. Even with the limp man by her feet, she couldn't look away.

CHAPTER 2

A thin, handsome man in a neat suit pulled her off the sidewalk. She'd seen him before when she nosed into the gallery. He always wore inventive fabrics, all snugly tailored. His salt-and-pepper hair corkscrewed wildly, and he manicured his beard. They had said hello in passing. She sensed that he was the manager or owner of the gallery, but they'd never spoken. When Rosewood bickered on the phone about the exhibit, she suspected it was with this man.

When he found Paire on the sidewalk, he introduced himself as Mayer Wolff. Paire was still shaking. She tried not to touch herself, because her hands and clothes were soaked in blood, and her hands didn't know where to go, so they trembled in the air. Ambulance sirens cut through the air blocks away, on their way but not there yet. Mayer threw his pinstripe jacket over Paire's shoulders and led her inside.

Mayer recognized her too. "Do I know you?"

Paire shook her head so they wouldn't have to make conversation.

She hadn't been confronted by violence like this since, well, since Maine, and she rolled her shoulders forward, the habit she'd acquired as a bullied tween in shitty little Abenaki. As Mayer Wolff led her into the gallery, she felt exposed. At this moment, Paire Anjou forgot she had just changed her name.

With her senses overloaded, Paire noticed movement around her without really absorbing it. The sign for the Fern Gallery, a green sprig, passed above her. The empress was the only painting that directly faced the window, mounted on a stand-alone wall with a six-foot alley between the art and the glass. As they passed by it she looked at the portrait bashfully, almost afraid it would catch her staring. She was in shock from what had just occurred outside but couldn't help her visceral reaction to the image. Possibly because she was in shock, she sought the opportunity to distract herself from seeing all that blood. Paire felt a turbulent rush in her stomach when her eyes found the portrait. The hands and feet, so elegant. The figure, so effortlessly poised.

Paire stared at the painting as long as she could as she walked past it, trying to see what had mesmerized the old man. The artist had used a bright palette and that red was bold as a fishing lure. Paire admired the craftsmanship, the technique behind the boldness, the control in the brush strokes. The woman's face was smooth, with a cold angelic paleness that seemed to have never seen the sun. Her robe was intricately detailed with minute strokes, adding an etched quality and including a few strands of gold thread at the bottom of the kimono where the hem was about to fray. It wasn't just that it was beautiful—*and God, it was*—it was that this was the sort of painting Paire would want to create had she the technique and the talent for capturing human expression.

Only after they passed the portrait did she take in the rest of the gallery. The two-story cathedral hall was floored with pine planks and walled with white plaster. Drenched in sunlight, the space had housed a sizeable assortment of postwar contemporary art during her last visit. She hadn't walked past the gallery in months, but all those works were gone. Technically, the gallery was closed while they installed Rosewood's show. Some works had already been mounted, and some leaned against the walls waiting to be hung. She recognized the large blocks of primary colors without studying individual pieces. At the back of the room, wooden shipping crates were stacked on a pallet.

A large man stood by the back wall, watching her with unblinking eyes. He was bulky, shaped like a pineapple, a marbled mix of fat and muscle. She wondered how many of them had been watching the front window when the man stabbed himself in the heart, and why it took them so long to react.

Paire was too curious to avoid looking over her shoulder to see the small crowd outside the window, who had wandered down from Seventh Avenue once they heard her scream. The gallery window offered a view of the dead hump on the sidewalk and the two bloody handprints on the glass. The blood was so bright, so stark against Manhattan's landscape of gray. The same red stippled her clothes.

Mayer sat her at a black swivel chair by a glass-top desk, clear except for a mega-monitor, keyboard, and a stack of papers with edges tight as a wrapped deck of playing cards.

Trace scents of paint hung in the air. She'd gotten used to these odors in her classrooms at school, and although it was fainter, older here, she could still identify the smells of dried oils.

He asked, "Did you know him?"

Paire shook her head. "I thought he might work here." Her voice was scratchy from screaming.

"Were you just walking by?" Mayer asked.

Paire didn't know how to answer that. She wanted to leave as soon as possible. Flight had served her well in response to adversity. There was no sign of Rosewood. *Where was he*, she wondered. She needed him. Her hands were shaking, and she needed him. But Paire sensed that if she admitted to coming here to see Derek Rosewood, it would only complicate matters and keep her trapped here longer.

"Didn't you see me?" she asked.

"I was in the back," Mayer said, looking Paire in the eyes.

She thought he was probably a kind man.

The large man against the wall said, "I saw everything." Paire detected no such warmth from him, a pink-faced older man with thin lips and bullet-hole eyes. Tall and bullishly bloated. His navy suit looked expensive, tailored in the utilitarian cut found on finance professionals. Possibly Brooks Brothers, probably custom. He tugged at his cufflinks and smoothed out the front of his suit jacket. His slick gray hair whitened at the temples, and a strong, square jaw was clearly delineated beneath the chin fat. His hands were thick, walnut-cracking vises, and under his suit she detected the muscles that had formed decades ago.

Sirens whined outside as an ambulance lurched to a halt on

the other side of the window. Two EMTs jumped out and hauled a wheeled gurney out of the back.

At the far wall, where the large man leaned and eyed Paire, a door opened to a rear office. Through the crack, Paire glimpsed shelves of pine crates.

A woman walked out from the back and approached Mayer at the desk. She was young, within a year or two of Paire's age. Petite too. She'd tied her hair in a French twist and wore a form-fitting, leg-revealing suit. She spoke to Mayer, sharp and angry—"I don't work here anymore"—and placed a magnetic security card and a few keys on the glass-top desk.

As she strutted out, Mayer made no effort to stop her. He and Paire watched her slip out the front door.

"Is that going to cause a problem for you?" Paire asked.

He shrugged. "Not a problem worth fixing. She's only been here two months, and was miserable the whole time. You can't please everyone."

Outside, the EMTs raised the gurney from ground to waist height. They'd tucked a white cloth tightly around the man's body, obscuring the head. Among the crowd of onlookers, a male college student videoed the scene on his phone.

She stared at her ankles. Blood freckled her dress and legs. When she rubbed a drop on her skin, it smudged. Paire shivered, and Mayer adjusted his jacket on her shoulders.

Another woman came through the rear office door, this time a blonde in a fitted black dress. She had the same trim, polished look and tied-back hair as the woman who had just quit, but she was more mature—Mayer's age.

Paire was worried that this woman would resign as well, but when she approached she gently smiled at Paire, revealing a mouth full of braces. The woman handed her a glass of water and introduced herself. "Lucia de Moraeas."

Paire didn't take the glass at first, showing a palm coated in blood, but when Lucia nudged her, she accepted the water.

Mayer asked Lucia, "Could you take her to the bathroom?"

Paire said, "I don't need to go."

He said to Lucia, "She's in shock. Take her in the back."

Lucia beckoned and Paire followed her to the back office. Her head still spun, and the room came in and out of focus, the noise outside fading in and out of clarity. She followed the grain of the floorboards, then raised her eyes to the woman's snug black dress and the effortless sway of her hips. When Paire walked with confidence she bounded on her toes, but her hips never moved like this.

They passed through the back office, a tight room the width of the gallery. Plywood and pine catacomb slabs held the Fern's remaining inventory. Paire supposed some of the postwar exhibit might have been boxed up back here. On the other side, a small desk and clip lamp stood by a heavy steel door, which presumably led out to the back alley.

"I think we have clothes," said Lucia.

Through another door, they continued to a small bright bathroom and stood at a porcelain sink. Lucia twisted the faucet and checked the warmth of the water before pulling Paire's hands into the stream. A diamond the size of a hazelnut sat on the woman's ring finger. Absently, Paire tapped the jewel with a finger.

Lucia remarked, "Don't place too much stock in these. It's just a mineral." In the mirror, Lucia tapped her braces. "But he did pay for these." She pointed to towels hanging on the opposite wall. "Use as many as you need. We'll buy new ones." Lucia said she would try to find some spare clothes, guessing Paire's dress size accurately before leaving her alone with the light hiss of tap water.

Paire threw the deadbolt and stripped down to her underwear while she rubbed the liquid soap into suds. The blood on her skin smeared, then slowly thinned, rouging her before coming clean. It wasn't going to come off all in one cleaning. In fact, she might need several soaks and showers to get all of it off, maybe more before she *felt* clean again. She sat on the toilet, lid closed, and tried to mop off as much as she could, monitoring the fading shades of crimson on her body and the deepening stains on the white terrycloth.

She heard more sirens, slightly muffled back here. Another car pulled up outside and the noise ended with an abrupt tweet. Footfalls on the pine floors sounded all the way back to the bathroom. She guessed several people had come into the gallery, mostly men, judging by the weight of their heels. One man had an exceptionally loud voice, and seemed to be arguing with Mayer. He sounded like the large man who had been leaning against the back wall. Back at the sink she turned up the water and tuned out the voices so they sounded like party murmurs.

The restroom had been intended for exclusive use by the staff. The décor resembled a bathroom in an upscale residence—literature by the toilet and a shelving unit with candles and plants. Trinkets littered the counter space around the sink, almost giving the impression of a voodoo altar. Paire casually inventoried the knickknacks—spare lipsticks, eyeliners, brushes, a comb, tweezers, dice, pens, and notably, a leopard-print clutch purse that contained two condoms. Ribbed, glow-in-the-dark. She imagined they might look like glow sticks when in use.

Paire listened to the murmurs outside, what sounded like Mayer recounting the last hour's happenings to whoever had just entered. Staring at herself in the mirror, she felt more like Katie Novis than Paire Anjou, once the clothes were off and the makeup was wiped clean. Her fingers crept into the leopard-print clutch and she withdrew a condom between her first two fingers, holding it like a cigarette. She tucked it into her own purse, inside her own wallet, where it snuggled against the New York State ID with her old Maine name on it. The condom was worth less than a dollar, and she chose to steal it because out of everything, she thought they would miss it the least.

Once the condom was in her purse, though, she immediately felt queasy that she'd done it. It was a tiny action, intended to placate herself by doing something that seemed a familiar behavior, but she still knew it was wrong. A moment later she opened her purse to replace the condom, but the door rattled.

Lucia called, "You okay in there?"

Paire panicked and placed the purse by her feet. She unlocked the door and opened it a crack. Lucia's hand, sporting that giant diamond, reached in with a hanger of clothes and a pair of shoes. Paire pulled them on in a hurry—a navy A-line dress and black pumps with a shorter heel than she would normally wear. She smelled the freshness of the dress, and felt the way her feet bent the leather, and she knew the clothes were new. Lucia and Mayer had bought these for her, likely from a shop nearby. Not cheap, not in this neighborhood.

When she stepped out of the bathroom, Lucia told her she looked great, and with a spare towel, wiped a little more of the moisture out of her hair. Paire thanked her by wrapping her arms around the older woman.

When they returned to the gallery, Mayer was locked in conversation with two uniformed NYPD officers, one of whom scripted notes while he listened. Two young men, one of Asian and the other of African descent. Both had bulky shoulders and hair trimmed a quarter inch from bald. They reminded Paire of guys she might meet at a club.

Lucia tried to hand a scrap of paper, which Paire identified as a sales receipt, to Mayer, probably for the clothes she was wearing. Before Mayer could take it, the large man appeared from behind and snatched it out of Lucia's hand. He towered a head and a half above Paire.

The police turned their attention to her. The officer without the notebook asked, "You found him?"

The big man answered for Paire. "Found him? She watched it all. Did everything but kill him herself." His voice was so much louder than everyone else's. "Sure you didn't know him?" he asked Paire, taking over the role of interrogator.

"She didn't know him," Mayer said. "No one here knew him." He crossed his arms and kept his distance.

Lucia stood behind Mayer, even further removed.

Ignoring the police, the pink man asked Mayer, "What are you going to do about Georgia?"

Paire heard herself ask, "Who's Georgia?"

Mayer said, "The woman who quit."

"Leaving you minus one employee the day before the opening. How's that going to work?"

The officer with the notebook felt compelled to ask, "Did this Georgia know the man outside?"

The banker answered as if all of this bored him. "She didn't know him. Mayer didn't know him, Lucia didn't know him, and whoever *this* is didn't know him. No one here knew him. If you want to know why that man killed himself, look into his background and you'll probably find a long history of emotional distress." He turned back to Mayer, about to speak, when he realized that the officers hadn't gone anywhere. "We've said everything we have to say on the subject. You have our contact information. You can leave us."

One of the cops pointed at Paire. "We don't have her information."

The banker looked at Paire. "Well, give it to them!"

Mayer gritted his teeth at the banker, but didn't protest. Lucia found a stack of Post-Its and a pen, and Paire scribbled a name and cell number.

One cop led her aside and asked her to describe the incident while his partner took notes. Steps away, Mayer engaged in heated whispers with the banker. Lucia busied herself across the room with the shipping crates, pulling out more framed Rosewoods for the exhibit. They tried to pretend a man hadn't just died in front of them.

Paire told them what she could remember. She asked what the man's name was, but they hadn't found any identification. She showed the officers her phone images, and emailed them to one of the cops in case they could use them.

As they spoke to her, Paire slipped a hand into her purse and felt the condom between her fingers as if it were a charm. She'd never fainted, so she didn't know how her body would feel before going limp. But it might have felt like this—the chilly sweat on the forehead, the weak hands, too weak to make a fist even if she tried.

Surreptitiously, Paire sniffed herself, and even in the new clothes she smelled briny from the blood.

When they were finished, one of the officers said, "I'm sorry you had to see this, Katherine."

Paire cringed. They called her by the name on her Maine license.

The police left her at the side of the gallery, away from Mayer and the banker as they volleyed heated words, and on the other side of the room from Lucia. Paire pulled out her cell phone, and on the sly took a photo of the big man. His face had the hue of boiled ham. She sent it to Rosewood with the message: *At the Fern waiting for you. Get me away from this man.* She didn't want to say much else, especially about the dead man. She just wanted to leave, and she couldn't just walk out. The two cops were combing over their notes by the front door to make sure they'd asked all the right people all the right questions.

Lucia circled the room, keeping as much distance from the banker as possible. When she got to Paire, she said, "You can go home soon, and this will be over. I promise."

Paire was grateful for her warmth. She thought that when the braces came off, Lucia would have a beautiful smile. "I've never seen anyone die before," she said. Even with her family history, this was true.

"I know, honey," Lucia said, rubbing her back.

Paire asked about the man arguing with Mayer. "Is that your lawyer or something?"

Lucia smirked at the notion. "His name is Abel Kasson." She said his name hesitantly, as if repeating a curse. "He's not with the gallery."

"Who is he?"

"Money. And that's all he is."

"Where the hell is Rosewood anyway?" Abel Kasson asked Mayer, loud enough to hear from across the room.

Paire wondered herself.

The two police officers excused themselves and stepped outside the gallery, where they commenced talking to the bystanders who still clustered around the window. A few of them stared at the painting instead of the bloodstains on the sidewalk.

With the Fern free of law enforcement, Abel Kasson raised his voice to Mayer. "You know why that person killed himself? All you have to do is stare into that painting for five minutes to figure it out. I've told you for weeks to take that thing down."

Mayer's voice strained to remain calm. "You don't own this gallery."

"For the next month, I might as well own it. Now take it down before it kills someone else." Kasson gestured to Paire from across the room as if she were a prop. "I saw the way she was looking at it. She'll be next."

This stirred up serious ire in Paire. Abel Kasson might be the first bully she had met in New York. His combination of contempt and dismissal reminded her of the vermin she'd encountered in Abenaki. Her spine straightened, and for the first time since she arrived at the gallery she found the clear, bold voice she had adopted in Manhattan. With Paire Anjou's voice, she called to Kasson, "Who the fuck are you?"

Her brashness made the man smile. Perhaps he thrived on conflict. In her experience, some bullies needed adversaries. He said, "Tomorrow night, a new exhibition of the acclaimed guerrilla artist Derek Rosewood will delight critics and crowds alike. And I'll be the one who made that happen."

"A man just died," Paire said.

"Not my business. Not your business." He pointed to the shipping crates. "See those? That's my business."

Her mouth twitched as she considered that this man might have some connection to Rosewood. Her phone pinged.

Rosewood had texted her back: *Meet me towards Seventh. Idling.*

She was confused. Rosewood was supposed to be here, but he wasn't. Nor was he going to come and get her. Just the same, this was an excuse to leave, and she would have taken any.

Kasson spoke to the gallery owner. He pointed out the window at the lingering crowd. "In an hour or two, all those people will be gone, and by morning, with a little pressurized spray, so will the stain on the sidewalk." Mayer glanced at Paire, and when Kasson caught him looking, the big man said, "This person isn't worth consideration."

Rosewood pinged Paire again. *At a hydrant.*

Paire took this moment to bid her farewells. She walked to Mayer and grabbed his hand before hugging Lucia one more time. "Thank you for the kindness."

Third ping from Rosewood: *Don't tell anyone I'm here.*

"No thank yous for me, I suppose," said Kasson. When Paire curiously cocked her head at him, he explained, "For the clothes."

Of course she'd seen Kasson snatch the receipt, but she hadn't fully considered that he'd paid for her dress and shoes.

Paire Anjou had been blessed with the art of defiance. Facing Abel Kasson, she kicked off one shoe at a time. They rested on the floor straight on their heels, perfect as a store display. She slipped the dress off her shoulders, unzipped the side, and let it tumble around her ankles. Without taking her eyes off his, she stood in her ivory underwear, the tops and bottoms still stained with a few spots of blood. With the banker struck mute, she turned and proceeded out of the gallery, clutching her purse beneath her arm. Her barefoot steps were inaudible, and she felt somnambulant as she passed through the crowd to Rosewood's idling taxi.

CHAPTER 3

On the ride back to Brooklyn, Rosewood had given her his T-shirt, so he was nude from the waist up and she below the hips. Rosewood was thin without being skinny. Only the tiniest fold of flesh rippled against the top of his trousers, where a wispy trail of sandy hair continued from where his zipper ended up to his navel. He cradled her head in his hand, and his touch stopped her from trembling.

This chivalry had been part of Paire's immediate attraction to Rosewood, because he was so different from the boys she knew in Abenaki. New Englanders were predisposed to a raw-edged rudeness, and Rosewood was painfully polite, greeting her with a "Ma'am," or sometimes more cheekily, "Good morning, Miss Anjou." Rosewood had spent the largest chunk of his childhood in Virginia, and he still carried a bit of the accent. When he was playful, the accent thickened.

She liked that he didn't sound like a boy from Abenaki. There were no rude taunts, no compliments that seemed like threats about her tight ass, certainly no waggling his wormy cock at her like the captain of the lacrosse team had in her junior year. Rosewood's manners seemed all the more alien to a girl like Paire, who expected some degree of cruelty from boys.

Paire rushed through the blunt details of what had happened at the Fern Gallery. Rosewood occasionally diverted his attention to the blood on her underwear and the smudges on her skin that hadn't come clean. He reached out to touch her leg, and she pulled it away at first, then gradually extended it to let him place warm knuckles over her knee.

Rosewood smiled easily with a large Anglican grin, the kind of horse-toothed smile she associated with tabloid photos of Prince William. When she saw his teeth Paire's heart quickened, and she was throbbing now something awful—part pheromones, part adrenal overload from the Fern. Possibly the lingering memory of that painting as well. Whatever brought them on, pheromones got to work in the back of the taxi, surging as their skin brushed and eyes met. She could be angry that he hadn't been at the gallery when he was supposed to be, but she didn't bring it up. Paire was new at boys, and thought a show of temper might jeopardize the relationship.

"You just let the dress drop," he said.

"It's not a big deal. I'm *au naturale* when I do studio modeling."

Their jowly driver peeked into the rearview at her, but there was nothing to see now that Rosewood's shirt covered her.

The taxi drove past the midpoint of the Brooklyn Bridge. Rosewood squeezed her knee, and her fingers crept on top of his as she looked out the window at the river and blurred thatches of riveted steel.

When she turned back to admire Rosewood's profile, she considered him prettier than she. He didn't have her high-bridged nose, and he looked so young for his age. He was thirty-two, but his satiny skin had made her think he was twenty-five when they met. With luminous hazel eyes and plump lips, his features seemed feminine. Even his cheeks were smooth. When he stopped shaving he tended to grow whiskers around his chin and a few on his upper lip, but not enough to scratch her when she kissed him. He dressed in T-shirts that he designed, which also made him look young. When she got him naked she found bruises from all the slips and scrapes he endured during his installations. She gravitated toward these imperfections when she probed his body with her fingers and tongue.

"He killed himself over that painting?" Rosewood asked.

"You've never seen it?"

"I've never been to the gallery, Paire." Now she was shocked. He shrugged. "It's a big city, and I'm never around there. It's not like it's in Chelsea, and it's not a major exhibition space. The show got thrown together pretty quickly, and Kasson chose the space. Honestly, I didn't want to show there, but he said we could do more with a small space."

"So you know Abel Kasson."

"Everyone's got a debt." He stroked her scalp and stared out the window.

"You didn't come inside because you didn't want to see him," she said, more confrontational than usual.

"You just met him. Would you want to run into Abel Kasson if you didn't have to?"

She repeated what Lucia had told her. "He's the money."

"He's funded a lot of shows," he said. "He's from an old money family in New York. You ever hear of Kasson and Kasson?"

"Nope."

"It's an investment bank that was around for a hundred years. I think they call them bulge bracket companies, but basically a multinational bank. They specialized in carbon emission trading. I guess you can trade on carbon emissions now."

"So he runs a big company." Because of her own family, Paire was repelled by affluence.

"He *ran* a big company. It went bankrupt in 2009 when all the other banks folded. So now he's just a crazy rich guy who fills his time pretending to be a curator. He's bankrolled a lot of artists. You should see his collection. Shit, you should see his apartment. It's like Tut's tomb in there."

She watered down her opinion. "I got a strange impression from him."

"He's a horrible person, that's why. He paid a hundred thousand dollars to get out of a rape trial a few years ago."

The taxi driver looked over his shoulder at them. Paire was surprised he could hear them through the Plexiglas. "Why would you take his money?"

He grinned. "So he doesn't have it."

There went her endorphins again.

Rosewood's grin fell, and he amended himself. "I wish I'd never met the man."

They cut through Brooklyn Heights and pulled down Pierrepont Street, a quiet block within walking distance of all the stores on Montague. Rosewood lived in a brick three-story brownstone with proud brown slab steps and a teak door that looked as if it had been carved from a single hearty slice of tree. He'd bought the place two years ago, after Macy's decided to carry his clothing line. To Paire, he confessed that the pristine brick reminded him of the military housing he grew up in. Now that it was April, the window boxes sprouted daffodils, yellow as the taxicab.

When they got out the cab lingered longer than it should have, and Paire pulled Rosewood's shirt down over her ass.

Inside, the place was sparse and tidy to a fault, a legacy of Rosewood's army breeding. All the books were shelved as vertical as the Chrysler Building. They reflected in the gloss of the wood floors. The art on the walls—not all of it his—served as the primary decoration. The entryway had been custom painted by a compatriot of his, an anonymous street artist in the UK. Although it had been rendered in spray paint and stencils, it recreated the elaborate pattern of a cathedral's rose window.

Rosewood didn't display much family memorabilia. Despite framed photos with friends and a large photo of him and Paire looking goofy—her in a tuxedo and him in a wedding dress—he didn't showcase photographs of his parents.

Other than his lingering traces of Virginian dialect, not much about him hinted that he was the son of a southern general. Paire had to forage for evidence of this connection. In the walk-in closet he had given Paire for her things, he'd left a few boxes of his own. She rummaged one night when she was alone and discovered a collapsible spring baton, the sort that riot police use to beat back angry mobs. One flick of the wrist and the black wand extended to a sixteen-inch spring coil, weighted at the tip. She slapped her palm with it lightly, and it hurt as if she'd caught a softball barehanded. The right snap would shatter bone.

More alarmingly, she found a black revolver with a long thin muzzle and a walnut handle, some war relic, which she might have thought was a harmless replica except for the scattering of brass bullets that ran loose in the box. It was the only direct link she'd ever found to his military ancestry.

Paire couldn't complain. She'd moved in a few months ago and there wasn't anything in plain sight that might connect her to Maine. In her closet she kept a sealed box with memorabilia from her time with Gilda, mostly sketchbooks and photographs. In another she kept a hat that Gilda had bought her. She didn't wear it, but last winter when the snow had reminded her of Maine's harsh winters, she had taken out the hat and held it under her nose. She sniffed for traces of a wood fire from the house where she had lived. They weren't comforting, just familiar.

Paire trudged up the stairs and into the bathroom. There, Rosewood removed her final garments and drew a lavender bath. While she soaked, she sponged off the blood and sour sweat. The warm water enveloped her, steam floating across the surface.

"I can't smell him," she said, relieved. The lavender purged the scent of the old man.

Rosewood brought her a glass of ice water to drink. "Water on the outside, water on the inside. Water cleanses throughout."

At last she was able to rinse off the discoloration on her skin from the blood.

Rosewood kept her company as the water cooled, sitting next to the bathtub with his head resting on the porcelain. They sat for a time, holding hands over the rim. The drain leaked around the plug, so the water level sank until eventually Paire was naked and damp in the empty tub. When she closed her eyes, she savored the warmth of his skin. She felt safe.

"Is there someone from home you might want to talk to about this?" Rosewood asked.

She withdrew her hand from his. He knew she didn't talk about Maine.

"Not your dad. But your aunt," he urged. Paire covered her

nipples with her forearms and sank down. Rosewood got the hint and changed the subject. "What did the man look like?"

"The way he looked at that woman, it made him seem so breakable."

"You mean the painting."

"What did I say?"

"The woman."

She nodded and heaved herself out of the tub.

Once she got dressed, they went to an upscale restaurant on Montague. Corniche. They both liked it because a muralist had painted the walls so it appeared that diners were overlooking a cliff above a glacier canyon. Over drinks, she could almost forget about what she'd seen that afternoon. But when she looked at her fingernails in the glow of the table's flickering candle, she thought about the painting. That woman's hands and feet. The red dress.

While they read over the menus, Paire predicted what Rosewood would order: a filet, prime rib, or flank steak. Sometimes she'd chide, "You're going to have a heart attack when you're forty," even though his body metabolized red meat the way a coyote digested garbage. He surprised her when he said, "They've got lobster."

Paire flinched. *Lobsters.* How far did she have to move to get away from lobsters? "So?"

"So, I haven't had it for a while. What do you think about a couple of lobsters? Seafood night. It'll make you feel like you're back in Maine."

She supposed it was her fault. Paire didn't talk about Maine, and Rosewood never asked much about it, possibly because he himself never talked about Virginia. She was too ashamed to speak. Everyone had idiosyncrasies, and this was one of hers. Lobsters. The scourge of Maine. She'd never mentioned how much she hated them, or the particular reason why she hated them, but why should she? When did the opportunity present itself? *Everyone has something weird they're afraid of,* she told herself. *Even Oprah is afraid of balloons.* But if she explained why she hated lobster, it would require talking about her parents. Talking about Lake and Cissy Novis would mean talking about their crime, the trial, all of it. Rosewood still didn't know about any of it, and she had no intention of telling him. Instead, she stated flatly, "I don't like lobster."

Rosewood tried to keep things light, to distract her from what she had been through today. "How can you not like lobster?" he teased. "You're from Maine."

"I just don't." Her tone said *leave it alone*. He might not have cared one way or the other about lobster, but once she rankled, he could tell she was hiding something. On another day he might not have pursued it, but today he was curious. Perhaps now that this girl had moved into his apartment, he wanted to know more about her. When they were making polite conversation during their first dates, he'd asked about her family and she had lied and told him that her parents had died in a commuter train wreck. Signal failure. Other than a few superficial details, she'd never had to delve that deeply into the specifics.

She could see how frustrated he was now. After bathing her, after listening to her go on about the sad man and the painting, his jaw tensed when she wouldn't divulge anything behind the banal topic of food choices. Just as irked, he said, "Maybe I'll just order lobster, and you can have whatever you want."

"Please don't." She thought about high school, even as far back as elementary school, when the kids used *lobster baby* as an insult. Out of context it sounded ludicrous, but after years of torment these tender places remained raw. After what happened this afternoon, she would be more prone to outbursts.

"You don't have to eat it." Somehow, behind a guise of politeness, this was evolving into a fight.

"I don't like lobsters. I don't like eating them, and I don't like watching them being eaten. I know it's weird, but it's important." Two other tables sandwiched theirs, and the patrons inches away from them sensed the heat in their conversation. Table right masked faces with menus, while table left pretended to watch the street traffic on Montague outside the window.

"How about this—I won't order the lobster, if you tell me why you don't like them."

Paire wouldn't look at him. She brimmed with rage and shame, that he would have the balls to snoop into her secrets, and that she still couldn't divulge them.

"Please just order something else," she fumed.

"Just tell me," he insisted, just as angry, eyeballs bulging.

Her temper popped. "They're my natural fucking enemy, all right? What the hell do you want from me?"

"Christ, Katie—"

"Paire!" This split the air like a firecracker. Chairs around them skidded on the floor.

"Paire…" Rosewood's disappointment made Paire shrivel, mainly because he sounded so much like Aunt Gilda. He reached for her hand but she slipped hers below the table. "Just tell me something."

The more he nudged, the less she wanted to give him. Her affection for Rosewood could be mercurial. Maybe she didn't trust Rosewood, and that made her wonder if she should start looking for a new sublet. Crossing her arms, she asked dismissively, "What do you want to know?"

"Tell me something about your parents."

The patrons to the right took their eyes off the street and glanced at them with interest.

"You already know about them. They're dead." This was only half true. Her mother was dead, and her father might as well have been. Prison had left him a breathing corpse.

From the few truths she'd told him, he knew their names were Lake and Cissy Novis. Lake was Jewish, Cissy Episcopalian. How a Jew had ended up in Maine was a matter of odd luck. When Paire was critical of her looks, she would lament her *Jew nose*.

"Before the train accident, did something…*bad* happen?"

Leave it to Rosewood to ask something that invasive in a public place.

"No one touched me in a bad place, Derek."

He hated being called Derek, and frowned when he heard it.

A few of her dates leaped to the next conclusion, the one Rosewood was forming. She saw him thinking about her dead mother, and the epiphany glossed over his face. "Did something happen *between* your parents?" Like this was a quiz show. At least he worded it more artfully than others.

"My father never hurt my mother."

Some boys had continued to the next logical thought, that if she hadn't been abused, and one parent hadn't killed the other, she was simply a rotten girl who didn't appreciate her family. They assumed she had abandoned her filial duties, and then wondered if she lacked the capacity to love anyone. The way Rosewood looked at Paire cheapened her.

Rosewood must have sensed she was close to a tantrum. Whenever they got close to these subjects at home, especially on the rare occasion when she knocked back a few cocktails, she might turn on him. The girlfriend who moved out six months ago would apparently huck stuff across the room when they fought, but that wasn't Paire. She curled up like a sleeping fox, quaking with anger just visibly enough that he wouldn't be able to fall asleep next to her. When he would try to talk her down, she murmured with the same vitriolic tone that she used now. "Please order something else."

Tonight, he would not placate her. He ordered the lobster. "It's my choice," he said, now just as tense as Paire.

She didn't hide her anger. "Well, you've got your autonomy, I'll give you that. Now look where it gets you." Paire got up and left the restaurant, and Rosewood dined alone.

When he came home an hour later, Rosewood found her in the bedroom. She sat on the floor with her back to the wall, madly scratching at her sketchbook with a pencil. They looked at each other without saying anything. Rosewood slid down the wall and sat next to her, looking over her shoulder as she scribbled. She had scribbled the profile of an old man.

"Is that what he looked like?"

"As close as I can get it." It was very close. She rendered his sad, shrinking face in exquisite detail as she remembered it, his eyes squinting from the pain as steel punctured his heart. Heavy shadows hung under his cheekbones. She successfully captured the depth of his frown lines.

"I'm sorry," he said.

Paire stopped and laid down her pencil, flexing and stretching her cramped fingers. She reached behind her and brought out the gun she'd found, its dark barrel pointed near but not at Rosewood. She worried that the weapon might discharge by accident, sending a bullet through the plaster wall and maybe a next-door neighbor. She might shoot herself in the foot while pointing the barrel to the floor—if she blew off a digit down there, that meant a life without open-toed shoes. She kept her finger off the trigger. Paire was fascinated by its weight and the shine of metal.

"Fuck!" Rosewood pushed the barrel away from them both, so if it went off, it would shoot across the room, and probably pick off one of Takashi Murakami's Mr. DOB characters, which resembled anime versions of Mickey Mouse. "Don't play with that." He'd never shown her the gun, but didn't accuse her of rifling through his possessions.

"It's not loaded. At least, I don't think it is." She was calm, but the fact that she held the gun made Rosewood tense, and edge a few inches away from her.

"What are you doing?"

She asked plainly, "Where did this come from?"

Rosewood quickly explained, "It's my grandfather's sidearm. My dad gave it to me because he thought I might need it in New York."

"This is part of your family heritage. Why would you keep it hidden?"

"Because it's dangerous," he said.

Paire rested the revolver on the floor. She wrapped her arm around his, wanting to feel safe with this man, her intoxicant in their relationship. A deep breath later, she said, "That's why I don't talk about Maine."

CHAPTER 4

By Rosewood's opening reception the next evening, someone had cleaned most of the blood off the sidewalk. A faint smear remained, something that might be more obvious in daylight, Paire thought. The Fern ended up choosing *HERO*, and Perseus proudly held up Hussein's severed head in the front window. A small crush of people gathered outside to admire it before entering the reception.

While she would never say this to Rosewood, especially tonight, when they arrived, Paire was disappointed that the woman in the red kimono wasn't still on display. She'd been thinking about the portrait all day, and wished she had taken a shot with her phone yesterday. Details of the painting stayed with her—the lushness of the crimson, the faint craquelure on the surface of the pigment. She wanted to see it again.

She and Rosewood timed their entry late, so they could walk into a crammed room. They locked elbows and entered the muggy warmth of the Fern together. The gallery looked different in the evening. Mayer Wolff had trained moody spotlights on each of the hanging works but dimmed the overheads, and cast green accent lights toward the ceiling to give the room the atmosphere of a parlor. The place was a forest of bodies. A DJ spun beats in the corner, and some of the girls Paire's age danced in stilted movements within the limited floor space available. Paire had difficulty skirting past without rubbing some part of her body against them. Standing a half head shorter than most, she felt like a pinball. Even in their finery, she smelled a few sour armpits.

They'd both dressed up tonight. Rosewood wore a trim-fitting navy suit, and he'd bought Paire a fitted black gown with embroidered embellishments. They made frequent stops as Rosewood shook a lot of hands and hugged people he knew. While he made small talk, she looked around the perimeter of the room at the works on display.

Paire recognized some of Rosewood's pieces, but some were new to her. All Rosewood's work had a consistent voice and feel, so she could have picked them out at an invitational. He liked primary colors and used a checkerboard palette of red and black for many of his pieces. Most of his images were inspired by war propaganda posters. The men's faces had square jaws and cliffs for cheekbones.

Her favorite Rosewood series was his least political. In five images, he explored the theme of laughter. All of his subjects were caught in various stages of laughter, from shy tittering to hysterics. They were silkscreened and printed in red, white, and black. The concept was simple, accessible, and to Paire, inspirational. At times, an artist found the sweet balance between authentic self-expression and commercial marketability, and this was it. Rosewood had once explained the work to Paire, saying, "Every person has what's known as mirror neurons that allow us to empathize with people based on their facial expressions. When someone's crying in a movie, we feel sad, right? We absorb the emotions that people wear on their faces. So, when someone sees this series, they have to love it. They smile back. They can't help themselves."

Hearing him dissect it took away some of the magic. Still, it worked. The portion of the crowd who stood in front of his *LAUGHTER* prints all smiled as if they'd been injected with vitamin B boosters. Paire felt like the series was his most honest work, because the lack of inhibition in the laughing men and women manifested Rosewood's own desire to be free of constraints.

In a space between bodies she glimpsed Mayer Wolff from across the room, embroiled in an argument with Abel Kasson. Mayer looked the way she remembered, tallish and thin, dressed in a silhouette-shaping check suit with a purple necktie. His adversary in the argument sported a bland wool suit that stretched around his middle and wrinkled at the joints. Kasson's face looked bloodshot, and he sweated at the temples. The two men argued by the rear wall, where one piece of work had been mounted and veiled with a blue velvet curtain—the only piece of work that wasn't on display tonight. Guests milled about it, trying to peek around the edges, only to be shooed away by Kasson.

"What do you have tucked behind there?" Paire asked Rosewood.

"No idea. We didn't talk about doing any kind of reveal. It might not even be mine." Rosewood kissed her forehead and gently tugged her toward the two bickering men. "Might as well get this over with."

When they reached the back wall, Kasson broke off his argument and bear-hugged Rosewood, who kept his hands in his pockets during the embrace. A beat later, the businessman stared at Paire. Perhaps owing to the fact that the last time he had seen her she had been in her underwear, he regarded her with a distant familiarity, and didn't immediately place her face. Mayer was the one who asked the couple, "You two know each other?" For the first time, Paire introduced herself to Mayer. They shook hands. His were warm. She didn't offer hers to Kasson, but he didn't seem to expect a handshake or a hug.

Kasson seemed amused. "I'll be damned."

Mayer looked unsettled. She wondered if he might have been just as disturbed by yesterday's events, or if he were simply agitated from the argument with Kasson. He asked, "How are you feeling?"

She gave him one of the smiles she'd perfected in the mirror. "Fine." What else was there to say, especially at an occasion like this?

He said, "We threw away your clothes. They were too…" *Bloody* was the word he probably wanted to use. "We thought you wouldn't have wanted them."

"No one thought we'd be seeing you again," said Kasson, likely implying that he would have preferred not to see Paire Anjou tonight.

Mayer said, "It was brave that you tried to save him."

"Some people are beyond saving," Kasson commented.

Mayer said, "If it makes you feel any better, I went out for a long night of drinking. I've never seen anyone die before."

"Me either," she confided.

"You call yourself New Yorkers," Kasson huffed.

Paire tried to ignore him and stepped closer to Mayer, so that it might seem like she, Mayer, and Rosewood were speaking in an intimate triangle, with Abel Kasson eavesdropping from the outside. "Do the police know who he was?"

"As it happens, yes. His name was Nicola Franconi."

The art world thrived on dropping names. She was afraid to admit that she didn't know it, and looked at Rosewood to see if her boyfriend was familiar with it.

"I've heard the name, but never met him," said Rosewood. Paire could tell by his falter that he had no idea who this man was either.

Mayer said, "He was the executive director at the MAAC."

Just a few blocks away, the Museum of Asian Art and Culture, otherwise known as the MAAC, was a museum that constantly fought to encourage more attendance in a town dominated by American and European art. She'd heard great things about it, especially the architectural feat of the building design. The collection spanned several centuries and several civilizations, from artifacts such as Japanese samurai suits of armor to modern painters from the People's Republic. She kept telling herself she needed to go one of these days. MSAD students even got in for free, and she hadn't yet made the time.

"So he ran the museum?"

"That would be the director. But he was the second in command. He's been around for a while. I've come across the name, but I never met him. We don't exactly work with the same artists." To Abel Kasson, Mayer said, "I'm surprised you didn't know him."

"Don't be so surprised," Kasson shot back.

"He was getting up there. Seventy-eight years old. I spoke to the folks over at the MAAC, just to connect. They said he'd already tried to retire a few years ago, but after taking nine months off, he came back. He was one of those people who couldn't stay idle. When I told them what happened, everyone was shocked. No one saw it coming."

"You think it was because of this?" Paire pointed to the curtain, envisioning the woman in the red kimono. "She's behind here, isn't she?"

"How did you guess?"

"It's the only thing that could have been back there."

Kasson bullishly inserted himself into the group, shouldering Paire to one side so he could fit into the circle. In Paire's esteem, he was too sure of himself. In a room full of lithe twenty-somethings, he should have felt like an outcast. Instead, he postured like an old gangster, the Godfather of the lot, who would remain long after the young crowd around them had evanesced. "Here's another casualty in the making. Get in line, miss." Paire did her best to smile, but that sheepish half smile came out of her, recalled residue from Abenaki.

"Mr. Kasson," warned Mayer.

"You know it's a fake," said Kasson, speaking to Mayer and Rosewood, now taking his turn to ignore Paire.

"Pretty sure the executive director of the MAAC would have disagreed with you," said Mayer.

"A crazy man in a position of authority is still a crazy man. It isn't a real Qi." He pronounced it *chee*.

Paire clarified with Mayer, "That's the name of the artist?"

"Short for Qi Jianyu. But he just went by the single name. *Qi*."

Rosewood perked up. "Not *the* Qi?"

"There's only one," said Mayer.

Paire felt like she was trying to comprehend a foreign language.

"Shit," said Rosewood, starting to sniff around the edges of the blue velvet curtain. "Why would you want to hide something like that? That's like finding the Holy Grail and keeping it in the pantry."

"It's hidden because it's *your* show," Kasson rebuked his donee. He told all of them, including Paire, "We were having a disagreement on this very topic. I've bought out the gallery, which includes the wall space this counterfeit is currently occupying."

"The terms of our agreement make exception for this one piece." Mayer explained to Rosewood, "Mr. Kasson and I have had this discussion on many occasions. The donor—"

"An *anonymous* donor," Kasson said.

"—is paying generously for us to assure that it will continue to hang. I've made a special provision to obscure it during this reception. All we're doing tonight is rehashing a disagreement that was resolved weeks ago in a contract." He gestured with his chin to the surrounding crowd. "And we're making ourselves look bad in front of guests who are here for *him*."

Kasson wouldn't let this drop. "You also promised that you'd be fully staffed for the event tonight, and you haven't replaced what's-her-name who quit. I've come to assume that your agreements are flexible, depending on their convenience." Kasson noted to Rosewood, "You should care about this."

"Why should I care? Finding a Qi is like finding a living dinosaur. Why wouldn't I want to see it? I want to tear down the curtain myself."

Paire couldn't be sure if Rosewood was that eager to see the painting or if he just wanted to agitate his benefactor. She also noticed that the crowd started to gravitate around them. They formed a spectator line around the artist, and around the curtain, expecting something to be revealed. They probably assumed that the blue velvet drape was covering the latest Derek Rosewood, the jewel in the crown for this exhibit. Ever the agitator, Rosewood seemed delighted by the idea of giving them something truly unexpected. "It's not like one piece will take away from the whole show," he insisted.

"You take for granted how secure your own notoriety is," Kasson warned.

Paire asked, "Why are you so sure it's a fake?"

Nerves frazzled, Kasson blurted, "Because there hasn't been a real Qi on the market for years. Mayer, remind me, what's the date on this one?"

"1980."

Kasson explained to Paire as if educating a granddaughter—a granddaughter whom he disliked—"Qi lived in exile. He was from Beijing, came to the States in the seventies, and then went back to

China. In 1980 he wouldn't have been in America. He didn't produce anything new in that decade, or any time following 1977."

Paire said something she considered an obvious possibility. "What if he'd painted it in China, and had it shipped to the United States?"

Kasson ridiculed her with laughter in a way she hadn't experienced since Abenaki. Her face flushed, and when she looked across the room at her favorite series of Rosewoods, suddenly that series of five seemed to be sniggering at her as well. He said, "You've seen the piece. The liberties he's taking, the sensuous quality of the figure. You think that would fly in China in 1980? *Please.*"

Mayer folded his arms and played with his beard, what seemed to be a method of placating himself so he wouldn't tell this man to go to hell. He said for Paire's benefit, "You're right. This was shipped from China. We've got all the documentation to prove provenance. It's real."

"Provenance can be forged, often more easily than paintings," said Kasson.

"An expert confirmed it for me."

"What expert—your anonymous donor? You've staked your professional reputation on the artistic equivalent of Al Capone's vault."

Paire leaped at the opportunity to contradict Kasson. "Al Capone's vault was real. There just wasn't anything in it."

"Aren't you cute to remember?" Kasson turned to Rosewood. "Remind me why she's here."

"Say that again, I'll rip down the curtain." Rosewood raised his glass in a mock toast. The Virginia accent crept out. Her heart melted when he protected her.

Paire wasn't a good judge of these things, but couldn't tell who would win if a fight broke out. Rosewood was nimble, but Kasson was so much more substantial that the artist might fit inside him.

Kasson sneered at the younger man. "Watch where you step." He looked Paire up and down again, this time wolfishly, possibly titillated by imagining her in her underwear. "Miss, what's your name again?"

"Paire Anjou." She let the words flit off her tongue.

"You don't say. What a wonderfully whimsical name. Light. Playful." He looked at Rosewood. "Fleeting."

Rosewood didn't hesitate. With that line of guests already gathered for the reveal, he dragged a corner of the blue velvet drape, fast as ripping open a shower curtain. The hooks that held it up couldn't withstand the force of the tug, so the entire cloth came off the line and jumbled on the gallery floor.

A smatter of applause erupted from the people immediately around them, who didn't know what they were looking at but assumed it was a new Derek Rosewood, something in a completely divergent style. The applause rippled throughout the crowd, until the entire room was turned in the direction of the canvas, and clapping as hard as they could without spilling their drinks.

Paire had been greedy to see the woman again but was unprepared for how it would affect her. The flash of red in the pigment recalled all that blood when Nicola Franconi had expired on the sidewalk, but just as quickly the memory of that violence faded, and she stared at the artistry with a hungry appreciation.

The painting hung higher on the wall than Rosewood's pieces. The woman's feet dangled at Paire's eye level. She stood close and sniffed the aged paint, noting traces of oil that stood out from the collective musk of pressed people. Her eye caught a tiny brushstroke of white, which, if she backed up a few paces, would simply look like a fleck of sunlight glinting off a pedicured toenail.

The placard mounted to the right of the frame read:

> **Qi**
> *The Empress Xiao Zhe Yi, Seated* (1980)
> Tempera on wood
> On loan from anonymous collection

She watched to measure the painting's impact on Rosewood. Rosewood often took in masterworks of art with either disinterest or disdain. She was almost certain the only reason he had pulled the curtain was to silence Abel Kasson, with the added benefit of confusing the crowd that had come for his work. *Always keep them thinking*, he might say. He might not be thrilled if guests went wild for the single piece of artwork that wasn't his, but maybe he'd be delighted if it stirred up more controversy. Paire tried to read his expression. She thought he might be fishing for the right thing to say that wouldn't pop her balloon. Something other than, *This is it? Someone killed himself over this? What's all the hubbub?* Ever the pedagogue, he might break the empress down into her elements, make academic comments about the lighting, criticize the gold-leaf frame for being too ornate for a modern painting, note that it was derivative of some artist she'd never heard of.

But Rosewood did none of these things. He stood fixed to the floor, looking up into the empress's self-assured expression the way a child might look at his first lunar eclipse. His mouth slightly open, Rosewood smiled involuntarily, his eyes shiny with rapture.

Instead of looking at the empress, Abel Kasson glared contemptuously at Rosewood. Mayer wasn't looking at the empress either. He turned his body away from the painting and regarded the crowd. When she could force her gaze away from Her, Paire did too. Now that the painting had been unveiled, everyone in the hall pressed more tightly together, moving in as close as they could. As if someone had tilted a box of marbles. They pushed against Paire, and the heat off the wall of bodies overwhelmed her. She felt the herd might actually pin them against the portrait. They all gaped at the empress without considering whose toes they might crush. The chatter that had filled room died out, making the pounding synthetic kick drum seem all the more invasive. Possibly sensing that his music was too loud for a room this quiet, the DJ lowered his volume so that the beat merely haunted the reception, lingering in the background as a soundtrack to enhance whatever contemplations and fantasies this painting inspired.

Mayer edged away. At first Paire thought he was stepping aside to let his guests have a better view of the empress, but he kept walking away, and she caught a glimpse of Lucia waiting for him by the entrance to the Fern's back office. She wore a taupe dress that clung to her in the same way Paire's did, showing off obliques that framed her stomach like parentheses.

With Rosewood distracted and Abel Kasson sizing her up broodingly, Paire decided to work her way out of the crowd as well, toward the front window. She elbowed a few people who were too transfixed by the portrait to notice her. Her face felt hot and damp by the time she reached open air.

By the front door, she looked at the mob from behind. The cluster around the painting reminded her of a science video she'd seen of sperm vying to fertilize an egg. On the other side of the room, Mayer and Lucia confided to each other in whispers, nodding at the empress. The way he leaned into her seemed overly familiar for an employer. He didn't need to whisper so close, now that the conversation in the room had petered out. Yet his lips hovered so near the woman's ear, and his hand touched her upper arm with the easiness that only comes from having touched something many times before. Lucia's left hand was suspended in the air just over his chest, possibly wanting to play with the purple tie. Paire could spot that Godzilla diamond from all the way across the gallery. For the first time, she noted that Mayer didn't wear a ring.

Scanning the room, Paire saw one other person at the Fern Gallery who seemed unaffected by the Empress Xiao Zhe Yi. The woman wandered apart from the rest of the gathering, at the front of the gallery with Paire. Turned away from the rear wall and facing the opposite direction, the woman strolled around the entrance, casually looking over Rosewood's pieces. She stopped at one of the hyena-people, the one in the *LAUGHTER* series that Paire herself favored out of the five. Anywhere from twenty-six to forty years old, she wore a beet-burgundy gown that seemed too formal for the reception, even among those who had come in suits and cocktail dresses. This woman was dressed for an award ceremony. Straight black hair cascaded to the middle of her back like a horse's tail. Slightly taller and more slender than Paire, her curves were less ostentatious. A slit in the fabric showed that her legs were toned but not muscular, and her skin was pale like Paire's. When the woman turned her face, Paire saw she was Asian. Because of her perfect oval face, Paire immediately thought she resembled the Empress Xiao Zhe Yi. She dismissed her observation a moment later, and judged herself harshly. *Can't tell non-Caucasians apart*, she thought. But as the woman rotated into full view, Paire was struck by the resemblance. They had the same lips, naturally contoured in a pout. When she looked back a second time, the real-life woman was looking right at her. She'd caught Paire staring. The woman politely smiled, then, possibly made uncomfortable by the lingering glance, sauntered out the door.

Paire followed.

She stepped out onto an almost vacant sidewalk and a refreshing blast of night air. All of those who had lingered outside the Fern to admire Rosewood's *HERO* in the window had since migrated inside. The DJ's muffled beat sounded behind the quavering glass. A few steps down toward Seventh, a taxicab idled, roughly where Rosewood had picked her up yesterday. The woman was already getting in. Paire saw a sliver of leg lifting off the asphalt as it withdrew into the vehicle. Her toes, clad sparingly in matching burgundy heels, looked perfectly pedicured. The leg disappeared, and a hand with long fingers closed the door. The taxi pulled off.

Paire looked down at her feet, realizing she stood over the spot where Nicola Franconi had expired. She could see how the blood had discolored the concrete like a dried puddle of oil.

Mayer suddenly appeared beside her, far enough that he didn't startle her, but close enough that Paire knew he had come outside for her. He looked concerned, as if he'd rushed out there to prevent some kind of disaster. His face was flushed, and when he coughed into the air, his breath came out like a cloud. In April, the temperature at night dipped low, and in that moment Paire noticed she felt cold. She shuddered. Mayer took off his jacket and offered it to her, just like yesterday. She politely refused. Lucia came outside as well and stood by Mayer, looking equally troubled.

"Is everything okay?" Paire asked, unsure why she was getting so much attention.

"Fine, fine," said Mayer. He looked past Paire, presumably toward the taxi.

All three of them turned to watch it, catching the last glimpse of yellow as it hooked around the corner.

Mayer seemed relieved to see the cab drive out of sight. He asked abruptly, "How would you like a job?"

Paire tilted her head, wondering if this was a joke.

He continued, "Listen, you're in art school. I assume you want to get into the business, right?"

Paire looked over at Lucia, who nodded to assure her that this wasn't some kind of prank.

"You stood your ground against Abel Kasson. If you can assure me you'll keep your clothes on while you're on the job, I'm pretty sure I can teach you everything else." His hand warmed her when she shook it. "Come by tomorrow and we'll work out schedules."

Rosewood rushed outside to join them. He spoke to Lucia and Mayer at once. "Good night, folks." Cheerful but insistent, he took Paire's hand. "Let's go." He hailed a passing cab, and she barely had time to thank Mayer before she was led into the back of the taxi. As they peeled off, she saw Mayer step close to Lucia and cradle the back of her head during a slow kiss.

In the taxi, Rosewood kissed Paire hard, ignoring the driver's eyes in the mirror. The veins in his neck pulsed and his temples throbbed. The color of his skin changed—even in a dark cab she could tell—and his hands were cold. The blood had left his hands and gone to his head and groin.

As soon as she shut the front door, his hands were on her, unzipping her dress and unlatching her bra. First, it was the familiar touch she knew, his arms holding her tightly from behind, lovingly, with a touch of apprehension. But tonight he felt stronger, his body warmer. His fingers rolled across Paire's lower back, arms, legs. He stripped off his own clothing as if it were on fire. For Paire, it felt like being with a different man. His fingers dug deeply into her muscles, and the sensations were pleasant, his vigor a refreshing novelty. But Paire felt strange, because at this moment he felt like a stranger.

They never made it to the bedroom, but sank to the floor in the entryway, right beneath the stenciled rose window. Paire shut her eyes and in her willing blindness felt the heat coming off the man. Gently, his hands cupped her ears, and his mouth met hers in the dark. His lips were soft, and she opened her mouth just as softly to welcome him. His scent was light and clean. Heart thumping, she felt the fine hairs on his legs and wrapped her arms around his narrow back. They came together aggressively, angrily. Paire submitted to it just as much as Rosewood. She hardly noticed the scrape of the pine boards against her shoulder blades.

When they went to sleep upstairs, Rosewood whispered, "I love you." It was the only time he'd said it, and it felt like an apology.

CHAPTER 5

On her first day at the Fern, Paire immediately went to the bathroom and slipped the glow-in-the-dark condom back into its leopard-print purse, hoping no one had noticed its absence. She'd bought a suit for the job, something that mimicked what Lucia might wear, a shoulder-augmenting three-button navy suit with purple trim, something that understated her cleavage. She tamed her synthetic red hair by pulling it back into a French twist. One small step into the art world, one giant leap away from Katie Novis.

Officially, she was a fine arts consultant. Her primary responsibility was to learn everything about their art collection. Almost all of the Fern's wall space was taken up by Derek Rosewood pieces, but the gallery kept a storage unit in Long Island City that maintained an appropriate climate for paintings—seventy-five degrees, fifty-five percent humidity. An impressive inventory of work was housed there, with the Picassos, Mirós, and Lichtensteins she remembered from first visiting the gallery.

"I've been working here for five years, and I don't know everything we've got in the archives," Lucia told her. The woman's braces quickly blended into her face, and Paire couldn't imagine her without them. She had kissed two boys with braces, later cleansing with mouthwash to purge the rancid metallic taste. Lucia seemed more hygienic, and Paire liked to imagine her flavor was sweeter.

Paire memorized everything she could about the artists' biographies, birth and death dates, education, anecdotes of how they were inspired—everything a potential buyer needed to know. It felt like another class. Her favorite one.

During one of her breaks, Lucia said, "This is as much about art knowledge as it is about salesmanship. And buyers don't want you to prattle on about technique. They want to know about the lives of the artists and the history of the work. They want the story behind the piece."

To test her memory, Lucia quizzed Paire when the gallery was slow. Once, as Paire entered a buyer's bank account numbers into the database, Lucia asked, "Where and when was Miró born?"

"Barcelona. 1890. And he died on Christmas Day in 1983."

"Where did he go to school?"

"The School of Fine Arts at La Llotja and Galí's Escola d'Art."

"Give me a nicety," Lucia said.

"He was an accountant for a few years until he had a nervous breakdown. The business world almost killed him."

Lucia raised a finger to her lips. "Don't editorialize, especially about that. Most of your buyers will be suits. Over time, you'll meet a lot of them."

Paire asked, "Are they all like Abel Kasson?"

"No one's like him," said Lucia.

Naturally, Paire tried to find out about the artist Qi. The Fern didn't keep much information, other than the shipment documentation from the gallery in Beijing that had apparently sent the painting to the United States after he'd died two years ago. The documents were written in Chinese, so she couldn't make sense of it. Information on the anonymous donor, presumably the same party to whom the painting had been shipped, was kept confidential. Paire had to find out what she could through her own research.

Qi Jianyu was born outside of Beijing in 1942, and was discovered by Americans in the early 1970s. Some famous people, notably Andy Warhol, raved about his work, and he moved to New York, where he enjoyed a short burst of fame before moving back to China in 1978. Paire couldn't find anything about his life after that, nor any record of where in China he might have lived or how his career developed. She found only one photograph of him, probably from the seventies, where he posed with a tall white man in horn-rimmed glasses who seemed to be leaning away as they stood together. The artist dressed in a rumpled black suit, a shorter man with a round face and an ecstatic, wrinkly grin, even though he would have only been thirty or so years old at the time. Other than his smile, there was nothing notable about his features. He seemed plain by all accounts, neither thin nor heavy, handsome nor ugly. She thought about walking through Chinatown, and how many times she might have passed a man with his physical characteristics and not noticed him. She suspected that a man who took on a mononym would have wanted to stand out somehow, and she supposed he had to funnel everything through his work to have any sort of voice at all.

Neither Mayer nor Lucia talked about the empress, even with it hanging on the back wall, unceasingly looking over their shoulders. Neither of them looked at the portrait much. Mayer angled his desk so he sat with his back to the painting. Occasionally, when Paire caught one of them stealing a glimpse, she'd notice them linger for an extra moment. Lucia tended to run her tongue over her lower lip when she stared at it. Mayer shifted in his chair in a way that suggested an uncomfortable bunching around his pelvis. The few times when work shifts overlapped and all three of them were at the gallery together, the painting made Mayer and Lucia forget their discretion. They looked at the painting together and then exchanged devouring stares.

The more she worked at the Fern, the more aware she became of the relationship between Mayer Wolff and Lucia de Moraes. That Lucia omitted any talk about her husband told Paire a lot about her marriage. No longer entranced by the braces, Paire noticed other things, such as the fingertip bruises on her arms, the ones she'd only see when Lucia came in and before she dabbed on cover-up in the bathroom. Despite her collection of trinkets in the staff restroom, there wasn't a photograph in the lot of her and her spouse. When Paire searched through her other belongings—just looking, not stealing—she found three stray photos of her family, friends, and what would probably be sorority sisters. Lucia didn't have braces in these photos, and bore an unusually prominent overbite with large spaces between her teeth when she smiled.

Neither of them ever spoke about their affair. Mayer wasn't married, but he didn't talk about his personal life. Lucia seemed more the type who would spill her secrets, yet she talked about anything and everything but Mayer. The lack of gossip worked out well for Paire. She didn't want to talk about her relationship with Rosewood either, largely because it might open up all sorts of questions about her background, so it seemed best that everyone's affairs and upbringings were latched in lockboxes.

Her awareness came from watching the two of them interact during the shift overlap. Mayer scheduled two people on the same shift. But in the half-hour overlap time, when Lucia was coming and Paire was leaving, she saw how they stole glances at each other. Lucia would stare at him a few seconds too long, chin down, her lips puckering involuntarily. Mayer might smile slyly at her, easing his mouth into a grin while he exhaled what seemed like a grateful sigh. They had their own code of glances that communicated their emotions when they couldn't touch, and maybe it was Paire's imagination, but these seemed more overt as time went on and the empress presided over the room.

Paire tended to avoid looking at the painting when others were around, because she was afraid that if she ever looked she'd end up staring for too long. Even when she avoided it, an irrational sense crept into her, as if the empress noticed when she was being ignored. Being in such close proximity sometimes gave Paire periodic shivers. Even with her eyes closed, she could have sensed the empress in this room. Against the Fern's white walls, the empress's crimson robe flew like a battle flag. Noting how it served as an aphrodisiac to Mayer and Lucia, and Rosewood too, she'd come to believe the painting had a pheromonal hold over people. And she worried that if she stared too long she might not be able to control her own behavior. If it made some people horny, if it made Nicola Franconi stab himself, she worried what actions it might provoke from a name-changing kleptomaniac like herself.

When Lucia quizzed her by mentioning, "Qi," even the name of the artist made Paire flinch.

She pretended that she had to think hard to retrieve the information, when she could have rattled off the biographical data like her social security number. "Born in Beijing, educated at CAFA. Lived in New York for five years and then moved back. Possibly lived in Beijing for the rest of his life, but we don't know more than that. He was reported dead two years ago."

Lucia asked, "Anything special about his technique?"

"I thought you didn't want me to dwell on technique."

"In this case, it's part of his story."

She remembered a smattering of what Mayer had told her. "He painted using tempera, just like they used in Renaissance frescoes. He believes—*believed*—it lent a timeless quality to the work."

Lucia played with her ring, which slid loosely on her finger. "Good. What's so special about this piece here?"

"*The Empress Xiao Zhe Yi, Seated*, is the only work from Qi currently on display."

"Where are the others?"

"No one knows."

"Vanished. You might say, this is the last known Qi in existence." She asked, "What can you tell me about the subject matter?"

Paire remembered the short description of the piece that the Fern kept on file:

> *The Empress Xiao Zhe Yi (1854–1875), also known as the Jia Shun Empress, was married to Emperor Tong Zhi, a member of the Qing dynasty of China.*
>
> *Talented at poetry, literature, music, and painting, she was favored by the Emperor above his other wives. This sparked jealousy in the Dowager Empress Cixi, who ordered the Emperor and the Empress to separate. The Emperor Tong Zhi died of loneliness, and the Jia Shun Empress, hearing of her husband's death, committed suicide.*

When she did a little more digging, some articles contradicted this summary. First, the Empress Xiao Zhe Yi wasn't the wife of

Emperor Tong Zhi of China, but his imperial consort. Similar to a wife back then, but not the same. The Dowager Empress Cixi was Tong Zhi's mother, a woman who ruled China while her son was too young to take on the responsibility. She controlled his power and his relationships, and did force the emperor and empress to separate. However, contrary to the gallery's blurb, the emperor didn't die of loneliness. After the separation, a palace eunuch encouraged him to "cure" his loneliness with trips to brothels outside the Forbidden City. He contracted syphilis from prostitutes. The Dowager Empress Cixi blamed the young empress for his death, and ordered her food supply to be cut off. The young empress either committed suicide or died of starvation. Rosewood might have been right. Freedom and control seemed to be at the heart of everything.

Paire found an image of the Empress Xiao Zhe Yi, an antique portrait in which the empress sat in a similar pose to the Qi portrait. In this painting, the hands and feet were hidden. Other than the face, one couldn't see a square inch of skin. Her legs weren't spread as far apart, and the loose imperial robes covered up any feminine curves. The garment featured two embroidered dragons that were ready to fight each other, but lacked the vibrant reds found in Qi's painting. The young empress's face was gentle, oval, and pale, too soft for cheekbones, with a wide, flat nose. She was beautiful, but not the same woman as the one hanging in the Fern.

Paire answered Lucia, "She was a real woman, a real empress from China. She was young and beautiful. An artist. She died when her true love died." She remembered the woman she'd seen during Rosewood's reception, and tried to recall how closely she resembled the woman in the portrait, or if she simply wished that the Empress Xiao Zhe Yi had a human incarnation.

The next day, when she was on shift with Mayer, she asked him, "Who gave this to us?"

He answered, "I'm not allowed to say, but you might meet them at some point."

"Did they really insist that it remain hanging during Rosewood's exhibition?"

Mayer said, "You live with him. You really call him Rosewood?"

"It's what he likes to be called."

He returned to her question. "The conditions of this donation were very specific, and the party gave us a lot of money. So it stays on the wall."

"But the donor doesn't want to sell it."

"The donor just wants to let people know it exists." He swiveled in his chair so that he faced it. Losing his willpower, Mayer marveled at the work, his shoulders dropping with a giant toke of air. "You know, you start looking at that thing, you can't stop. It's dangerous. Abel Kasson was right about that."

Now that Mayer was staring at the empress, Paire took the liberty of looking as well. She stepped close to the canvas, breathing on the paint. "So you can't sell this. But if you were to *try* and sell this, what would you say?"

Mayer seemed to appreciate her playfulness. He rose from his desk and joined her in front of the gold-leaf frame. "All right. First, it's unique. This is the chest of gold that you hope to find in a treasure hunt. The history of the artist alone makes it almost priceless—I would say *almost* only because for the moment, I'm trying to sell it. In truth, it really is priceless. But for me, what makes it special is the work itself, not the provenance. Forget that it pays homage to Chinese tradition. What you should notice is how it *deviates* from Chinese tradition. Take a look." Mayer raised a finger, careful not to touch the pigment. "Bare feet. You'd never see those in a royal portrait. And you'd never see the legs so defiantly spread, like she's straddling the back of a chair. The cheongsam—well, I don't even want to get into the symbolism of the patterns in there, but you've got an eagle and the Statue of Liberty hidden in the embroidery. Let's just say these are not Chinese images."

"You mean the kimono?"

"Kimono are Japanese. She's Chinese, and she's wearing a cheongsam. You can tell by the way it's cut up the sides, not folded like a robe."

Paire looked more studiously at the embroidery in the garment, and the intricate stitching started to reveal shapes and patterns, not just floral vines. The brushwork created the perfect illusion of stitching, white relief atop the flowing red backdrop. She found the Statue of Liberty and the eagle's spread wings. Then she spotted a peace sign, the dove's foot inside the circle. She even made out a face with hollowed cheekbones and glasses, similar to the photograph she'd found of the artist standing next to the tall American. She wouldn't have noticed any of it if she hadn't stood very close, trying to pick it out of the details within the jungle of simulated needlework.

Mayer continued, "Those symbols would have gotten him into trouble in the People's Republic. American symbols. The way he renders those images in the embroidered vines in the cheongsam, I'd say he was hinting that the insidious nature of the political ideology works its way into everything, even clothes. Even art. Especially art. It probably would have created a stir in China, especially at the time."

"Even something this subtle?"

"In Communist China, life as an artist was—and is—a completely different world than it is over here. Especially in Qi's time, if you were an artist, you worked to serve the values and ideology of the State. In a sense, you would be a propagandist. When Mao spoke at the Yenan Forum in 1942, he cribbed from Lenin and said that art needed to serve the people. There was no exploration of individual expression. That kind of expression in art would have been unheard of. So when Mao was in power, artists adhered to the style favored in China at that time, which was socialist realism, or realism that depicted socialist ideology. Ironically, that style came from Europe—essentially, French nineteenth-century realism, later co-opted by the Russians, who added a little moodiness to it. But I've already told you this."

"Tell me more."

Mayer shrugged. "An artist in Beijing in Qi's generation would have been taught Western techniques, such as oil painting, which was a Western invention. So, the use of tempera could be seen as a commentary from an artist who was forced to create using Western techniques. It's a petulant move. He could have stuck with oils or acrylics, but he used egg-based tempera, almost to throw the obvious adoption of Western techniques in the faces of those who mandated them. Tempera is a relatively delicate paint that ages and cracks, that you can only work in thin coats, with no knifework or thick brushwork. It's limiting because it's so hard to work with. You need a solid surface to work on because it cracks easily. As a result, Qi didn't paint on canvas. He painted on wood. And not just any wood. He used Chinese red birch for his boards, from the western part of the country, towards the Himalayas." Mayer wound a ringlet of his hair around his finger. "Have you ever seen a red birch tree?"

"I haven't."

"They're elegant. When you see them in nature, they have peeling brown bark that comes off the trunks like paper. The grain is light and mild, and a perfect stand-in for canvas. What Qi is saying—or what he might be saying, which I'm fabricating for the purpose of selling this piece of work to you—is that, despite being forced into an artistic style based on Western tradition, under that veneer is something distinctly Chinese." He pointed to the bottom corner. "See the chop?"

"Come again?"

"The way he signs his work. Round about this time, artists would still use a *chop*, or a wax seal, to stamp their work instead of a signature. He's using that here, the red stamp right in the corner. But you can see he's also painted a signature, like a Western artist, right below it. He's mashed up East and West as much as he can. And maybe that was the sort of commentary that the State might forgive." He gestured again across the canvas. "But the American symbols, the way she's posed, the overt sensuality—that wouldn't fly in China. And that makes the piece even more fascinating for me."

"What does it tell you?"

"I don't know. Maybe this was painted for a private collection, but I can't imagine that this would ever have been displayed in China. Not in public. Not in 1980." He rubbed his beard. "And then there's the possibility that Kasson's right, and this is just an exquisite forgery."

He stared at Paire, possibly interested in how close she stood to the piece. At a museum, a guard might instruct her to step back, but here at the Fern, colleague to colleague, he'd allowed her the proximity. Mayer warned, "You could lose yourself in the embroidery patterns alone. And the way she looks at you, she's almost daring you to."

Paire wondered if any of the story was true. She found it hard to believe in history, because like any story, it always changed depending on who was writing it. But she wanted to believe it. She knew the model in the painting wasn't the actual Jia Shun Empress, but in her imagination they were the same person, as if Qi finally gave the woman the proper rendering in 1980, and anything before that had been cartoon illustrations based on hearsay descriptions.

In the story she chose to accept, the young woman was kept apart from a man she loved. When her man died, she had added her death to his to spite the person who had separated them. In the portrait, the empress's expression evoked a sense of loneliness, certainly. But more than that, she possessed a defiance that came from having lost what she cherished. Once the thing she dreaded most had befallen her, nothing else could frighten her.

Paire remembered how hopeless Nicola Franconi had looked when he plunged the letter opener through his ribs. She imagined that he had been so consumed with the Chinese bride that he had volunteered to die if he could not possess Her. That he would be attracted to Her was the most natural thing. The woman in the painting was a beacon for lost souls.

When no one else was in the gallery, Paire patrolled the perimeter, trying to minimize the clack of her heels on the floor. She scrutinized each Rosewood to find something new she might appreciate. She lingered whenever she got to the hyena people in the *LAUGHTER* series, staring at the different ways the lips parted, how much teeth each of them showed.

She took advantage of her window time to watch stray people, some of them likely classmates, walk past the Fern. When she made eye contact and smiled, occasionally they'd come in and she'd chat them up. When the street was empty, she studied the quiet brownstones across the way, looking into the black windows for traces of movement, occasionally seeing a figure drift behind the glass. Sometimes she looked down to the pavement just outside the Fern, where a slight discoloration in the concrete was the only indication that blood had been spilled there.

At the window, she also appreciated whatever limited sunlight filtered down between the high-rises. Manhattanites didn't see much direct sun on either side of noon. The high-rises diffused sunlight like the canopy of a redwood forest, so the street-level pedestrian was treated to a hint of sun through reflections and a general brightening of the sky. When she looked up from the front door, she craned her neck for a hint of blue. The odd thing was how the reflected sunlight managed to enter the Fern gallery.

In her first-year art history classes at MSAD, Paire had learned that the temple of Abu Simbel in Egypt had been engineered so that twice a year, on his birthday and his coronation day, the sun would shine in through the shadowy chambers and illuminate the face of Ramses's statue. In a similar fashion, sunlight bounced around the tight glass-and-steel labyrinth of New York and found a way to glint off the empress's eyes.

Paire would saunter toward the back of the Fern until she reached the empress, fooling herself that the crimson cheongsam was something that just happened to catch her eye, something that ignited a fledgling interest instead of a surge of delight. Her skin always prickled as she approached. After ensuring that she wasn't being watched by Mayer or Lucia, she combed the woman's face, closely studying the brushwork.

Her heart surged just to look at her. The way the empress stared out from her sun-soaked spot on the wall, she seemed genuinely regal, as if everyone else were just a guest in the court. Paire resisted the impulse to kneel. When she turned away she still felt its ghostly summons, like a faint whisper in the wind.

One of Paire's primary duties was to sort through the mail, and within a few days she'd opened several letters concerning the painting. A woman from Iowa who had visited New York for the first time several weeks before wrote that her arthritic knee had been pain-free since she saw "the young Japanese queen." A man from Connecticut sent his résumé and a headshot, and offered the Fern a thousand dollars to forward the contact information of the model who sat for the portrait.

The letters paled in comparison to the uninhibited fits of revelry from those who absorbed the empress in person, and this helped Paire control her urges. *There but for the grace of God*, she'd think. Within the first week, she could spot gawkers in the front window.

Mayer would point them out too. Possibly he did this for his own amusement, but Paire wondered if he might be warning her as well. "Look. There's another one," he said at least once per shift.

Once, a college boy slouched on the sidewalk just outside the window, loitering in a tightly zipped windbreaker with a half-open backpack sliding off his shoulder. He kept his back to the window, and occasionally turned to look inside, past Rosewood's *HERO*, all the way to the rear wall. If he was an MSAD student, Paire didn't recognize him. He seemed about her age, but his face had a virginal sheen to it, still glossed in adolescent oils. While not at the ideal proximity for viewing, the boy would have been able to gain a general impression of the red cheongsam bursting off the back wall.

She tried to make an excuse for him, defending herself in the process. "He's just waiting for the bus."

"No one takes the bus in Manhattan. And buses don't run on this street anyhow," Mayer reminded her.

Paire stepped in front of the painting, interrupting the line of sight between the boy and the portrait. When he turned again for a glimpse, he fluttered his eyelids, as if he'd been snapped out of hypnosis. He seemed ashamed of having been caught staring, and walked away briskly.

"You'll get used to it after a few weeks," Mayer said. "You know, there are people who faint in front of the *David* in Florence."

"I did know that." She'd learned that bit of trivia in her art history classes.

"No one knows why that happens, but it happens. Everyone loves the empress too. Don't act surprised, and treat them as if they're the first person to notice it. Some people have extreme reactions. Nothing like Franconi, but you'll see some notable reactions from time to time. Roll with it."

The next day, a toddler in overalls led his mother into the gallery and stumbled all the way to the portrait, leaping as high as possible while swiping at the bottom of the birch board until his mother caught up and swept him up in her arms. His face looked as if he had just tasted chocolate for the first time. When his mother pulled him away, he bawled loud enough to shatter crystal.

On a sadder occasion, a morbidly obese man stopped in front of the glass and glared at the back wall. He'd been drinking a gigantic soda, and after a long stare at the window, he dropped the plastic cup, letting it splash on the pavement by his ankles, where the cola mixed with the blood residue left by the old Italian. The man wept in blubbering, convulsive torrents. Mayer stepped outside to speak to him, and the giant man's forehead came to rest on his shoulder, soaking into his suit coat. Whatever words were exchanged, Mayer seemed to comfort him enough that he could move on.

Paire spotted an old woman outside the window, petite and skeletal with a spiny hunched back, dressed in jeans frayed at the knees and a shirt with the red-and-white check pattern of a picnic tablecloth. She pressed herself up against the glass, as if no one would notice. Mayer barely reacted. "Don't mind her. She's a regular."

The woman stretched out her arms, pressing palms flat against the glass. She pushed her body into the window as if trying to embrace the building. Smooshing her cheek on the window, she began swaying on the pane. It wasn't a sexual reaction. Her gyrations stemmed more from some sort of divine bliss. This went on for several minutes.

Paire dubiously asked, "She's a regular?"

"Been coming here a few days after the Qi went in the front window. She's harmless. It's a shrine for her. Watch. When she's done, she'll kiss the glass and go."

The woman eventually gave the glass a tender peck, and shuffled toward Seventh.

Of all the eccentric behavior that happened around the empress, the incident that most startled Paire happened at the end of the week, involving one Phyllis from Arkansas, a mountainous housewife in her fifties dressed in a floral muumuu and tennis shoes. The empress hooked her like a trout and reeled her into the gallery. Her eyes glazed, she plodded through the Fern and stopped a foot before the painting.

Paire said hello to her. Without taking her eyes off the canvas, the woman extended an unsteady hand. "Phyllis." Her voice wavered with a prominent rural accent.

"Welcome."

Phyllis spoke automatically as she glanced over the painting. "There was an airfare deal, so the tickets were cheap. Keith asked why I wanted to come to New York City, and I told him I wanted to see something I couldn't see in Arkansas." Phyllis heaved a longing breath and took in the woman in the crimson cheongsam, while her Pledge of Allegiance hand covered her heart. "This is it, isn't it?"

"She's unique," Paire affirmed. In moments like this, Paire played the part of the distant admirer, pretending the portrait didn't have just as resounding an effect on her.

"Who's the artist?"

"A man named Qi."

"Is that right?" Phyllis mused, almost giggling while her eyes traced the edges of the canvas. In the background behind the empress, Qi had painted a small window deep inside sepia shadows, revealing tree branches with pink petals. "Cherry blossoms," observed Phyllis.

"That's right."

"Where's Mr. Qi from?"

"China."

Phyllis didn't take her eyes off the tempera. When Paire had first noticed the tree, she thought it strange, since she'd always thought of cherry blossoms as being Japanese. But when she looked it up, cherry trees grew in China too. If Phyllis made the same assumption, she kept it to herself. She just commented, "Is that right?"

What happened next felt as haltingly quick as a hiccup. Phyllis closed her eyes and moved her lips in what might have been a silent prayer. Paire didn't speak because she didn't want to interrupt her moment. She expected that when Phyllis's prayer was over she would trudge out of the Fern like the rest. But instead, Phyllis wilted.

Paire had never seen anyone faint. The woman's knees gave out first. The hand that covered her heart dropped to her side, and Phyllis's head swayed as if supported on a swan's neck. She tumbled into Paire. The woman was heavier than she, and although Paire managed to hold her for a moment, her ankle rolled and the two women toppled clumsily to the ground.

Mayer rushed to them, ready to phone an ambulance, but Phyllis came to almost instantly. Paire rolled out from under her and jostled her head, gently calling her name, and the woman blinked as if she'd woken up to birdcalls.

When Phyllis realized what had happened, her face flushed. "Oh no," she said. Taking in her surroundings, she was visibly mortified. She reached for the hem of the muumuu and pulled it down to maintain her modesty, even though it had only risen to midcalf. "Oh no." Mayer insisted that they call a doctor, but Phyllis refused. "Just need some fresh air." When she left the Fern, Paire was certain she would look over her shoulder, but Phyllis couldn't bring herself to look at the empress, lest the painting send another wave of overwhelming ardor crashing over her.

When Paire closed at night, she shadowed Mayer or Lucia when one of them set the alarm by the back door. Each time she would open the door and peek into the narrow alley behind the building, a corridor of painted gray brick just wide enough for a car to lop off both its side mirrors. Paire was too new for them to trust her with keys or alarm codes. Lucia had told her, "Don't take it personally. I was here two years before Mayer gave me the access PIN."

Sometimes while Mayer or Lucia turned off the lights in the back office Paire stood out in the gallery alone, where she could take a minute and savor a private viewing of the empress. The rest of the time in the gallery she had to suppress her desire to look at the painting, but when the space was hers for these few seconds, her temperance was rewarded. Paire approached the portrait within touching distance, and took in some of the finer details of the cheongsam. At times, she considered that she'd only ever thought of her mother as a two-dimensional portrait, something she stared at in frames. Then she would immediately wipe away that thought.

In the Qi piece, the stitching looked so realistic that she wanted to press her finger into the pigment to test it. Studying the patterns, she found more shapes, in the same way one might make their own constellations of the stars. Paire found something that looked like the Venus symbol, the circle atop the cross. She saw something that might have been a Chinese character, but when she leaned in close she recognized the symbol, the interlocking N and Y that marked the logo for the New York Yankees. She closed her eyes and smelled the paint, which to Paire was scented like perfume. These moments were a guilt-ridden satisfaction, much like a sugar addict stuffing her face with a private stash of cupcakes. Her audience with the empress was an indulgence so audacious it made her lightheaded in anticipation and guilty afterward that she took so much pleasure from it.

During these moments she took photos with her phone, which she would later use as reference to draw the Jia Shun Empress. Sometimes, when flipping through her photo stream, curiosity would get the better of her and she would swipe through images of Nicola Franconi. There he was, still standing, almost warning her to stay away. Yet she always came back to the empress and sketched her at night, in Rosewood's bed.

Paire started working on the hands, trying to recreate those pianist fingers. She couldn't get enough of them. She sketched pages of feet. By the weekend, Paire needed a professional manicure and pedicure. She marveled at the polished skin and nails of her fingers and toes, and compared them to her drawings and photos of the Empress Xiao Zhe Yi. At some level, Paire recognized that she was becoming too emotionally attached, but just as Lucia and Mayer had fallen in love by accident, Paire formed her own taboo adhesion. She allowed herself the exhilarating decadence of becoming the empress's caretaker.

When Paire went to her regular studio modeling gig, the professor seated her on a plain wooden stool with her hands on her hips. The seated pose was easy to hold, but the wooden seat dug into her ass, and Paire's right buttock would fall asleep. She wore a red silk robe bought for fifteen dollars in Chinatown. The professor told her she could improvise poses, and she kept the robe partially on her, opening it across her middle so that the edges of the fabric framed her nipples. She dared to sit with a wide stance like the empress, so the rows of scribbling students would be able to see the most private expanse of skin from her chin down to her feet. Paire sat a little more proudly than usual, and hoped the class would take special notice of her fingers and toes, buffed to a satin luster.

CHAPTER 6

Rosewood and Paire stood at the base of an indoor rock climbing wall. The facility had once been a warehouse in the industrial interior of Brooklyn and had been gutted, leaving only the brick superstructure and windows that let in a cascade of sunlight. The giant room now housed an artificial landscape of cliffs, with multicolored plastic holds bolted on the sides.

Since Paire didn't own shorts, they had to buy her some along the way. She had on her loosest T-shirt, which had a quote stylized in old typewriter lettering: *Adventure must start with running away from home. William Bolitho.*

The harness fit too snugly around her hips, and she wasn't used to the sensation of being gripped and pinched in those places, at least not like that. From where she stood on a bouncy mat, a rope rose from the harness like an umbilical cord, all the way up the wall, some fifty feet above them. She'd picked out a red rope, naturally choosing crimson when she had the chance. Rosewood fastened it to the belaying device and a few screwgate carabiners. At the top of the wall, the rope fed through an anchor, and descended back to Rosewood, who served as her belayer.

"Are you ready for this?" he asked.

"Sure," she said, sounding more confident than she felt.

"If you fall, it won't be very far. I'll anchor you."

Paire understood why they were there at the rock wall. Or at least, Rosewood had explained his reasons for bringing her here. Every night, she'd been dreaming about the empress. It was always the same scene. In her dream, the empress was a real, flesh-and-blood woman instead of a painting. The Jia Shun Empress stood on the far bank of a river while Paire watched from the opposite shore. Her bare feet sank into the mud. Rather than slipping in it, she was glued to the bank securely by it, so she wasn't afraid of being so close to the water. Between them the river was a rapid, silty flow, thick and chocolaty like the Mississippi. Paire could smell the rich clay stirred up by the scour. Unlike a real freshwater river, it also carried the trace scent of sea salt in a brisk breeze she'd only felt on Maine's stony beaches. Another step and she could be carried off. In the water, several multicolored buoys bounced along the surface, pulled by the current, but not carried off, because they were anchored beneath the water. She recognized them instantly—they were lobster traps. This made the water even more dangerous than the current. She didn't want to cross. It was safer to stand glued to the clay bank and admire the empress from a distance. Still, when she beckoned to her with those long, perfect fingers, Paire couldn't refuse the invitation. She stepped forward, hearing the audible suction as her foot ripped out of the mud. The moment her foot landed in the river Paire was pulled as if caught in a snare. Her body slipped into the water. She flapped her arms to fight it, but she felt the moisture envelop her, then hood her head, clogging her mouth and nose, deafening her when it flooded her ears. She struggled against the current as it spun her. When she found the surface of the water, she bobbed like one of the buoys, fighting for air even though she was only dreaming. Something caught her leg. The lines from the lobster traps had wrapped around her ankles. The ropes led from the buoys down to the caged traps at the bottom of the riverbed. Water splashed in her eyes, but occasionally she caught glimpses of the woman in red on the far shore, who stared back impassively. Paire kept swimming in her direction, against the underwater tether on one ankle, then another. She couldn't break free from those lines no matter how hard she kicked. The ropes caught her arms next, preventing Paire from treading water. The buoys clustered around her. The ropes pulled slowly but firmly until her head sank under the muddy water. She opened her eyes under the river and saw nothing but a brown murk, and her limbs thrashed wildly against her restraints as she sank to the bottom, where the graveyard of lobster traps waited for her. Paire lost sight of the empress while gasping for her life.

What this meant for Rosewood was that Paire kicked him in bed every night until she woke him up. Two nights before, when her dream had startled her awake at three, she found Rosewood already up, flipping through her sketchbook, looking at pages of hands and feet, and, more damning, sketches of the empress's face.

At the climbing wall, she looked at the top and wondered how much it would hurt if she lost her grip.

"I better not fall," Paire said.

"You might fall, but you won't get hurt."

Rosewood had described the climbing gym as a "useful distraction." As she pulled at the harness around her hips, she dwelled on the word *useful.* "When am I ever going to use this?"

"You'd be surprised," Rosewood said.

She looked up at the wall. Fifty feet up, and she knew it would look even taller when she was at the top looking down. The only help she'd have getting up there were those multicolored grips. "I'm having doubts about this."

Rosewood placed a hand on her back, between the shoulder blades, where Paire was convinced he could feel how forcefully her heart was pumping. He said, "You're letting that thing get the better of you." She remembered how Rosewood ignited when he first saw the empress, how he had to rush them home and strip down in the foyer. Had he forgotten about that, she wondered.

"You know me that well?"

"I've known you long enough to see a change. You've never reacted like this to anything else. By process of elimination, it's the Qi." He spoke so tartly she wondered if he might actually be jealous of what the empress evoked from his girlfriend. Rosewood wouldn't say it, but he must have noted that Paire had never had reactions like this to his work, artistically or otherwise. He added, "Don't fixate on any one thing. It won't liberate you. It's more likely to keep you trapped."

She didn't want to admit any allegiance to the painting, but she found herself making excuses. "It's not a bad thing to be inspired."

"You're kicking me in your sleep. I need to get some rest."

"This is going to make it better?" she asked.

"It's training. Trust me," he said. "Remember, jugs are your best friend."

"Excuse me?"

"The big holds on the wall, the ones that are easy to grab. Those are jugs."

"Seriously?"

"Chalk your hands." He handed her a white ball, the size of a baseball, and she rolled it around her palms and fingers until she was fairly certain they were dry.

"I feel ridiculous," she remarked. This was true, but more because she'd overdressed for the occasion. Despite the shorts and loose T-shirt, her vibrant hair and beet-red lipstick were too dazzling for athletic gear. This gym was not the place for fashion statements. Some of the other climbers to their left and right smirked at her.

He leaned into her ear and urged, "Climb."

She started up the wall, reaching for a green hold, then digging a toe into a pink mound of plastic. Her shoes were different from anything she'd ever worn, and resembled ballet shoes with hard soles. The moment her other foot rose off the ground, the first slipped off, and she stumbled on the blue mat and tumbled into Rosewood. Agitated, she said, "What is this supposed to help with?"

"Concentration. Don't use your toe unless you have to. Use the inside of the foot. Your foot should be turned out like a frog."

Rosewood had tried having a conversation with Paire about the Empress Xiao Zhe Yi, but she didn't like to talk about the painting, because she didn't want to admit her fascination with it. So last night, when her rabbit kicks woke him up, he forced the conversation without ever mentioning the Qi by name. "You know how much a painting is worth?" he asked.

"As much or as little as someone's willing to pay for it?" she responded.

"There is no inherent value to art. I know I'm not supposed to say that, because it's how I make my living, but it's the truth. Nothing that I sell is going to cure cancer, or feed people. Nothing that I make will create a solution for real-life problems."

To Paire's regret, her first thought was: *maybe that's just your work.* But she wouldn't say this. She wouldn't hurt him. She knew what he was doing. The same way Rosewood had recognized a change in Paire, Paire too saw a change in how Rosewood looked at her, with a measured pity for how she fawned over the empress. Not even the painting itself, for he was never at the gallery when she was actually aweing over it, but the secondary images of it, the photos on her cell phone and the sketches in her pad. When he diminished the value of his own work, he was trying to wean her off her reliance. She had to tread carefully to spare his feelings. "What's the value, then?"

"Art stimulates thought and emotion. If you're lucky, it can stir up a cultural dialogue. Once people start talking, start bickering with each other, there's a chance that they can figure out real solutions that make progress."

This might have been the role of Rosewood's work, but she questioned whether this was the function of all art. Nevertheless, she played along. "If that's the case, isn't there a value for whatever sparks that dialogue? Building momentum from inertia, and all that?"

"As much value as anything else that can change the way people think. But no more, and no less."

"So, as much or as little as someone is willing to pay," she said.

Since their conversation hadn't convinced Rosewood that she was any closer to abandoning her obsession with the Qi, he ended up suggesting an activity where they wouldn't have to talk, where she would have to focus on something right in front of her, instead of daydreaming about the painted birchwood on the Fern's rear wall.

She reached for the green hold again. He placed his hands on her back and whispered in her ear. "Try two hands," he suggested. His arms didn't envelop her but his touch felt like its own kind of embrace, the whisper in her ear intimate as a mattress confessional. She liked it. She wondered if all this effort from Rosewood came from a desire to keep Paire all to himself. If so, she welcomed the attention.

She grabbed the plastic nub with both hands, and hoisted her foot onto the pink hold.

"Roll your foot into the wall," he said.

She lifted her other leg and found a blue knob. Her shoe kept slipping. "Don't go for the round ones—they're the slopers. They're harder to stay on, because there's no edge. Find the ridges. Those are the incuts—good for hand-holds."

She wasn't following everything, and her eyes kept darting up and down the wall, unsure where she should focus. Someone to her left knew what she was doing, and spidered up the wall.

Her left foot found a blue ridge, and she felt a moment of balance, with both hands fastened securely onto jugs, her feet sufficiently froggy.

Rosewood coached from the floor, "Remember, if you can climb a ladder, you can climb a wall."

For this moment, she felt good, her mind blissfully free of anything to do with the Fern Gallery. She moved upward slowly but steadily, ambling from hold to hold, maintaining her balance. The clarity lasted only a few seconds. A vision of the empress flickered into her thoughts. Her focus now disrupted, her hand found a sloper, and she tilted off-balance. Her left foot slipped, and after a few flaps of her arms, she fell off the wall. Paire had climbed about twenty feet off the floor, twice the height of a basketball rim. She panicked when she realized she was going to plummet to the floor. Her body tensed, preparing for the impact, which assuredly wouldn't be as pain-free as Rosewood had promised. But she stopped in midair. After her moment of lurching panic, the rope caught her, and Paire dangled in the air by her harness.

She rotated on the rope like a Christmas ornament until she faced Rosewood, whose gloved hands secured the rope. He smiled up at her. "Not so bad, right?" She smiled down at him. She liked trusting him like this, and for a briefest moment, her brain stopped flooding with thoughts of the empress.

That morning, on the taxi over to the climbing gym, Rosewood had tried to address her attraction to the Qi again, this time more directly. He approached the subject gently, so he wouldn't embarrass her. "What do you like about it?"

Paire had wondered the same thing herself ever since she'd first seen the portrait. She wondered if the allure was simply a consequence of having watched a man die in front of it. Rosewood might have questioned the inherent value of art, but that painting was at least worth someone's life, because that was the price that someone was willing to pay for it. But the more she learned about it, the stronger her attraction became. She admired the strength she saw in the woman. She wasn't an empress, but had been a real person that the artist had dressed in costume. "I like that this woman gets to be someone else."

Paire had hinted that she wanted to separate herself from her past, but she'd never told him why. While the taxi jostled them on the way to the climbing gym, he took a guess. "I know you don't like to talk about your family. I get it. How many times do you hear me talk about mine? And that's fair enough. It's healthy to know who you *don't* want to be. Look at me. I don't want to be a soldier."

Paire knew more about Rosewood than she heard him share with others because she was nosy enough to ask about his family and he never evaded her questions. When he was fourteen his parents had enrolled him at West Point Academy. His father had wanted him to pursue the family trade, but Derek Rosewood had inherited his mom's slight build and pretty face, and didn't fit in. Perhaps he was born with the predisposition to rebel against authority, or perhaps he'd learned it through living with Grant Rosewood, a domineering man, who, in the photos Paire had seen, towered above the rest of the family, with heavy arms and shoulders like shot puts. Derek Rosewood got himself expelled from West Point by repeatedly showing up to class naked, the way it was rumored Edgar Allan Poe got himself tossed out. As she remembered this story, Rosewood had said, "It's trickier to know who you *want* to be. And you're only going to find out if you get out and experience as much as you can.

As an artist, that's also how you're going to find your voice. At least, that's what I did."

The taxi rounded a corner, and she saw the sign for the gym. Dover Cliffs. "So if I hate this?"

He said, "Then at least you tried it. But it would pay to be good at this."

"Why?"

"Because you can apply it to other things."

Paire didn't think he was being fair. Most of her life in Abenaki seemed to be a long string of things she knew she didn't like. Just two years out of Maine, she was just starting to get to know what she *liked*. She liked Rosewood. She liked cozying into his warmth at night. She liked getting support and mentoring from an established artist. She even enjoyed the occasional leer from strangers, giving her more attention than she ever got in Maine. She liked creating, even if it was only on her sketchpad. She hadn't had the time to learn much more than that.

Having thought about her family again, her anger propelled her. Paire started back up the rock wall, and scrambled up the sides more confidently, trying to do the scary thing, even if she fell. She found the jugs and insets, avoiding the slopers. When she thought about her feet, she concentrated more on how she placed them, and less about silly things like whether her toenails could match the glow of the empress's.

After the crime, the one she didn't like think about, which put Lake Novis in prison and left Cissy Novis dead, Katie Novis was taken in by her grandmother, Gilda Abington. *Of the Abenaki Abingtons*, she'd joke to herself. She always remembered Gilda as a spinster, a creaky woman with a perpetual frown who had shriveled in her decades of Maine salt-winds. At one point Gilda had been married to John Abington, twenty-two years older than she. John Abington had founded Abington Press, a publishing house that specialized in children's books. The press brought the beloved Claymore character, an illustrated cartoon armadillo, to the childhoods of a generation. *Claymore the Courageous Armadillo. Claymore Wonders Who's in the Dark.*

Claymore Goes to City Hall. Just a sampling of titles. Abington Press had built a small empire around these titles and other kids' books. Even Rosewood had once referenced Claymore in passing, but Paire didn't dare explain her family's connection to the Claymore books. She never mentioned the name Abington.

John Abington passed away several years before Katie Novis was born, so she never knew him. When he was alive, he apparently split his time between New York and Maine—the house in Abenaki was considered the summer house when it was built. Gilda didn't like New York, and as Katie later found through research, was reluctant to spend time in the city where she knew her husband kept mistresses. After they'd been married twenty years, Gilda started staying up in Abenaki, and the two lived in separate cities. When John died, Gilda took over the estate, and held a position on the board of directors for Abington Press, although Katie suspected that she served more of a figurehead role. She never spoke of the publishing business around the house.

John and Gilda had one child, Cecily Abington, Cissy to most. Once her parents had separated, Cissy spent most of her time with her mother in Maine—at least until Cissy's late teens, when she was transferred out of the house and into the hospital.

When Katie was taken in by her grandmother, Gilda was a widow, alone in a gigantic Queen Anne mansion on the Atlantic coastline. Buffered by pines on one side and a rocky cliff on the other, it overlooked a tempestuous set of breakers that churned white foam on the calmest days. Gilda's master bedroom was a round room in the second story of the bulky turret that faced the ocean. On the first floor of the turret, Gilda kept a round library and office, where she spent days leafing through books. Katie had considered Gilda largely asexual, a nun without the habit. If her grandmother had been lonely, she'd never let on. True to her New Englander roots, she didn't talk about her emotions.

From a young age, Katie wandered around the grounds, logging a good hunk of time in a pear orchard cloistered by a wall of pines. John had had it planted, so Gilda almost never visited. The fruit grew small and tasted almost sugarless until the moment each piece dropped from its tree and turned soft on the ground. They grew Bartlett, Seckel, and yes, Anjou varieties, and sometimes Katie treated herself to the occasional edible plucking. In the orchard, Katie didn't have to look at that pale yellow house and see the silhouette of her disinterested grandmother in the windows. She didn't have to think about Abington Press, Claymore the armadillo, or her parents. This was the safest place she knew, and so long as the weather stayed north of twenty degrees, she braved the winter to sneak out to her private place.

Gilda had made attempts to wipe her daughter out of public record. She couldn't control every reporter, but when Lake Novis was on trial, she kept the story from hitting the press. It only leaked out to a few outlets outside of Maine, and never spread as wide, or as sensationally, as it could have, especially when it was attached to the Abington family. Gilda had gone so far as to purchase and burn copies of the newspapers that ran coverage. She burned them right in the pear orchard, and when she told Katie about it years later, Gilda's story inspired her granddaughter to make her own purge fires when she turned klepto in high school. Her efforts didn't stop local rumors and whispers, but Gilda did what she could to wipe Cissy's name out of memory. When Katie Novis changed her name, she felt like she was extending these efforts, effectively ending the Abington family line.

Rosewood occasionally asked why Paire didn't visit her Aunt Gilda, but the truth was Gilda didn't want her to visit. Last year, when Paire first started school, she tried to call Gilda every week. At first Gilda merely offered a few terse sentences before making an excuse to end the call. After a while, she didn't pick up.

Paire wrapped her arm around the top of the rock wall. She'd scrambled up all fifty feet, and felt a little dizzy when she looked down at Rosewood, still anchoring her with both hands choking the rope. The height shouldn't have bothered her. The cliffs at Aunt Gilda's were more than one hundred feet above the churning ocean.

"Now fall," Rosewood called to her.

"Excuse me?"

"We'll teach you how to rappel later. Just drop. It's easier than you think."

Paire's heart pounded.

"Let go."

Funny, Paire thought, the whole purpose of this trip was to keep her from dwelling on the painting. More important, it was to keep her from stewing about all the things that made her susceptible to the draw of that painting. The things she hated about her past. This had failed. As she hung from the top of the wall, she distinctly remembered the cliffs outside the Queen Anne in Abenaki. How, when she had wandered close and looked over the drop, she'd hoped Gilda would show some concern, even a tap of the window from inside the house.

Arms outstretched and eyes closed, Paire dropped backward from the rock wall, first feeling a knotting in her stomach when she fell, then feeling liberated as her body breezed through the air. For an instant, she abandoned her fear. She was doing the *scary thing*, the ultimate scary thing, and though terrified for her life, her other worries vaporized. It was bliss.

The sensation didn't last long. When Rosewood successfully belayed her, the rope tightened and Paire dangled in the air. She felt a slight melancholy.

Rosewood lowered her gradually to the floor, and Paire kicked at the wall whenever it felt like she might collide with it. All the way down, she thought of her mother, who had died at the end of a rope.

Cissy Novis had hanged herself. The police would later determine that she'd first tried in the bathroom with the bedsheets, throwing them over the shower curtain rod and twisting the fabric as tight as she could. The knot was never tight enough to choke her, and although Cissy was petite like her daughter, when she let her weight drop, it broke the rod. In the garage, Cissy found rope and threw it over a crossbeam. She stood on two plastic milk crates and kicked them away, and according to accounts, twisted about like a worm on a hook for fifteen minutes until she finally expired. The police found her in a floral dress she almost never wore, something that flared out at the knees like a Doris Day housewife's dress.

Katie had once asked Gilda, "Why'd she do it?"

Gilda's minimal response had a sense of duty to it, as if she were trying to imprint a message onto Katie. "Some cookies come out of the oven wrong. When that happens, the only thing to do is throw them away."

Paire felt her shoes touch the floor, and a moment later Rosewood's hand on her back. She felt less inhibited than she had moments before, and kissed him. "My parents were both criminals. They did bad things. That's why I don't talk about them. That's why it's easier for me to think about what I *don't want* than what I *want*. Because I don't want to be like them." She felt her shoulders relax as she said this.

Rosewood mulled this over as he unscrewed his carabiners. He made no show that this was the first time she'd told him one of her big secrets, but he smiled sheepishly to himself. "You know, the best way to cure a phobia is to expose yourself to the thing you're afraid of."

"Do the scary thing?"

"They call it exposure therapy."

Her mind flashed back to dinner a few weeks ago. "You want me to eat a lobster?"

"That's not what you're afraid of," he said. "I want you to break the law."

CHAPTER 7

Roughly forty feet underground, Paire and Rosewood stood on the platform of Wall Street station.

The subway wasn't always reliable, but they timed it so the train dumped them on the platform just before three thirty in the morning. At that hour, the only other person in sight was a homeless man bundled into a sleeping bag under one of the benches. No cops.

As with most New York subway stops, faint, harsh light glinted off the tiles. Despite the fact that the station was in the heart of the financial district, it was grimier than most. Two trenches flanked the central platform. Across the rails, too far to touch, the white tiles were flourished with a strip of red-and-white checkerboard. *Wall Street* had been spelled out in microtiles that reminded Paire of ancient Greco-Roman mosaics.

They dressed in identical beige uniforms with MTA badges embroidered on the sleeves and reflective strips looped around their waists and upper arms. To make them look more like authentic MTA uniforms, Rosewood and Paire had crudded up the knees and shins with spatters of paint, which, from a distance, looked like mud. Paire thought they looked a bit like firemen's uniforms. Their worker boots were heavier than anything she was used to wearing. They carried yellow construction helmets, and each of them toted a satchel: a bulky duffel for Rosewood, and a long black tube for Paire. Nothing big enough to resemble the "suspicious package" that subway riders were warned about.

A few minutes later, two others stepped off a Brooklyn-bound 2 train. They wore matching MTA uniforms, so even though Paire had never met these men, she knew they belonged to the group.

Charlie and Humberto. After another five minutes, a Bronx-bound 3 let off laggard Lazaro. Paire was highly aware that she was the only woman in the bunch.

The other three were older than Paire but younger than Rosewood, somewhere in their mid-to-late twenties. Humberto had walnut skin and black whiskers hanging off his chin. Charlie was a redhead with freckles on the backs of his hands. Lazaro had insomniac rings under his eyes and a piercing through one eyebrow. They were all thin, and their gender-neutering uniforms draped off them. Paire was nervous their youth would give them away. For example, people might notice that Charlie's baby skin had never seen a day of manual labor. She'd trussed up her hair to minimize it, but her crown of artificial red seemed like a bullseye tonight.

"You're shaking," Charlie said to Paire. Irish accent, she noted.

"Am I?" She looked down at her hands.

"Just a bit," said Humberto.

"Try not to do that," said Lazaro with a scratchy voice, looking around the station.

Rosewood said, "Act like you belong here. That's how people get away with it." He seemed so hungry to be here, more vibrant than she was used to seeing him. She wondered what this gave him that the money and notoriety couldn't provide.

He pulled out two-way radios from his satchel, yellow-and-black hunks of disposable plastic that resembled gigantic bumble bees, and handed them out. "Equipment check."

Everyone turned knobs until pinpoint green lights glowed on all of them. They spoke into their radios to test them.

"Hakuna matata," said Rosewood.

"Hakuna matata," repeated Charlie.

"Hakuna matako," said Lazaro.

"What's that?" Humberto asked.

"It means 'no ass' in Swahili." Lazaro tugged his uniform against his skinny behind and wiggled it.

"Hakuna matako." Paire chuckled, and the laughter helped settle her nerves.

Rosewood spoke to them with patriarchal authority. "So I guess these all work." He was more serious tonight, without the lilting playfulness Paire had come to expect.

They walked with Rosewood in the lead, marching together in his wake. Surrounded by a team, she felt both safer and more conspicuous. Her steps started to bounce again, as if she were walking across a trampoline. She fingered the collapsed spring baton in her uniform's roomy side pocket, the one she'd dug out of Rosewood's closet. Rosewood himself had advised her to carry it, *just in case*.

They trotted up the stairs to the mezzanine, which looked similar to the platform level, but with no trenches and more light— essentially a long corridor of white tiles, dusty from knee-level down. They carried their gear to the corridor's midpoint and set down their bags.

Rosewood pointed at the boys with his radio as he designated roles. "Humberto, Charlie—spotters. There and there." He sounded more serious than she'd ever heard him.

They strapped on their plastic yellow helmets—Humberto had scratched his up to make it look used—and jogged out to the far ends of the walkway. They stood like sentries, looking out for cops, MTA security, or concerned citizens.

Rosewood addressed Lazaro. "Let's set up the scrims." Then to Paire, he said, "Unpack the goods."

On their knees, Lazaro and Rosewood hastily unzipped the small pile of black bags and cases, their expressions reminiscent of surgeons cutting out a tumor. Segment by segment, they pulled out hollow aluminum tubing that they twisted together in seconds. Paire guessed they had done this so many times that by now it had become rote. The tube segments jointed together until they created two rectangular frames. As if pulling a magician's handkerchief from a bottomless pocket, they drew lightweight silk out of the bags and fitted it over the frame until it was taut. Within a minute they stood the structure upright so each one served like a changing screen. The scrims obscured them from the ends of the passageway. Neither of the men looked anywhere but at their work, but Paire couldn't help but occasionally peek from behind their screens, up and down the corridor to make sure Charlie and Humberto were still at their posts, keeping them safe.

While they set up the scrims, Paire unzipped her own duffel and pulled out supplies. First, the bucket of paste that she and Rosewood had boiled up the night before. Unlike traditional wheat paste, the secret ingredient was Teknabond, which Rosewood explained made the work "hurricane resistant." His words. She pried the lid off the small plastic bucket with a screwdriver. The mixture was still grayish blue and had the consistency of chowder. Another bad association with Maine.

Out came the brushes, rollers, and paint tray. By the time she laid out the painting materials and poured the paste in the tray, Rosewood and Lazaro were already finished assembling the scrim. Lazaro moved with the fluidity of a short-order cook.

She had just finished sliding the fuzzy foam tubes over the paint roller cages when the men took them, slathered them in the paste, and began spreading a thin coat on the tiles.

From Charlie's end of the corridor, Paire heard the distant pounding of heavy heels. Then yakking. When she looked, Charlie was talking to a drunk couple. She couldn't hear words, just complaints as Charlie redirected them to a detour. The man was in his fifties and wore a leather motorcycle jacket. His companion was a woman in clunky combat boots that rose above the knee and purple lipstick that glowed, even at a distance. She was rocky on her heels, and he had trouble standing in place, staggering back and forth as he argued with Charlie. The couple might have fallen over if they hadn't been supporting each other.

"Don't pay attention to them," Rosewood muttered. "Eyes on the prize."

While they painted, Paire uncorked the long black cylinder and laid out the panels they had printed back in Brooklyn. First drawn, then scanned, enlarged, and printed, the full design measured twenty feet across. They'd had to cut it into five panels to transport it, trimming the edges with X-Acto blades. She unrolled each panel and configured them on the ground.

Having finished slopping on the paste, Lazaro and Rosewood took each panel and carefully applied it to the wall, rolling more paste over it to glue it to the tiles.

This was going so quickly she could barely keep up. She unzipped a flat parcel and took out the stencils. Drawn, traced, and meticulously cut apart with blades, she handled them as delicately as lace. Two designs. Three panels for one, two for the other. She laid them on the floor. The first design was six feet long, the second just under four feet. This was the part she had needed to practice at his studio multiple times until she got it right. To the right of the boys' wheat pasting, she chose an open space of tile, and while considering for the moment that this would be the moment she was truly breaking the law, jiggled an aerosol can and sprayed a coating of adhesive to the paper stencils. Lazaro and Rosewood were affixing the fourth and fifth panels while she mounted her stencils on the wall, panel by panel. The tall one the size of an adult. Next to it, the short one the height of a child. Not so firmly that they'd tear when they peeled off the stencils, but firmly enough to give the designs firm edges and prevent overspray.

A man in his thirties stumbled into view. His face soot-stained and sporting a jungle of beard, he wore an outer layer of military fatigues. Paire tried to ignore him, but he was louder than the drunk couple. He shouted obscenities at Charlie and gestured wildly, cocking his arm as if threatening to punch him, but not actually taking a swing. She assumed he was crazy. Frustrated that he couldn't walk down the hallway, he paced in a circle in front of Charlie, who held his arms up to blockade the man, as if fending off a bear. At the other end of the corridor, Humberto looked on with interest, but didn't leave his post.

The pasted portion of the mural hung in place, the goop drying and cementing it to the tile. Rosewood stepped back and cocked his head to make sure the panels had come together properly. Paire handed him and Lazaro two cans of black spray paint, and they rattled them to stir up the mixture. The final touch.

The man in the fatigues barked something at Charlie and stormed off.

They dusted black spray paint across the stencils, their hands gliding over the paper. Then Paire packed the paint rollers back in the satchels and hammered the lid back on the paste jug.

Their radios came to life for the first time. "Heads up," said Charlie through the speaker.

Paire's chest felt icy. At the end of the hallway, a short man in an MTA uniform with a moustache approached Charlie. A real MTA uniform. A real MTA guard. Charlie left his radio on so others could hear.

Lazaro said to Paire, "Don't look."

"Eyes on the prize," repeated Rosewood as he sprayed the bottom of the six-foot stencil, unfazed by the confusion. "Almost done."

On the radio, they heard the MTA man ask Charlie, "What's going on?"

"Light patchwork on the tiles," said Charlie.

"Where's the notice?" More combative this time.

Charlie stalled. "You got plenty of notice."

The MTA man sighed, likely exhausted and in no mood for an argument. "Just show me the papers."

Paire heard a ruffle of documents as Charlie procured what she knew were forged permits. If this got to trial, she imagined what kind of sentence she'd get, whether she would see the same judge with the Benjamin Franklin spectacles who'd approved her name change. She worried that in New York impersonating public utilities workers might be misconstrued as terrorism, and whether this transgression might somehow fall under the Patriot Act. She looked down at her hands, and they were indeed shaking visibly. The guys had stopped painting, but were waiting a moment for it to set.

"We should go," she said.

"Just a minute," said Rosewood.

Paire heard rustling on the radio. She suspected the MTA man was reading through Charlie's documents, trying to determine whether they were authentic.

Rosewood nodded to Lazaro and they peeled off the stencils, rolling them as they went, and stuffing them, crumpled, into a duffel.

Humberto appeared next to them, making Paire jump. "We've got to go."

Rosewood said, "Charlie's taking care of it."

Humberto nodded to the other end of the hallway. "Not the permits. We have police on this end."

Rosewood said to Paire, "Grab a bag. Don't look up. You're exhausted from work." He looked at the stretched silk regretfully. "Leave the scrims up."

Paire took just a second to look at what they had just completed. The twenty-foot pasted mural created the illusion that a hole had been cracked in the wall, giving the viewer a look behind the tiles. Within the crevice, a huddle of stringy, muscular workers clustered together. Their arms pushed up over their heads, they held up riveted girders, which bowed from the weight of the city above. The shape of the opening formed a perverse smile, and the sallow workers with ashen faces seemed like rotted teeth. Beside the crack were two characters, rendered in spray paint, staring into the gaping hole in the wall. The tall one was a fat businessman—not Abel Kasson, but close enough that when Kasson saw it, he'd note the comparison. He stood beside the chasm like a circus barker, with a cane pointed to the exposé. The second character, a boy at the man's feet, held up a dollar's admission to the peep show.

Humberto waved to Charlie with his radio, and when Charlie lifted the talk button, he said as calm as a flight captain, "We're going to wrap it up here." Down the hall, Charlie immediately turned on his heels and walked toward them, leaving his fake documents in the hands of the MTA man.

"Where the hell are you going?" shouted the man, his Queens accent coming out more strongly.

In a few seconds Charlie reached the others, and they briskly walked en masse back the way they had come, bags in hand. As they rounded the corner, they passed two uniformed officers. They weren't the same officers who had spoken with Paire the day Nicola Franconi had stabbed himself, but they were similarly bulky, with shaved heads. Rosewood said hello, trying to sound fatigued. Paire wanted to sprint but had to be content with walking at a deliberate pace. Rosewood had told her several times not to run unless they absolutely had to.

The MTA man, still dumbfounded by what was happening, shouted after them, "Hey!" Possibly he didn't want to antagonize a group of five, alone in an underground corridor at three in the morning. His voice seemed apprehensive, questioning his own judgment in trying to stop them. But once the team rounded out of sight the police turned the corner and came into view, and he found new courage. "Stop them!"

"Drop the bags," said Rosewood.

He ran, and they followed.

The boys all ran faster than Paire, and she had to push herself to keep up. They had longer legs, and more practice dodging the police. The boots didn't help. They clambered down the stairs to the subway platform, their uniforms rustling.

When mapping their exit, they'd anticipated a couple of routes. One would be to step on the next train out of the station. The other was to exit the station up the stairs to the street. Neither option availed itself. Paire could hear shouting behind them: the two cops and the MTA man. They were only a few seconds behind them.

Rosewood looked up and down the platform, scanning the scenario for a blink before he said, "Onto the tracks."

He hopped into the trench. Their accomplices dropped down into the tracks as well. Spurred by the shouts of men behind them, Paire planted her hands on the yellow safety line and climbed down. Her boots sank into slippery, packed dirt between the ties. The practice on the rock wall helped a little with her balance, but she still fumbled for footing. They started down the tracks, all of them careful where they placed their boots. She tried to plant her feet on the railroad ties but didn't always find them. Her boots sank in the loose aggregate and debris—soggy newspaper, an empty Coke bottle, brown paper bags, and empty cardboard coffee cups. She looked over her shoulder and saw the two uniformed officers charging at them, with the moustached man catching up on the stairs. Running as fast as the tracks would allow, she slipped, and rocked off balance. She would have fallen if Rosewood hadn't caught her arm.

"Keep to the right," Rosewood urged, cautioning her to avoid the electric rail. Had she fallen, she would have braced herself on the electric current.

They sped forward, down the length of the platform. Behind them, the officers jumped down into the trench, possibly intrigued by the challenge. She heard the sound of their boots crunching gravel and garbage.

She could hear her own breathing and feel her lungs begin to pinch, but she was so frightened she wouldn't dare stop. Lazaro was out in front, followed by Humberto, then Charlie. Rosewood had trailed behind with Paire to make sure she could keep up. She charged as fast as she could without risking another tumble, and they made it all the way to the end of the station and disappeared into the shadows. The subway tunnel turned into a mineshaft, sparsely lit by the dimmest bulbs.

They all slowed in the dark. In the lead, Lazaro crept daintily on the ties as if tiptoeing on lily pads. Paire kept her arms stretched to the sides so she wouldn't slip, using the weak tunnel lights as beacons.

The men behind them shouted after them, the predictable "Stop!" and "Police!"

Once they were in the darkness, their shouts bounced around the tunnel, making it hard to determine the point of origin. Hard breathing from the rest of the group blended into a symphonic wheezing. Someone coughed, maybe Charlie. The air tasted damp. Her nose dripped.

They kept going in silence for another minute before Rosewood said, "Slow down." Under a faint light, she saw him look back the way they had come.

She looked and listened.

"They're not following us. It's too dangerous. They don't want to get shot in the dark, and they don't want to get hit by a train. They'll call it in." She could still see a pinpoint of light where the tunnel behind them opened into Wall Street station. She expected to see flashlight beams bouncing around in the dark, but the officers had climbed out of the trenches.

Her lungs stung even more now that they slowed down to a walk. When she caught her breath, she asked, "So why are we still on train tracks?"

"We're finding an exit."

They rounded a bend, after which they lost the light from Wall Street station.

They hadn't prepared for this, and Paire had no idea if anyone knew what they were doing. When they passed under the next tunnel bulb, she looked to the others to see if they had the same confidence as Rosewood. Humberto seemed at ease, while Charlie and Lazaro looked edgy.

The acrid smells in the corridor mixed mildew, rubber, hard water, and charcoal, as if she were standing inside an abandoned smokestack. She tried to calm herself by listening to their footsteps, scuffing along the trash and gravel. Their boots tramped through more water, a section of subway that had flooded, or never drained. They sloshed through a two-inch marsh. The liquid seeped in through the worn stitching in her heel, and she felt cool moisture dampen a sock. Paire imagined the liquid might be brown as milk chocolate.

Then she heard a new noise. Scratches on the wooden ties. Small creatures moving hesitantly, scrambling as they scurried away in the dark. Paire kicked something soft with her boot and gasped.

"Just kick them away," Humberto called back. "They can't bite through the boots."

Her breath quickened as another scrambled over her toe. Heavier and substantial, maybe the size of a burrito. Her fear had subsided, and turned to anger. She spoke softly to Rosewood, trying not to sound volatile, lest the rest of the crew regret having a tagalong. "You knew we might have to escape through the tunnels."

"Of course I did."

"Why didn't you tell me?"

"Honestly, I thought this would be a deal-breaker for you."

She remembered a furry gray rat she'd seen in Union Square with a hot dog nub in its mouth. Tried to remember how cute she thought it was at the time. "They carry disease," she said, stunned that this didn't rouse him.

"It's not my first time in a subway tunnel."

Every few steps, she felt something bombard her boot. Paire stepped on something soft, and it squeaked like a dog toy. She cursed to herself, too loudly, and lurched away. The squeaking magnified. Actual squeaks, chittering in the dark. A sonic irritant, like Styrofoam. Thousands blended together, possibly warning each other that intruders were tramping through their nest. The scraping of one hundred thousand toenails across the ground sounded like they might be tearing their own tunnels through the earth.

Rosewood called out to the group, "I'm going to turn on a flashlight, so I can check the map. If you don't like rodents, don't look down." A moment later a strong, wide beam burst through the darkness and up through the arched ceiling. He angled the light on a paper map of the subway grid. "The beauty of Wall Street station is that it's a short jaunt to other lines. We crisscross the tracks and we'll come up at another station. By this map, it won't be more than twenty minutes or so."

She looked over his shoulder at the map, and then couldn't stop herself from looking down at the tracks. The railway teemed with rats. All around them, hills of rodents tumbled over each other. They didn't look cute anymore. Their humps undulated in oceanic ripples. The flashlight glossed the grime on their pelts. Paire suppressed her gag impulse so she wouldn't seem weak in front of the others.

"Like kicking through autumn leaves," said Humberto, staying in the lead.

Paire tried to imagine it that way, but the density of the pack made her feel more like she was trudging through snow. The rest of them pulled out their flashlights and shone them across the nest, revealing how far it extended down the tunnel. Humberto seemed to revel in the thrill. When he swept his boot through the mass of rodents, rats flew through the air, only to be absorbed somewhere else in the mischief.

Paire flipped her spring baton to full extension and swatted at the rats by her feet. She batted away bodies, but more just filled the open spaces. She accidentally knocked her shin with the tip. At another time and place she would have paused to nurse the pain, but nothing stopped her from flailing the baton through the pack as she moved forward.

Over the screeches of the rodents she heard a distant whine of heavy metal.

The rats must have heard or felt it too, because a few moments later they skittered away from them, diving under the rails and finding holes wherever they could scoot, hidden except for earthworm tails. Vermin cleared a pathway on the tracks in just a few seconds. The absence of rat noises made the next shriek of grinding wheels that much louder.

The tracks vibrated. Not just the two railways, but the ties in between. A deep, low rumble filled the passageway. A faint light began to illuminate it.

"Stay high and avoid the rails," said Rosewood, his voice elevated. He crossed the tracks first, bounding over the first and then the second electric rails. Lazaro followed a moment later with a few impala hops. With the rumbling growing louder, Humberto signed the cross over his chest when he jumped. Charlie skipped over the first rail, and then lost his balance, almost falling backward into the live wire before he found his balance again. He leaped as high as he could over the second electric rail, and Rosewood secured his landing by grabbing his forearm and slapping him on the shoulder.

The whole passageway grumbled now, but Paire hadn't moved.

Around the bend, the first, then the second headlight of the train came into the view, rambling towards her.

"Jump!" Rosewood shouted to her, more insistent than ever. Worried, even.

She stood rooted to the ties and stared down the train. In that moment she considered her motivations for moving away from Abenaki. She thought that by fleeing Maine she might have a chance of outrunning the crazy, but given where she was, she wondered if crazy just clung to her. Maybe it was impossible to evade it.

"Move!"

The train raced toward her, lurching unevenly on the tracks, the way a runaway calash might teeter from the uneven draw of maniacal horses. A few more seconds and she might not even feel the impact.

They were all shouting her name. Her new name. Not Katie Novis, but, "Paire!"

This jogged her back to the present. She vaulted as high as she could over the first electric rail. As the train passed, its wind across her back gave her the added push to jump the second rail. As she launched over the electric current, she considered that just a few inches would mean the end of her. Not so different from the cliffs in Abenaki. Not so different from the near-death when she was a child. Her life had always been gifts of being in the right moment, at the right place.

When she landed, Rosewood held her close and prolonged the embrace. "Please don't do that again," he said into her ear, just loud enough to be heard above the grinding of steel. Lazaro slapped her on the back. They all watched the train rush past them, one of the conductors staring wide-eyed at them as he flew by. The grumble faded, until the tunnel was again vacant.

The group moved forward silently. A few rats scurried along the tracks, but nothing compared to the nest they'd trodden through. Paire didn't have to swat any with the baton.

A light appeared after a bend in the tunnel. Not as bright as

Wall Street station, but definitely some kind of station, which meant they could climb out of the pit.

Rosewood confirmed, "We're here."

When Paire saw the platforms, she asked, "What stop is this?"

"City Hall."

"It looks closed."

"It is closed. This station has been abandoned for years."

As they pulled themselves out of the ditch, Paire took a look around the station. A few electric lights illuminated the platform dimly, but they gave off a fraction of the light compared to an active subway stop. They reminded Paire of flaming sconces in a castle.

"Someone must have found the lights," said Charlie, pointing to a series of iron chandeliers that dangled above them.

She asked, "Are they usually off?"

He shrugged. "Hell if I know. I've never been here. None of us have."

Rosewood said, "Beautiful, though, isn't it?"

The station was magnificent, with the most elaborate tilework she'd seen in the New York underground. Its sweeping arches might have seemed more appropriate in a Tuscan wine cellar, and a portion of stained glass allowed filtered light to shine down from the street. Even at this hour, street lights found a way down here.

"We're under City Hall?"

"At this very moment," Lazaro said.

Paire found an exit sign and headed toward the archway that might lead them back to the street.

Rosewood stopped her. "We have to wait."

"For what?"

"It's about four thirty now. We'll wait another hour or so, when the first commuters start hitting the sidewalk. Then we'll walk out of here in plain sight."

"You're worried the police are still following us?"

He said, "They might not come after us in the tunnels, but we just vandalized Wall Street station. Someone's going to call it in. If we pop up a few blocks away, and we're the only people outside, someone's going to find us. It'll pay to wait another hour."

"What do we do in the meantime? Trivial Pursuit?"

"Take advantage of being in a place most people will never get to see."

Paire had to pee, but she supposed she could hold it a little longer. All five of them slid down the platform walls and stared up at the glow coming through the stained glass. It was cold, and she pressed against Rosewood for warmth. They listened to their own breathing. Now that they were safely cloistered, they all relaxed. Lazaro began giggling with relief, at first an accidental release, and then a fit of elation. Charlie joined him. Paire could still feel her heart close to bursting, but she gave in to it too. The laughter was infectious, all five of them releasing their tension in seizures of hysteria. Just like the *LAUGHTER* series.

She asked, "So how close did we come to getting busted, anyway?"

"Honestly? Pretty close." Rosewood seemed at ease again, and that put Paire at ease. "But we've come close a few times."

Lazaro nodded, indicating that he'd been there for those occasions. His eyebrow piercing gave off a molten reflection.

Charlie noticed something before the others. "Shit." At the far end of the platform, a group of three men wandered toward them.

"They did follow us," said Paire, immediately terrified.

"That's not the police," said Rosewood. He echoed Charlie's sentiment, "Shit." He stood and snapped to attention. Paire and the others stood as well. She wondered if they needed to run again.

As the men came closer, she could see they didn't wear uniforms. They dressed in tattered clothes, reminiscent of the bearded man who had barked at Charlie back at Wall Street station. From both the dirt and the dim light, they seemed to be sepia-toned, so that when they came toward them they created a mirage, as if a daguerreotype had come to life.

"What is this?" she whispered.

Lazaro leaned into her ear. "Ever hear that myth about the mole people who live underneath the city?"

"It's no myth," said Humberto.

The head man was taller than any of them. All three of them wore beards, but the tall one's beard matted and corkscrewed more than the others. His muscles had atrophied slightly from age, but his shoulders were broad, and his jaw clenched. With his two men flanking him, he waltzed up to the group with hands folded behind his back. His musk soured in her nose.

Of the two with him, the one on the right looked jumpy, not from nerves, but with a twitchiness that might have been a byproduct of drug use. Paire knew a fight would be five-to-three, but these men were tougher. She imaged how they must look to these people, five skinny college kids in their shiny beige uniforms with a spritz of stage dirt to act the part. They might seem cartoonish.

The front man spoke in a low, whiskey-scarred baritone. "Are you really MTA?"

"Of course we're not," said Rosewood, possibly trying to curry favor by hinting that they were all subversives.

"Then you really have no reason to be here." The man unclasped his hands from behind his back, and when he folded them over his groin, Paire saw that he held a sizeable hunting knife. Even in the dim light from the stained glass, the steel gleamed. The twitchy one darted his eyes, staring hungrily at Paire. She wondered when last they'd come across strangers down here, and what might have happened. City Hall station might have been a Venus flytrap where unsuspecting dupes were lost and digested.

"We'll be here for an hour, and then we'll leave," Rosewood declared firmly.

"Not with those clothes and whatever you've got on you," said the leader.

For a fleeting moment, Paire hoped that this might all be one big joke, and that this was one of Rosewood's many contacts in the art world. At any moment the two of them would bust up laughing and give each other man-hugs. In order to keep her skin from prickling, Paire dreamed they would shoot the breeze over a shared bottle of hooch.

Charlie's reaction dissuaded her of this fantasy. He whispered to Rosewood just loud enough that the rest could hear, "We're dumping the clothes anyway."

Rosewood pretended not to hear him. "We're just passing through. This doesn't need to go wrong."

The man stared. Apparently he wasn't planning on bantering with any of the soap-scrubbed surface folk. He stepped closer, with the knife pointed at Rosewood's navel.

Rosewood raised his arm and leveled his grandfather's service revolver at the man's chest. The skylight faintly glinted off the metal, but between the dim light and the speed of the movement, several seconds passed before everyone realized that a pistol had been produced, and in the quietude of this abandoned station, any number of men could be murdered without attracting any attention from above. When he cocked the hammer with his thumb, the mechanical double click bounced off the tiles and all the station's hard surfaces with a wintery reverberation. "How wrong do you want this to go?"

The twitchy one turned and sprinted down the platform. Moments later, the second man tapped the leader's shoulder and backed away. After considering his options, the leader lifted his hands in a *you got me* gesture, and wiggled the blade in his right hand, as if to say that he could possibly have still driven the tip of that knife through Rosewood's abdomen, if it were worth the bother. He paced backward a few steps, pivoted, and strolled in the opposite direction.

Noting the expressions of the other men, Paire was convinced that none of them had known that Rosewood was carrying the weapon.

Rosewood said to her, "That's why I keep this."

They spent the remaining hour somberly watchful on the platform, with their backs against the wall, afraid to talk in case they drew more unwelcome attention. The adrenaline had ebbed, and they all seemed exhausted. Lazaro looked like he was on the brink of nodding off, his head between his knees.

Around five thirty, the stained glass brightened as the sun came up. Rosewood walked to the platform edge, checking to make sure other mole people weren't watching them. "Let's lose the uniforms."

They kicked off their boots. Paire didn't want to touch hers with bare hands because of the rats. She undid the laces with her cuffs over her fingers. They all unzipped their uniforms, letting them fall around their ankles, and then kicked them off into a jumble at the wall. Underneath, each of them wore some kind of business suit. Paire had a trim-fitting charcoal two-piece that she had worn to the Fern just the day before. She stepped out of the uniform, which rumpled in a cloth doughnut at her feet. Inside each of their uniforms, they had strung dress shoes around their necks, and they slid on the shinier footwear. Wing tips for Rosewood. Low heels for Paire. Rosewood tucked the pistol in his waistline, hidden by the suit jacket.

Once dressed in office attire, they headed for the exit. A thick chain and padlock blocked the main entrance to the street, but they pried open a plywood door until the crack widened enough for a person to fit. Sunlight shone through the gap.

They skipped up the stairs to the street, into a gloomy overcast morning. City Hall's French portico stood steps away from them. Commuters already rambled down the sidewalks. Most didn't look up.

Without saying any farewells, the boys walked in three different directions. A half block away, Humberto hailed the first taxi. They were back to the plan, reconnecting later when everyone was home safe.

Rosewood lifted his hand for a taxi, and one slowed for them. When they slid into the back, he asked, "How was it?"

She fought for words. "Rat-*tastic.*"

"It's all right to be scared. That's part of it. It's what makes it fun. You'll see in a day or two, when your nerves settle down. When you're willing to step outside the bounds of convention, you can be exactly the person you want to be. You'll be free."

She nodded, wondering how much of this was for her benefit, and how much Rosewood needed this to preserve his own sense of independence. She stopped thinking, and enjoyed the safety of sitting with Rosewood's arm wrapped around her. Paire fell asleep on his shoulder on the ride back to Brooklyn.

CHAPTER 8

Abel Kasson paced next to the front window at the Fern. "How long?"

A woman in a white lab coat answered him from the back of the gallery. "It won't be any faster if you keep asking." With a white mask strapped to the lower half of her face, she blended into the gallery walls.

Mayer stood on the other side of the gallery from Kasson, talking to patrons. By now, almost as many people gummed up the Fern as had attended Rosewood's opening reception.

The open space in the rear half of the Fern had been transformed into a makeshift laboratory, complete with microscope, computers, and a tilted drafting table where *The Empress Xiao Zhe Yi, Seated*, was being examined through a macrolens. The images captured through the camera had been blown up and displayed on an LCD monitor. Dr. Sarabeth Friederichs, a forgery expert handpicked by Kasson, buzzed around the examining table. She'd set up her equipment yesterday, and was still conducting tests.

Paire greeted anyone who looked in her direction, but most of the guests orbited around the authenticator. Kasson had just come in an hour ago, and she'd been trying to avoid him.

The Wall Street station mural had gone up three nights ago. After the terror faded, the experience exhilarated her, emboldened her. But it made her feel more exposed. She wondered if the police would examine their scrims and the duffels they'd left behind, and somehow track them down to Brooklyn Heights. The press had covered the stunt, and New York's mayor was debating whether to paint over it or leave it up. The police hadn't been close enough to see their faces, and the sketch of Charlie that came from the moustached MTA attendant looked so generic it might have been a Harvey Ball smiley.

Rosewood had pushed Paire to join the crew because he said she thought she needed pushing. He saw the way she longed to become someone other than Katie Novis, even if he didn't understand why.

Paire had indulged him because she hoped he was right. She still felt a little of Katie Novis in herself. When she stepped out of the shower naked, without the new clothes and without the makeup, the mirror told her that a simple costuming, even a legal name change, couldn't completely alter who she was. The occasional stunt with Rosewood might, like a benign form of shock treatment, add up to a cumulative jolt that would leave Katie Novis dead and forgotten in Abenaki. At the Fern today, she felt foundationally different about herself. Tectonics were shifting.

Two days before, Mayer had consented to an art authenticator after a long and flush-faced shout-bout with Kasson. The banker insisted that the Fern Gallery was intentionally exhibiting a counterfeit work of art to draw more foot traffic. The morning after their installation had gone up, Paire observed the argument with a thrill, even a lick of defiance when Kasson shot her a look at the desk.

Word got out about the test, and a crowd began to gather at the gallery. Who had alerted them was anyone's guess. Both Mayer and Kasson denied calling any attention to the spectacle.

The expert headed up Friederichs & Strauss, a firm in New York that specialized in fine art forensics. The white lab coat was Kasson's suggestion— Friederichs muttered something about how she usually worked in jeans. Early on, she had complained about the people milling around. Mayer finally set up a perimeter of orange traffic cones so that looky-loos wouldn't get close enough to interfere with the testing. Kasson alone crossed the line, looming over the woman's shoulder periodically in case he spotted the clues that would reveal the hoax.

Paire was going to chalk all of it up to student traffic, but older patrons turned up too. Reporters showed up, primarily writers for trade press. Since most of the nation's fine art press kept their editorial headquarters within fifteen minutes of the Fern, their writers wandered over to see if the hubbub was worth reporting. Kasson began pacing on the outside of the crowd, an electron to their nucleus.

Mayer didn't look happy to have reporters ask him questions, but he faked congeniality better than Kasson. Currently, he was talking to a writer from *Perspective*, the biggest art journal in the United States. She wore stilt heels and horn-rimmed glasses. Hunched slightly at her shoulders, she had the posture of a sunflower stalk and spoke with the vocal timbre of a four-year-old. "Does it concern you that you might have a forgery in your gallery?" she asked Mayer.

Some of the spectators sidled up to hear from the director.

Possibly spurred on by Kasson's glare, Mayer threw on a folksy charm. "We're resolving an important question. Qi is a forgotten but important voice in twentieth-century art. This portrait right here could be the only known work in existence. If it's real, everyone should know about this. If it's not real, it's just as important that we don't give anyone false hope."

If Paire hadn't known otherwise, she might think the idea for testing had sprung out of Mayer's head.

"So, do you know much about what she's doing?"

They studied Friederichs over at the drafting table. The scientist looked up from her eyepiece for a moment, appeared irritated, and then refocused on her work.

"I'm not a forgery expert, but so far she's used microfluorescence, where you beam X-rays to reveal the spectrum of most of the elements in the pigments. She'll see if the author used multiple layers. Forgers can sometimes build up multiple layers of paint to reproduce the exact style of the original. In this case, where there is no original that we know of that a forger would work off, we'll at least know if there's anything underneath."

"Do people still use black lights for this kind of thing?"

"They can, but nonfluorescent paints can be used to nullify the test."

Before they opened that day, Mayer had vented to Paire about how bad the gallery would look if everything went tits up. The testing put the Fern's reputation at stake. But to the casual observer, Mayer seemed to relish the attention.

"Are the X-rays dangerous for us to be around?" the reporter asked.

"Not at this level."

"What is she looking for? What's the tell-tale?"

"Ultimately, we want to verify that the artist is, in fact, Qi. To do that, we want to conduct a number of tests to make sure this conforms to his typical style. In this case, the artist used a traditional egg-based tempera—pretty much egg yolk and vinegar—the same thing Michelangelo used. The pigment testing is primarily done to make sure he used that."

"Will she be able to date the painting?"

"The dating and pigment analysis isn't as important as you think. In theory, you could possibly test for mitochondrial DNA traces from the chickens that laid the eggs, and check to see whether those chickens came from China or the United States. But that wouldn't help us."

The reporter adjusted a handheld recorder closer to Mayer's chin. "Why not?"

"Because we're not entirely certain whether Qi was in China or the United States when he painted this. In this case, provenance—documentation of who owned this painting and when—is just as important as the pigment analysis."

"So what does the provenance tell you?"

"That it was shipped from a gallery in Beijing to the United States. They claim to have had it, but not shown it, since 1981. According to the documentation, it passed through customs when Qi Jianyu passed away two years ago."

"So, isn't it time to look for Chinese chickens?"

This made Mayer laugh. "You'd think, but there's the chance

that the documentation itself was faked, which would call the provenance into question." He frowned after he said this, possibly regretting having introduced the notion. "So she'll look at things like how the painting is dressed. You consider the frame, and the surface the artist used. In this case, we already know that the wood matched the kind of wood Qi would have used—Chinese red birch."

Paire noticed that Mayer's talking to the reporter disturbed Kasson, who paced in his corner like a fresh fighter waiting for the bell.

"So that's not a canvas?"

"You can't use canvas with tempera. The surface bends and the paint cracks. There's already a little crazing on the painting, which you wouldn't normally see on a piece this young." Mayer's voice was drying out from all the talking. "Sometimes you get forgers that try to reproduce this effect, even sticking a painting in the oven, but if this one was faked, they weren't trying to create the impression of antiquity. I'd imagine it was stuck in poor storage conditions."

The reporter stared at the monitor, and Paire recognized the expression, the way her eyes lazily fell on the folds of fabric in the LCD monitor. The empress had the power to enchant the weak-willed, even on a television screen. "I'm confused. How will you know it's authentic?"

"I'd imagine the doctor is looking for stylistic idiosyncrasies. The quirks that would be unique to Qi. We know he was left-handed, so she'll be making sure the brush strokes came from a left-handed artist. She'll look at the composition and make sure it's consistent with his other work. That sort of thing."

"Didn't you say there weren't any other works from Qi?"

"Not that we know of."

The writer slid her glasses back up the bridge of her nose. "Then how do you know what his idiosyncrasies are?"

From the drafting table, Dr. Friederichs called out, "I'm not looking for any of that. I found what I'm looking for."

Everyone who wasn't already looking turned toward the examination table. The crowd at the front of the line inched past the traffic cones for a closer look. Her hand sheathed in a latex glove, Friederichs tugged lightly at something, then moved the macrolens over the area until it came up on the LCD. "A hair."

On the screen, the dark thread looked like a wet reed that had washed ashore. Half of it was embedded in the paint, trapped in the pigment. Almost as if it were growing out of the birch board, the hair looped in the air and sank back into the paint, somewhere around the empress's big toe.

Kasson chimed in from across the room, suddenly interested. "What are you going to do with that?"

Refreshingly, Friederichs was as unimpressed by Kasson as she was by everyone else, despite the fact that he'd hired her. "Good old-fashioned DNA testing."

"What are you going to test it against?"

No one had an answer. Not Friederichs, and not Mayer. Members of the crowd glanced at each other, and then looked to the scientist for a suggestion.

A woman stepped out of the crowd. "You can use me," she said. *Breakfast at Tiffany's* sunglasses. Scarf tied under her chin. Loose wool coat that hid her figure.

• • •

The crowd instinctively stepped away from the woman as she revealed her face and hair. The woman Paire had followed out to the street at Rosewood's opening reception.

A deep breath ballooned in Paire's chest, and she expectantly held on to it. In the daylight the woman's face seemed more remarkable. Three full dimensions of the face on the birch plank. Paire crept behind the scientist so she could compare the empress with the real woman. Her skin was a few shades darker, her features more sharply defined on a body more athletically trained than the Empress Xiao Zhe Yi. She was older than Paire by at least a decade, but bartenders might still have asked for her driver's license. Her glossy black hair was longer than in the painting, but only by a few inches. In the perfect oval of her face, Paire noted a few lines around the eyes, not necessarily wrinkles, from where the baby fat of her youth had evaporated.

The woman noticed Paire looking at her. She lingered for a moment, her eyes running down the contours of Paire's figure, and gave an almost imperceptible smile.

Mayer must have helped stage this, because he showed no surprise when the woman revealed herself. He stared over at Kasson, who seemed ready to pop from displeasure. "This is our benefactor."

The woman stared at Kasson. "Melinda Qi. I'm his daughter."

Paire had expected English laced with a hint of Chinese accent, but Melinda spoke with a crisp American cadence.

Kasson looked as if he'd caught someone trying to pick his pocket. He cut across the room to stand an intimate distance from the woman. Others stepped back, but Melinda stood her ground and looked him up and down, warning him with her eyes.

Kasson could not feign his usual off-putting congeniality. He stared at her threateningly, his head angled down so his eyes bored into her. He extended a hand and said his name.

Melinda looked at his hand but kept hers folded at her waist. He frowned when he was denied, and spoke. "You sound like you grew up in the States."

"Good ear," she said without humor. Paire liked her.

"How old would you have been when he painted this?"

"I would have been four," she said.

"Older than I thought." He smirked. "So you'd have no memory of this."

"Memory is all I have of my father," she said.

"Memory's a powerful thing," he said. "It can play tricks on you. Make you believe things that aren't real."

"Take my blood and see what's real," she said.

Kasson made a grand gesture toward the portrait. "The woman in the painting is you. We can all see that."

She replied, "It doesn't surprise me that a man like yourself would have difficulty distinguishing between Asian women. But the truth is, the woman in the painting more closely resembles my mother, and I closely resemble her. That is how she would have looked in 1980."

"She was in the States with you, correct?"

"Sharp as a tack."

"How would he produce this from across the Pacific?"

"Memory's a powerful thing," she said.

He shook his head, exasperated. "How are you so sure someone isn't playing a cruel trick on you?"

"Because I know what cruel tricks look like."

Once his intellect caught up to his rage, Kasson stepped a pace backward. He adjusted his cufflinks. His face had turned a blistering pink, but he said nothing more. Kasson cut through the crowd to the front door, his typically percussive footfalls now soft as slippers.

CHAPTER 9

The break-in happened a day after the coverage ran online in *Perspective*. The burglary had been low-tech. Someone hurled a stone through the front window. Nothing was taken, not even Rosewood's *HERO*.

The Fern's alarm system immediately triggered a call to the police, as well as to Mayer. By the time Mayer made it to the gallery, two patrol cars were splashing twirling blue and red lights across the block's brick façades. The burglar had long gone.

When Paire came to work the following morning she saw that a cantaloupe-sized hole had been smashed in the window, with a network of cracks spidering out from the center. The hole let in a draft of early morning spring chill. Pedestrians would now have an eye-level peephole that looked onto the Empress Xiao Zhe Yi. The cracking textured the rest of the pane, obscuring the Rosewood that hung right behind it. Her face framed by the snaggy edges of the hole, Paire marveled at the trail of glass pebbles on the floor inside.

"Who even finds something this size in New York?" Mayer said in the retelling. He showed Paire a stone roughly the size of a guinea pig. "It's not like these are just lying around on the street." Paire wondered herself.

The stone had smashed through the front window at a merciful angle and velocity, so it didn't damage any of the artwork. It had landed in the middle of the floor, steps away from the desk. The police had marked the spot with an X of black electrician's tape.

"The alarm must have scared him off," Mayer guessed. Paire had once heard the alarm by accident, because when she set it one night without Mayer's supervision, she forgot the code, and the siren clanged through the gallery loud enough to set her ears ringing. "That's the volume they use to get dictators out of churches."

Mayer had been there all evening, and he was dressed casually— at least, casually for Mayer Wolff, in a loose cotton shirt with jeans and biker boots. He hadn't groomed his beard, and while it was close-cropped, the hair seemed more brambly than usual. Deprived of shower and sleep, Mayer looked tired, and to Paire, older.

Lucia was there too, dressed in a white polo shirt and shorts, so her long, tanned legs goosebumped from the cold. She'd pulled her hair into a brioche at the crown of her skull and wore Mayer's coat over her shoulders. Lucia sat next to him at the desk, leaning her head on his shoulder, her arm tucked through his. Paire had never seen them touch like this in public.

Similarly sleep-deprived, Lucia lifted her head when Paire opened the door. She groggily disentangled her arm from Mayer's. When she rose from her chair, she slid her arm across Mayer's back as she walked away, until he clasped her hand and kissed it softly.

"Paire's smart enough to know what's going on, and I'm too tired to pretend." Mayer stood and held Lucia's face in her hands. He pressed his lips gently against hers, resting his forehead on hers afterward. Lucia's eyelids batted and she brushed his cheek with her hand. Paire couldn't help but note the ring on Lucia's finger when she touched Paire's shoulder on her way out. "He's the good one in all this," she said.

Paire felt like one of two nurses changing shifts.

She pretended that she had seen nothing out of the ordinary, and sat down next to her boss. They both looked through the hole toward brownstone steps across the street. "Do they have him on camera?"

He gestured around the room. "Do you see any cameras, Paire?" The way Mayer said her name had changed since they'd met, from skepticism (*is that really your name—Paire?*), to the tone of a pedagogue addressing a student, to this one, that of one peer addressing another. And as a peer, he could be curt with her without worrying about hurting her feelings.

Paire hadn't thought about the Fern's security system beyond the alarm keypad. "I thought it might be built into the walls somewhere, like a nanny cam."

"We've just got the rock to go on."

"Nothing was taken?"

"Nothing was touched, as far as we can tell. None of the paintings are even crooked." He rubbed his eyes and sipped a gigantic iced coffee.

"Is there a chance that it's just vandalism?"

He seemed incensed that she would even ask him this, as if the question implied that the collection in the gallery might not be worth stealing. "It would be a strange coincidence that the story ran online yesterday, and this happens. Although, to be honest, I'm not sure how many people would have read it. It's for art wonks. Also, I'm hard-pressed to believe that an art wonk would be fool enough to think they can smash-and-grab an art gallery."

"Are you sure they wanted the Qi?" Paire said this to try and be fair to the vast Rosewood collection that covered most of the walls, but the moment it left her lips she knew it was an asinine question.

The way Mayer looked at her confirmed it. He lamented, "Now that people know it's real, it's become a commodity. *The last Qi.* That has value. And people will want anything that has value."

Two workers with beards and big stomachs entered the gallery. The patches on their gray uniforms read *Moby Glass Repair.* Several weeks ago, Paire wouldn't have given them a second look, but after the night at Wall Street station, she scoured over their uniforms to see if they looked too new, with creases in the fabric or wear that came from a hastily rubbed stain. One of the men couldn't stop staring at the red cheongsam on the rear wall. This relieved Paire, because the way he stared indicated that he'd never seen the painting. A thief wouldn't ogle the empress in front of the gallery owner.

Mayer snapped his fingers in front of the man's nose to jostle him out of his trance.

"You might want to think about sturdier glass," said the lead man.

Within a few minutes they signed forms and began removing the broken pane. Mayer took *HERO* off its mount and leaned it against the rear wall, just under the empress.

The Fern opened at the regular time. Three people waited outside the gallery right at ten o'clock, waiting for Paire to unlock the door.

One was an MSAD student who had read the article. He gushed with enthusiasm. "I got to admit, I never heard of the guy. Where can I see more of his stuff?"

"No one knows," she said.

The other two, professionals in suits, one young and one old, had also read the article and wanted to see the piece for themselves.

Paire stood with the group as they took in the empress. The older man cleaned his glasses so he could view the portrait with clear lenses. When he saw Perseus holding up Hussein's head in *HERO*, he asked, "Who is this fella?" From his intonation, she thought he might really be saying, *what the heck is this dreck?*

Over the morning, more people than usual drifted in and out of the Fern as the workers removed the glass from the window, hammered it to bits on the sidewalk, then plucked the stray shards out of the window frame with gloved hands.

Paire made small talk with the patrons. Sometime before lunch the foot traffic dwindled, and the workers mounted a new pane. Apparently, a cinder block could bounce off this one.

In the lull, Paire asked Mayer, "Should we let Melinda Qi know about this?"

"Mel knows." Mayer rolled his head from side to side to stretch his neck.

"Is she worried?"

"Not as worried as she should be," he said. "I told her to take it back. That thing should be locked in a fortress." Paire stared at the royal with the bare feet, and imagined a blank, white wall. Her heart sank at the thought.

"But the Qi is good for business."

"I'm going to admit something that you can never repeat. I

want potential *buyers* in here. The Qi doesn't attract buyers as much as armchair enthusiasts. Since I think of art as having an educational and inspirational value, I don't mind those people coming by too, but they don't help the business, because they're not going to buy. Always remember, there's a difference between an art gallery and a museum. The foot traffic has gone up in the past few months, but our sales have stayed flat."

"What about the contract you signed with Melinda? Didn't you make money off that?" She felt uncomfortable referring to the woman by her first name, when she still hadn't officially met her. Paire wanted to say *Ms. Qi*, but thought she'd sound like a kiss-ass.

"Mel paid me to hang the painting for three months. She gave me decent money, the equivalent of a commission I'd make on a Lichtenstein. So I thought it was a good deal. I'll admit I was enticed by the idea that we'd be the ones who'd bring Qi back into the public eye. But that contract is up in a few weeks, and I'll be happy when this goes away. This is more trouble than it's worth."

Mayer must have recognized how deflated Paire felt and added, "I'm also thinking about Mel. She doesn't have much to remember her father, and I don't want her to lose this. The Fern isn't secure enough for this piece. People will try to acquire this, legally or illegally. On top of all this crap…" he gestured to the window, "…on top of Nicola Franconi…the third-party authentication…on top of all that, there are the bids I have to turn away. If we keep dangling this out there in the public, and keep saying no to enough people who want to buy it, someone's going to find a way to take it. For me, that means fixing more broken windows. But for Melinda, it might mean losing a family heirloom."

"What bids are you turning away?"

He smiled languidly. "Now that we've verified this is an authentic Qi Jianyu, lots of people want to buy it. Once you place value on something, people are going to want it for themselves. I've gotten several bids, but the first one I can't ignore was emailed to me this morning."

"From who?"

"Guess," he said, expectantly.

"I have no idea," she said, and then a horrible thought surfaced. "No."

When he saw her expression change, he smiled. "He's an avid collector, you know."

"How much?"

"Too much."

"Have you told…" Paire still fumbled with the correct name, "Melanie—Mel?"

"I've sent her the information, although I know she doesn't intend to sell. It's a nonissue." Mayer looked around his gallery at all the exhibition pieces that hung in the wall space rented by Kasson. "I can't wait until we get these Rosewoods out of here, and I can cleanse this place of that man. No offense to your boyfriend."

Paire made a silent promise to herself not to repeat this when she got back to Brooklyn.

Startled, Mayer and Paire looked toward the entrance at the same time. That someone opened the door was no surprise as people had trafficked in and out all morning. But the mass of the silhouette in the doorway and the force with which he yanked the door open alarmed both of them.

"Turds," said Mayer under his breath.

Kasson marched to the desk, and Mayer stood up so fast Paire thought his chair might topple. "I'd think you'd be a little happier to see me," boomed Kasson. "If I hadn't challenged the authenticity of the piece, people might never have found out about it, and by association, this gallery."

Mayer frowned. "You didn't have to come in. I forwarded your request."

Kasson's voice seemed to rattle the plaster. "I assumed that you gave my email the attention it deserved. That's why I came in." He placed a briefcase on the desk and flipped two brass latches, opening it like a clamshell to reveal piles of money. More than Paire Anjou or Katie Novis had ever seen at once. Gilda had money, but she never had the audacity to trade in cash.

Paire smelled the ink on the bills. Perhaps owing to her criminal pedigree, Paire considered how easy it would be for someone to steal this money. All it would take would be a larger man. Or a smaller man with a weapon. Maybe even Paire with a spring baton. Crime happened so quickly.

"There are other things to spend this money on," Mayer said.

"I only have eyes for her, Mr. Wolff."

"How about a villa in Tuscany?"

Kasson scratched his chin. "I already have one." Paire didn't know if he was joking or not, but tried not to wince when he winked at her. "Just be a good broker and make your client some money."

"It's not for sale, and if it was, you couldn't afford it. She would always price it out of your reach."

"Well, that seems unfair. If she doesn't want someone to own it, why would she show it? It's like Tantalus. Putting it on display for the world to see, but not letting anyone have it. Why would someone do that?"

"Maybe she's sentimental."

"Maybe she's selfish."

"We don't even have a register in the gallery," said Mayer, rubbing a palm across his uncombed beard. Paire noticed he had dropped the *Mr. Kasson* when addressing him.

"I can't be the first person in your career to pay in real money."

"You're the first person in a while."

"What do you do when it happens?" Kasson asked.

"We run to the bank." Mayer massaged his temples, this time with both index fingers. "Why do you even want it? You thought it was trash."

"I thought it was *fake*, not trash," Kasson corrected. "You don't see an artist like Qi that often—"

"—or ever," Mayer jabbed.

"You'd neglect your duty as her representative by not presenting this offer?"

Mayer gazed down into the briefcase, skimming over the stacks of banknotes. "How much is this?"

"The same amount I emailed. Call her."

Mayer phoned Melinda Qi while standing at his desk, staring Kasson in the face.

When Melinda picked up, Paire heard Mayer's side of the conversation. Melinda's voice through the speaker was tone-only, a neutral hum devoid of peaks and valleys. He talked through Kasson's offer, and when he repeated the dollar amount, Paire's eyes flared. She looked again into the open briefcase, trying to count it all within a few seconds.

Mayer gave Paire a quizzical look, a reaction to something Mel said. Kasson's meaty fingers drummed on the lid of the briefcase.

Mayer disconnected. "She'll discuss it."

"Smart girl," said Kasson. "When is she coming?"

Mayer bent over the desk, scribbling on a Post-It. "She finds you repellent, so she refuses to be in the same room as you." He pointed to Paire with the pen. "She'll talk to Paire." He gave Paire the Post-It, palming it so that Kasson wouldn't glimpse what he'd written. "Go there."

With no pockets to stash the note in, she clenched it in a closed fist.

Kasson's face flushed, and he now hovered over the desk in her direction.

"Are you sure?" Paire said to Mayer.

"She asked for you. And I can't leave the gallery. Or I should say, I'd feel safer if I remained in the gallery." He glanced over his shoulder at the empress, as if to check that someone hadn't sneaked behind them all to try and nab it. Mayer locked eyes with Kasson. "I'll let you know what she says." When Kasson refused to budge, he looked down at the money. "If you can't wait, I have a few Derek Rosewoods I can sell you."

• • •

Paire had expected to go to Melinda Qi's home, but the address Mayer had given her led to the MAAC.

The Museum of Asian Art and Culture sat only a ten-minute walk from the Fern Gallery on Sixteenth Street. Paire had passed it once or twice, but it wasn't a block she walked regularly. When she arrived today, she looked with fresh eyes at the façade, surprisingly large for such a narrow street. Nicola Franconi had been this museum's executive director, right up until the day he stabbed himself in front of the Fern. Paire had since researched a bit about the museum.

The building had been commissioned back in the seventies to Chinese architect I. M. Pei. At the time, Pei was finishing the John Hancock Tower in Boston. Opened in 1977, the building had a giant glass mirror that reflected the old John Hancock building, and enjoyed a short infamy when the glass panels dropped to the sidewalk like guillotine blades. Pei wouldn't be commissioned for the Louvre Pyramid until 1984.

This was a more modest building, squeezed in between his major projects. The MAAC opened in 1978, and, echoing much of Pei's larger body of work, the structure was a geometric puzzle of glass and steel, built on a concrete foundation. The ceiling ushered in a generous amount of sunlight, especially for a building in Manhattan. A staircase of concrete slabs anchored to the wall seemed to hang in midair. At the ground level, an artificial pond introduced a meandering coastline of water that interrupted the straight lines.

The museum curated modern artists from Asian countries. The only artist whose work Paire recognized was Takashi Murakami, and only because of the Murakami hanging on Rosewood's bedroom wall. The rest were unfamiliar. Whenever she'd been exposed to Asian art, she'd seen historical artifacts—samurai armor, or Katsushika Hokusai's *The Great Wave off Kanagawa*, which Paire would recognize because it had been screened onto Gilda's favorite coffee cup. Her teachers tended to skip over Asian art, and New England museums typically housed it in dimly lit corners.

Everything on display at the MAAC had been created within the past century. By the entryway, Paire was drawn to a series of bronze sculptures that covered much of the atrium floor. Each sculpture formed the head of an animal. Each head had been severed and mounted on a pike, its mouth agape. The collection formed a circle, a morbid sort of Stonehenge. Paire stood at the center and examined the faces of each. Goat. Monkey. Chicken. Dog.

She'd bent to look inside a pig's mouth, thinking about *Lord of the Flies*, when a voice whispered in her ear, "If you touch it, you have to eat it."

Melinda Qi appeared next to her, giving Paire a start. She wore a bright yellow dress, belted at the waist, which showed off her shoulders. The cheongsam in the painting didn't reveal the arms of the empress, so even though Paire acknowledged that the portrait had captured a different woman, the similarity between Melinda Qi and her mother was so close that when she looked at her bare arms and crisply defined deltoids, she enjoyed a quick thrill from sneaking a peek at something heretofore unseen.

"They're all from the Chinese Zodiac." Melinda pointed around the circle, making a pistol with her finger and play-shooting each of the animal heads. "Twelve of them—ox, tiger, rabbit, dragon, snake, horse, sheep, monkey, rooster, dog, pig, and last but not least, rat. This was in Central Park a couple years ago. Do you remember it?"

Paire found her voice. "I wasn't in New York then. Who's the artist?"

"Ai Weiwei. You know him?"

The way she asked made Paire feel like she should, but she shook her head.

"You should get to know him. He designed the national stadium for the Olympics back in 2008."

Paire felt uncomfortable at her own ignorance, and her confidence ebbed. "For some reason, I thought I'd be coming to your home."

"What makes you think I don't live here?" Paire froze, unsure how to react, until Melinda laughed. "That's a joke." Paire envied how easily she laughed, like a ripple in the water. She said, "I have a meeting with the executive director."

Paire was suddenly uncertain of something she knew to be true. "Isn't the executive director dead?"

"Not this one. Places like this always have someone waiting in the wings."

"Why are you meeting?"

"I suppose because this is an Asian art museum, and because I'm an Asian artist."

"You're a painter too," Paire said.

"Ceramics."

The next question slipped out. "Did your father ever have any pieces here?"

Melinda looked distant for a moment, maybe lost in a memory. "By the time this place opened, my father had moved back to Beijing."

With a carefree gait, Melinda led Paire outside the zodiac circle of severed bronze heads. Paire knew she was supposed to discuss Abel Kasson's bid, but now that they were together in a private moment, she wanted to talk about anything else. "Is the museum going to show your work?"

"With any luck." Melinda walked delicately on her heels, so that even on the concrete floor the tap was no louder than the collision of two marbles. Paire's heels knocked loudly on the concrete as she kept pace. The other woman's body seemed both lighter and stronger than Paire's.

"Is there a way for me to see any samples of your work?"

Melinda abruptly pivoted to face Paire. "If you want, you can see several samples of my work. Would you like to see my studio?"

When Paire answered, she hoped she didn't sound too starstruck. "I would."

"Good. That makes me happy." They continued past the modest queue at the ticket counter, where a bored attendant was having difficulty swiping someone's credit card. They rounded a corner out of the main flow of traffic. At the end of the hallway stood another security checkpoint that marked the entrance to the administrative offices. Presumably, Melinda wanted a quieter place where they could discuss the large sum of money at stake. Instead, she said, "I should probably head to my meeting."

"What about…" Paire didn't want to say Abel Kasson's name, because it might tarnish their interaction. "The offer?"

"I'm going to refuse it, of course," Melinda said, with notable satisfaction.

"Why are we meeting, then?"

"I wanted to get Abel Kasson off Mayer's back. Did he actually bring in a suitcase full of cash?"

"He did."

"What does that amount of money look like?"

"The briefcase was pretty full."

She laughed. "I'm interested that he's taken an interest."

Paire started to feel comfortable with her, and stopped worrying how every word needed to convey the proper esteem. She realized that they'd stopped by another sculpture. Another bronze bust.

Melinda said, "The truth is, I wouldn't mind getting rid of the thing. It's a painting of my mother, and I have a bad history with my mother. Of all my father's paintings, it's the one I would have wanted the least. I don't want it in my house."

Paire asked, "Do you want to sell it?"

"Not to him. Don't get me wrong. I don't have anything against money. And ultimately I may not want to keep the painting. But it can't go to that man. Can you go back to Mayer with that message?"

Paire nodded.

Melinda continued. "There's a history between us." She reached up to the bronze bust and gently patted its cheek.

Paire sucked in and held an inhale, thinking an alarm might sound or some guard would bark at them, but nothing happened. This wasn't part of the exhibition, but a bust sculpted in tribute to some museum bigwig.

Melinda lightly touched Paire on her arm as a farewell gesture, and continued to the administrative check-in. Paire watched the sway of her hips as she moved down the hallway. Faintly, she heard Melinda announce herself to a brown-uniformed attendant.

She looked more closely at the bust. A man with glasses. His head was the size of luggage, and not a carry-on, either. When they had approached and she only glimpsed it in her periphery, she assumed that he was Asian, but she noted the distinctly Anglo eyes behind the glasses. The man had a thin face and sunken cheekbones, and pronounced folds around his mouth that looked like his lips were held in parentheses. His wispy hair had been styled to seem heroically windblown. She recognized him. He had stood next to Qi Jianyu in the photograph she'd found. In the casting, his face looked not old, but older than he would have been in the photograph, maybe by another decade. The sunken cheeks were the giveaway. The plaque didn't mention the artist, but identified the man the sculpture intended to honor:

Gabriel Kasson
1929—
Industrialist, Philanthropist, and Founder of the
Museum of Asian Art and Culture

CHAPTER 10

Melinda Qi's home and studio had once been a warehouse distribution center in Long Island City. To Paire, it looked like an old prison. A thick iron fence topped with razor wire corralled the property. One entered the brick compound through a loading dock with several gates, all freight-width. A narrow open-air dirt courtyard stood between the compound's two main buildings. Some of the windows had been shattered, and others fogged up from the murky smog of industry. Only the high windows were clean and clear, as if they'd been replaced recently. Paire guessed that Melinda lived behind the clean ones.

Paire arrived in the evening, when the neighborhood seemed abandoned. The scariest places in New York were areas without people or the constant hum of traffic. She checked over her shoulder every few seconds and pressed the doorbell to the Morse code rhythm for S.O.S. until Melinda jogged out to the front gate.

Mel gave her a warm hug and a tour of the compound. Building A was her living area, building B her work area. Apparently, multiple artists used the studio, but she was the only one who lived there. As they walked through the secluded lot, the moon and lights from adjacent buildings gave just enough light for Paire to make her way through the gravelly dirt without stumbling. Mel knew her way around by heart, even in the dark.

Paire wanted Melinda to be taller. She still hadn't completely distinguished this woman from the figure in Qi's portrait, and when she had envisioned the empress in the flesh, she imagined someone a foot taller than she, a long-limbed prima ballerina. Melinda was only two inches taller than Paire at most. Her tousled hair also unsettled

Paire. A few tendrils escaped a loose bun and drifted about her face. Unlike the defined comb streaks in the empress's hair, Melinda's hair settled wherever the wind blew it.

Mel unlocked her studio door, and the steel moaned as she slid it open. Instead of the paint fumes Paire knew from Rosewood's studio, Melinda's smelled of clay and loose-lidded jars of glaze. "This is where I work," she said. With the flip of a switch, a string of overhead lights flickered, illuminating a vault the size of a small barn. Paire gasped. She had entered an urban Eden. Mel's studio was a literal sculpture garden, overgrown with gigantic ceramic flowers, each one taller than the ceilings in Brooklyn Heights. Hearty, succulent leaves fed into trunks that twisted like frayed rope. Robust blossoms at the tops exploded in tropical purples, oranges, and reds. The petals, fleshy lips. Stamens as long as stork beaks. Beneath the lights, all of them bore a glossy sheen from the ceramic glaze. Paire thought of Audrey II from *Little Shop of Horrors*. All of them possessed a monstrous beauty.

The organic, earthy odors seemed out of place here, where the flowers didn't need soil, and would never die.

"You made all these?"

"Made here and fired in the kill."

"Kiln?"

"It's pronounced *kill*."

Paire didn't believe her.

She said, "Trust me. This is what I do."

"Can I touch them?"

"Just don't hang off it."

Paire stroked the cool, smooth surface of the nearest stalk.

At her request, Melinda explained how she created her giant flowers. "The first step is constructing a metal armature. The clay's too heavy, and these things would collapse without it." Melinda showed her one in the corner, a woven skeleton of thick wire. She used copper, which could withstand higher temperatures without melting. As she walked around the armature, she tended to it as if it were a real plant, preening the leaves, making slight twists to the wire to bend the petals this way and that. She used a stepladder to adjust the pistils and stamens at the top of the stalk.

"Once the armature is set, you pack on the clay." Polymer clay, which fired at lower temperatures. She explained how she glommed clumps of clay onto the wire, fleshing out the form. Once it achieved the proper bulk, she massaged the clay with her thumbs until the grooves of leaves and rooty veins emerged. She carved out details with knives and other tools. Mel showed Paire a table of instruments that resembled antiquated dental tools.

"Once it looks the way it should, I bake it." Melinda employed three men to help her roll the packed armature across the dirt on a wheeled pallet and load it into the kiln. "It's the riskiest part of the process. We never do it in the rain, and we move like sloths."

Paire lightly ran her fingers over a petal. "Then the glaze."

"Then the glaze," Mel repeated.

Paire was fingering the sublateral veins on the underside of a leaf, and Melinda's face came into view beside hers, staring at the spot Paire had focused on, possibly trying to take in her own work the way a newcomer might see it.

Melinda stood closer, as close as Rosewood might stand when they were together.

Paire felt the need to talk. "Why didn't you become a painter like your father?"

"Because he was too good at it, and I didn't want to compete with him."

Paire said, "Your father was in a different country. Did it really feel like you were competing with him?"

"It's not a competition he started, but it feels like a competition because I'm working in the arts. It's a strange feeling to be both inspired and intimidated by the same person. There are times when I don't want to be an artist at all, just so I can separate myself from him."

"Then why do you do it?"

"Because it makes me feel good. I was the kid everyone copied in art class. It made me feel good to be good at something, so I kept at it. Now, it's the only thing I can imagine doing for fourteen hours a day. I assume you're an artist."

"I'm trying to be." Paire thought about her sketchbooks, and how she had yet to develop an authentic voice, or a body of real work. She had so much work to do.

"Why do you do it?"

Paire had to think about how to put it into words. "It's the only thing that makes me forget about everything else."

Melinda led Paire back across the courtyard to the kiln. Like her studio, the entrance was marked by a steel door, but this one opened like a submarine hatch, with the spin of a steel wheel. Once it spun freely, the artist yanked a heavy lever, and the metal groaned as the door swung heavily on its hinges. There were no lights inside the kiln, but enough light from the courtyard shone inside for Paire to get a sense of it. Inside, the room was more than twice her height, stacked with silt-stained yellow bricks and a domed ceiling.

Paire commented, "It's like a giant igloo."

"It is, isn't it?"

"Is it safe to go in?"

"Of course it is." The inside was musty and smelled of ash. Two of Mel's flowers loomed in the shadows, like giants ducking their heads.

"So they get fired here?"

"Fired here, and hauled back to the studio to get painted."

"Can you show me how you paint them?"

Mel looked at her guest, perhaps gauging the sincerity of her interest. "We'll see."

After the tour, Melinda and Paire returned to building A, the living space. They sat at a garage sale walnut dining set, which felt out of place on a poured concrete floor. Their voices bounced around on all the hard surfaces.

Mel poured Cabernet. Paire didn't drink much, but she thought it rude to abstain. With a body just north of a hundred pounds and a low tolerance, she felt tipsy after two glasses. When she was drunk, she became giggly. Her vision softened, and the physical distinctions between Melinda Qi and the Empress Xiao Zhe Yi further blurred. She was fascinated with everything the empress was saying from across the table.

Mel rubbed a finger around the rim of the glass, as if trying to make the goblet sing. "What do you know about my father?" Paire averted her eyes, and she apologized, "I'm sorry—that's not a fair question, is it?"

Since they had met at the MAAC, Paire had found out more about Gabriel Kasson, Abel Kasson's father. Gabriel had worked with the United States Ambassador to China during the Nixon administration. His official title was Special Assistant to the National Security Advisor. He accompanied the President and First Lady when they visited the PRC in 1972. Paire found a photo of Pat Nixon in a bright red coat, shaking hands with officials at a school in Beijing. In the background, looking deathly serious, was the face cast in bronze at the MAAC. Gaunt cheeks, glasses, and breezy hair. In the photo, he held his topcoat tight against his chest while the breeze played with his hair. A few articles that covered his career mentioned the trip to China, but most pieces summed up his life in a paragraph describing a businessman who collected art and founded the MAAC. At some point, he was the president and CEO of Kasson and Kasson, the company that would declare bankruptcy in 2009.

Paire didn't know how much she should say about Qi Jianyu. She felt too much like a stalker already. "I admire his work. At least, the one piece I've seen." She intoned the word *admire* to convey a passing interest in his work.

Melinda playfully squinted through her maroon liquid at Paire. "If that's the only one you've seen, you ain't seen nothing," she said. "I only wish I had more to show you."

"Have you seen others?"

"Here and there," she said. "The popular pieces all had a similar theme. Painting modern people in ancient costumes. It was a simple idea but the execution made it special. I liked to think he was trying to show us that the figures we hold up as icons are just as human as the rest of us. But the effect was the opposite. The way he rendered his people, he took ordinary people and made them iconic." She sipped the wine with a gentle slurp. "Look at my mother. She wasn't someone people would line up around the block to see. But up there on the birch board…"

Paire had barely touched her second glass of wine. Since Melinda had already emptied her third, she sipped more to catch up, feeling like she might soon be too buzzed to keep track of the pour. "Did his other paintings have the same effect on people?"

"That and worse. That old man who killed himself? He wasn't the first." She saw how Paire's face shrank at the memory of Nicola Franconi's body curling up on the sidewalk. "I'm sorry to bring that up. It was horrible you had to see it." Melinda sighed. "I've seen what my father's paintings do to people. I should feel guilty that I let something loose that can cause that kind of damage. But you know what? It makes me jealous. Because I would kill to create work so gorgeous that someone would stab themselves just to ensure they've captured that memory for the rest of their lives."

Paire's stomach twisted. That last comment would seem like an overstatement if she had not seen the man die herself.

Mel smirked at Paire. "I don't hate my father for creating work that's better than mine. It inspires me to be better myself. But having his work is a burden, and sometimes I feel like art shouldn't be a burden. It should bring joy."

"Why a burden?"

"Bad things happen around those paintings. There's a curse around that thing. Something my father sealed in spite. More bad things are bound to happen as long as it's out there." Since Paire wasn't touching her wine, Mel reached across and took a sip from her glass. "Abel Kasson? He's a volatile man. You introduce that painting to that man, something wrong is going to come of it, it's just a matter of when. Knowing that catastrophe is going to strike, that's a burden." Gauging Paire's reaction, she added, "Sometimes I want to relieve myself of that burden."

Paire wasn't sure what to say. Now that they were talking about

Qi Jianyu and not Melinda Qi, she felt like she was representing the Fern Gallery again. The conversation turned back to business, and she felt self-conscious about being a little drunk during a business conversation. She spoke with the ostentatious overenunciation a child would use to impress grown-ups. "So are you trying to sell it?"

Mel said, "You don't want me to, do you? I can tell."

Paire thought, *No, not to Abel Kasson. Not to anyone.* But what she said was, "Wouldn't you want to keep it? It's a part of your father."

"It's like having the ghost of my father in the room. The ghost of my mother too, because she's in the painting." She rolled the stem of her glass between her fingers. "You probably had a good relationship with your parents."

"You'd be surprised," Paire said.

This seemed to intrigue Melinda. "What was your father like?"

Paire felt like she needed to say something, rather than let the question hang in the air. "I only met him once."

"What was he like?"

"Like talking to a mannequin."

"Tell me about him."

Either because of the wine or because she felt compelled to extend their time together, Paire told Melinda Qi things about her father that she'd never divulged to another New Yorker. Not even Derek Rosewood.

• • •

Lake Novis got out of prison when Katie turned thirteen. The prison told Gilda when it released him, and even provided an address. Katie found it in the mail.

Up until then, Gilda had titrated information about her father, determining what dose to give her depending on her age. Until she was six years old, Katie was told that her father was an explorer. Botswana. Papua New Guinea. Gilda might have kept lying to her, but once she got to school, Katie heard rumors about her father. They grew more barbed the older she got.

At six, she learned that her father lived in prison, but she didn't fully grasp what a prison was at the time, or why someone would live there. She wanted to visit, but Gilda refused to bring her, either because she thought it would be unsafe or because she didn't want to be seen in a correctional facility. Katie wanted to write, but her grandmother wouldn't divulge the specific prison that incarcerated Lake Novis. When she turned eleven and was allowed internet access and her own library card, Katie learned that her father was at Maine State Prison, about halfway between Abenaki and Bar Harbor.

Thanks to Gilda's efforts to suppress and destroy the media coverage of the trial, she wouldn't read much about the crime itself for another year. The prison didn't let unaccompanied children visit the inmates, so she sent letters. She never received one in return.

Gilda had purged the rest of the house of photographs, so she didn't know what her mother or father looked like. Given the lack of evidence, from time to time Katie wondered if her parents had existed at all. When they talked about the Immaculate Conception at Christmas, Katie got to wondering about her own birth, whether she might have just bloomed into existence, or, since she was a Darwinist, dragged herself out of the sludge in a local cranberry bog.

Katie had rummaged through all the storage boxes in the attic for some traces of her parents. At the bottom of a crate of books, she finally found a letter tucked inside a copy of the Bible. It had been used as a bookmark. Trifolded and left in the envelope, the letter wrapped around a crisp photograph. *From Cissy to Gilda*, with a postal stamp from Caribou, Maine, farther north than Montreal. The letter read, *Please be happy for us.* Cissy scrawled her signature in a loopy cursive, with a pigtail in the *C*.

Katie kept the photograph under her winter sweaters. On some nights, she looked at it before she slept. Lake and Cissy Novis. Her parents had been a pretty couple with smooth skin. They mugged for the camera, cheeks pressed together, intentionally foolish. Her father's front two teeth folded over each other slightly, but not enough to damage the impact of the smile. Her mother blew a kiss with the same swollen lips that Katie had inherited. The date had been written on the back. At the time the image was captured, they would have been in their early twenties. They glowed with joy.

On Katie's thirteenth birthday, Gilda honored the day with a cupcake and a candle. The lackluster celebration and Katie's simmering adolescent discontent gave her the excuse to be testy. While she forked the cupcake, she asked, "When am I going to see my father?"

"I don't know," Gilda replied as she had when Katie had asked a hundred other times. "I'll get back to you."

That response had staved off follow-up questions for years. But on this night, Katie launched a forkful of frosting-coated cake into the air, hitting Gilda square in the chest. Her grandmother gasped. For the first time ever, she truly looked at her granddaughter. Whether she admired her spunk or worried about her volatility, Katie couldn't be sure. But she had the woman's attention. Katie spoke in a bolder voice, one that she would use more as Paire Anjou. "I know he's out."

"So, the jig is up," Gilda said.

"Were you ever going to tell me?"

"You don't want to meet him. He's not..." Gilda chose her words carefully. "He's not someone you would want as your father."

"How do you know?"

"He's not a good man."

Katie said, "I don't care. He's my father."

Gilda said, "He's not right—mentally." She added, "Never was."

"He's your son-in-law."

"All the more reason you should listen to me."

Katie had made up her mind. "I'd like to decide for myself."

Grudgingly, Gilda finally consented and chaperoned the visit to Lake Novis's single-room flat in Portland. Gilda didn't seem surprised when Lake answered the door, but Katie was struck dumb. Her father was much thinner than in the photograph, as if he'd stopped eating the day they put him away. He looked as though he'd been embalmed. For the occasion, Lake wore a waxy suit that seemed dug out of storage, possibly the same suit he'd worn during the trial. It didn't fit him.

"Hello, Katie." He didn't speak much, but when he did, he wouldn't rasp anything louder than a whisper.

She shivered when he spoke her name. With his cornstalk body looming in the doorway and his sad, sagging expression, she felt like she was being called home by death.

Katie Novis didn't rush to hug her father, nor did Lake thrust his arms out for an embrace. With Gilda as an arbiter of sorts, they sat on the couch and conducted a businesslike interview. Looking back, Paire considered something that Katie hadn't noticed at the time, which was that Lake's daughter looked remarkably like Cissy Novis. As such, Lake had a tough time keeping his eyes on her.

In the dank room with water-stained wallpaper, Lake kept the curtains drawn, and in the faint orange light he appeared like a mirage. Her father leaned forward with his arms on knobby knees. His suit cuffs rode up and she noticed thin slivers of scars on his wrists.

She said, "I wrote letters." She waited for that miracle breakthrough where Lake would spark at the sound of her voice. Her earnestness would melt him, and they could begin a new relationship with his teary apology.

His dreary voice sounded like dribbling rain. "If you want to hate me, I deserve it."

With that, he confirmed every rumor she'd heard about him. The truth that smeared the Novis family name. The crime that made everyone in Abenaki treat Katie like guano. The reason she would run off to New York and change her name. He confirmed it all, with no visible contrition. Lake didn't want a second chance with his daughter. He wished to be forgotten, with the hope that whatever pain he'd caused would die with him.

Father and daughter didn't look at each other. Instead, both kept their eyes on Gilda, and Katie hoped that she would say something that would reach her father. Instead, Gilda detached herself from the conversation, presiding over the ceremony like a totem.

Katie hesitantly asked, "What are you going to do for work?"

"The prison has a program. They're setting me up with the parks department. I'm going to pick up litter."

"Do you miss Mom?"

Every person in the room fidgeted, including Katie. She'd never known her mother, and had never referred to her as *Mom*—it was a term far too intimate for a woman who only existed in images. Lake had gone to prison too soon for him to be comfortable with being a father, and had possibly never referred to his wife as a mother. Gilda shifted in her seat and scratched at her nude nylons.

He rubbed his eyes as if he were going to cry, but he seemed so weak, Katie thought the meeting might just be exhausting him. "Of course," he said. "Every day."

"Are you sick? You look sick."

"I'm not sick."

"You're skinny enough to be sick."

"I'm not sick."

"It would be weird if you were sick like Mom. I mean, what would the odds be?"

"What?" Now they both sensed more tension from Gilda, who hiked up her shoulders and kept her eyes somewhere below the coffee table.

"You know, the leukemia."

Gilda looked queasy. Prison seemed to have dulled Lake's mind, but he looked at Gilda and Katie understood the unspoken communication between them, some secret they shared but would keep from her. Lake directed the next question to his daughter while reading Gilda's expression. "How much do you know about your mother?"

"Not much."

Even in his beaten voice, his passion for Cissy was evident. It was perhaps the only lingering passion in his life, and he grew more animated when he talked about her. "Then you should know your mother was the perfect woman. She honestly was. If you think nothing else about either one of us, think that. She should be the one here. I should be the one that died." She noticed his crooked teeth, the front two folding over each other. They had yellowed with age and tobacco, and seemed symptomatic of a failing body.

She didn't even know why she asked, but in her burgeoning teen rebellion, it just came out. "Then why didn't you?"

His response might have come from the cumulative frustration of the past thirteen years, and leaked out like a surrender. "Because there is no justice."

• • •

Melinda jogged Paire out of the memory. "How did it make you feel?"

"Like I wanted to be stronger, so I wouldn't turn out like him."

She smiled. "I like that you gave yourself a name." Melinda placed one of her heels on the table and rolled up her hem. "I gave myself this." She pointed to her ankle, and Paire saw a square tattoo the size of a postage stamp. Her vision dulled by the wine, the design looked all squiggles from across the table. She found herself looking at the glossy skin on Melinda's taut calf. Then Melinda smiled by raising a single corner of her mouth.

"That's pretty," said Paire, not knowing what else to say. "What does it mean?"

"It means *me*. I made it. It's an artist seal." Paire remembered Mayer mentioning this, but Melinda explained, "The same way Western artists sign their work, Chinese artists create a seal, or a chop, to make their work unique. It's a little archaic, but I like the idea because instead of a scrawl, I can make my own name seem prettier."

Paire looked closer. What at first glance appeared to be Chinese characters were interlaced letters: *M, Q,* and *I,* or M. Qi. Melinda said, "A version of this gets pressed into the clay before I fire it."

"You use a chop like your dad."

"I was bound to pick up some of his habits," Melinda said.

Paire stared at her bare foot. The clean toes nestled into each other, satin skin on each of them. Paire wanted to touch them, to feel the feet that she looked at every day on the rear wall.

Melinda watched the way she looked at her. Dropping her foot, she leaned into the table and turned her hands so the palms faced the ceiling, offering them to Paire. She smelled like lavender. Paire wasn't sure what to do with her own hands, and folded them around the stem of the empty wine glass. Melinda reached over and unlaced Paire's hand from the glass. The younger woman breathed in a loud lungful of air.

"Why did you invite me here?" Paire asked. She understood the answer when the woman's hands enfolded hers.

Melinda rose from her chair to lean toward her. Paire froze. Her fingers pressed down into the walnut, cold and stiff. As the woman's mouth drew toward hers, she knew she had the option to say something, to excuse herself and fumble through a polite apology. She supposed she didn't want to hurt Melinda Qi's feelings by rebuffing her. But she also wanted to know how those lips felt. As her face drifted closer, Melinda's teeth nibbled at her lower lip, and Paire wondered why she herself had come. Even if this woman wasn't the empress on display on the Fern's rear wall, she was the daughter of a legend. That was some kind of royalty. Then Paire understood that she was here not so much to see the empress, but to be seen *by* the empress. To be recognized by this woman.

Melinda's fingers, soft and narrow, burrowed through her hair. The back of Paire's scalp tingled. Her lips involuntarily stiffened into a pucker, but she willed herself to relax. Melinda's mouth lacked the sharp bristles that boys grew. She didn't find the sensation unpleasant, but she didn't fully enjoy it either. This was a strange, new sensation, and she found that she allowed it to happen more than participated.

Melinda sensed Paire's hesitation. She lingered, her mouth brushing against Paire's lips, then drew back to look at her quizzically. "That was a new thing for you, wasn't it?"

Paire nodded. She wondered what her expression conveyed to Melinda, whether she seemed scared, shocked, or hesitantly aroused.

CHAPTER 11

Paire stood looking at a couple of cavemen. More accurately, a caveman couple, replicas of a male and female *Australopithecus*. The man slung his apelike arm over the woman. Given their nonchalant slouches and vacant expressions, she considered that the pair might be a nude, ancient version of a couple strolling down Bedford Street in Williamsburg.

She stood at the entrance of the Hall of Human Origins, a large round room in the American Museum of Natural History. Paire had never been to this museum, mainly because it didn't feature art, and because she had seen her share of dusty taxidermy dioramas at the Dorr Museum in Bar Harbor. Today was Saturday. Tourist day. People flowed past her like spawning salmon navigating round a rock in the riverbed. She wore another neutering uniform, black pants and a white short-sleeve button-down shirt that billowed out under her breasts, pillowing her figure. A chestnut-brown wig, bunched in a ponytail, hid her red hair. No makeup. The badge sewed onto her chest labeled her as museum staff. She wasn't used to being invisible, not since she'd moved to New York, and while the point of this exercise was to blend in, it made her uncomfortable to see so many people amble by her without so much as a momentary ogle.

Paire waited for a voice to come through the two-way radio clipped to her belt.

While the patrons passed by her at the Hall of Human Origins, Paire looked at the display of glass cases, and wondered if Melinda Qi's ceramic flowers were taller. A baby stroller rolled into her ankle, and the mother hastily apologized. Paire thought that she looked at her funny, as if wondering whether a woman that young and that slight had any business being a security guard.

At any moment, Paire would hear a voice on her radio, and she would have to spring into action. At any point until then, she had the option to walk away. They would have broken no laws. But this was a delusion. At any moment, one of the regular security guards might waltz by and spot her as an imposter. She'd slipped on the uniform just minutes ago in the women's room, and despite what she'd been told about the patterns of the guards, she wasn't certain whether she could trust what she'd been told. A small miscalculation in timing, and someone would haul her off the floor.

Rosewood had assured her that this stunt would be safer than the last. The crowds would make it safer. "It's worse when it's quiet, because you stand out. The more you stand out, the more likely someone's going to spot you. Here, we'll lose ourselves in the masses." Rosewood had also promised that this installation would take less than a minute to complete. "It'll be over in a blink." Paire didn't know if she believed him.

While she waited, she thought about her drink with Melinda Qi, and how much could happen in a blink.

Paire's belt radio buzzed, and brought her out of her reverie. She couldn't tell how long she had been standing there in her uniform.

"Close off the room," Rosewood said through the speaker.

She snapped to attention. "Closing the room."

Across the Hall of Human Origins, at the other entrance, she recognized Lazaro in a matching uniform. He wore glasses and a dreadlock wig that hung down to the middle of his back. He'd removed his eyebrow piercing, but his hat looked ridiculous, ready to topple off his fake hair. Amid the quiet buzz of the people, he'd already started to steer people away, and asked those at his end of the room to exit.

Paire stretched out her arms to maximize her size. "Excuse me, folks, we're going to have to ask you to clear the room for a few minutes."

A few heads turned. A chubby family kept waddling toward the *Australopithecus* case.

Paire felt emboldened, even imperious. "Excuse me. *Excuse me.*" The authority she projected surprised her. "It'll just be a few minutes. We need to clear the room. Clear the room, everyone!"

If they were clearing the room, that meant that elsewhere in the museum, specifically under the blue whale exhibit, Charlie had forced himself to vomit in the hallway and collapse on the floor. Diversion. Rosewood would have stayed long enough to ensure that guards had been drawn to help him. If need be, he had alerted guards in adjoining rooms so they'd come running. Hopefully, this would give them enough time.

People shuffled out slowly, some glaring. They were confused, but couldn't ignore the authority of the uniform. Maybe some out-of-towners who associated New York with terrorism suspected a bomb scare, and those were the ones who hustled out without question.

Paire's voice hardened to shoo out the stragglers, who did eventually turn and stroll out of the room. Savoring her command over the crowd, she understood the wild thrill of transgressing the law.

"There we go," she said. "Thank you for your cooperation."

Not everyone went quietly. A man with a crew cut in a Pittsburgh Steelers sweatshirt said, "We paid good money for these tickets."

"It'll just be for a few minutes, sir. Thank you for your assistance."

Now that someone had spoken up, another woman in bright pink found her voice. "We came a long way for this." This woman was closer to Paire's age, and with her tone tried to convey that despite one of them being a guard and the other a ticketholder, they were connected by the bond of womanhood.

"You'll be back inside before you know it. The museum thanks you." Imbued by her own audacity, Paire felt more confident with every patron she bossed around.

She avoided eye contact with these people, so none of them would realize there was a human being somewhere behind the robotic monotone. To usher them out faster, she began a mock conversation on her radio. "Yes, sir, they're headed out now. I know it's urgent, sir. I'm doing my best."

Other than a stray protest, the room cleared with a soft trample of feet, sounding like the faint, low vibration of drum skin.

By the time she looked behind her, Rosewood had already crept in past Lazaro and knelt by the *Australopithecus* display. He hadn't dressed in uniform like them, but wore a costume that obscured his features: a trucker's baseball hat advertising Prize Pig Ale, aviator sunglasses, and fake beard, almost Amish. All of them wore some kind of disguise, something to fool the cameras when they played back the footage. Paire hoped it would work.

When she turned back toward the great exodus, someone was standing his ground on the other side of the threshold, looking past Paire as Rosewood worked. He was a local. From her short time in Manhattan, Paire had learned how to spot a local from an out-of-towner. The locals, like this one, were the ones that looked completely unimpressed. A trim, college-aged kid with thick black glasses and a groomed beard, he wore flannels that opened to a frayed T-shirt.

"So he gets to stay and we don't," he said, acting like he was entitled to know whatever she knew.

Rosewood had once said that after the World Trade Center attacks, New Yorkers felt they had an implied duty to investigate unusual activity themselves.

"What's he doing in there?" he asked.

"Sir, we'll open the room in a few minutes. Please." Calling someone her age *sir*. She felt ridiculous, and he smirked at her. Paire gestured down the hall, in the direction the rest of the patrons had shambled.

"Seriously, what's going on?"

"You know I can't tell you," she said.

"Do you not know?"

Shit, she thought. He was challenging her just for the sport of it.

Paire allowed herself a quick glance behind her. In seconds, Rosewood had unfolded a piece of white plastic and laid it on the floor. Across the room, Lazaro gesticulated to his own strays who insisted on staying in the doorway. As if they really cared that the room was closed. As if the Human Origins exhibit were a real draw, she thought. She'd never been here, but even she knew that people came for the dinosaurs and the space stuff. No one cared about the caveman mannequins. She felt the only reason that this punk was hassling her was that she had taken away his privilege of roaming free among the halls. Rosewood might have been right—freedom was everything to some people.

"How much are they paying you?"

Fuck. She wished she had her spring baton. If she didn't have on her costume, she wondered if he would be more or less likely to talk to her, or if it would just change the tone of their awkward engagement.

He asked, "Seriously, you really don't know why you just cleared out a room?"

Paire stared at him without speaking, which she didn't want to do, because she felt as if he looked into her eyes he might have a better chance of identifying her in a lineup. "Is there something in here that's dangerous? Too dangerous for me but not for you?"

Christ, she thought. She knew assholes like this in high school, who had to start shit just to see how far it could escalate. Now she was stuck with one of them. She had never been good at facing them head-on.

All she had to do was mention a *suspicious package—probably a prank*, but the moment someone cried *bomb scare* in a crowded museum, the severity of the crime would dramatically increase.

The kid asked, "Maybe I should ask another guard?"

She sighed, trying to threaten him without raising her voice, to make it seem like causing him harm would be a matter of tedious routine. "Not a bad idea. If we need to detain you, other guards would help."

"Did you just threaten me?"

"In fact, I did." Paire scowled at him, now looking into his eyes so he could understand the depths of her disinterest in him. "It's my job to clear the room. If you get in the way of that job, I can and will detain you. We keep a room in the basement, and you can call a lawyer and sort it out. We don't normally have to resort to that, so I can't say how long you'll be in there. But you could just leave now and save us the trouble."

"Bitch," he said, and walked away.

Behind her, Rosewood moved fluidly, rolling out the white sheet of plastic onto the front of the glass case with the caveman couple. Somewhere, this might have tripped a silent alarm. To the right of the Australopithecines, he unrolled a six-foot illustration of a biped, humanoid figure. A moment later, he affixed a small, rectangular placard that matched the others at the museum.

Rosewood used a six-inch ruler to smooth out the bubbles, and was finished. Without stopping to admire the work, he crossed the room back toward Lazaro, and the two disappeared around a corner.

For a fraction of a second, Paire admired what Rosewood had installed. Similar to the style of stenciling he'd used back at Wall Street station, this was a preprinted decal in black and white, printed on thin, white plastic. A mild adhesive held the plastic to the glass, but it would peel off easily, without leaving any residue. Only a handful would see it before the real museum guards pulled it down, but Rosewood had captured a camera phone shot of it himself. The image would later be posted and shared among a larger audience.

Rosewood had illustrated a bearded man in rags. The man's cheekbones protruded with the same inelegance as the hominids in the cases. His chin tucked down toward his clavicle, and his downcast eyes evoked the same sense of shame that all of these depictions of early man shared, as if they all knew they weren't the final step in evolution. The difference was that Rosewood's man was modern, possibly nomadic, definitely undomiciled. An overcoat hung off him and made Paire think about Russian peasantry. The placard text closely matched the font that the museum used for their signage, naming the subject with the same scientific detachment as the other exhibits: *Homeless Erectus*.

When Paire first met Derek Rosewood, he'd spoken about the role of the artist as a social agitator. She'd believed him at the time, and she was sure that others still thought of him that way. When they took a gander at this illustration, those people would marvel at the biting commentary on how the privileged gawk at humans behind glass cases while ignoring the real crisis of humanity happening right outside these tourist attractions. They would be indignant at others' inclination to objectify the disenfranchised. Before she really knew Rosewood, she would have been one of those people. Now, she saw it for what it was—a mischievous prank. She loved it.

"If you're not already moving, get moving," Rosewood's voice said through her radio.

She realized she'd been lingering, and headed toward the exit. Momentarily stopping in a corner between the cameras, a corner they had identified in previous walkthroughs, she went into the same bathroom where she'd changed. In the handicapped stall, she stripped off the uniform top the way she had in practice, along with the belt. Pinching herself as she undid the clips, she slid off the wig, bunched it all, and stuffed it in the trash. At the mirror, she undid her ponytail, shook out the red hair, and hastily applied scarlet lipstick.

When she came out of the bathroom, people looked at her differently, the way she liked being looked at in New York.

She had to pass the Hall of Human Origins to get to the exit. A collective of people had already gathered to see *Homeless Erectus*, and a few camera flashes reflected off the glass case. Real guards in real uniforms kept people at bay with outstretched arms, and Paire felt some pride that she had aped their mannerisms accurately.

She continued out through the Grand Gallery, underneath the sixty-foot Native American canoe that hung from the ceiling. She almost made it through the doors when a guard called to her. "Ma'am. Ma'am. *Ma'am!*"

She froze in her tracks and slowly pivoted. A large guard stood within arm's reach. She saw the embroidered museum shield before she looked up at his face.

He gave her an expectant look. "You know this is an exit only. If you want to come back, you'll have to go through another entrance."

Paire exhaled.

"That's all right. I'm ready to go outside."

CHAPTER 12

Abel Kasson marched into the Fern Gallery. "I enjoyed the bit at the museum. I especially liked how Derek Rosewood chose not to mock his benefactor this time." He cast his eyes down at her legs. "You look healthy, like you've been getting some exercise."

"I've been rock climbing," Paire said.

Kasson patted his stomach fat. "You'd never know it, but I was a handsome man when I was younger. An Olympian body. I may have packed on some insulation, but I'm still strong all over." He winked at Paire, and she broke eye contact. Unable to control herself, she shivered. "See? That's what I mean. I can't spark any magic in you. But the day you walked into the gallery, I saw how you changed when you saw *Her*. You were bewitched by that painting. You still are. I can see it in you."

"You're the one who wants to buy it." Normally, this would have been Mayer's sort of response, but his impatience with Kasson had rubbed off on her. Her tone had changed since she'd last spoken to Kasson and was rougher, more defiant.

Paire suspected Kasson had chosen this time because he knew Mayer wouldn't be there.

"Of course I want to buy it. The empress bewitches me, same as you." He stole a lingering glance at the portrait behind her. "This is why I want to talk to you. Because you understand as I do the—well, *unnatural* allure of this work. And because you have Mayer's ear."

"So you're hoping I'll pass a note to Mayer for you?"

"He will listen to you. *She* will too. The fact that she was willing to talk to you and not Mayer is telling. She's comfortable with you, or at least, more comfortable with you than the rest of us. She might listen to reason."

In truth, Paire hadn't spoken directly to Melinda Qi since that awkward kiss.

She thought, *If you really wanted Mayer's ear, you'd talk to Lucia.* She wondered if Kasson knew that Mayer and Lucia were a couple, but she would never hint at it aloud. "I think you'd be better off making your own arguments."

"There's something in it for you," he said.

"A bribe?"

"In your profession, they would probably call it a *commission.* But I'm not talking about money." He leered at her. "I'm saying that it's in your interest to get rid of that painting."

"How's that?"

"You see what happens to people around it. Mayer's been able to shut himself off from it, but you haven't. You're never going to own it—you must realize that—and if you don't own it, all you're left with is a constant temptation eating away at you. It will slowly poison you, like living next to a power plant."

"Do I seem like I need help?" She sounded as tough as she could.

Kasson shook his head in mocking amusement. "You're going to wake up with six toes and a prehensile tail, and you won't even understand how they got there."

"If you know it's so dangerous, why do you want it?"

"I have two things in my favor. First, I can control my own urges. I've reached an age when I'm not governed by my passions. Others—like you, for instance—will surrender to them like an addiction. And second..." he savored this, "...you're never going to have her. Because I will."

"You have as much chance of owning that painting as I do."

"Is that a fact?"

"That's what I've been told."

At this point Kasson must have understood that she was not going to help him. "There's always a way, Miss Anjou. Just don't get too attached. You'll miss her when she's gone."

CHAPTER 13

Early that evening, Paire and Rosewood lay on their mattress. She could smell the toxic stench of fear on herself. Her armpits reeked of skunk and spoiled milk. She didn't usually smell like anything, and this was a point of pride for Paire. Stress was giving her B.O. To cloak it, she'd borrowed some of Lucia's perfume.

Rosewood was too polite to call attention to the bad smells, so he asked about the good ones. "Are you wearing new perfume?"

"It's Lucia's. For what it costs, it could be liquid gold."

Over the last few weeks her stress had mounted. Kasson had been right. The painting seeped into her day by day, heightening her preoccupation with it.

Her escapades with Rosewood and crew gave her a whiff of elation that lasted a few days, during which she stopped dreaming about the Empress Xiao Zhe Yi. But then, as they always did, the dreams returned. The same dream with the rushing river, where Paire drowned in the current. Starting on the banks of the river, and ending when Paire was lost in the tangle of lobster traps. When she woke, the imagined smell of the empress clung to her, a complex perfume of babies and the lilacs she'd remembered from Abenaki.

Paire had continued compulsively rendering hand and foot sketches, as if every day might be the last time she saw the portrait. When she drew the face, the lips were too thick, the eyes slightly Europeanized. More like Melinda. She despised her sketches, and referred to them as "cave paintings." Just the same, Rosewood taped them up on the walls, a vast feathering of drawings on the eggshell plaster across the bedroom. The face seemed a composite of the

Chinese empress and Qi's daughter, and failed to capture the essence of either. But it was enough to remind Paire of both.

Paire had become insatiable for Rosewood's mouth, and when he went down on her, his tongue circling her clitoris, she stared at the hand-drawn face on the wall, a distant cousin of royalty. When she came it was sometimes with the woman, not the man.

She had felt closer to Rosewood after his guerrilla stunts, bonded together by ordeal. Sex intensified with the thrill of the crimes. They wore each other out, eager to celebrate the success of their survival.

They lay naked on top of the sheets, Paire feeling pungent. In her guilty reverie, chest still billowing from the sex, she said, "My dad was in prison." She had shared this with Melinda Qi, but not with him.

"I'm sorry. That's the worst thing that can happen to someone." She was surprised. "The worst?"

"To be captive? I'd rather die," he said. "So he's out now?"

"They let him out when I was thirteen. He was in for twelve years."

Normally someone might have asked, *So, what did he do?*, but Rosewood said, "Is that why you're afraid to take that painting? You're worried you'll get put away like your dad? Worried you'll be like him?" They had joked about stealing the Empress Xiao Zhe Yi. In passing. Nothing serious. Maybe she liked to joke about it more than Rosewood.

"That's part of it, sure."

"Was he a thief?"

"Not exactly. But he was a criminal," she said.

"Did he hurt people?"

Now that she'd come out with it, she regretted having said anything. "Tried to hurt someone."

"Twelve years. That's a big hurt."

"Yes, it was."

"Was it your mom?"

"No, she was already dead." Again, she immediately regretted having said this. The street sounds from Pierrepont suddenly seemed louder. Traffic, random shouts, and dog barks distracted her like gnats.

Rosewood gently pressed his palm against the side of her head, stroking her cheek with his thumb and then coiling her hair around his fingers. "Do you think we're hurting anyone with these installations?" he asked.

"On the contrary."

"It's not so different," he said.

"You're trying to convince me to commit a crime."

"I'm trying to get you to make a decision. I'd be satisfied with whatever choice you make."

By now, Paire had told him everything she knew about Qi and the Kasson family. She'd assumed that as a prominent artist, Rosewood would have heard the story, but he hadn't heard squat. He'd only been to the MAAC once, and other than receiving money from Abel, he had no interaction with the Kassons.

She had also told him about the kiss with Melinda. This wasn't a confession. Paire didn't feel like she'd betrayed Rosewood, but she felt strange about the experience. How abruptly she left, and whether she had hurt Melinda's feelings. Of course, in the retelling, Paire had been a passive participant, which was mostly true. But she omitted that once the initial shock of the other woman's lips passed, Paire Anjou might have, for just a few moments, kissed back, softening her own lips and even opening her mouth just enough so her tongue might flick against Melinda's. Paire didn't know what purpose it would serve to tell Rosewood this—either it would titillate him or it would hurt his feelings. When she asked, "What do you think?" he had said, "I'm in the art world…I've seen two women kiss. How do you think she feels?"

In that moment, when Rosewood worried about Melinda rather than stewing about the relationship, or worse yet, succumbing to erotic fantasy, Paire knew that she loved this man.

She thought about how safe she felt resting beside him. How easy it was to play with dangerous ideas.

He asked, "Kasson said he was going to steal it himself?"

"Not exactly, but there are only so many ways you can acquire a piece of art. If not by purchase or trade.…Do you think he would? He's mostly hot air."

"I don't know. You don't get to where he is without doing something bad. He has influence, and he makes things happen. I'm not saying he's going to break into an art gallery himself—although I'd sure like to see what that would look like—but he's got enough people on payroll to do it for him."

"So I should steal it before he does?" Her brain spun as she imagined herself in the Fern, dressed in some head-to-toe unitard.

"Melinda Qi told you that painting is a burden. I think you'd be doing her a favor."

She teased, "How do I know you don't want it? Something to hang up next to the Murakami."

"I couldn't care less about the painting. It's just a painting. If you learn nothing else from me, learn this—a piece of art only has value because of what people ascribe to it. Qi's work is impressive, but the world will keep spinning without it. I'm more interested in seeing you become the person you want to be, and that happens when you take risks. Sometimes big risks. And I'm warming to the idea because it would have more value to you than it would to either Melinda Qi or Abel Kasson. You draw inspiration from it. That says something."

Paire couldn't believe he was talking so casually about this. "I can't do it."

"Then don't."

They lay in a comfortable sloth, where the words spilled out effortlessly between them. She said, "I get the sense that Mel's going to get rid of it somehow—she'll either cave to Kasson's bid, or it'll go somewhere else. Maybe a museum. Maybe storage."

"You might not see it again," he said, without much emotion. "That's the upshot, isn't it?"

This was exactly the dilemma. At some point, that painting would be sold, stored, donated, or stolen, and Paire's inspiration would vanish. Selfishly, she allowed herself the delusion of picturing what the empress would seem like here in the apartment, hanging over the bed, serving as an aphrodisiac to them, and steering her ability to find her creative voice.

"I thought you didn't want me thinking about the painting. I thought that's what the rock climbing and the guerrilla stuff was all about."

"All that stuff was giving you a taste for what you can do on your own. The more you become your own person, the less likely you'll be to obsess over someone else. All I'm trying to do is help you make your own choices. That is the very essence of independence."

"You think I obsess over it," she said.

"I'm teasing you a bit, but there's a bit of truth to it, don't you think? If it's gone, you might pine over the thing even more. *She's the one that got away!*"

She poked him between the ribs. "Stop it."

"I'm just trying to get you to recognize it for what it is—an impressive piece of work, but not the be all and end all. I think it's important that you demystify it, so you can move on."

He was being gentle with her, but it still stung. It stung because she couldn't deny the obsession. Paire afforded the luxury of weekly manicures and pedicures now, to try and perfect her hands and feet the way she'd seen those depicted on the birch board. "Another pedicure," Rosewood would comment each time.

Now he said, "You think that painting is magical. In the short term maybe that's not so bad, because it's motivated you to create your own work. But sooner or later, you'll realize it's not all magic. Something is going to prove it to you. That's not a bad thing either, because at that moment, you'll realize that creating something that good doesn't have to come down from the mountaintop. It's just as human as eating and crapping—and that means it's within your reach too. But the downside is that I'm worried it's going to wreck you when that happens. Now, maybe Melinda Qi will take it back into her collection where no one will ever see it again. Maybe she'll sell it, and you'll realize it's just another commodity that gets bought and sold. When that happens, your heart is going to break."

Paire imagined how she would feel hearing that news, and knew he was correct.

"Something is going to pop the bubble. If it has to happen, and I think eventually it will happen, maybe it's not so bad that you have a hand in it, so you can prove to yourself that great art is human and not divine."

She stared at the wall across the bed, the blank space next to where the Murakami hung. The empress wouldn't feel right next to Mr. DOB. She would need her own wall. Paire pictured how the woman would look, red cheongsam daringly open, confidently presiding over them. How that would look when she woke up, and how it might energize her. The work she might create. The endorphins made her tremble, and that surge of pleasure scared her. She made excuses for why they shouldn't steal the painting. "I'd get caught."

"I'd help you."

"*We'd* get caught."

Rosewood laughed and softly pinched her earlobe. "We infiltrated a national museum. Do you really think we couldn't get in and out of a tiny gallery? It's not the Met."

"The security system is good."

He feigned surprise. "Oh, they have one of those? So they don't keep the door open at night and let the raccoons in?"

"No. It's seriously good."

"You set the alarm at night. So you can disable it."

This had recently changed. Paire had now worked at the Fern Gallery long enough for Mayer to trust her. Whoever was closing with Paire, be it Lucia or Mayer, took turns shutting down the computer and gathering up paperwork while the other person went to the back and armed the system. In theory, she could leave it disarmed. It would be quite simple, really. "They have cameras."

"I have a ski mask," he said.

"So now you're the thief, instead of me."

"If you want me to be. I would do it for you. I just need you to ask. Embrace your freedom of choice."

The hair on her arms rose. Talking like this made her feel a little drunk. Paire's heart jumped. She was struck by how easily Rosewood might risk himself for her. They kissed softly with wet, open mouths. "So I would unlock the back door too, I suppose?"

"No, too obvious. You lock the back door. I would bust open the door with a crowbar. A break-in like any other. Except when I get inside, the alarm won't sound. I could steal a few pieces, a few Derek Rosewoods," he sniggered, "so it wouldn't be too obvious someone was just after the red queen. It'd just seem like a straight-up art robbery. You've already had one attempt. Is it so hard to imagine someone would try something more sophisticated than a rock through the window?"

"All this on a night that I just happened to forget the alarm?"

"You'll only be guilty of incompetence."

Rosewood had started talking about the plan in definite terms, swapping out *woulds* for *wills*. She started getting anxious at how real this plan could be, and fished for things to say to stop the conversation. "Prison."

Rosewood said, "Galleries get robbed all the time. They wouldn't install fancy alarm systems if they didn't."

"They'd figure out it was me. You. *Us.*"

"You'll probably lose your job, but you can get another one."

She propped herself on her elbows, more alert. "Do you even like that painting?"

"I've said I like it."

"But it's so different from your work."

"That doesn't mean it's bad. Far from it. He did everything right with that one."

"Do you like the idea of owning it?"

"I like the idea of doing something bold together. For me, it's not so different from what we've been doing. I think it's romantic. I'll put the question back on you. How would it make you feel?"

Paire hemmed until she came up with, "Every time I see her, she makes me want to be a better artist."

"Is that all she makes you want?"

She rolled so she leaned her back against his chest, lost in thought for a minute. She thought about the face of the empress, the blushing lips painted with a pout. The woman in the painting was real. She was two real women, actually. Both the mother of Melinda Qi and the Empress Xiao Zhe Yi herself. They had blended into a figure who seemed larger than life, somehow both regal and rebellious. But when she stopped dissecting the portrait and identified what made Paire Anjou keep staring every time she entered the Fern, she said, "I'd like to be that strong." Paire interlaced her hand in his, and the two admired the twine of fingers.

Rosewood lightly stroked Paire's face, and when she shut her eyes, he gave her closed eyelids the lightest brush with his fingers, running up and down the mohawk ridges of eyelashes.

She said, "I wouldn't want anyone to get hurt."

"That's why we'd do it at night."

She imagined what might be possible, allowing herself the fantasy of pulling off another stunt, but this time for her and not Rosewood. She enjoyed being the primary focus of this. Because of what they'd done in the subway and at the museum, she even allowed herself to think of this as something other than a crime. Rosewood had been helping her to see how social convention, even legal convention, wasn't always clear-cut. Maybe this could even be positive. Melinda would be relieved. Kasson would stew over this novel sensation of loss.

Paire reminded herself that they were still just playing, conjuring up a plan in their blissful, postcoital reverie. She was still high on the rush of possibility, basking in what she had already done with him. But the more they talked, the more plausible it seemed, and the closer they got to attempting it.

"We're still talking hypothetically."

"What else would this be?" he said slyly, circling her navel with his fingers.

She applied some of the knowledge she'd learned from Rosewood over the past couple of months. "The back entrance. That would be the entry and exit point."

"That's how I'd do it."

"It's not a canvas. You couldn't cut it and roll it. It's solid birch board. And not a small one at that."

"I've had to move flat panels like that. You can dress as a trash collector, and wheel out a trash bin. For something that size, you could mold two trash bins together. From the outside it would look like you're just wheeling around two plastic tubs, but on the inside the center divider would have been cut away, so you'd have one large rectangle to stow it."

"You'd be in Manhattan wheeling that around. Pretty obvious."

"No one looks twice at the trash man. Not in this town."

"So you'd take it on a subway?"

"We'd have a van. The driver would get a call and pick up the trash man and the tubs. Plenty of room in a van for all of it."

She got excited. "I'd be driving the van?"

"You'll be at the library, or anywhere plenty of people would see you. You'll be nowhere near this." This made sense, but she didn't like the idea of having to sit out.

The scenario was quickly becoming real. She thought it might actually be possible. Paire kept imagining the portrait on their wall. She knew she shouldn't want it—it wasn't fair for one person to own something that valuable, to hide it away from the world. But she did want the Jia Shun Empress, and the more possible it became to acquire the painting, the more exhilarated she became. Her mind scrambled with conflicted thoughts, between conscience and covetousness. "I wouldn't want to hurt Mayer."

"The Fern has insurance. He wouldn't be in business without it."

"He'd feel violated." *I know I would*, she thought.

"From what you've told me, it sounds like he'd be relieved. That thing brings all those weirdos into his place, including Abel Kasson. I think he'd be glad to be rid of it. It's an albatross."

"You think Mayer would be happy if we stole from him?"

"I'm saying he won't cry when it's gone."

She wondered if the guilt of a crime would be too much for her to bear, especially with a father who had already spent twelve years in prison. She would be just like Lake Novis. The thought revolted her. She thought she'd grown out of her klepto phase. She'd also never wanted anything this badly. Time seemed to slow whenever she looked at that painting. Other sounds died down, and there was only the empress, humming in her head.

Rosewood's plan seemed flawed. She might have stolen trinkets from students and lit fires in the orchard, but she'd never committed a crime this serious. Paire might give herself away when the police questioned her. The police could read people's reactions—that was their job. They'd be able to tell she had something to do with the robbery just by how she fidgeted in her chair. She might give herself away with an eye tic.

Paire lay on her chest on the bed, her arms hugging a pillow as if it were a giant teddy bear. Her ankles crisscrossed in the air. She imagined the Jia Shun Empress above her bed, anticipating such a time the way some women dreamed of their wedding nights.

CHAPTER 14

Paire sat in a small room with glass walls.

The MSAD library had been rebuilt in the mid-nineties, with a modern two-story open-air reading room, surrounded by a perimeter of conference rooms. Intended for study groups, each one came with a sliding glass door that soundproofed group conversations. Paire sat in one of these rooms, pretending to focus on her laptop. Each chamber looked like one of the taxidermy dioramas at the American Museum of Natural History. When people passed, some squinted at her with a passing curiosity, and some shot dirty looks because she was hogging a room intended for groups. Maybe they were just struck by the yellow dress.

Paire wore a bright canary dress when she closed the Fern Gallery with Lucia. That night, she wanted to be remembered, and the yellow dress stuck out. Someone at the library desk asked, "Special night?"

They had waited five days, until Paire was scheduled for the closing shift. In the meantime, she and Rosewood had turned the Brooklyn Heights flat into a war room, sketching out the plan on the same giant pads they used to map out Rosewood's guerrilla installations. They printed a crude floor plan of the gallery and maps of the neighborhood. Talking through it step by step, Rosewood played secretary, scribbling with squeaky markers and taping the sheets on the walls, so they could view their entire scheme at a glance.

They'd gone shopping together for the necessary supplies: janitor's uniform, gloves, a four-wheeled dolly, two plastic trash barrels, a crowbar, hacksaw, hammer, duct tape, small zippered case for the tools, and a bandana. All bought with cash, from different stores. Same as they'd done when they shopped for Wall Street station.

The planning invigorated her, even though it meant risking everything she'd built in New York. Paire would be an obvious suspect. If they weren't caught in the act, the police would find their way to Pierrepont Street. They would want to search Rosewood's flat, which at the very least meant she wouldn't be able to hang the empress in the bedroom the way she'd daydreamed. But she'd already broken laws in New York and gotten away with it. And the reward would absolutely be worth it, she told herself.

Paire had trouble sleeping. When she was awake, watching her boyfriend sleep next to her, she imagined that he might wake up, and they'd share a moment of epiphany, where they would both admit this was a foolish errand conceived by a pair of crazies.

They reviewed timing until she had memorized the sequence of events for the evening. She would close the gallery at seven and immediately head to the MSAD library. She'd stay there until it closed at midnight. That's how much time she needed to kill. Rosewood would arrive at the Fern around ten thirty, not so late that he'd be the only person on the street.

He'd told her that she had to stay in sight. Make small talk with the librarian so that someone could say they saw her. The police would know it was a ten-minute walk to the Fern, maybe even a two-minute cab ride. She should make a few phone calls, enough to show she was engaged when the robbery took place. GPS tracking would place her back at the library. Once it closed, she needed to go back to Brooklyn.

"The police will eventually want to talk to you. You'll need to fake surprise when it happens," he'd told her. "Mayer will blame you for not setting the alarm. Prepare yourself for that." She practiced what she would say, rehearsing until her story sounded natural.

For those five days leading up to this evening, Paire had difficulty talking to Mayer and Lucia. At different points, they both asked, "Are you all right?" Paire felt like a bell diver with a knot in her air hose. She reminded herself to feign nonchalance—less Novis, more Anjou.

That night while working her shift with Lucia, she thought of calling it off. All it would take was a phone call. But Paire didn't call Rosewood. Whenever she stole glances at the rear wall, she wanted the empress more than ever. The red cheongsam was always in the corner of her eye, an ever-present crimson blur. Soon it would belong to her.

When they were closing, Lucia finally cornered her while the computer monitor blinked to black. "You've been different, and I know what it is."

Paire's blood chilled. She'd just returned from the back office. The alarm remained unarmed. Lucia said, "It's the break-in."

Paire felt her sphincter tighten.

Lu continued, "That morning after someone threw a rock through the window. You saw Mayer and me together. I know you knew about us before that, but we'd never been so open about it. You've acted differently since then."

Had she? She hadn't made up her mind to steal the painting until later. *What's wrong with you?* Rosewood might have scolded. *If you act guilty, you're going to give yourself away.*

"It's not my business." Paire bit her nails, the ultimate irony for a girl obsessed with her hands. All of those manicures were for naught, and in the final week before the burglary, her ragged fingertips looked as if she'd just clawed her way out of a grave.

"But it makes you uncomfortable," Lucia said.

Paire wanted the conversation to end, so they could finish closing and she could leave the Fern. "I think you make a good couple. It's nice to see people in love."

Lucia stared down at the large diamond on her left hand. "Mayer's a good person. I hope it doesn't change the way you think about him."

"You're both good people," Paire said.

"Are you kidding? I'm a shit." The depth of her shame surprised Paire.

"You're not a shit." Paire couldn't help but steal a glance at the wall clock. She worried about how long this conversation might stretch.

"My husband doesn't beat me or anything, if that's what you're wondering. He's not a drunk. He's not abusive." Paire remembered bruises on Lucia when she'd first met her, but didn't contradict her. "He's actually sweet, in his own way. He works too much—he's a doctor. Did I ever tell you that?"

"You never talk about him."

"He's a rheumatologist," Lucia said proudly.

"I can't remember…"

"Arthritis."

"That's right," Paire said.

"His name is Enrico de Moraes." Paire had always assumed that Lucia had kept her maiden name, even though she didn't look like she had an ounce of Latina blood in her.

Almost breathlessly, Lucia said, "He can be distant. He takes his work too seriously. And the hours—*the hours*…"

Paire shifted her weight from foot to foot, wishing she could sit down. She thought about the alarm system panel by the back door, its blue block letters glowing DISARMED. "A girl gets lonely," Lucia said. Possibly realizing how coy this sounded, and wanting to seem earnest, she rephrased, "I got lonely. And here comes this handsome man of the world. I mean, look at him—Mayer's *dashing*. Don't you think?"

Paire hadn't ever considered dating a man that much older than herself, so she had never spent much time considering whether Mayer Wolff was attractive. She supposed he was, thinking about the wild hair, the closely cropped beard along his strong jawline, and the fine fabric suits. Paire nodded. "Absolutely."

"You have to understand. Mayer never intended to steal me away from my husband."

The way she loosely spilled this confession, Paire wondered if Lucia might be drunk, but didn't smell alcohol on her.

She didn't know what to offer the conversation. "Do you love him?"

"Which one?"

"Either."

"That's the thing. You know how you can love more than one person?" Lucia studied her face.

Paire thought about the question. Rosewood referred to people like Lucia as polyamorous.

This struck a tender spot. In her heart, Paire knew she had come to love Derek Rosewood. And as she admired the empress on the wall, the feelings the painting conjured closely approximated love. Maybe she wasn't so different from Lucia.

"You're lucky to have choices," she said.

"I guess I am." Lucia smiled, flashing her braces.

Paire knew the braces would come off in only a few more months. She wondered if Lucia would mark that moment as a new beginning in her life, when she could make some of the harder decisions about her relationships.

Lucia turned off the lights slowly, and the room grew incrementally dark as the bulbs were extinguished one by one, and the only light shone in from the street. The two women hugged on the sidewalk after Paire had slapped the padlock on the entrance. Lucia lingered in the embrace.

• • •

In her terrarium at the library, Paire tried to do some schoolwork. She was writing a paper on an artist of her choosing, and she had picked Lempicka. Paire liked the urgency in the faces she painted. Everyone in her work radiated with purpose. It was the same confidence that attracted her to the Empress Xiao Zhe Yi. *Girl in a Green Dress*, from 1930, appeared on her laptop monitor. The woman's dress was a shade of green she hadn't seen elsewhere, but made her think of emeralds. Her white-gloved hands tipped a wide-brimmed white hat, and to Paire, her severe expression conveyed a resilience that Paire not only admired, but aspired to. This was the woman Paire wanted to be in New York—stylish, glamorous, yet confident enough not to lose her own sense of self.

At this moment, she felt completely divorced from this ideal. She had written two pages since she arrived, and it was all garbage.

Around eight o'clock, she started to get cold feet. She tried to call Rosewood, even though he'd told her in no uncertain terms that they couldn't speak the evening of the robbery. "We'll seem like we're colluding," he'd said. "Which we are." She definitely couldn't leave a message, or text him, but she tried him several times. Now, just after ten, she thought about going to the gallery to intercept him. He warned her not to be anywhere near the gallery. "If you're near the gallery at all tonight, it will hurt your alibi. So only do that if you want us both arrested." As panic settled in, she felt helpless. The crime would take place, and she couldn't prevent it.

Rosewood had modeled the navy blue uniform with SANITATION printed in block letters across the shoulder blades. A small clump of cloth from his pocket unfolded into a matching navy hat, which he pulled down to his eyebrows.

"Sexiest janitor I've ever seen," she'd said. It seemed stupid now.

They molded together two gray rectangular trash barrels, so their hulls formed a flat wall when stacked side by side. Cutting away the center, they created large plastic tub. With the lids on top, the bins looked like any others. The *getaway garbage*, they called it. Her heart had raced when it was finished, because more than the rest of their props, this container demonstrated their joint determination to steal the Empress Xiao Zhe Yi from the Fern.

Despite the stray people that milled about the library, Paire felt alone. Her mind churned with thoughts and fears. She felt ashamed at how badly she wanted the empress. Her skin prickled as she anticipated reconnecting with Rosewood at the end of the night. Then she agonized about the consequences tomorrow, when Mayer tore his hair out, when the police asked her how she could forget to arm the security panel.

She imagined what she might say to the cops, envisioning the same pair of officers she had met when she was slicked with Nicola Franconi's plasma. She would claim that she was distracted. Lucia's confession about her affair with Mayer had overwhelmed Paire. That's what she could say. This would misdirect the police. But she felt inhuman entertaining this. When the police spoke to her, she would do what she practiced with Rosewood. Feign mortification. Except that she wouldn't have to fake it at all. Right now, she was very much ashamed of herself. She called Rosewood another time to try and call the whole thing off. Voicemail.

Paire was caught in something she could no longer stop.

She had tricked herself into thinking of Derek Rosewood's installations as *rule-breaking* instead of *law-breaking*. But they were all crimes, this one simply more blatant than the rest. Paire Anjou's worst fear was coming to life. She was becoming her parents.

• • •

As a teen, Katie Novis sniffed out her parents' ugly history on her own. Gilda Abington had purged Lake Novis's trial from the press, but Katie found a reporter at the *Portland Press Herald* who periodically wrote about the Abington family. After teaching herself to drive before legal age, she brake-lurched her way down to Portland with one of Gilda's extra vehicles.

At the *Herald* offices, Katie asked for Wayne Braden. She waited in the lobby for hours until she caught him on a coffee and tobacco break. Wayne was tall and bulky, with thick glasses and a receding hairline. Once he saw her, he was empathetic. In retrospect, he must have wondered whether Cissy Novis's daughter had inherited her mother's illness. Several times, he asked if she needed to see a doctor.

After some encouragement, as well as her insistence that Gilda Abington had not put her granddaughter up to this, they went to Wayne's office and he answered her questions. Wayne had been one of the victims of Gilda's purge. Perhaps he spoke to Katie because he felt it would only be fair for the girl to know the truth, and perhaps he just wanted to get even with Gilda Abington for expunging so much of his work.

Wayne described Cissy Novis as an eccentric child. From a young age, she had conversations with imaginary friends, or, as Wayne described it, "You know, ordinary weird kid stuff." Then, more serious incidents occurred here and there. At a fundraiser, she lit the drapes on fire, causing little damage but a lot of hysteria. She wounded the family dog with a pair of scissors because she said when she was alone with it, the corgi turned into a crocodile and tried to eat her. Cissy started psychiatric care when she was twelve. The Abingtons kept it quiet. Doctor visits were given the code name "dance class," in case someone had to explain where their daughter was.

Cissy Novis escalated her problematic behavior when she hit puberty. She stole from some of the local shops on Abenaki's King Street, named not for the British monarchy but for William King, the first governor of Maine. Some shopkeepers overlooked it. The Abingtons had to pay others to keep mum. They returned the stolen items, and once, they brought Cissy for a staged apology. When she got her license, Cissy pilfered spirits from the house supply and drove drunk around town with one of the unused family cars. This was considered another forgivable eccentricity, until she crashed a Bentley into the courthouse.

"When you look at photos of her from the time, you'd never think she'd be anything but the perfect daughter. She looked like a porcelain doll. I mean that part in a good way. She was beautiful, like you." Wayne said. Reading Katie's discomfort, he said, "You don't see it yet, do you? Don't worry, you will."

After the courthouse, the Abingtons tried inpatient therapy. Cissy was committed to the Portland Center for Psychiatric Care. Wayne believed that once she was out of the house, the family, and in particular Gilda, felt relieved. Cissy's parents were more visible in public. Wayne showed Katie photographs taken during this period, and Gilda smiled more freely than she'd ever seen.

Lake Novis was an attendant at the hospital. Wayne explained,

"They have plenty of rules to keep the men and women apart, but people break rules, and things happen."

Five months into the pregnancy, Cissy's belly began showing, and the hospital couldn't ignore it. It didn't take long to identify the father, and the hospital fired Lake Novis. The Abingtons were furious.

"They might have sued the trousers off that hospital, if it wouldn't mean a heap of bad press," Wayne said.

The family kept this a closely guarded secret, so he had to speculate about the next bits to fill in the gaps. Wayne knew the Abingtons didn't favor abortion to begin with, and by the time Cissy got home she was into her third trimester. The plan, he supposed, would likely have been to keep Cissy under a sort of house arrest until she gave birth, then find an orphanage for the baby. With an acute sense of irony, Wayne said, "That's how we do it in Maine." But Cissy ran away. She found Lake Novis, and they drove north to Caribou. Lake pumped gas until the baby was born. He eventually held up his own gas station for three hundred dollars, and occasionally held up liquor and convenience stores. The full roster of those robberies would come out during his trial. They gave the baby Gilda's middle name, Katherine, but Wayne couldn't be sure if this was to honor her mother or spit in her face.

This was how Katie Novis learned the circumstances of her birth. Not only was it statutory rape, Cissy Novis might not have been able to establish the mental competence requisite for sexual consent even if she had been of age. Katie had come into the world as the daughter of a rapist and a criminally dangerous schizophrenic. The story would only get worse.

• • •

Sealed in her library conference room, Paire dialed another number, and connected on the second ring.

Melinda Qi said, "I'm surprised you called." She hesitated, her voice tinny through the speaker. "But happy you did."

"I'm sorry for how I left the other night." Paire felt a rush of relief cascade down into her gut. "I hope I didn't make you feel bad."

"I misread the situation," said Melinda, now atonal. Possibly Mel had hoped Paire was calling because she'd enjoyed that kiss and wanted more.

"I think you're wonderful."

"And?"

"I wasn't in the same place, but that doesn't make you any less..." she tried to find the right word, "...it doesn't make you any *less.*" Paire felt like she needed to add something, to steer this talk to something more benign. Even now, she was slightly dumbstruck that she'd even placed this call. *The things guilt can make us do*, she thought. "I loved your work. I wish I could create something that unique on my own."

"Are you calling on behalf of the Fern right now?"

"I'm calling on behalf of myself." Paire remembered watching how Melinda's hips swayed as she walked down the long corridor to the Museum of Asian Art and Culture administrative offices. "I never asked. How did your meeting at the MAAC go?"

"Well."

"Are they going to show your work?"

"I wasn't there to talk about my work." Mel paused, giving Paire a moment for her stomach to squirm. "Are you in touch with Abel Kasson?"

Paire frowned as she thought about the banker. "Only when he comes by to harangue us. I'm not calling you because Abel Kasson wanted me to."

Melinda warmed. "So I can trust you, then?"

Absolutely not, Paire thought. *I am stealing your painting right now.* "Of course you can."

Static filled a long pause. Paire had reached the point of shame where she didn't want to attract more attention, so she didn't talk. She folded her spare arm across her body and squashed her boobs against her ribs. That old habit from high school.

Melinda said, "Give me your email. I'm going to send you something."

Paire gave it to her, and waited. A half minute later, a message appeared in her inbox. No subject. PDF attachment. Paire opened it and scrolled through a legal document. It had been scanned askew, and the Courier type ran downhill.

"What is this?"

"A contract between my father and Gabriel Kasson."

Paire skimmed the contract for details, but ultimately the signature page told the story. Two scribbles, one in English and the other in Chinese characters Paire couldn't understand, ran above the typed names of Gabriel Hartford Kasson and Qi Jianyu. Dated February 23, 1973.

Paire remembered the photo of Pat Nixon in Beijing, the red coat bursting out of the gray wardrobes of the Chinese and Americans. Somewhere in the background, slightly out of focus, the lean pillar of Gabriel Kasson looked on through his thick-rimmed spectacles.

"Did they meet during the 1972 Beijing visit?"

Melinda said, "So you did look him up."

"What is this contract for? An art commission?"

"In 1973, Gabriel Kasson spent a lot of money to commission a museum in Manhattan. He made a point to secure a prominent architect. With enough money, they hired I. M. Pei to design the building. That was a score. The museum was built for the primary purpose of housing the works of Qi Jianyu."

"You're kidding." Paire wanted to call bullshit, but didn't risk speaking ill of the woman's father. Just the same, she waited for Melinda to tell her she was joking. "That doesn't make any sense. A building that big was built to house one artist's work?"

"He had a lot of work. Gabriel Kasson was a fan. A big fan, with a lot of resources and influence."

Paire stated the obvious. "But the museum isn't showing any of your father's work."

"Correct."

"So where is it?"

"That's the big question, isn't it?" Melinda asked. "It all disappeared. No one knows where. It's probably boxed up in the archives. And with a museum like that, the archives could be in the basement, or they could be in some offsite facility. Point is, no one's seen that work for decades. But the Kasson family owns it."

Paire scrolled through the document, trying to pull out details. "Is that what's in this contract? The museum deal?"

"Oh, God no. That's just the contract that got him out of China." Melinda narrated as Paire read the text. "My father lived outside of Beijing, and he was poor. He didn't read English, and only spoke enough to get by on stilted conversations. He never read the terms of this contract, but as it was explained to him, this was going to give him a new life. That contract promises my father a house, a new car, and a nice salary every year until he dies. That contract also commissions twelve new original works to help open a new institution dedicated to promoting modern art from Asia. Effectively, a new exhibit to open what would become the MAAC."

Paire was confused. "That sounds like a good deal."

"That contract also states that every piece of work he produced would become the property of Gabriel Kasson. Every nickel he could generate off his work would go into Gabriel Kasson's bank account. And upon his death, all of my father's estate would transfer to the Kasson Foundation. That's what that contract says. Even if he could read English, he might not have been savvy enough to navigate the legalese. But he signed his life away without knowing it."

Paire wondered where Rosewood was right now, and if she could get him to respond, whether she might still call off the theft. Her insides felt rancid. "He figured it out when he got to the U.S."

Mel said, "Pretty soon afterwards. There's always been a big Chinese community in New York. Someone helped him figure it out. Turns out, my father was just another servant. Just the help. Not so different from a gardener who grew the right ivy to ornament a mansion. So he did what any sane rebel would do. He refused to paint."

"Just like that?"

"He produced some half-assed pieces to fulfill his contract, but they were nothing compared to what he had been doing in Beijing. He told Gabriel Kasson that he was homesick, but the truth was he painted crap out of spite. Kasson knew it too. The museum opened with a little fanfare, but the critical reviews of my father's new work were lackluster. Pretty soon after, the museum decided that to make money it needed to showcase other artists, so they did. My father's work came down, and got tucked away. That was the end of his flash of fame. That was the end of him."

Paire repeated what she'd read. "Then he went back to China."

"That's how the story ends." Mel paused. "Funny. The way they talked about it, you'd think it was this big political power play. Mao had died by then, and China had the new *open door* policy. It was a coup to get a Chinese artist to come back to Beijing, and a big slap in the face to America. But it had nothing to do with politics. Gabriel Kasson had exploited my father, and my father didn't want to be exploited."

Paire wanted to call Rosewood so badly she'd have used telepathy if she could. She had set her golem in motion and now she couldn't reign him back in. "The Empress Xiao Zhe Yi—the painting of your mother..." Paire trailed off.

"Is the last known piece from my father."

"Did you always have it?" Paire remembered the date. 1980. After Qi had moved back to Beijing.

"It came to me after he died. And that's the only reason it's on display now. My father had hidden it for years."

Paire stared at her yellow dress in a reflection, grateful that Melinda Qi wasn't sitting across the table from her right now. Dogs could smell fear and people could smell guilt. She would have to pretend not to be twisting inside. She sent an email to Rosewood, knowing he would get it on his cell. *STOP.* She knew police would discover it when they investigated, but she didn't so much care.

"Does Mayer know all this?"

"He's seen the contract," said Mel. "He's kept Abel Kasson

at bay." Mel laughed without much humor. "It's been a pleasure watching *little Kasson* whipping himself into a frenzy. He knows what that painting represents. It's the family secret. For decades, the Kassons have been able to make the world forget about my father." Paire couldn't help but think of Gilda destroying the stories about Lake and Cissy Novis. "That painting could be my father's revenge. It could be the one time in New York where poor trumped rich, or where a Chinese family got one over on whitey. No offense."

Paire wondered aloud, "Who was Nicola Franconi?"

"The man who stabbed himself? I didn't know him. I assume he worked with Gabriel Kasson, but I've never met the man." Melinda sounded defensive, like she didn't want to be blamed for his death.

Paire hadn't heard back from Rosewood, but she assumed by now he probably had the painting. The thought comforted her. Because if they possessed the painting, they could return it to Melinda. If they couldn't give it to her publicly, they could always break into that compound in Long Island City and find a place to leave it. Like a baby on a doorstep. Police might probe, but if the portrait went back to its owner, it wouldn't be a protracted investigation.

This was a simple and elegant solution. Paire was even proud of herself. For the first time all night, her shoulders dropped and her belly filled with air.

• • •

Paire treated herself to a taxi ride instead of the subway. Rosewood hadn't texted her, but she would see him soon enough. Once she explained everything, he'd probably be angry with her. She wouldn't blame him, considering the risk he'd taken, but he would come around. They'd move beyond it, she was certain of that. Or at least, she kept telling herself so.

As her taxi pulled in front of the brownstone, she couldn't see any windows lit up. The whole place was dark, and her heart sank. But it wasn't yet midnight. He was planning on dropping off the painting at another location. So she waited up for him.

Over the course of the evening, her adrenaline ebbed. The immediate panic faded and a more insidious dread crept into her. Her nerves made her hands tremble. She never made it to the bedroom. Sometime around five, she passed out for an hour on a few sofa throw pillows in the first-floor studio. She woke up when the sun came through the windows, and downed a liter of water to quench her dry throat. No messages on her phone. Her morning call to Rosewood bounced to voicemail.

Rosewood never made it home.

Her shift at the Fern started at ten, but she felt compelled to arrive early. She wanted to prepare herself for running into Mayer. Less triumphant this morning than she had felt when she came home the night before, she rambled into the city on the subway like everyone else. It sprinkled this morning, and the drips from all the folded umbrellas made the floor of the car slippery.

Two police cars were parked in front of the Fern, their blue swirling lights dancing throughout the gallery. Paire walked across the street from the entrance, prepared to stroll past and then come back, but she saw cops inside, and she needed to know exactly what happened. Yellow plastic tape drooped down like Christmas tinsel across the windows and door. She half-expected to see broken glass, even though Rosewood had said he would enter through the back.

Inside, two police officers examined the floor behind the desk. It made sense they would be here, but it amplified her sense of dread. Her hands were shaky, and she thought about heading back to the subway, but it would seem more suspicious if she didn't come into work. She had to do the hard thing, even if her body trembled.

Now that she was here, she needed to face Mayer. She wouldn't be any more prepared than she was at this moment. With other people in the room, he might not blow into a rage. But Mayer wasn't with the officers. Likely, he was in the back office, where the rear door had been pried open, wondering how much it would cost to repair. Her blood drained from her forehead as she understood that she was responsible for all of this.

Paire didn't have keys for the front door, but it wasn't locked.

She walked under the tape and pushed it open. The lights hadn't been turned on. Sunlight hadn't made it into the Fern this early, and but for the blue lights, the gallery was still a cave.

"What the hell are you doing?" said one of the officers angrily.

She'd hoped these would be the same policemen whom she'd met right there at the Fern, the day Nicola Franconi expired on the sidewalk. The ones who would remember her, who would be sympathetic. No such luck. These were tall white guys, one WASPy and the other southern Mediterranean, both with the same closely shorn hair. They wore loose raincoats, and the blue flickers of light glinted of their waterproof sheen.

Paire felt as if she should be formal with them, but wasn't sure what title to ascribe. *What do I call them?* she wondered, *Police, or detectives?* "I work here," she said, trying to sound calm but coming off scared just the same.

"You can't be here, it's a crime scene!" the dark one barked.

She hadn't expected so much anger.

The Nordic one walked up to her and flashed identification: NYPD DETECTIVE molded in brass, with an unlikely duo on New York's crest—two historic characters in a coonskin cap and feather headdress. Paire wanted to leave, but she worried that the same way running can trigger hunting behavior in a predator, walking out the front door would mark her as a suspect in the crime.

Mayer needed to see her there. She needed to hug him and prove her allegiance. He wouldn't be thinking of this as a good thing, but Rosewood was right—this robbery would be the best thing that ever happened to him. He'd never have to worry about the weirdos again, and never have to bat away Abel Kasson's unwelcome solicitations. But today, she just needed to comfort him.

"Wait," said the blond, "You really work here?"

She faked entitlement. "Of course I do. Why else would I walk straight into a crime scene? Where's Mayer?"

The empress was missing from the rear wall, leaving a vast expanse of white plaster. Three Rosewoods were missing, including one of the smilers. The thief had left *HERO* in the front window.

From behind the back office door, Paire overheard a third policeman say to a colleague, "Caught fuckin' on the boss's desk."

A fourth voice said, "He was the boss."

The detective in front of Paire called to the back of the room, "Shut up!" Then to Paire, he said, "You probably shouldn't be here." His voice lost its abrasion, and that alarmed her even more.

Something was wrong. A coldness crept through her. Panic gave way to numbness. Whatever was behind the desk drew her. Her arms dropped to her sides, and she moved toward it.

The detective tried to block her path with wide arms, the way she had effectively sealed off the Hall of Human Origins. "I can't let you back there," he said. His widespread arms stopped her for a moment.

Paire dawdled, swaying on her heels. She needed to ask something that would give her an excuse to linger. She could have made an observation, something to prove that she belonged here. *They took the Qi* would have been the most obvious one. Instead, something in the man's tone—but worse, some smell in the air— made her ask, "Was someone hurt?"

Two steps to the left and she saw it. Behind the desk, a dark hump stretched out on the floor. Just the contours stood out first. Then pant legs and men's shoes. Paire made a noise she'd never made before. A pitiful squeak. Something much more appropriate to Katie Novis.

She lunged toward the desk. The detective blocked her, yet despite his size he struggled to keep her back. She recognized the shoes now. Two-tone wing tips, way too formal and way too expensive for Rosewood. Pinstripe trousers. She had seen Mayer Wolff wearing these just yesterday, when she came in to start her shift with Lucia. Mayer had seemed buoyant. When he left, he had told them, but more told Lucia, "I'll see you later."

Paire shifted in the opposite direction, breaking right. This time she was too quick for the detective to stop her, and she escaped his blockade.

"Don't!" he warned. He snatched at the air, but wasn't fast enough to grab her arm.

She ran toward Mayer, but as she rounded the desk, another figure on the floor stopped her.

She saw the legs first. The desk had hidden them. Women's legs. Lucia's tone, tanned dancer's legs, bent at uncomfortable angles. Her feet were bare and still. Her cheek rested flat against the wood floor, and one eye stared at the rear wall, its lid slightly drooped. Her mouth had frozen agape, so Paire caught a glimmer of silver from the braces. Lucia wore the same crème cocktail dress she'd had on when they closed the gallery together. A bullet hole as wide as a coffee mug ruptured the freckled skin between her shoulder blades.

CHAPTER 15

Rosewood didn't come home for the rest of the week, nor did he answer his phone. Paire didn't work, because she didn't have a place to work anymore. She missed a few classes, and muddled through homework. Her professors understood, and let her out of a few exams.

She attended both funerals. Mayer had a closed casket, Lucia open. The embalmers put on rouge, which Lucia never wore.

Paire drank quite a bit.

Whenever she returned to the apartment in Brooklyn Heights—Rosewood's apartment, really—she felt like she was breaking into a tomb, stewing in the smells of unwashed underwear and the coal mine odors of her school charcoals. She kept the lights on at night. Within a week her bedsheets were coated with a gritty film, and she tossed uncomfortably in the whipped tousle of fabric instead of sleeping.

Sometimes she threw spasmodic fits that came and went like afternoon thunderstorms. Tears and plenty of screaming. Neighbors pounded on the wall until she quieted down. Once, she wailed long enough to get the hiccups.

Paire missed everything about Rosewood, even the simple warmth of his body. But she was also afraid to see him. The next time they saw each other they would have to address the consequences of what had happened. Rosewood had planned everything to the last detail, and he seemed so sure of himself when he left in his janitor's uniform. Given how that evening played out, Rosewood might blame Paire for endangering him as much as she had blamed him for his recklessness.

More than anything, Paire wanted to confirm that the shootings had been accidental. She didn't know how she would cope with her role in two deaths, but it would be some comfort if the tragedy had been unintentional. She couldn't believe Rosewood would have gunned them both down in cold blood. He had turned down a career in the military, a life of violence, to be an artist. *Artists don't kill people*, she told herself. Well, there was Caravaggio. And she'd heard a theory that British painter Walter Sickert had been Jack the Ripper. How well did she know Derek Rosewood, anyway?

Rosewood was probably suffering worse than Paire, grappling with the complex regret of the deed and relief at having survived it. At least, this is what she wanted to believe. When she saw him, they would comfort each other. One couldn't simply right the wrong of murder—and as she voiced the word in her head, the deed attained the necessary gravitas—*murder*—but by having her co-conspirator in the same room, she would at least feel less alone in the act. Her guilt would be somewhat alleviated by distributing the onus of blame.

For all she knew, Rosewood might be hurt, even dead. In a place like New York, it would be hard to imagine that someone could find a corner to die where the body wouldn't eventually be discovered. Then again, Rosewood had navigated them to the abandoned City Hall subway station. An entire subterranean network sprawled underneath Manhattan. But if he'd been hurt, the police would have found his blood at the Fern.

Paire wanted to know he was safe. And although she would be too ashamed to admit it aloud, or even dwell on it in her mind, she wanted to see the Empress Xiao Zhe Yi. She wondered if the portrait had made it through all this without injury.

To protect himself, Rosewood might have destroyed any evidence linking him to the crime. Paire imagined the empress engulfed within the snake-tongue flames of a landfill bonfire, and it made her nauseous.

The student center had one of the last pay phones in the city, and she tried Rosewood's cell whenever she passed by, hoping that calling from a different number would have made it safe enough from him to pick up. The calls never connected.

Since her professors had given her a temporary reprieve from schoolwork, she had more idle time to dwell on her predicament. The police hadn't talked to her since they let her go from the Fern that morning. Eventually, they would come around. They would find it interesting that she lived with famed street artist Derek Rosewood, someone who coincidentally was exhibiting at the very gallery where she worked. Bells would ding in their heads.

The press gave the killings some attention, but it wasn't a big enough story to draw more than passing curiosity. Fine arts just wasn't front page news, even when you threw theft and two bodies into the story. This relieved her.

Paire weighed her options. She might run away herself. She wouldn't be as successful at hiding as Rosewood. A world traveler with installations in twenty-three different cities, he could have abandoned the empress in a dumpster and flown to Bhutan, for all she knew. Being a leader in an underground movement might have earned him enough contacts to remain underground. Paire had moved to New York and changed her name, but she didn't have Rosewood's connections. She'd never been outside the United States. She thought about another massive city where she could lose herself among the millions. Maybe Los Angeles. She found herself thinking about this option the way a tongue probed a canker sore.

She stopped dressing with her usual flair. Since the crime, she chose muted greens—a color that made her feel safe. The color that had made Katie Novis feel safe. No faux fur, no leather pants. She left the peacock vintage apparel at home, and tried to be as inconspicuous as possible.

Paire spent Memorial Day weekend suffering under the year's first heat spike in the city.

To pass time, she leafed through all of Rosewood's personal belongings in the closets. Eventually, she dumped out the boxes and cluttered the floors. Ostensibly, Paire tossed through his personal effects to find clues to where he might have gone. But she ended up combing through everything to better understand the man she had been living with. She flipped through scrapbooks and tossed them aside. She read a stack of letters from his father, General Grant Rosewood, surprised that Rosewood would have kept them. Each letter was a handwritten novella, a stack of paper so thick that, folded, barely fit into the envelope.

His father had an authoritative editorial voice. Most of the letters accomplished two things—reporting on the weddings, deaths and ailments of immediate relatives, and urging Rosewood to stop embarrassing the family with his artistic endeavors. After a while, they all read the same. Disappointment committed to the page. More interesting than the letters were the envelopes. On each one, along with the cluster of stars-and-stripes stamps, a return address in Virginia.

CHAPTER 16

By nine in the morning Virginia was too warm for a jacket. The sky seemed overly expansive without the skyscrapers. Fresh off the train, sun lightly toasted Paire through the glass of the taxicab.

In the mirror back on Pierrepont, she had rehearsed her story for General Grant and Bethany Rosewood, memorizing each fictitious detail that made it seem plausible—when the baby was due, who her doctor was, that sort of thing.

She chose Saturday morning to visit them. Hopefully, the parents would be sympathetic to a young girl coping with an unplanned pregnancy. If the General stayed consistent with the tone of his letters, he'd want to preserve his family's honor and tell her where to find their son.

The neighborhood had been built exclusively for the military. Most of the houses were brick buildings modeled after colonial Williamsburg. The Rosewood house was like many others in the neighborhood, a three-story brick fort with no decorative moldings, no architectural accents. The kind piggy number three would have slapped up to keep out the wolf. She wondered if this was the military's way of designing suburbia: pragmatic homes with equal plots of grass in front and the identical swing sets for the kids in back. Two rows of mottled sycamores lined the street, towering over a sidewalk that no one seemed to use. Aside from the occasional silhouettes in the windows, she didn't see or hear anyone. No car motors growled, no kids screamed, no pets yapped at the back doors waiting to empty their bladders in the back yards.

Paire hopped out of the cab and strode to the front door. She trembled with anger but not fear. She worked to muster up the necessary emotion—tears—to sell her fake pregnancy to the Rosewoods, and managed to produce a narrow streak down her cheek. She rang the doorbell, once, twice briefly, then longer the third time, until she heard a rustling somewhere in the brick box, the shuffling of someone trying not to be heard. Her finger rode the buzzer for a half minute longer. Somewhere upstairs a face flashed in a window, but when she looked up it retreated from the glass.

"Hello!" Paire called, politely at first. She brazenly repeated in a sing-song voice, "Helloooooo?"

More shuffling from upstairs. Whoever was up there didn't want to be disturbed. Then it struck Paire that it might not be the General up there. No self-respecting military commander or his attorney wife would be driven into hiding by a twenty-year-old girl. Only an overgrown boy would hide like that. Derek Rosewood was up there.

Paire seethed. His parents were obviously absent. And if he wasn't man enough to answer his own door, she would go in and get him. The garage next to the main house was open, and Paire rummaged through it until she found the right tool to gain entry. It wasn't like her to break into a house, certainly not a military home, but she didn't second-guess herself. Fleeting thoughts merely ran through her, such as, *If I'm arrested, would I go to regular prison or military prison?*

She looked for a ladder but instead found a toolbox, and lugged it to the back of the house. A sliding glass door marked the entrance to the Rosewoods' kitchen, locked but without the bars she'd find over the doors in Brooklyn. Likely, they never thought someone would have the balls to burgle a general's home. She would go through the back entrance, just as Rosewood had suggested when they planned the Fern robbery. When she looked up, Paire caught a slightly longer glimpse of a familiar face.

Paire might have used the spring baton but she had left it in New York. From the box, she pulled out a large wrench, a foot of solid steel, and wielded it in front of the glass door, invigorated by the promise of destruction. She felt the foolish and furious sensations of having been duped, and ached to smash something. If this was what it took to rouse that little squirrel from the tree, so be it. Paire wound up, arcing the wrench over her head and shutting her eyes so glass pellets wouldn't fly into them.

"Stop!" Rosewood yelled from upstairs.

Paire froze midswing. When she opened her eyes, the business end of the wrench was an inch from the glass.

He hung out of the upstairs window. Neither of them acted surprised to see the other. Rosewood seemed to have aged ten years in the past few days. The first thing she noticed was that his head was completely shaved. *Another cheap disguise*, she thought.

"Are you stupid? You're going to break the glass," he said.

"That's the idea."

"Jesus Christ. Hold on." He vanished from the window, and appeared at the kitchen door a minute later. He wasn't happy to see her, and didn't pretend otherwise. "Get inside."

Paire heard a fleck of the general's genes in his bark.

The most off-putting thing for Paire was that there was little different in his manner. He spoke to her as if nothing awful had ever occurred. She had worried that confronting Rosewood might unleash his inner savage, but he was the same man she knew, with the puffy lips and brimming confidence.

Paire had the upper hand, and they both knew it. She made herself comfortable on a kitchen stool and leaned on the butcher-block counter, twirling the wrench on its head while she stared him down. If things got ugly, she would use the wrench as a club, and aim for his knees.

"I was going to tell your parents I was pregnant," she said.

"Why?"

"Thought they'd feel sorry for me and help me find you."

"Well, you're out of luck. They're away."

"Away at the grocery store, or out of town?"

"Business trip for my dad. My mom tagged along."

"Happy coincidence," she said.

"No coincidence. They didn't want to be in the same house as me. But to their credit, at least they didn't turn me away. Or turn me in. Why are you here?"

Paire was coy. "Aside from the baby?"

He was angry, and an explosive look of potential retaliation flared in his eyes. "Are you fucking stupid? Imagine if you broke a window and the cops came. The two of us would be in a police report together. Someone would get to thinking."

He was acting like this was still part of the plan, like they'd worked this all out in New York. Her blood heated and her palms felt steamy. She tightened her grip on the wrench. "Do you even give a shit about what you've done?"

"You have no idea how much of a shit I give about that. This has ruined me," he said, achingly. He looked at Paire with the same hatred she had reserved for him, as if she had pulled the trigger.

He slouched more than usual, and ambled over to another stool, far enough away from Paire that they couldn't touch each other, even if she reached for him. He seemed strung out, sleep deprived. He spoke languidly. "I didn't want to hurt anyone." Until this moment, Paire had held out a micron of hope that someone else had charged into the Fern and shot Mayer and Lucia. She'd been hoping it had been Lucia's husband. Rosewood's confession dashed her hopes.

"Then why'd you bring the gun? Why would you bring that fucking gun?"

"To scare people in case I needed to." Back in his home state, some of his southern accent returned. "You didn't tell me there'd be people there. There shouldn't have been people there."

"You think I knew there would be? *Christ*." He had crow's feet, and she'd never seen wrinkles on him. His obvious stress made her dial back her indignation. "How did it happen?"

Rosewood let out a deep, regretful sigh. "It happened fast. I was already in there. They came through the front, kissing. Lucia was the one who saw me, but Mayer rushed me. He didn't know it was me until he got close. I pulled the gun to scare him, but he didn't stop. It just went off. Scared the shit out of me. I didn't mean to squeeze the trigger. It was all reflex." His hands raked his thighs, and Paire wanted to believe he was telling the truth.

"So what happened with Lucia?"

"Are you recording this?" He looked her up and down for any unseemly bulges from recording devices.

"I'm not recording anything."

"Show me your phone."

Paire pulled it out and powered it down before resting it on the counter.

Rosewood wouldn't look at her. "I don't remember the second shot. She moved. Looking back, she was probably just trying to help Mayer. The gun went off. I know I must have squeezed, but it just happened. I didn't mean it. She moved, and my hand squeezed."

"Reflex?"

"It happened so fast. A couple of seconds."

"If it was an accident, how come you were more accurate with the second shot?"

Rosewood rubbed the back of his neck. "For days, I've been trying to pretend nothing happened, that I never shot anyone. Down here, it's almost possible to think it was a dream. That sounds stupid, but it's the truth. I don't know if you ever felt like distance helped wipe away something bad." Of course he would know this was exactly how Paire felt when she left Maine. She resented that they shared this impulse, but she stopped twirling the wrench. "My Dad trained me to shoot low. I wasn't aiming. You get that close to someone, the bullet's going to go someplace important."

She continued, a touch softer than when she started. "So, what happened after?"

"I did mostly what I planned to do. The van picked me up."

"Who drove?"

"Lazaro," he said.

"Where did you go?"

"We drove to Long Island. Made a bonfire and burned everything."

Paire suppressed a gag when she thought of the empress in flames.

He said, "Not the paintings. Everything but the paintings." Rosewood's complexion seemed slightly gray as he looked out the back window to a trimmed lawn. Maybe he wanted to cry, but he managed to resist the urge.

Paire realized that she'd never seen him cry, not even a little tear at a movie. Maybe years of living with the general had trained him out of it. She tried to keep her poise. "Where's the art?"

"I did everything I'd planned." He said regretfully, "I handed it off."

"I don't understand."

"Paire, I didn't rob the place for you."

She didn't understand.

"I did it for someone else. I had to do it."

Her breath might have iced in midair. She didn't fully comprehend what he'd told her until she let it absorb for a moment. The shootings had been accidents, but Derek Rosewood had always intended to betray her.

"Who?"

Rosewood didn't answer.

"We lived together," she said.

"You lived in my home," he said, slightly resentful.

"Why are you telling me this now?"

He frowned. "Because this has destroyed my life. As hurt as you're feeling, it's nothing compared to what I have to live with, or what I have to do now."

"You killed two people." It felt grotesque for her to say this aloud.

"You could turn me in, and I'd go to prison. And you'd go to prison too. You can decide to do that, and I won't stop you."

"What's your plan, then? You're a public figure. You can't just disappear."

"You'd be surprised how easy that is. People forget pretty quickly."

179

They sat in silence until she couldn't stand it. "You think the shaved head is going to hide you forever?"

"I shaved it for the army," he said flatly. She scanned his face for a trace of bullshit, and as far as she could tell, he wasn't lying. "That was my deal. I needed protection, and my dad offered me a deal."

"He's making you go to war?"

"We're not at war. He wants me to continue the family legacy. He sees honor in it."

"Aren't you too old?"

He scowled at her. "You can enlist until you're thirty-four."

"They'll send you someplace hot. You can't stand the heat." Without trying to, she started feeling compassion for him. The acceptance of his punishment indicated how desperate he'd become.

"I'll go to jail otherwise."

She ruminated about all this, trying to make sense of it. "Were you hired to rob the Fern?"

"You could say coerced. That would be more accurate."

Paire was close to hysterical, and Rosewood might have sensed it. He spoke slowly and softly, trying to do his best not to provoke her.

"Were they going to pay you?"

"Yes," he said.

"Then you were hired." She squeezed the wrench in her hand. "You're rich. You didn't need the money."

"I needed the money *more* because I'm rich."

"That doesn't make any sense."

Rosewood's fingers swirled at his temples. "Everything I do needs to be funded. The flat in Brooklyn Heights—you think I bought that outright? With the loads of cash I got from my military family? Every piece of my work, every business venture, needs money. And the more money I need, the more I'm indebted to the source of that money."

"*Poor baby.*"

He squeezed his eyelids shut and slowly stretched his head side to side. "You need to know that I really liked you, Paire. I mean, really. I still do." There was something that resembled affection in the way he looked at her now, but it failed to match any of his loving gazes back in Brooklyn. His face was apologetic. A beggar's woeful simper.

She fumed, "Who gives a fuck?" She clenched her jaw. "Where is the art?"

"I handed off the Qi to him, and that's the last I saw of it."

"So, it's just gone."

"It's his now." His breath shortened, almost panting now, as he tried to articulate his next thoughts. "Don't go after him. He's crazy. He comes across as a blowhard, but he's more dangerous than you think. When he found out about the shooting, I thought he was going to kill me—he gave me these." Rosewood lifted up his T-shirt. Several bruises, purple as eggplants, stained the skin above his ribs. Bigger than a fist. A shoe might have seeded these wounds. "See this?" He lifted a gauze bandage to reveal a four-inch stitched gash in his lower abdomen. "He sliced me with a jackknife. He said it would *remind me of my incompetence.* He said if he saw me again, he'd kill me. Really, I think if my father wasn't who he was, he'd have finished me that night."

A cold thought washed over her, but she wasn't ready to accept it. She asked, "Who are we talking about?"

Derek Rosewood looked at her in awe, shocked she had to ask. "Abel Kasson."

She rushed to the kitchen sink and puked, dripping an orange stream into the basin.

Rosewood stood from his stool but didn't dare approach. He made no noises behind her, but the lack of motion gave her the sense that he hadn't moved anywhere. When she pulled her head out of the sink, he looked concerned, standing with his open palms facing her, the universal sign of a peace offering. His expression of fear and contrition might have been the last thing Lucia ever saw.

Something ruptured in Paire. She hurled the wrench, not at Rosewood, but at the back door. They both watched it spin in boomerang spirals. When the metal hunk hit the glass, the door shattered, and they both flinched at the noise. It would have been the loudest noise in the neighborhood. The glass fractured in large hunks, with one jagged four-foot slice crashing down to the carpet like one of I. M. Pei's John Hancock windows.

"Call me a fucking cab," she demanded, sliding up onto the kitchen counter, ankles dangling and shoulders rounded forward.

CHAPTER 17

Paire was eating a hummus wrap and watching the people across Park Avenue.

At the corner of Park and East Seventy-Fifth, a homeless man watched a stream of taxicabs cruise down toward the MetLife building that stoppered the road at Grand Central. The thin white man had a beard like an oriole nest. His loose-fitting raincoat stiffened in places from urine stains, and he staggered as if he were adjusting to an artificial hip. Not one of the mole people she had seen in City Hall station, but similar.

Several times now, he'd passed under the green awning of an apartment building. The building stood eleven stories, with a limestone and brick façade and the sort of elaborate carvings and gargoyles normally appended to churches. The round-faced doorman shooed him away, each time more agitated than the last. Although he was dressed in a black coat with gold trim, and a hat that made him resemble an airline pilot, the uniform's ill fit made the doorman seem more comical and less authoritative.

The doorman threatened to call the police the last time, but the threat didn't sink in. The homeless man stared at him, then through him, then focused on his face with a vague recognition, as if trying to recall where or when he had last seen the doorman. He slurred, "I just want some shade."

"You have to find it somewhere else." The doorman might have wondered the last time this man had been indoors.

"The coat's too hot," said the bearded man.

"Then don't wear it." The summer heat had really kicked in that week, and in the middle of the day, it seemed too hot for everything.

Truth be told, it was too hot for doorman uniforms too, but the doorman sweated in his anyway. He tried to be understanding and pointed west. "The park is a couple blocks that way. All the shade you want."

"But this is right here."

"You can't be here."

"Why not?" The bum sounded drunk. Smelled drunk too, once one could smell beyond the piss. The doorman grimaced when the odors hit him and fanned his nose.

"Because you can't." The doorman stepped closer, demonstrating how much larger he was. "Please don't make me make you leave."

Something registered. Maybe he sensed that he might be in danger, but the raincoated man stumbled back, and eventually turned to amble in the direction the doorman had pointed.

When the homeless man rounded the corner again and passed under the awning, the way a fish crosses across an aquarium window, the doorman clenched his jaw and balled up his fists.

The doorman might have charged at him to run him off, but he didn't get the chance. A second man breezed past the doorman. A redhead in a popcorn-white suit, he was slightly taller, slight of build, and in his twenties. He strolled leisurely, possibly taking a late lunch. The degree to which he was clean and buffed made him look European.

The businessman made it to the street corner when the homeless man approached him and asked a question too subdued to hear, but he performed the universal pantomime for bumming a cigarette. Perhaps caught off-guard, or simply generous of spirit, the redhead dug out a pack of cigarettes and gave away a smoke. The doorman smiled to himself. Maybe he was surprised to see that someone in Manhattan still smoked. Definitely European.

The man in the suit pulled out an impressive silver lighter that reflected the sunlight, and showed off an elaborate etching reminiscent of a Wild West revolver. After accepting the light and puffing a few clouds, the homeless man grasped the businessman by the hand, smearing grime on the French cuff, and tried to take the lighter away from him.

At first they almost looked like they were playing. The suit smirked, as if dealing with a child who was adorably misbehaving. But when the bearded man pulled harder, they tangled. To push him away, the executive boxed him across the ear with an open palm. This knocked them apart a few paces, just long enough for the businessman to return the lighter to his pocket. The doorman marveled at the spectacle, unwilling to get involved.

After taking a moment to collect himself, the raincoat man rammed his head into the other's chest, knocking him hard on his back to the pavement. He wheezed and fought for breath. It looked like it hurt. With his opponent immobilized, the bearded man fished inside the suit jacket until he found the lighter. Once he palmed it, he bolted in the direction of the park.

The doorman rubbed his hand across his jowls, and let out a long breath. He smiled and then chuckled mildly. One man tackling another for a lighter, almost like black-and-white clips of slapstick violence he'd seen from silent films.

But the man in the suit didn't get up. Moments went by, and then he let out a deep, primal scream of terror and agony, the sort of gravelly howl that shreds vocal cords. He lifted a hand, and his palm was red and wet.

The doorman gasped. He looked back into the lobby. Technically, they were supposed to use the desk phone for emergency calls. At least, that's what the union told them. He started to walk inside when the man called, "Help me," and perhaps it didn't feel right to abandon him. The doorman plucked out his mobile and rushed to the businessman on the sidewalk.

When he stood over him, the doorman covered his mouth with a hand when he saw a red patch on the man's stomach. The blood spread in a dark cloud across his shirt.

"He stabbed me," said the man, astonished. He spoke in a foreign accent. Maybe British or Irish. With the stress in the voice, it was hard to tell.

"Let's get you inside," said the doorman. He tried lifting the man to his feet, but the movement made him scream even louder.

He shook his head in protest. "I can't get up."

The doorman lowered himself to his knees, prepared to use his mobile, but the injured man clutched the doorman's wrists tightly. He shivered convulsively with the pain.

The doorman placed one hand on his shoulders to comfort him, and wrenched one arm free to dial his phone. The emergency operator had barely picked up when pedestrians began to collect. Paire walked across the street so she could mill about behind them.

This stretch of Park Ave didn't get much foot traffic this time of the afternoon, but just like ants who've smelled a drizzle of honey, people were drawn by the commotion. The doorman suddenly found himself surrounded by a small cluster of people, all wanting to help, all asking questions while he was on the phone. *What happened? Did you stop the bleeding? Does he need CPR?*

The emergency dispatcher now repeated her questions in his ear, and the doorman stammered through an explanation of what happened—something about a homeless guy, a stabbing, and no, he didn't see a knife.

A taxicab screeched to a stop right by the awning. Not one of the city's yellow cabs, but a gypsy cab, beaten to crap with a lunar surface of dents in the body.

A young Latino driver sprang out of the car, skinny with a white tee and camo pants, with an overgrown chin beard that rounded like a microphone windscreen. "What happened?"

The doorman was still trying to explain things to the emergency dispatcher. He made the universal brush-off gesture to the cabbie, as if sweeping dust with his hand. The way he had tried to shoo away the bearded man. It proved just as ineffective.

The gypsy driver said, "Throw him in the back. I'll get him to the hospital."

The doorman wouldn't be swayed. Possibly, he was comforted by the idea that professional paramedics would take the injured man.

The driver snapped his fingers in front of his face. "Jesus Christ, man! We don't have time to fuck around."

The doorman didn't want to hang up. He made an excuse for why they should wait for an ambulance. "The blood. Your seats," he said.

"Does it look like I give a shit?" The cabbie seemed upset, and his energy possibly made the doorman wonder how quickly the man on the ground needed a doctor. The driver knocked the phone out of his hand. "Get him in the back and I'll get him to the hospital in two minutes."

There was no time to think this through, especially not with the driver barking at him.

"Get his shoulders. I've got the legs. *You!*" He pointed to a spectator, a lean, tanned woman dressed in yoga gear with a rolled rubber mat tucked under her arm. "Open the back door, please." Back to the doorman, he said, "Ready? One, two, three, and *lift.*"

The injured man quaked as they raised his body off the ground. He pressed his hands against his stomach.

Behind all of them, Paire Anjou slipped into the building lobby, unseen by everyone in the sidewalk gathering. Paire had dressed down today, in jeans and a T-shirt, with a dark brown wig pulled back in a ponytail to hide the red hair. She wore bookish glasses and kept her chin tucked down.

She knew several people in the crowd. Charlie was in the suit, his blood no more than corn starch and food coloring. Humberto drove the gypsy cab, which they'd gotten on police auction for three dollars and would be able to ditch and burn if they had to. Lazaro played the homeless man. *Homeless Erectus.* By now, he'd probably stripped off the raincoat, and would shave off the beard as soon as he found a razor and a bathroom. Some of the bystanders were Lazaro's contacts, people she'd never seen but seemed game to help out the cause.

Paire acknowledged from the outset that the plan was reckless. Crude and dirty, there would be no janitor's uniform, no hollowed-out trash cans, no insider to turn off the alarm system. Her actions would be driven by impulse. Lazaro and the rest of them didn't seem to mind.

Dressed as a UPS deliveryman, Lazaro had already visited the building several days ago to find out where the doorman kept the keys, where the service elevator was located, and the specific floor of Abel Kasson's apartment.

With the doorman now occupied, Paire headed straight for the mailroom and pinched the right keys off a hook board. The fastest way to get to the flat would have been the elevator, but elevators made noise, so she climbed the stairs that led to the back entrances to each apartment. She ascended fifteen flights before she arrived at the rear entrance to Kasson's flat. Her face felt hot and damp by the time she reached the landing.

None of them had ever been inside Kasson's flat, but they knew he occupied the entire floor, as did every other tenant in the building. Paire didn't know what alarm systems might be in place. Once she unlocked the door, she might set off a motion sensor. The doorman might have the alarm codes, but she didn't. If this happened, she was prepared to sprint through the apartment to see what she could find and let herself out the emergency exit. They were relatively certain no one was home, but not absolutely. They'd called at various times of day from pay phones, noting when Kasson picked up and when he didn't. They had even called right before they arrived. The call to Kasson's home went unanswered.

In the satchel she'd brought with her, she kept a crowbar and a spring baton in case she needed to smash anything. Doors or people. She hoped she wouldn't have to use them.

The steel door reminded her of the rear entrance to the Fern Gallery. She tried several keys before she felt the top bolt slide and the tumblers fall into place. Even though she was fairly certain no one was home, she opened it gingerly, just wide enough to get inside. She walked in through a kitchen the size of the bedroom in Brooklyn Heights, with black-and-white mosaic tiling and granite counters that had been swabbed until they shone. Floor-to-ceiling windows looked out across other rooftops along the Upper East

Side, and she caught a glimpse of the Central Park tree canopy between the buildings.

She listened for sound and heard nothing.

She looked around for alarm systems and didn't find any.

Paire left the door open, in case she had to run through it on the way out. After passing through the kitchen, she entered a long corridor. Kasson had a railroad-style flat, where the central hallway served as a spine, leading to various rooms. A narrow Persian runner covered a beige wall-to-wall carpet, running from the kitchen down to another set of windows on the other side of the building. A half dozen doors, all shut, stood in between. Paire followed the sunlight.

The carpet muffled her feet, but she still crept slowly, in case her foot landed on a squeak spot. All down the corridor, Kasson had hung pieces of art. One of Derek Rosewood's laughers hung between the doors, and she couldn't remember if this was one of the pieces taken from the Fern.

The hallway led out to a grand living area, possibly half the footprint of the entire flat. Like the kitchen, the windows stretched floor to ceiling, overlooking Park Avenue. At the center of those windows, a set of French doors could open onto a shallow balcony lined with balustrades, not deep enough to sit a table and chairs, but enough to step out and admire the view. A marble fireplace adorned the center of the wall, opposite a burgundy leather sofa and two wing chairs. Above the fireplace Kasson had hung a vintage oil painting of a mounted hunting party, the dogs going wild for a pheasant they had scared out of the brush.

The room was so cluttered with knickknacks Paire needed a moment to take them all in, almost forgetting that she was trying to get out as soon as possible. Kasson had filled the room with art and collectibles: an Italian mantel clock, a Napoleon III gold leaf console, a child's colonial American rocking chair. A stylistic mishmash. More things for Kasson to collect. *Here* a black lacquer chinoiserie Louis XVI commode with bronze d'ore mounts, *there* a Victorian fainting sofa, none of the items with so much as a scratch in the wood or an ass-print on the cushions. The inlaid bookshelves, traditionally reserved for books, were cluttered with all sorts of trinkets, from a small jade Buddha to a handheld football video game from the 1980s. An autographed baseball from what appeared to be the entire 2000 Yankees. Hummel figurines of a nativity scene.

She almost missed it, but a corner of wood grain peeked out from behind a worn pirate trunk. Chinese red birch. Paire noted the artist's chop on the back, otherwise she might have overlooked the bright wood grain camouflaged among the artifacts. She had expected to find it on audacious display over the mantel, or in a bedroom, where she'd planned to hang it. But since Qi's last surviving work was a source of shame to the Kasson family, it made sense for them to hide it. She was just relieved he hadn't destroyed it.

Her heart raced to be so close to it again.

The frame had been removed, so the side of the wooden board had been stripped of ornamentation. She lightly placed her fingertips along the edge of the wood and turned it around. She leaned it against the wall, stepped back to admire it and check that it hadn't been forged. She was no expert, but she'd been snorting distance from the tempera enough to recognize the texture of the brushstrokes. This was the real deal.

Producing a large white plastic bag from her pocket, Paire sheathed the birch panel.

On the way out, she briskly stepped sideways like a fiddler crab, maneuvering the portrait awkwardly back to the kitchen. She moved with less caution. Her feet fell more heavily on the carpet. And she made more noise. The floor creaked.

And when it creaked, one of the doors opened—only an inch, but Paire froze. She heard the knob squeak as it turned. Pure chemical panic. She held her breath, afraid to look behind her to see who might be in the doorway.

Paire thought about running. She could easily make it to the kitchen. The back entrance was twenty feet away. But in her moment of fight-flight-or-freeze decision making, she remained rigid on the infinite Persian runner. Resting the painting on the floor, tipped against the wall, she reached inside her satchel and found the spring baton. A snap of the wrist and it sprang to from seven to sixteen inches, telescoping down to a weighted tip designed to fracture bone.

With some will, Paire turned to face whatever was in the door crack. She couldn't see much. But it was a person. The hallway was dark, and the light behind the door silhouetted a figure—a man, she guessed by the height. Not Abel Kasson. She couldn't make out features, other than one dull eye hogging the gap, but she knew it wasn't the banker. The eye looked at her, glanced at the baton and the white plastic wrap around the empress. Then back at the baton.

The door slowly closed, more quietly than it had opened.

For a moment or two the corridor was silent. Then Paire remembered to breathe. She gathered up the painting again in a wide embrace and retreated to the back door, closing it just as delicately. As fast as she could, she ran down the steps and burst out of the building's service exit, avoiding the doorman completely.

• • •

Twelve hours later, Paire emerged from the Fifty-Ninth Street Columbus Circle station to the heavily trafficked rotary at the southwest corner of Central Park. She carried a bulkier duffel, her arms spread wide to tote the large panel wrapped in plastic. To fit in, she wore a hoodie and sweats from the John Jay College of Criminal Justice, located just a few blocks away. If a cop stopped her, maybe he'd be less suspicious. Because the school specialized in everything from correctional studies to forensic psychology, the school mascot was a bloodhound. Specifically, a bloodhound with a deerstalker hat.

Across the street, the curved façade of the Time Warner Center rose up from its spacious lobby to the two towers that housed the Mandarin Oriental. The bottom four stories were occupied by a glossy retail mall, with floors too smooth to run on in new shoes. By this time of night almost all the lights were out, and the rows of shops had all pulled down their theft-deterrent gratings. Gigantic ornamental orbs dangled from the lobby ceiling, each of them her height. The red, white, and blue accent lights hinted that Independence Day was coming up.

A young man in a matching bloodhound sweatsuit met her on the sidewalk, outside the lobby doors. They nodded to each other without stopping for hugs or handshakes, and she shadowed him as he walked down Broadway and rounded the corner.

"You shaved," she said. This was the first time she'd seen Lazaro without facial hair.

He rubbed his bare chin. "I was happy to be rid of that thing. And that shower felt like an orgasm."

"Everything go all right?" she asked.

"Fine. Dropped off the cab, cleaned it, and swapped out the plates." He nodded to the plastic-wrapped birch board. "I see everything went smoothly on your end. Anyone see you?"

She lied. "No."

"No dogs or anything?"

"Just in and out."

"Where's the fun in that?" he joked.

She smiled. "Can I ask you something and have you promise not to get offended?"

"Sure."

"Do you do this because you're an artist, or because you're a criminal?"

She wanted a serious answer, but he just laughed softly. "We're going to be right around the corner."

They came to a service entrance around the rear of the building. He knocked *shave-and-a-haircut* on the door and they waited.

"When does Rosewood get back?" Lazaro asked.

"I don't know. I don't even know where he went this time," she said. Her body gave a slight spasm that someone might mistake for chills.

"He's like that."

The door was opened by a bulky man with curly red hair whom Paire had never seen before. Because of the hair color, she wondered if he and Charlie were related. He wore a security guard uniform.

Lazaro asked Paire, "You have it all?"

She dug out a roll of cash as thick as a scone, and handed it to the guard.

"I'm blind for fifteen minutes," he said. "Can you work with that?"

"Yes."

"After that I have to call the police. That'll be bad for both of us."

"I understand."

Lazaro shook the man's hand. "I'll leave you to it," he said, and left them both.

Paire lingered for a moment as he walked away from them, wanting to thank him but remembering that all of these stunts had gotten her into this trouble in the first place.

The guard extended a hand. "Joyce."

She didn't know if that was a first or last name, but didn't ask.

Because of his jowls and the beard, at a quick glance he had the look of someone who might carry extra weight around his middle, but he was lean. An old scar ran through an eyebrow, and the tip of a vine tattoo peeked out from underneath his uniform collar. "Get inside," he said.

They hustled down a service corridor lit sporadically with yellow bulbs. Toting the birch board between them, Joyce carried the front half as he led at a brisk pace. They entered a service elevator, open and waiting for them, and he pressed the top button. "You realize right now I'm in the men's room with digestive troubles."

The doors closed and the cables lifted them.

"Cameras?" she said.

"The video files will be deleted." He checked his watch. "I disabled them right before I opened the door. They'll be down for a few minutes, but the power outage will trigger an alarm and a backup system will come up in about ten minutes. That's also when the police will be coming. Work quick."

The elevator doors opened to scaffolding that looked down over the eighty-five-foot atrium. Between the metal grates, she could see straight to the floor. Joyce sped up, and they hastened across the catwalk to the window, a wall of glass that looked out onto Columbus Circle, down Central Park South and into the lush treetops. If she were high enough, she might be able to see Kasson's building on the other side of the park. Even at this hour, a few people were coming out of the subway stop, and two yellow taxis spun around the rotary.

When they reached the window, Paire unzipped her duffels and unwrapped the plastic. Gazing down through the grating, she became acutely aware of how high she was, possibly as high as Gilda's backyard cliff in Abenaki. Previously, this height might have terrified her, but after weeks of rock climbing she performed without hesitation. At a Derek Rosewood pace.

Behind her, Joyce cooed as he took in the empress for the first time. Even under the pressure of his own limited time, he couldn't help but dawdle for an extended glance.

Paire had reframed the birch board in a simple ebony, and screwed sets of twin eye hooks into the top and bottom. She retrieved two fifty-foot coils of hanging wire, and a small bolt of ruby-red fabric, as close as possible to the hue of the empress's cheongsam.

She speedily wrapped one end of the hanging wire through the eye hooks at the top of the painting, twisting the ends the way one closes a bread bag. She latched two clips on the red fabric to the eye hooks at the bottom of the frame. Then she and Joyce quickly lowered the painting down from the scaffolding, unwinding the wire yard by yard. Down into the abyss they lowered the portrait. The red sash unrolled and hung from the birch board like Superman's cape.

Joyce asked, "How do we know it's not crooked?"

"Like this." Paire dialed her cell phone, steadying the wire in her other hand. Out by the statue of Columbus, the tiny figure of a man in a hoodie sweatshirt stood out in the rotunda. Lazaro was still out there, hoodie and all. He picked up his phone and muttered into Paire's ear.

She repeated to Joyce, "A little up on the right." They made adjustments. "No, *your* right." She let some wire go gently through her fingers until he said, "That's it. We're good."

After disconnecting, she tied off the wire to the scaffolding, wrapping each end around itself like a caduceus.

"We're good?" Joyce asked.

"Let's go."

She tucked everything back in the duffel and they raced back to the elevator and rode it back down to the ground level. When the doors opened, Joyce slowed down. "You know how to get back to the exit, right?"

She nodded.

"So there's the other thing we have to do now."

She didn't understand, but the unexpectedness of the statement made her nerves hum.

Joyce tapped the crown of his head with two fingers. "About here."

Lazaro hadn't explained this part to Paire.

Joyce said, "You got to hit me."

"I've got to get out."

"I'm a security guard here. You don't hit me, they're going to find a way to blame me." He pulled out two white strips of plastic and tossed them on the ground. "When you're done, zip tie my wrists behind my back so they find me like that."

"Will you lose your job?"

He laughed. "I was going to lose my job anyway. You knew that, didn't you?"

"Why did you do this?"

"Because it seems like it's worth it. Now hit me. You don't have any time." He turned to face away from her. "Do it from behind. That way I don't have to give a fake description of some other perp. I never saw you. You crept up on me from behind."

"I don't want to do this."

"You've paid for it. Get it done."

Back in Abenaki, Katie Novis had tried to fight bullies, but she was too petite to do serious damage. Then again, Katie Novis didn't carry a telescoping spring baton. She found it in her duffel and snapped it open. Her hand shook.

"I don't think I can."

"You must have someone you hate bad enough. Pretend I'm them."

Paire took his advice and imagined a host of people she would have wanted to club in the head. A stream of faces flickered through her mind like spinning numbers on a roulette wheel. Surprisingly, instead of her mother or father, school bullies, or even Derek Rosewood, she landed on Abel Kasson. She took a deep breath, and as she mustered the strength to swing, Joyce interrupted. "One thing. Don't kill me." He looked over his shoulder and they smiled at each other. "Come on."

The spring baton came down against the side of his head near the top, around where he had tapped his fingers. Although he was a foot taller than Paire and possibly a hundred pounds heavier, his shoulders dropped and his knees buckled. Joyce dropped to the floor, flumping along the right side of his body. Flecks of blood sprayed over her clothes. Paire gulped in shock. She remembered Nicola Franconi, and checked that Joyce was still breathing before she tied his hands and ran out the exit.

CHAPTER 18

By morning, every major national news outlet covered the scene. This time, it was front page news.

According to the media, the security guard, who was not named in the piece, was knocked out from behind and then left tied up on the floor while a person—or *persons*—broke into the Time Warner Center. Other than a mild concussion, he had received no injuries. The spectacle was so visual in nature, the morning shows even ran it. CNN rotated footage every hour. The painting had been stolen from a local gallery during a theft that had left two people dead. Presumed missing, the painting had turned up in one of the most visible locations in Manhattan. The photos that circulated around the web caught the striking image of the piece. Taken from one of the mall balconies, the empress dangled halfway to the floor, with New York as its backdrop. The sash that draped a red tail from the bottom of the portrait bore an embroidered message on both sides, so that it would be readable from the front and the back. The message was a dare for discovery:

WHO AM I?

• • •

Within a few days, the story gained even more momentum. Paire followed it casually.

A few reporters had called Brooklyn Heights and left messages for Rosewood. While not a suspect in the Fern Gallery shootings, he was still exhibiting at the gallery when everything happened. Now that he had announced his retirement from the art world at thirty-two years old, he was someone reporters wanted to talk to. Paire unplugged the phone.

Most articles pieced together a chronicle of the forgotten artist who called himself Qi. They quoted Melinda Qi in a number of pieces, and she helped fill in the blanks to connect her father with Gabriel Kasson.

Melinda discussed how the vast inventory of her father's work had been purchased by the Kasson family. She hinted that his works might be hidden among the crated stacks at the MAAC. She even allowed the media to reprint the contract signed by her father and Gabriel Kasson, which helped fuel the story. The press loved a villain.

So far, Abel Kasson hadn't made himself available for comment.

Rumors speculated that Melinda herself had orchestrated the stunt at Columbus Circle, which would have connected her to the shootings at the gallery. Her response had been quoted in an article in the *Wall Street Journal*: "You'd probably want to look at someone with greater resources and more free time."

Paire hadn't spoken to Melinda since the evening of the robbery, back when she'd phoned from the school library. She had wanted to speak to her ever since, but wasn't confident she could connect with her without conveying remorse, and possibly confessing. Instead, she followed Melinda through online news alerts, and imagined her voice behind all those quotes.

A few days into the media frenzy, another development unfolded. The Empress Xiao Zhe Yi vanished from the evidence locker. Paire didn't know whether or not this would please Melinda, but it twisted her insides.

She read the news on the most sweltering day of the year. Montague Street was steamed by a swampy heat she'd rarely known in Maine. People walked as if they were learning their first steps, their slick skins pinned under the enormous thumb of the heat. Even the traffic slowed down, as if the cars themselves were exhausted.

That day she had been visiting vacant apartments. She needed to move out of Rosewood's flat, if for no other reason than it wasn't hers to begin with. In the past two days she'd seen three apartments, the most promising one in Carroll Gardens with a Fashion Institute of Technology student close to her age. To make a favorable impression on possible roommates, she dressed up in a stylish green cotton chemise whose color closely resembled the sprig on the Fern's marquee. It was too heavy for a day like this, and perspiration soaked under her arms and beneath the folds of her breasts.

As soon as she returned home to the brownstone, she knew something was wrong. Her door had been knocked open and the doorframe splintered where the lock had torn through the wood. Someone had smashed his way into the place. Later, she'd consider that she could have retreated and called the police, but given her involvement in a number of crimes, she didn't see the police as a viable resource.

Instead, she grasped her collapsed spring baton and pushed open the front door with her finger.

On the first floor, a heap of broken belongings had been shoveled to the center of the room like a compost pile. These were mostly Rosewood's possessions, but some of her things were mixed in too. They'd all been torn, cracked, and split. Everything had been pulled from the edges of the room, artwork ripped off hooks and smashed. Kitchen drawers were pulled out, utensils bent and then cast to the floor. Canvases, whether blank or painted, had been slashed, and the wooden frames snapped by boot heels. Everything had been collected, destroyed, and deposited in the pile. From upstairs, someone had pulled clothes off the hangers, brought them down here, and shredded them. She recognized some of Rosewood's scrapbooks, pages torn out and photo prints reduced to strips. It seemed as if the center of the room had opened like a drain, drawn the contents of the flat, and then clogged with the mass of possessions. The pile reached her navel, the right consistency and height for a pyre.

As she examined the pile, Paire found traces of her belongings, all broken. She came to the sickening realization that nothing had been stolen. Everything had simply been vandalized. The intruder had taken care to ensure each object was properly ruined. Her easel, for example, wasn't a fragile structure, but it had been hurled at the wall—most likely several times, from the dents and divots that tore into the plaster—and dismembered at the joints. She pulled out the hand-shredded ribbons that used to be her wardrobe. At this point, she couldn't distinguish between shirts and skirts. Even her tube socks had been cut into calamari rings with a pair of shears. Corners of ceramic dishes crunched underfoot, and from the stegosaurus ridges of glass in the walls, she surmised that her glasses had burst like Molotov cocktails. The entryway mural had been soaked with fluids, and the paint ran.

She noted slashes in the sofa and chairs. Their fibrous and cottony filler spilled out like entrails. None of her usual sitting places existed, so in the dim sunlight that seeped in from outside, she sat in the corner of the room that seemed the cleanest. She felt violated, but wasn't moved to scream. Not while her adrenaline kept her alert.

The smell, a soupy concoction of paints, thinner, toiletries, food, and perfume might have been toxic. Paire's nose ran from the fumes. She wiped it on her sleeve, since the toilet paper in the bathroom had been run off the roll.

She continued to the kitchen. They hadn't stored much food in the fridge, but all of it now decorated the walls.

When she composed herself, she started to count her belongings to see if there was anything within the pile that could be salvaged.

She was scavenging fastidiously when a voice said, "It's nice to see you wearing green again."

Abel Kasson walked soundlessly down the stairs. He'd dressed down today. No suit. Instead, he wore a pink polo shirt that stretched over his stomach and golf slacks. The country club clothes seemed even more offensive in a room filled with trash. In the heat, and likely from the exertion required for this destruction, he'd sweated through every inch of the fabric on his body.

Paire was terrified, but she found the baton in her purse and snapped it to attention. Occupying his particular spot at the base of the stairs, he blocked her path to both the front and back doors. Without an immediate exit, she tried to mask her fear with spite. "You do all this yourself?"

"Ambition is a family curse." He held a pair of shears, and snapped the blades together for effect.

"Not the only family curse, though."

"When I first met you, I envied your blissful ignorance. In nature, the animals that live the longest are the ones that are ignored by predators. Being a wallflower can be an evolutionary advantage. You should have stayed that way. You were much safer when I couldn't remember your name. The old one or the new one."

Panic surged through her like venom.

"You know how I knew I could exploit you?" he said. "Because you're a kleptomaniac." So, Rosewood must have shared that with him. Her guts knotted. "Except you don't steal things to own them or to sell them. You steal things so you can destroy them. But a thief is a thief. Once I gave you the right excuse, it was like lighting a fuse on a rocket."

With that confident, vanquisher's smile, Kasson was in complete control. He stepped closer, ready to charge at her at any moment. For the first time, Paire was happy that Joyce had forced her to club him with the baton. Otherwise, she might not know what it felt like to use it against a man. What level of strength it took to make it hurt.

Kasson stood on the other side of the trash pile, but started to work his way around the perimeter toward her. Paire took a step whenever he did, to keep her distance, as if they were manning opposite positions on a clock face. She kept an eye on his shears, and remembered Rosewood's stomach wound.

Kasson said, "I hear he's going into the army. Maybe they'll send him to Afghanistan or some other shithole of a place."

"He might die over there."

"You might die right here."

Paire stiffened, and wiggled the baton so she could feel the slight undulation of the weighted tip.

Kasson snapped his shears. "In the end, we're only accountable to ourselves. He made his own choices, just like you made yours. Whatever the reasons for obsessing over that painting, you're accountable for all the choices you made to get it."

She gestured to the pile between them. "So this is what, retribution?"

"This? No. I was just trying to find what you've taken, and I got carried away. Where is it?"

Paire was confused. "What are we talking about?"

He seemed exasperated that he had to explain himself. With a free hand he swabbed the sweat from his face. "The painting. It's gone missing. Where is it?"

So he doesn't have it, she thought. "You think I could have broken into a police storage locker?"

"Is that so hard to believe? You've been shadowing Derek Rosewood for months, and just broke into the Time Warner Center. Not to mention my home."

Paire was actually relieved to hear this. As soon as she'd heard that the painting had gone missing, she'd assumed that Kasson had bribed an officer to steal it back for him. In the same moment, she felt vulnerable that he could link her other recent break-ins. She didn't try to deny any of it. Someone was in his home when she was there. Someone had seen her. "I don't have it," she said.

"Clearly." He looked around. "You don't have it *here*. But that doesn't mean you don't have it. Where is it?" His temper rose. He kept advancing around the circle of debris, and she kept retreating.

This wasn't going well. If he didn't believe her, there was no answer she could give that would satisfy him. Instead of repeating the truth, she verbally parried while she figured out how to escape. "Why would I tell you when you have a weapon pointed at me? Say I have it hidden somewhere. Say I was that crafty. And I knew you might even show up here one day to throw a tantrum because you can't control every wrinkle of universal space-time. Say all that. Why would I tell you, when I'd be giving away my only point of leverage?"

"You'd tell me out of desperation. That's what they all do." Kasson looked through her and snapped his shears.

Paire's flailing attempt at self-preservation was an empty warning. "If you hurt me, the police will be all over you."

He hesitated for just a moment. "Let's find out."

Kasson sprinted around the pile, faster than Paire could have anticipated, with a strength and agility that shouldn't have come from a man of his bulk. The speed his body remembered from when he was an athlete. She didn't have time to defend herself against him. In the second she was afforded, she readied herself to block the hand with the shears. But Kasson didn't use the shears. He punched her with his other fist, bringing his arm down like a cudgel on the top of her head. The force was deadening. The shock plunged into her jaw, her neck, and down through her ribs. She crashed against the carpet—too thin to cushion her—and her skull smacked with a sparkling pain.

Kasson stood over her. Other than a slight heaving in his chest from the exertion, he had reverted to his poised reserve. He said plainly, "I just assaulted you. Let's see if the police come running." The stinging in her head was too intense for her to speak. "Where is it? Quick now, before I use my other hand." The twin blades of the shears opened like crocodile jaws.

Paire clambered to her knees, her head still sparkling from the blow.

Kasson enjoyed his triumph, and the top half of his body puffed exultantly. He only took his eyes off her for an instant, never expecting her to do anything but succumb.

Snapping her wrist, Paire lashed out and caught Kasson in the shin with the baton.

He yowled and stumbled back, until he tumbled into the wall. He rubbed the hurt shin with his unarmed hand.

Paire climbed to her feet. Dizziness kept her from walking a perfect line, and she zigzagged away from him.

Kasson's jowls clenched. His face flushed, and the blood vessels in his neck seemed tumid to the point of rupture. He rushed at her, too fast again. He swiped at her with his bare hand, and caught her on the ear before she could dodge him.

She bent at the waist as what sounded like a mosquito mezzo-soprano sang in her ear canal.

His hand closed around her throat. With sumo momentum, Kasson marched Paire back into the window. He almost carried her, and his fingers smelled like talcum.

She kicked her knee up to his groin, but she only grazed his testicles, and he guarded himself for the next kick by pivoting his hips. Kasson didn't seem like the type who would actually kill someone himself, certainly not in a public place like this. But he wasn't the impassive strategist she'd come to hate. He seemed feral. As his thumb pressed into her windpipe and her eyes fogged, she knew he had no intention of stopping. In a moment she wouldn't be able to talk, wouldn't be able to breathe. The other hand, the one with the shears, brought the tips up toward her eyeball, grazing her lashes.

Knowing this might be the last action she made before she lost consciousness, Paire brought the baton down on his wrist as hard as she could. She heard something snap. Maybe his forearm, or maybe it was wishful thinking. She couldn't see well enough to know where she'd connected. But he howled. The shears dropped to the floor. With effort, Paire pushed him away with a leg. They gave each other room, taking restorative breaths, rubbing the parts of themselves that had been hurt. Each having inflicted pain on the other, they were both wary.

Kasson growled, "Tell me."

Her heart pounded, but Paire remained defiant. Her throat hurt from where he'd choked her, and stung when she spoke. "Keep looking."

He trembled with fury. "You have no idea the situation you put me in. This is a family matter, do you understand? This is my *name*, you little shit." Kasson bent down slowly to pick up his shears, but before he got to them she struck his clavicle. He swore something awful. While he absorbed the pain, she clubbed him on the head and shoulders. From the way he shouted and fought to cover his head, she knew she'd wounded him, but these were just bee stings to a bear.

After a momentary falter, Kasson regained his strength and charged, head down, and barreled into her chest. He knocked her flat on her back and the wind flew out of her lungs. Continuing on his own momentum, Kasson trampled over her and then clumsily tripped on some of the loose debris on the floor. He collapsed onto his belly and careened headfirst into the opposite wall. His skull collided with the baseboards. The floor rumbled with his weight.

Once air leaked into her lungs again, Paire rolled onto her side and fought to scramble to her feet. She tasted blood in her gums.

On the other side of the room, Kasson crawled on all fours as he found his bearings. He found a way to his feet, and stood before the front door. She might be able to run to the back of the flat. He was slow now, but her legs were just as wobbly.

She squeezed the baton until her knuckles blanched. "We've been making noise. How long do you think we can keep this up before someone calls the police?"

His round face flushed, its expression vicious. "As long as it takes for me to strangle you." He ambled toward her, hand cocked for a haymaker. But he was still groggy from the pain, and when he took a step toward her, he put an awkward, drunken foot forward.

Paire moved faster. She was so amped up from the fear, she stepped toward him and whipped the spring with all the power she had into the bridge of his nose. The cartilage crumpled with an audible crackle. His hands covered his face, and moments later blood seeped out between his fingers. She continued her assault. She couldn't afford to let him recover. He had a hundred pounds on her, and he was used to fighting. The briny fumes of blood diffused into the air and ignited something primal in her. She whipped the baton at the crown of his head. The weighted tip came down on the thinnest part of the skull. Kasson dropped to the floor.

Paire stood over the man, nerves jangling, panting in short, shallow breaths as she gawked over the fleshy heap. After a minute, when he didn't move, she slowly reached toward his neck, and pressed two fingers into his jugular. The pulse was barely there, but it was there.

Then she snatched her purse and fled.

CHAPTER 19

Paire clanged an iron gate with her shoe, because Melinda Qi's compound in Long Island City didn't have a doorbell to ring or a door to knock on. Through shouting and banging, she tried to approximate the volume of a riot.

She was trembling. Adrenaline had kept her going for the past few hours, and now it was wearing off, leaving her shaking like a junkie. Everything made her nervous right now.

Paire had nowhere to go. She felt hunted and, out in the open air like this, exposed and vulnerable. She couldn't call the police, and without the law as an ally, she had a drought of options. She was wearing the only remaining clothes she owned, and these were now torn in places and stained with blood, both hers and Abel Kasson's.

On her way there, Paire kept looking over her shoulders. Cabs wouldn't pick her up, not with all that blood on her. On the subway, her fellow straphangers gave her a wide berth. Suspicious of all of them, she wondered if they'd call the police, or if one of these strangers might be following her for Kasson, just to see if she'd lead them to the empress.

As she drummed against the fence rails, Paire began to cry. She held it back for as long as she was able. Then she curled slowly into herself like a wilting flower. She felt mortified for crying in the street, even an empty street, but was unable to stop. She slid down with her back against the bars and let the desperate sorrow consume her.

Melinda found her like that, leaning against the fence, holding one shoe in her hands. She was walking down the sidewalk, carrying groceries in cheap pink plastic bodega bags. Resting them on the pavement, Mel crouched and placed a hand on Paire's knee. "Do you need a doctor?"

From her tone, Paire couldn't tell if she was happy to see her or suspicious. They hadn't spoken since the night of the robbery, and so many things had changed since then. If Melinda Qi had a fraction of Paire's paranoia, she must have wondered by now if Paire had anything to do with these events.

"It's not all my blood." Paire had intended to diffuse Melinda's concern, but this only made it worse.

"We should go to the police," Melinda said.

"Please, no."

"Your voice sounds froggy." Mel looked under Paire's chin at the finger bruises. "Someone hurt you."

Her voice shook. "Can I come inside?"

Melinda looked up and down the street, likely wondering herself how much danger Paire might be in, and how much she'd be heaping on herself by harboring her. "All right."

She unlocked a number of doors in succession, first the gate, then the exterior door to her building in the compound, and then her apartment door. She led Paire to the dining table and gently tilted her chin so she could examine her neck. "Was this Derek Rosewood?" Apparently, she hadn't heard about his abrupt retirement, or his decision to join the United States Army.

Paire shook her head, afraid to provide another answer.

Mel understood. "Kasson. You wouldn't have come otherwise." She sounded deflated in this last statement.

"He was in my apartment." Paire corrected herself. "In Rosewood's apartment. I can't go back there. I didn't know where else to go."

"I'm going to run you a bath," Melinda said, moving into the adjoining bathroom.

"You don't need to."

Melinda turned on a thundering rush of water. "Too late. It's already running." She led Paire into the bathroom and left her alone, returning a minute later with a stack of clothes. "We're not exactly the same size, but close enough that T-shirts and exercise pants will fit."

Paire stood in the center of the sizeable room and folded her arms over herself protectively.

Mel said, "I'll give you some privacy," and excused herself, shutting the door behind her.

Paire threw the flimsy deadbolt to lock it. She hesitated taking off her clothes. She knew the bath would make her feel better, and that she needed to get rid of these clothes, but she still felt vulnerable, even in this gated compound.

When she emerged from the bathroom, Melinda was sautéing mushrooms and onions in the kitchen. "Food will help too."

"Sorry I came here. I panicked."

"Don't apologize."

Paire said, "I don't have to stay, but I wanted to warn you."

Mel smiled, but Paire could see she had frightened her. "About what?"

"You know the painting is missing."

"Good riddance," Melinda said.

"Abel Kasson is looking for that painting. He's going to come here."

"Did you tell him I had it?"

"No. But do you?"

"Paire, the painting was in police custody. How would I get it?"

"I don't know. But he thought I had it. It stands to reason that he'll approach you."

Melinda's face squinted as a thought landed, and a new dread washed over her. She left Paire for a moment to rush to her kitchen counter, where she thumbed through a stack of mail, leafing through several envelopes. "Where is it?" she asked herself. When she couldn't find whatever she was looking for, Melinda went to a pregnant bag of trash and tore open the plastic.

Paire watched as her host rifled through garbage, finding a postcard that had been smeared by grease. Back at the dining table,

Mel dealt the card so they could both see it. "Honestly, I thought this was from the Fern. It arrived yesterday."

The card was embossed, the print a tight script usually found on wedding invitations:

> *You are cordially invited to a private reception.*
> *Qi Jianyu Retrospective.*
> *Independence Day.*

Paire felt sick when she read the location. "I know that address."

Melinda looked just as unsettled. "And that means he knows my address."

· · ·

July fourth fell the next day. Just before eight in the evening, Paire and Melinda stepped out of a taxi at the foot of Kasson's Park Avenue apartment building. The city's fireworks would start soon. Paire wondered if they could hear them this far uptown. Right now it was just horns and a faraway siren.

The evening was warmer than any in Abenaki. The older woman wore a form-fitting black dress, and the younger wore a newly purchased white gown. Bare shoulders for both. They gave their names to a stocky Mediterranean doorman, a new face for Paire, and he showed them to the elevators. The front ones, intended for the residents.

They rode in silence, and Paire shuddered as the doors opened to the fifteenth floor.

Kasson's front door stood ajar.

Unnerved by the lack of party chatter, Paire held the elevator doors. "We don't have to go in. We can take the elevator back down. No one will know we were here."

"I have to," Melinda said.

"If he's in there, he might attack us," Paire said. She had left Kasson unconscious on the floor on Pierrepont Street. Now they were at his flat, and he had to be in there.

Paire had expected a crowd, and hoped they would be lost in that crowd, or that there would at least be other guests at the reception so that Kasson wouldn't erupt as soon as he saw them. Given the absence of sound, she expected that he was in there alone, patiently waiting for something to pluck a strand in the web.

"Stay with me," Melinda said.

Familiar with the layout from her earlier trespass, Paire led them into the flat, down the long Persian runner in the corridor.

Melinda pointed to the Rosewood laugher on the wall. "Is that—"

"Yep, that's his."

Paire didn't try to tiptoe tonight, and the wood creaked. She suspected someone down the hall listened. In her purse, she checked for her spring baton and rolled it between her fingers.

They came out into the living room. The outside dark, the interior lights turned the windows into mirrors. The French doors opened onto the balcony, and a few candles had been lit at the base of the railing balustrades. A fire crackled, the loudest sound in the apartment.

The room was almost empty but for a single man who sat in one of the wing chairs. It was not Abel Kasson.

"Hello, Melinda," he said.

He was a long, frail man in eyeglasses, with a wispy gray moustache. He wore a robe and slippers, as if he had expected to be alone tonight. His fingers crooked over the armrests like leafless twigs, the thumb of one hand absently tapping on the upholstery. He said to Paire, "I know you. You were here the other day. What's your name?" His voice was hoarse but demanding.

"Paire."

"Right," he said. "Another artist?"

"Trying to be," Paire said.

He said to Melinda, "She wasn't invited."

"And yet I'm here," Paire said.

The man looked away toward the fire, a small orange flicker dancing off two glowing pine logs. Following his gaze, Paire now saw the portrait. The Empress Xiao Zhe Yi sat just beside the hearth, leaning up against the wall, right next to a brass stand that held black-tipped tongs and a poker.

Paire recognized this man's face, but not from the peering eyeball she'd seen in the doorjamb opening. Studying his profile and sallow cheek, Paire saw the resemblance between this face and the bronze bust she'd seen in the lobby of the MAAC. The one that commemorated its founder, Gabriel Kasson.

"This is a party. You should sit down," he said.

Paire backed down the hallway, searching for a trace of Abel Kasson, then returned to Melinda's side when she found no sign of him. She clutched the baton in her purse, but had no cause to draw it. She touched Melinda's shoulder and gestured for her to sit down. They lowered themselves slowly onto the sofa, as far away from Gabriel as possible. As they sank into the cushions, a breeze from the open doors made the fire dance.

"This is the first time I've ever seen you," Gabriel said to Melinda. "You've grown up well. Your father wasn't a handsome man. You lucked out and got your mother's genes."

"What is this?" Paire asked.

"Are you her translator?" Gabriel shot at Paire, then said to Melinda, "I tried to track your father down, but I never got to him. Sometimes I wondered if he'd actually moved back to China or if it was all a ruse. I could never find an address for him." He sounded accusatory.

Mel finally spoke. "It's a moot issue. He died two years ago."

"That I did prove for myself. I tracked down a copy of the death certificate. Those can be faked, so I even found the man who signed it. I trust that he is dead. Wherever he ended up, he's not there anymore."

"So there you have it," she said.

"You ever visit your father in Beijing?"

Melinda stared hatefully at the old man. "Never made it."

"But you stayed in touch."

"He was my father."

"More so than your mother. I know you two had a falling out. She found out you liked girls."

Paire stood up. "That's it. We're leaving."

Gabriel turned his attention to Paire. "We're not even talking about *your* father, Ms. Novis. Don't worry, I know all about him, too."

Paire shivered when she heard her birth name.

"Do you still keep in touch with your father now that you've moved all the way down to New York City?"

No sense in denying anything. Paire said, "Only as much as I can stand it. So, not much."

"No shared vacations with him coming up, now that he's free again? No vision-expanding trip to Mont Saint-Michel? No long hike on the Appalachian Trail?"

Paire was growing irritated. "He wouldn't survive in the sunlight."

"Institutionalized for too long. Probably needs to keep himself to confined spaces." It must have been a Kasson family trait to poke at people's soft parts.

A man's voice boomed behind them all. "What the hell is this?"

Paire pulled out the baton and whipped her wrist so it stretched to its full length. When she turned, she saw Abel Kasson standing where the hallway opened into the living room. He had two purple rings under his eyes and a white bandage across his nose where the doctors had reset his bridge. He looked as shocked as they were. When he saw the spring baton he flinched.

Gabriel seemed amused. "She's brought a weapon! This is wonderful."

Abel Kasson saw the painting against the wall, and shouted at his father, "You had it?"

"It's not the first time I've had to keep something secret for your own good."

It would have taken someone of considerable influence to remove a piece of evidence from a police locker.

Gabriel said, "Let's all sit down. I can see everyone is itchy. But we'll get it all settled."

Abel stepped the long way around the two women and settled in the wing chair opposite his father. They flanked the two women at the center of the wide sofa. Paire and Abel traded looks.

"I don't want these people in my house," said Abel.

"I don't want to be here either," said Melinda.

"I wanted to be left alone," said Gabriel. "But you started it."

"Is that right?" Melinda said.

He waved at the empress. "You could have waited until I was dead to trot this out."

"I waited until my father was dead. I thought that was long enough."

Gabriel reached out and scratched the surface of the painting, scraping the tempera lightly with a fingernail. "At some point you should really go to Beijing. It's important to see where you're from. Your father ever talk about it? What it was like?"

"Sure he did," she said noncommittally.

"You can taste the soot over there. And that's coming from someone who grew up in New York. I remember back when there were more fireplaces in Manhattan. You could smell the ash in the air. But nothing compared to Beijing. I could feel my lungs crystallize when I was there. And I was only there off and on for a few years. I can't imagine what it would have been like for your father to have grown up there. The pollution that festered in his body. It's no surprise that I found him where I found him." Gabriel seemed to detect something interesting when he looked at Melinda. "Surely your father told you how we met."

The corner of Melinda's mouth twitched. Gabriel explained, "It was during the 1972 trip with Nixon. While the President was doing his thing with the Chairman, I was on duty with the First Lady. The trip was such a public spectacle, we had to run ourselves ragged with all the visits. Visits to schools. Villages. Hospitals. I met your father in a hospital bed. I thought he was delirious, because he had this goofy smile on his face, and he hummed to himself. Notably, the tune he was humming was a Beatles song. 'Help!' The melody was discernable, even though your father was no singer. The

Beatles were outlawed in China, as was most Western music. Luckily, no one on the staff recognized the song. I barely recognized it. I'm no Beatles fan, but even I knew that one. And to find a local in Beijing humming a rock and roll song…that was notable. It meant he had some kind of connection to the West, and clearly a fondness for it. That immediately piqued my interest." He adjusted his glasses and crossed his legs.

"Still, your father was a sick man in rags. He stank like he was moldering. I'd heard a lot about cholera outbreaks, and I was paranoid that the First Lady, not to mention myself, had been put in danger of contracting a communicable disease. I had words with the hospital staff. The doctors kept denying that it was cholera, but I had it in my head that it must be, and in my butchered version of Mandarin, I strongly urged them—let's be honest, threatened them—to move us out of the room. Your father was stowed in this hangar of a room crammed with beds, coughing like a miner with black lung. Whatever was going on, I was convinced it was contagious.

"I was in the middle of asking why the area wasn't quarantined when I felt something slip into my hand. A folded sheet of paper— someone from behind me slipped a note into my palm. Then a voice whispered in my ear—with a thick accent, but in English—"Just a snakebite, boss." Those were the first words I ever heard from your father. And it was a snakebite—he had the bandages around his ankle to prove it. A pit viper got him in the heel." Gabriel shifted in his seat and grabbed the poker. For a man his age—eighty-six years old, Paire had calculated when she looked up his biography— he seemed nimble enough with the brass rod. The fire didn't need tending, but he prodded the logs anyway. "I probably wouldn't have come back to see him, but the note he'd slipped me wasn't a note. I expected it to be some plea to help him defect. You get your share of those when you're doing that kind of work." For moments he seemed lost in memory, and murmured, "Not a note at all. Instead, he'd given me the most exquisite pencil sketch of the First Lady. He'd composed a quick drawing from across the room when we'd first entered. Moreover, he had given Pat Nixon wings, because he made her an angel. It sounds hokey, but the sketch was sublime. I hadn't seen art like this in China. I'd never expected to, but now that I had, it made me miss the art world back in New York. Especially back then, the art in China—at least, to me—was a composite of competing grays. You didn't see this kind of creative expression. You didn't have the arts like it existed in the West. If you were lucky enough to be an artist, you painted on behalf of the State, and the work you created was intended to honor the State and the People. To draw the wife of the President of the United States, and to make her an angel—playing with religious iconography, not to mention glorifying a political figure from another country—you just didn't do that in China. Then, to slip that drawing into the ambassador's hand while the hospital staff was watching. This man had a kind of daring that I'd never seen. I needed to go back and speak to him. So when we were done with the First Lady's events, I found a way back to the hospital, and after some protest, I paid off enough people for them to let me visit. Qi Jianyu. He insisted that I refer to him as Qi."

At this point, Gabriel pulled the poker out of the fire and examined the tip as it faded from red to black, a wisp of smoke trailing off the tip. Paire was afraid he would jab the birch board and sear the portrait. Abel stared expectantly at his father. He seemed to know the story, but was afraid to interrupt.

"We got to know each other over the next year. The President might have gone home, but I was still there." He turned to look at Mel. "Your father was a teacher at the university, and did his own work on the side with extra materials he pilfered from the school. Qi invited me to a village in the middle of nowhere, to some dilapidated hut that looked like it should have been condemned. He staged an exhibit for me in the middle of the countryside, hidden from everyone. Certainly illegal. It was gorgeous. Your father was begging for a chance at real freedom, and I gave it to him.

"You have no idea the lengths I went to for that man. I set him up with a home, a car, a good income that he could rely on every year. More than he'd ever make in China, I'll tell you that. I pulled strings to get him over here. That was no picnic. I transferred out of the embassy when Nixon ducked out of office in 1974, and it wasn't easy to figure out how to move one Chinese artist to the United States with all that transition. But still I did it. I convinced the most famous architect of the day, I. M. Pei, to design a building for me, and ponied up the money to pay for it all. All for your father, Melinda. You know how he repaid me? In sloth. As soon as he had a whiff of success, he wanted more of it. He wanted more money. More everything. He said he couldn't understand the contract that he had signed. But was it my responsibility to explain an arrangement that was clearly mapped out on paper? When he got to New York, the only thing he had to do was paint. And he refused to do it. After the millions spent on opening a cherry museum in the heart of Manhattan, he refused to do the job that I hired him to do. He felt like his freedom was compromised, even though I'd given him more freedom than he'd ever known."

Melinda kept her head down. Paire couldn't tell if she was disgusted by Gabriel Kasson's account of her father, or if some of this rang true.

"I opened the museum with the inventory we were able to bring over from China. This was a lot, don't get me wrong. But I'd expected him to create new work for this museum, and I only got a few slapdash pieces he threw together to fulfill his contract. I got crap. We opened with crap. And not enough of it, at that. I had to bring in more artists just to fill in the empty spaces on the walls. Your father seemed to feel he was entitled to be a billionaire just by stepping foot onto American soil. It doesn't work like that."

At this point Melinda finally asked, "What did you do with the work?"

"Once he moved back to China, it became clear that the museum wouldn't be able to showcase his new work. There was no new work to showcase. We had to make use of the space somehow, so we made room for new artists. I didn't know as much about art as I should have. Especially for someone who founded a museum. I had the passion for it, and the means, but I hired someone who knew how to curate. That's how I found Nico Franconi." For the first time, his gaze landed on Paire. "I'm sorry you had to watch him die. I guess guilt got the better of him."

Paire caught the effort in Melinda's voice as she tried to sound patient. "Where is my father's work?"

"It was in storage for a while, but someone was going to find it eventually. There was so much bad blood from when we opened the museum. So many people that took your father's side. I have to admit I was feeling a little vindictive."

Melinda raised her voice. "Where?"

Abel finally spoke. "He burned it."

Gabriel glared at his son, perhaps loathing the fact that Abel had snatched the punchline away from him. Abel said to Melinda, "My father burned all of Qi's works. Franconi helped him." His tone stated the facts plainly, without a hint of apology to her, but without a trace of satisfaction either.

Gabriel explained, "We had to erase the memory, to preserve our name. With a multigenerational legacy like the Kasson family, your name is your most powerful asset. We'd lost enough on our gamble to bring an unknown Chinese artist to America. We'd lost millions—and that's when losing millions meant something. We couldn't lose our name as well. So we destroyed your father's legacy to preserve ours."

Abel said, "There's nothing left, and that's the truth of it."

"Nothing but this," said Gabriel, gesturing to the painting with the poker, the black tip, assuredly still warm from the fire, inches from the surface. Melinda's mouth gaped, and a tear rolled down her cheek.

"The last remaining Qi," said Abel. To his father, he said, "If you'd let me take care of this, it would have all been over by now."

"Don't worry, it will all be over soon enough," said his father.

Paire scraped her nails on the sofa fabric and stared at the gathering clouds through the gigantic windows. They might be low enough to obscure tonight's fireworks. She heard a faint combustion through the window, and she couldn't tell if it was a crackle of fireworks or a distant gunshot, the way New York City seemed to clear its throat whenever it seemed too quiet. She asked, "Why are you telling us this?"

Gabriel shifted his attention to Paire. "I see the way you look at her. It's how I used to look at her. You should have seen Qi's other work, and how it affected people. How it drew out their impish impulses. The power that man had over his craft." He fingered the edge of the birch board. "There was a reason I brought the man overseas, and that was the power of his work. I'm too jaded now to look at it objectively, as is my son. Melinda here sees this work as a gateway to understanding her father. But you—*you*," he pointed at Paire, "you see the work the way people *should* see it. You marvel at it. It's glorifying for me to see. Because it tells me I was right all along. That he was a *master.* Such a master, in fact, that even one single work could earn him the recognition he richly deserved." Gabriel glanced fondly at the Empress Xiao Zhe Yi, brushing her face lightly with his fingers. With some effort, he stood up from his chair. Abel stood to help his father, but Gabriel shooed him away, so he sank back down. Gabriel bent and scooped up the painting, holding it by the edges of the frame, just as Paire had carried it when she had stolen it from that flat one week ago.

"Back then, so many people assumed that my passion for art was just another form of materialism, just more things to collect. But it was just the opposite. This was my escape from the regimented parts of my life. This painting ignites something in me, and I can see that it affects you the same way. The same way it changed people when they first saw Qi's work back in 1974."

Paire thought he might chuck the portrait into the fire, and she slid onto the edge of the sofa cushions in case she needed to dive into the hearth to save it.

Large as it was, and birch board at that, Gabriel held it like a kite. Pivoting away from the fireplace, he looked like he was waltzing with it. A gust from the French doors almost blew it out of his hands, but he held on tight. "It's heavier than it looks," he bubbled with his own audacity.

Paire wormed around on the cushions.

"Please be careful with that," said Melinda. Her voice wavered a bit as she gave in to her own turbulent emotions.

"Don't worry," Gabriel cooed, "It will be over in a minute. You don't realize what you have until it's gone. That goes for addictions, too." He retreated backward toward the open balcony.

Now Paire and Melinda rose from their seats. Abel rose as well, but circled around and stood between his father and the two women so they couldn't intervene in whatever Gabriel had planned.

"There's a good boy," Gabriel called to his son. The older Kasson walked out onto the balcony.

Paire needed to act. She approached, and when Abel tried to stiff-arm her, she swatted at his arm with the baton. Only this time, he was prepared. He grabbed her wrist and pinched her arm until the pain made her drop her only weapon softly on the carpet.

"This is senseless," Melinda implored. She moved slowly, creeping toward Gabriel like a stalking lioness. "Think about what you're doing. Think of what that work gives people."

Gabriel remarked, "It gives people cancer. This thing ruins people." But he admired the portrait just the same. "This is wiping the slate clean, for both our families. Nothing clings to you like shame. You know how to get rid of shame? To find someone to blame it on. And I'll have to be that person. I'm as good a choice as any."

Gabriel backed up with careful duelist's steps until the marble balcony railing caught him just under the buttock. The wind swirled around him. "You're all funny. I wish you could see yourselves. Here I am, perched on the edge of a window fifteen stories up, and you're all more worried about this thing." He made the birch board dance in the air. "Eventually, you'll thank me."

Paire remained stiff, petrified by the inevitable. Later, she would remember all this seeming like a hallucination, happening silently, without punctuation.

Gabriel folded his arms around the board, holding it to his chest in an embrace. Willing the strength in his legs, he sprang into the air, backward over the railing, like a track-and-field high jumper.

As he spun in an axel, his face looked peaceful, as if caught waking from a blissful dream. Quietly, he slipped into the night.

Melinda gasped.

A staccato shriek tore out of Paire.

Abel was the only one who moved, rushing to the balustrades, his hands holding the marble rail as if he were preparing to jump himself.

It didn't seem real until they heard Gabriel land. Over a hundred feet below, a jarring and meaty slap sounded as muscle and bones collided with the pavement.

Abel let out a low, grieving groan, the first noise from him that had sounded like regret.

CHAPTER 20

Abel Kasson stepped off the balcony, his face red as a blister. Tears clouded his eyes, so when he stared at Paire and Melinda he looked blearily about the room instead of focusing on them. He unfolded a jackknife from his pocket. Behind him, clouds lit up with an electric flash, and the first thunder rumbled seconds later. Paire heard a faint crackle from the fireworks that were being launched into the storm.

The spring baton lay across the room. The only thing within arm's reach was a couch cushion. Paire grabbed one and held it like a shield.

Incensed, Kasson came at her with the grace of a runaway boulder.

He moved even faster than he had at Rosewood's flat. Kasson plunged the knife into the cushion. The impact alone forced her back a few steps. The blade ripped out the white filler, and cotton billows fell to the floor. With his father had gone the last shreds of his composure, and Kasson was in a blackout rage. He stabbed and slashed at Paire in a frenzy, and she used all her strength to keep the cushion held in place.

Kasson slashed and caught Paire across the forearm. Too stunned to scream, her mouth opened in an inaudible gasp. Blood dripped on the carpet. He raised the knife above his shoulders for a killing stroke, but Melinda threw the fireplace tongs at him, which whacked him on his shoulder. A momentary distraction, but enough time for her to tug Paire's arm and encourage her to run for the exit. They both sprinted down the main corridor.

Rather than wait for the elevator, Paire took them through the kitchen to the service staircase. Kasson followed steps behind, hollering after them as he stumbled down the stairs. To stay ahead of him, they circled the turns so quickly that Paire felt dizzy. Or perhaps it was the blood loss from her arm. She drizzled on the steps.

Her bleeding might have saved their lives. Kasson was catching up, but he slipped on some of Paire's blood around the second floor, and tumbled on the landing.

When they got outside, Melinda was momentarily transfixed by the sight of Gabriel Kasson's broken body. He'd just missed crashing through the green awning. Blood pooled around the skull, and scraps of brain littered the sidewalk. He reminded Paire of Nicola Franconi, another man dead on the pavement.

The empress should have smashed apart on the sidewalk as well. But on the way down, the wind must have caught the board like a sail, and wrenched it out of Gabriel's arms. The gust carried it into the awning, where it tore through and lodged in the canvas. A corner of the birch board stuck through the fabric, just above their heads. While Melinda flagged down a taxi, Paire impulsively pulled down the painting, bleeding arm and all. She had to take it. She jumped up and caught the board, and her body weight dragged it through the canvas with a loud rip. The impact had scratched the tempera, scarring the empress's cheek, but she was otherwise undamaged.

A taxi stopped, and they climbed inside as Kasson barreled out the front door, holding the knife at his side. He might have chased after them as they drove off, but as they pulled away he froze at the sight of Gabriel Kasson, and fell to his knees beside the halo of blood around his father's head.

CHAPTER 21

The next morning, the empress leaned against the brick wall at Melinda's compound, next to the dining table. Melinda scrambled eggs with spinach. "You need to eat something," she urged. "It will help to keep the medication down."

They'd spent several hours the night before at the hospital while a doctor sewed up Paire's arm. She still felt woozy from the painkillers, the only reason she had been able to sleep at all. Paire lifted her bandage and examined the gash on her forearm. The stitches pulled every time she rotated her wrist. Doctors said it would scar. When it healed, it would stripe her arm lengthwise, and she wondered if some people would think that she tried to open a vein in the bathtub.

Against the wall, the empress's face had been marred with a few scars of her own down her cheeks, disfiguring the perfect oval.

They sat together while Paire forked through her eggs. Both of them stared at Qi's painting.

"She follows you with her eyes," Melinda said.

"She does. But I used to think that about my Brandon Flowers poster." She blew steam off her eggs. "What do you think it is about her?"

"My father used to say if you knew how they did it, it wouldn't be magic," Melinda said.

"You know Abel Kasson will come for this," Paire said.

"You're the one who took it with us. We could have left it there."

"I thought you wanted it."

"I did. But that's not why you took it."

"*Touché*," Paire said, staring down at her eggs and resenting the other woman's tone.

Melinda let the steam rise off her own plate of eggs without touching them. "The compound has the external gate, plus two locked doors to get in here."

"You really think that's going to stop him?"

Melinda looked at the empress against the wall. "Maybe we should destroy it."

"You could lock it up. It's easy enough to find a storage unit in New York," Paire said.

"None of that would stop him from finding us," Mel said.

"I doubt it."

Melinda stood and turned the birch board so it faced the wall. "Let's pretend for a few moments that it isn't here."

Not having any siblings or pets, Paire had never been charged with another's welfare. Not so much as a gerbil had ever shared her bedroom. Having something to care for stirred nurturing instincts in her that had been dormant. "We could leave."

"Not a bad idea. Not for both of us, but for you. You ever think about going back to Maine?"

This came as an affront to Paire, but she considered it for Melinda's sake. She had no home anymore and had lost her few possessions. Without family to support her, without Rosewood loving her and housing her, she didn't have anything left. The realization cast her into a deep gloom. Retreating to Maine would mean becoming Katie Novis again. A return to weakness. Suffering under the family taint. Even with the imminent threat of Kasson and the shame of Rosewood, the grief over Mayer and Lucia, New York still felt safer than Abenaki, if for no other reason than her doom was less assured here. So long as she could stay ahead of Kasson.

"I can't go back to Maine."

"You still have a father. That's more than I've got."

"For all practical purposes, I don't have a father." She remembered Lake Novis in his ratty chair, his gloomy eyes adrift to the yellowed wallpaper. He had resigned himself to death. He'd ebb away in that dark room, pining after his dead wife, until gamey smells heralded his passing to his neighbors.

There was a pause before Melinda asked, "How bad was it up there?"

"Some kids have it worse, but it was plenty bad enough for me. Would you call your father right now?"

"Of course I would."

"You loved your father," Paire said.

"I love him still, even if he's not alive."

"But he left you."

Melinda shrugged. "He stayed in his own way."

Paire asked, "Would you call your mother?"

"That's a little different," said Melinda. "You know I was disinherited by my mother."

"Some families do that," Paire said, hoping to convey a shared experience.

"My mom had old-country values. A gay child was a dead child. She died hoping I'd meet the right guy." Melinda added, "But even with that, I would probably call my mother if it would help us out of this."

Paire understood that whatever the turbulence with her family, Melinda had, at some point, known what it was to have loving parents. "I'm not saying my family is better or worse than yours. Only that I can't go back to them."

Paire saw Melinda's frustration. Despite her reluctance, she spilled it, so she could make Melinda understand why she needed to stay here, and why she had nowhere else to go. Kasson might very well murder them, and the need to keep secrets didn't feel important. For the first time in New York, Paire divulged the secret she'd hoped would never leave Abenaki.

* * *

After Lake Novis and Cissy married, they lived in seclusion in northern Maine, specifically, Caribou. There they had their baby in private. Gilda diligently kept reporters from printing news about their whereabouts, or the juicy scandal of how an institutional guard fertilized an inpatient.

During the trial later on, it would all come out. Even though the press stayed away, court transcripts told the story. As a teen, Katie Novis pored through these to try to get a glimmer of who her parents were. Neighbors from Caribou had testified. Some said that Lake and Cissy Novis had been "in wedded bliss" and that they were "wonderful neighbors." As one neighbor said, "I never heard a peep about them that indicated anything was wrong...you know, until *it* happened." But a few witnesses hinted at some misgivings. One said, "There was something off about them," and another, "They were gloomy. That's what I remember most."

In his own testimony, Lake Novis had explained:

> *Some people weren't meant to have children, plain and simple. Some people find out about these things and they rise to the occasion. We didn't feel that way. But we were stuck. Cissy was Catholic, I mean a faithful Catholic, so abortion was out. We figured we'd have to make the best of it. We both thought that the maternal and paternal instincts would kick in. We waited for them. But they never did.*

By the trial, Cissy Novis had already hanged herself in the garage, so she wasn't around to testify on her own behalf.

Gilda, however, had said, "Cissy was a challenging child, no doubt about it. Postpartum depression was probably the final factor."

Katie sensed when reading this that Gilda was trying to leverage the trial to clear her own name, to convince the world that while Lake and Cissy Novis might have been monsters, they didn't come from monsters.

By the time Katie Novis was ten months old, Lake and Cissy were depressed and fatigued. Cissy had overdosed on aspirin but recovered. Lake hungered for the intimate contact the couple had had before they became parents. They both wanted things to go back to the way they were before. Lake testified that Cissy had nothing to do with the "solution" that was hatched, but without Cissy to confirm or deny her role in the events that followed, no one with the exception of Lake knew for sure. Even Gilda speculated, when asked, that her daughter might have been complicit in the deed. Of course, attorneys demanded this statement be struck, but there it remained in the transcripts.

On the Maine coastline on any given night, buoys from lobster traps bobbed up and down on the water like tombstones in a flooded graveyard. Lake had set out on a foggy night with the child. The baby was wrapped in a blanket—less to keep her warm and more to keep her comfortable enough not to scream in the cold. Lobster boats occasionally patrolled the coastline at night to make sure poachers weren't hauling their traps, or competitors weren't cutting free the buoys. But Lake picked a night when the visibility was poor, and he could neither see nor hear any boats on the water.

He rowed out as quietly as possible, so that not even the drips from the oars would give him away. When he was far enough out, he found a buoy and pulled it into the boat. He hoisted the soggy rope and waterlogged wood as if playing tug o' war with the Atlantic.

The plan was to strip the baby naked, insert her in the trap, and lower it back down to the ocean floor. Once it was submerged, Lake would cut the buoy free, so the boats wouldn't haul it up with their daily catches. The lobstermen would consider it a lost relic of the trade. Eventually, lobsters would find their way into the trap. Captive and hungry, they would eat the food provided, their claws stripping the child down to nothing, even eating the soft bones until their exoskeletons bulged. If the trap was found at all, there wouldn't be anything left of the girl. Fishermen already had a name for a lobster trap that was lost at the ocean bottom. They called it a death trap. After leaving a window open in the nursery, Lake would call the police in the morning and claim his daughter had been kidnapped.

In the courtroom, Lake claimed that it had taken him a while to work up the nerve to load his daughter into the trap. He hoped that the chill of the water might push his daughter into shock, and that she would die quickly. He even said the *Sh'ma* before lowering Katie into the Atlantic, which the prosecution naturally doubted, since Lake "had never been a religious man, proving so by marrying out of his faith." Regardless, Lake had definitely hesitated, for had he not hesitated, he would not have been caught.

While the lobster trap sat on the bottom of the rowboat, tiny Katie Novis began crying. It was doubtful that the infant was cognizant that she was crying for her life, but Lake swore she was. She "shrieked like an eagle" into the night, and for this reason, another boat came upon them. According to Lake, it emerged from the fog like an apparition.

One of the fisherman on the boat testified:

> *I thought this guy was poaching from us. It was dark and foggy, so a couple of us were on the bow, shining flashlights into the boat to see what he was up to. We heard the baby, but we just thought he had taken the kid out on the boat with him. When we saw the kid naked in the trap, well, Jesus Christ, that was another story.*

Lake was plucked from the boat, and beaten by the crew of the fishing vessel. He sustained several fractured ribs, a broken nose, a sprained ankle, and some internal bleeding. Lake was unconscious for several days in the hospital, in which time news had reached Cissy of what had transpired on the rowboat, and the charges that her husband faced. Some would argue that her suicide demonstrated the shame that came with being a co-conspirator. Those of a more romantic nature would argue that she knew her husband was going to prison for life, and she couldn't live without him. Still others would argue that after months of postpartum depression, the dual tragedy of her daughter's near-death and her husband's near-crime sent her over the edge. Whatever the reason, she hanged herself while Lake was in his coma. He awoke to handcuffs and her death certificate.

Before she died, Cissy changed her will, leaving her money to her daughter. This might have been an act of contrition, or with Lake in prison, simply the most sensible allocation of her resources. The money passed to a trust. When Katie claimed the money on her eighteenth birthday, she vowed to leave Maine and never return.

• • •

Melinda soberly digested the story. She had no words of wisdom for Paire. All she said was, "You're welcome here, but it's not safe."

Paire suggested, "There are other places to go. It's a big country. We could always go someplace he wouldn't find us."

Melinda tilted her head back and stared at the ceiling while she considered whether to flee. She said, "I live in a fortress. I'd rather take my chances here."

"You could call the police." It took some amount of will for Paire to suggest this. If they involved law enforcement, they might eventually stumble across Paire's connection to the Fern shootings. But she was willing to call them if it meant protecting Melinda from Kasson.

"The Kassons bribed the police to steal this painting out of their own storage locker. I wouldn't trust them, would you?" Melinda had a point.

Paire mulled through ideas. Out of desperation, she asked, "If you gave him the painting, do you think he would leave you alone?" This sounded so ridiculous when aired aloud, she immediately burst out laughing.

In an involuntary release of nervous tension, Melinda joined her. Giggle tears dropped from the corners of her eyes. "Even if I could, I'm not sure I would. This comes down to two bloodlines, the Qis and the Kassons. Abel Kasson and I are the last of each line. If he wants to finish off my family, he's going to have to work for it."

Paire considered for the first time that she was the last of her line as well. That fact had mattered so little to her that she had changed her name without giving any thought to discontinuing the lineage.

Melinda thought aloud, "I could buy a gun."

Paire convulsively shook her head. "Have you ever used one?"

"How hard can it be? Kids use them."

Paire thought about how Lucia and Mayer had looked on the floor of the Fern. "You know how easily it could go wrong."

Melinda let it go. "Brady Bill and all—I guess it would take too long anyway. No guns, then. You lost your club back at Kasson's apartment. What was that thing?"

"A baton." Paire began to worry that they had nothing with which to defend themselves. "Do you have anything else we could use? Pepper spray or a Taser?"

Melinda smirked. "I've got kitchen knives."

Nodding to the birch board, Paire said, "We should at least hide it." A thought struck her. "That's our weapon."

CHAPTER 22

The two women were asleep in separate rooms when Kasson came. Paire lay on the sofa near the dining table.

Something woke her—a movement in the air, creak of a door, or crackle of human joints. Maybe she so readily anticipated his arrival that her body was programmed to wake at intervals. She smelled talcum. Paire reached for a paring knife under her pillow, but Kasson was already on her in the dark. He pinned her to the sofa cushions.

Kasson sat on the couch with her. Seemingly, he had been watching her sleep. The moment she sprang upright, his thick, talcum-scented hand clamped over her mouth. He pressed his own knife to her throat.

Kasson whispered into her ear, "Promise not to scream, and I'll let you breathe. Do you promise not to scream?"

She considered her options, and reluctantly nodded against the fingers.

"If you do scream, I'll have to slice your neck open. Do you understand?"

Again, Paire nodded. She was petrified, and had no snappy, spit-in-your-face retort. Kasson lifted his palm off her lips, but kept the knife tip pressed into her ribs.

Her mind raced. They had prepared all afternoon, but now that he was here, she panicked. She had expected to hear him fumble with the locks, or break the glass. He'd slipped in without a noise, and caught her by surprise.

"Where's Mel?" she managed to eke out.

Kasson said, "In her room." Paire called out Melinda's name in

232

the dark. A muffled voice called back, squabbling Paire's name with a gag in her mouth.

"Let me see her."

"You're in no position to make orders."

"I'll scream."

"And I'll cut you open." Kasson looked around the room. "Come to think of it, scream all you want. In this place, who would care?"

After staring at her with some amusement, he squeezed her arm like a tourniquet, and towed her light frame off the couch. Paire's legs were still asleep, and she stumbled as he dragged her into Melinda's bedroom. Kasson walked with a limp.

None of the lights were on, but he shone the way with a small flashlight, eventually spotlighting Melinda in a tight halo. She lay on the mattress, alive but bound, her wrists and ankles trussed with zip ties. A band of duct tape wound over her mouth.

"Why didn't you tie me up?" Paire asked.

His voice was so at ease, he might have been talking in his sleep. "Because you're the weak one."

Melinda kicked in vain to tear through the zip ties, and screamed hoarsely through her gag.

Kasson pulled Paire out of the room. "Show me where you have it."

"We mailed it off to the MAAC."

He slapped her hard and fast above the cheek. She'd forgotten how hard he hit, how much muscle was buried beneath his rolling skin. It took a few seconds for the pain to register, and when it did, her skin stung like a sunburn. "Don't worry," he said, "that won't raise a bruise."

"It was crated up and mailed off yesterday. I can show you the tracking slip."

Kasson's closed fist hammered into the girl's ribs. The air burst out of her lungs. Paire coughed and her eyes bugged. Winded, she fell and balled up on her side.

Kasson let her catch her breath. All the planning, and it came down to this. Paire had no choice but to tell him. "It's in the studio."

She led Kasson to the painting, out of the living quarters and across the compound in the moonlight. Paire couldn't see a light on in any of the adjoining buildings. She didn't even know what time it was, just that it was late enough that everyone in the neighborhood was asleep. He had timed his assault perfectly.

Hardly breaking the silence of the evening, they scratched across the gravel to the metal door, and with his limp, the flashlight beam bounced all over. When she threw open the door, a skunk stripe of moonlight shone through the room onto the empress. The portrait leaned against the far wall, behind one of Melinda's giant flower stalks.

"A vision in red," he sighed.

His knife dug a little deeper into Paire's ribs, but she didn't dare vocalize the pain. Kasson nudged her forward, close enough to prove that the painting wasn't a hoax. Once convinced, he withdrew the knife and was pulled toward the portrait, like they all were. He stepped in front of Paire—although not so far that he couldn't reach behind and slash her—and fingered the edges.

"Greater things have been erased from history," he said. "Julius Caesar burned down the Library of Alexandria." Perhaps for the first time, Kasson spoke to Paire as a peer. They shared a moment of silence together, Kasson likely reflecting on the work in front of him while Paire considered the imminent violence to follow. "He was a great artist. It's a shame," he said.

Possibly owing to his fatigue and injuries, and maybe even the lateness of the hour, Kasson took another step toward the portrait of the Empress Xiao Zhe Yi. Close enough to touch it. Still near enough to Paire to lash out and catch her with the knife. A collector like Kasson knew better than to run his hands over the tempera, but he couldn't resist. This thin coating of pigment was the closest thing to skin that he was going to get. Slowly, his massive body sank to his knees. He lowered the flashlight and knife to his thighs. Then, he leaned in and kissed the woman on the lips.

When he was finished, he cocked his arm and pounded his fist into the birch, smashing his hand against the empress's face. His first blow bounced off the wood, but he kept pummeling, faster and faster, each time more forceful. The pigment smeared, streaked with blood from his hand. Until her face became unrecognizable. Until Paire heard the wood crack. Until the plank split in two.

Paire ran. Fast as Kasson was, he was on his knees, and he reacted too late to catch her with the swipe of his knife. He chased her, but now that he was slowed by the limp, Paire sprinted through the door and clanged it shut behind her.

Paire spun the steel wheel as tightly as possible. Kasson pounded on the other side, which, given the thickness of the door, sounded like distant taiko drums.

She had trapped Abel Kasson inside Melinda Qi's giant kiln.

Back inside the living quarters, Paire cut Melinda free with a chef's knife and stripped off the duct tape, careful not to pull too hard. Melinda shook and dry heaved from nerves.

Paire's eyes watered from the stress, though she didn't feel any sadness or terror. "He's in the kiln." As Melinda had instructed her, she pronounced it *kill.*

They'd both discussed this scenario. While this was Paire's idea, Melinda had explained how it would work. Cremations took place at around 1,700 degrees, and the kiln heated up to 2,900 degrees. At that temperature, nothing would be left. Not even teeth.

Of course, it had all been theoretical. Now, as they stood outside the kiln, listening to Kasson's arrhythmic percussion, Melinda double-checked with Paire. "Are you ready to do this?"

"It's no more than they did to your family," said Paire.

"Can you live with this?"

"I don't see any other way," Paire said. "Sometimes you need to purge everything to start over. And nothing purges like fire."

Melinda lifted a tendril of the younger woman's hair. "We'll burn the painting too."

"There's not much left to burn."

A stiff breeze whipped through the compound, and when

it whistled through their ears, they couldn't hear the banker's muffled protests.

They hovered over the control panel.

"You remember how to work the controls?"

Paire tried to remember the sequence, what buttons to press and in what order. She turned the temperature gauge to the far right, until the needle pointed to 3,000. "Will this wake anyone up?"

"Not around here."

Kasson must have heard them out here, even though they barely spoke above a whisper themselves. His meaty hand thumped on the door, and Paire made out an obscenity. The C-word.

"He'll get louder when I turn it on," Paire said.

"Only for a little while."

Melinda rested her hand on Paire's back, and would have assuredly felt the girl's heart hammering away. "When you're ready, push the button."

Paire pushed a button the size and color of a clown nose. A motor spun to life. Inside, Kasson heard it, and sensed something was wrong. His pounding on the door grew feverish. Paire wondered if he knew what kind of room he now occupied. It would be black as a cave in there, and he might not be able to tell. To the layperson unaccustomed to such things, he might have assumed it was a storage room. Panic gripped him, but the real fear hadn't set in yet.

"That's it. You've done it."

"How long will it take?"

"A little while. Maybe forty minutes to get to that temperature."

"How long before it's over?"

"Maybe a few hours. It will be over before the sun comes up." Paire shivered. "It's getting cold."

"We should go back inside. The machine will do all the work."

"I don't feel right about leaving. I think we should stay here."

"You sure?"

"I want to make sure it's done."

Melinda went inside for just a few minutes, and retrieved a fleece blanket and two bottles of water. They sat on the gravel in silence, close enough to feel the heat from the kiln as if it were a campfire. Kasson slammed against the door even harder when the heat became intolerable. The pounding slowed down, each hit progressively weakening, until he stopped altogether. At some point, he shrieked at a pitch that Paire would have thought him incapable of, although it was quiet as a mouse's *eek* through the door. As soft as a lobster in a boiling pot. She imagined he had caught on fire. The empress would be burning as well. Paire pictured the thick man engulfed in orange frames, his leathery skin slowly charring and wearing off the bones. She wasn't unhappy when she imagined it, because it meant his suffering was close to an end. She wondered if he spent his final moments looking at the painting, content to be wedded to the woman in their tragic demise.

As the sun broke over Brooklyn's warehouses, Paire stopped the motor, and the two women sat together, warmed gently by the stacks of sweltering brick. Paire took hold of Melinda's hand for support, and eventually they went inside to sleep.

When the kiln cooled, Paire made sure she opened the door first. She was afraid that the body might not have completely burned, that Kasson's corpse would be half charred, wearing a twisted death grin. But it was just ashes in there, a small scatter of dust from flesh, bone, birch, and paint, which when swept up would approximate the size of a Cornish game hen. Melinda was right—not even teeth survived. The knife had melted.

They waited until that evening to discard the ashes, and did so in the Gowanus Canal, New York's unofficial dumping ground for the illegally deceased.

CHAPTER 23

Across the dining table, Melinda said, "I have something to tell you."

In 1979, it was reported that Qi Jianyu had left the United States and returned to China, where he lived for the remainder of his life as a professor at the University of Beijing. This report was substantiated through immigration documentation, a few stray photographs of the older Qi in what was unmistakably Tiananmen Square, and a written letter from the Chinese embassy confirming the artist's return to his country of origin.

The documents had all been forged, and the photograph doctored. The ironclad piece of evidence, supplied by the embassy, was authentic but untrue. Various offices in the Chinese government were simply happy to report that the artist had returned to China, because of the positive public relations impact. When they couldn't locate Qi Jianyu, they wouldn't recant their statement, because they didn't want to seem fallible, and twice embarrass the country by stating that its most famous modern artist at the time had, in fact, decided to stay in America. When pressed to back up their statement with proof, preferably a televised statement from the artist, they refused to comply. This was an American problem, and the official statement from the Chinese was that the location of one of its billion citizens did not warrant the full attention of the government.

As Melinda told Paire, the truth was that Qi remained in the United States until he died two years before. He lived anonymously in a flat in Chinatown just off Canal Street. Lost in seas of fellow Chinese, no one looked that hard for him. Once you stripped away the artwork, Qi was an unremarkable-looking man, dressed in generic chinos and golf shirts, his gray hair cropped to bangs in the front. Anglo-Americans didn't give him a second glance.

He lived apart from Melinda's mother, the couple having separated once her mother decided to disown their daughter.

Qi and his daughter visited in secret. They could never meet in public places, but she came to Chinatown. The owners of his apartment building provided Qi Jianyu a rent-free flat and a basement studio. In return, Qi taught art to neighborhood youth. Over time, he established an informal school in that basement. According to what Qi told his daughter, his student shows reminded him of the abandoned barn outside Beijing, where he staged anonymous art shows for the people who dared to create. He taught them so well that a number of his students had become successful artists. Others branched into forgery.

Upon his death, his students forged documentation to show that *The Empress Xiao Zhe Yi, Seated,* had been shipped from an art gallery in Beijing instead of delivered from Canal Street by courier to Melinda Qi in Long Island City. Again, the Chinese government failed to respond to requests to prove the authenticity of these documents. This was another American problem, and by then the Chinese government had no interest in dredging up anything more on Qi Jianyu.

When Melinda finished, Paire couldn't speak. A lump formed in her throat. She didn't know what she could or should say. Something comforting would be appropriate, but nothing comforting came to mind. No one had ever said the right thing when it came to the story of Paire's parents, so she had no way of knowing what the right words might be.

Eventually, Melinda said, "I need to show you something."

They walked across the compound to the warehouse where Melinda stored her finished flowers. They slid open a steel door, and lights flickered overhead above her gargantuan ceramic garden. Following Melinda through the bent leaves and drooping petals, Paire cut across the room as if fumbling through a corn maze. The rear wall of the vault was a large expanse of white drywall. Melinda had hastily constructed this years before, without even painting over the nails that pinned it in place. Melinda ran her fingers along the wall in the far corner of the room. Kicking gently at the plaster, she loosened a rectangular flap by their feet. A piece of drywall no larger than an automobile window had been sawed out of the larger wall and then refitted into place like a jigsaw puzzle. Something that small would have been overlooked. The outline of the hatch would have been indiscernible from across the room if the warehouse were empty. Behind the synthetic orchard, it was perfectly obscured.

Melinda gave it another kick, and the panel dislodged, coughing up a mist of dust.

They shimmied through the hole in the wall, Melinda on her stomach and Paire on her back. The next room was dark until Melinda switched on another bank of fluttering overheads. In a room the size of a squash court, pine crates aligned in rows like oversized dominos, up and down in aisles. They filled the floor.

"He never stopped creating. He just stopped showing," Melinda said.

"How many—"

"Two hundred and six."

"So the empress—"

"Was my least favorite. It was a portrait of my mother. So it was the piece I was happy to sacrifice."

Melinda picked a crowbar up off the floor and handed it to Paire, so she might pry apart a crate and see what was inside.

CHAPTER 24

The MAAC was jammed full of bodies tonight, all tuxedoes and cocktail gowns. It was November, and the sky darkened early, so at eight in the evening it felt like a crisp midnight. Manhattan was a cool monochrome of black, white, and gray this time of year. Inside the museum, the wardrobe of the guests mirrored the palette of the city.

Against a white backdrop, the color of the artwork popped out that much more. Around the cavernous hallways, the Qi retrospective exhibit filled up most of the wall space. They had miraculously found places to hang almost all of the crated works. Viewers gathered in rows around the perimeter of the great hall, breathlessly beholding the individual works and the cumulate impact of the artist's expression.

In the crowd, Melinda Qi was mingling. A reporter held a microphone under her chin to record her thoughts on her father's work. Melinda's teeth gleamed from across the room. She looked happy.

Paire watched Melinda but didn't want to intrude. She stood by the museum entrance, dressed in a gray curve-hugging gown. She wasn't avoiding the crowd so much as admiring a particular piece of work that stood by the entrance, next to the commemorative bust of Gabriel Kasson. The sculpture had been placed so that all the guests who paraded through the entrance tonight would see it.

A young man approached Paire. Probably her age. He stood next to her under the pretense of examining the same piece of artwork. He said, "Cheers," and they clinked glasses. He was Asian, with bronze skin and a gymnastic musculature that his dinner jacket couldn't hide. With a shaved head, his cheekbones seemed more prominent. Paire thought he was handsome. She'd always been dopey for cheekbones.

"Do you know someone?" he asked.

"I know a few people," she said coyly.

"This was a tough invite to get. What's your connection?"

"I used to work at the Fern Gallery," Paire said.

The man's eyes flickered in understanding. By now, everyone in the room had heard about the shootings at the Fern.

"I'm sorry."

She didn't want him to feel guilty for bringing it up. "What brought you here?"

"Qi used to teach me in his apartment complex. I was one of his basement kids." He sipped his champagne. This could have been a boast, but he stated his connection to Qi Jianyu without bragging.

"So are you an artist or a forger?"

The way he laughed reminded her of Lazaro's reaction when she had asked whether he was a criminal. She smiled at him.

He asked, "Did you see the big flowers in the next room? Apparently, that's his daughter's work."

"I've seen them. They're beautiful," Paire said.

"I really like this one," he said, pointing at the sculpture in front of them. "But it doesn't look like anything from him or his daughter."

"It's from a different artist," said Paire.

He read the artist's name on the plaque next to the sculpture. "Funny name, but I like it. Think it's a man or a woman?"

"A woman," she said.

The sculpture in front of them was a six-foot statue of a suit of armor. A samurai suit. Of Japanese, not Chinese, inspiration. Poetic license. It had been crafted tile by tile out of ceramic back in Melinda Qi's studio in Long Island City. Using Melinda's process of fabricating an armature first, a mannequin had been built, then the suit of armor painstakingly fabricated from individual ceramic tiles. The toughest challenge was getting the glaze right, so when it baked it was the right mix of black with hints of deep red and speckles of mottled sea green.

"I like that the armor has breast plates contoured for a woman."

"I like that too," she said.

The man commented, "The armor plates, what do they look like?"

"Lobster shells."

He laughed. "Maybe. Do you think?"

"Yes. Lobsters," Paire said, edging closer to the man, her shoulder softly brushing his arm.

ACKNOWLEDGMENTS

A few years ago I wandered into the Weinstein Gallery in San Francisco, and first learned about the artist Rudolf Bauer. While this book is a work of fiction, I took some inspiration from the relationship between Bauer and his benefactor, Solomon Guggenheim. Maria Echavarri was incredibly generous with her time, providing details about their relationship and pointing me to additional resources.

Several people helped give me a better sense of what life might be like for an artist in China during the 1970s. In particular, Jeff Kelly provided a wonderful overview, and shared stories about his wife, acclaimed artist Hung Liu. Raman Frey gave me insights and pointed me to influential artists from the period. Christina Hadley gave me a better understanding of what it's like to work at an art gallery, and Rachel Ralph fielded questions about the state of contemporary street artists, as well as technical questions about guerrilla installations. I'm also grateful to a certain New York firm for indulging my questions about the techniques used to identify art forgeries. To provide some of Paire Anjou's backstory in Maine, I drew from several friends who live there, especially from my old friend Crash Barry, who told me stories about his experience on lobster boats.

I'm indebted to Randall Klein at Diversion Books for continuing to believe in my writing. The entire team at Diversion Books has contributed to the success of this project, including Mary Cummings, Chris Mahon, and Sarah Masterson Hally. Jennifer Skutelsky provided her expertise editing an early version of the book. Special thanks to my agent and champion Jill Marr for being a fierce advocate and a warm counsel.

I wouldn't have written this book if I hadn't grown up as the son of two painters, Philip and Virginia Dolan. They taught me how to appreciate art, and gave me the desire to create my own. I feel blessed to have a community of friends and family who support me. To my niece and nephew Hannah and Graham, you guys both give heaps of joy. Finally, thank you to Sabrina, for being proud of me whether I win or lose.

ALEX DOLAN is the author of *The Euthanist* and *The Empress of Tempera*. In addition, he hosts the show *Thrill Seekers* on the Authors on the Air Global Radio Network. He is an executive committee member of the San Francisco Bay Area's Litquake festival, and a member of International Thriller Writers and Sisters in Crime. He has recorded four music albums, and has a master's degree in strategic communications from Columbia University.

Visit www.alexdolan.com

Keep reading for
an excerpt from

THE
EUTHANIST

Available now!

CHAPTER 1

Every autumn is tarantula mating season around Mount Diablo. Horny male spiders roam through the twiggy grass to find their soul mates in a sort of spider Burning Man. They say spiders are more afraid of us, but that's bullshit. They don't even see us. They incite terror with their furry little legs and never know the havoc they wreak in our lives. If you were like me and grew up having nightmares about tarantulas, you would probably avoid the area like a nuclear testing zone.

Normally I'd have steered clear, but on this day I was driving through spider country to see a client. Bugs shouldn't scare a grown woman, but driving here made me nervous. A shrink once told me being afraid of spiders meant I wasn't aggressive enough. Then we talked about my stepdad.

He asked, "What is your stepfather like?"

"He's the sort of man who places a dead spider on your alarm clock to see how you react."

"I don't understand the metaphor," he said.

"It's not a metaphor. My stepfather put a dead tarantula on my alarm clock when I was nine. So when it went off, I hit the spider instead of the clock."

My doc dropped his notes. "Why the hell would he do that?"

"Because he's a fucking sociopath. He sat by my bed when it happened, I think just so he could see the look on my face."

"How did you react?"

"How do you think? I screamed my head off."

The shrink had eyeballed me the way that a psychic magician looked at a spoon he wanted to bend. I think he was wondering if

I was lying, and if not, what he should do with me. "Do you speak to him?"

"Not since he went to prison."

After Gordon's spider stunt, big hairy bugs petrified me. The alarm clock wasn't the only time he pulled that crap either. He hid another one in my underwear drawer, and another at the bottom of a Balinese tin box where my mom held her "guilt" chocolate. The fear wasn't irrational, not if you half expected them to pop up like Easter eggs. I still shake out my shoes in the mornings, in case there's one curled up in the toe. Once I was old enough to have my own apartment, a Zen chime dinged across the bedroom in the morning, so I had nothing to slap on the nightstand.

Because of my fear of spiders, I cautiously rounded the hairpin turns through the foothills of Clayton. Hands at five and seven o'clock. One of those fuckers came out of nowhere—a brown spider the size of my fist boogied across the road. If I'd seen it coming, maybe I would have sped up and smushed it under a tire. But it flew into the road like it was in the Olympic trials, and, for whatever reason, I jammed on the brakes. On this vacant road with the paper clip bends, the car *erked* to a standstill. The spider paused. Tarantulas are predators themselves, so they know what hunting behavior looks like. It sensed the enormity of the vehicle, its hot breath and growling motor hovering over it. For a moment, it might have actually been afraid. But then it skittered across the asphalt and into the wild brush off the shoulder. Maybe later when it wooed its amour, it would recount this story so it could get some spider cooch.

My hands strangled the wheel, forearms buzzing with the motor's vibration. I hated myself for being spooked.

Behind me, the driver of a matte brick truck blasted the horn. I found the honk comforting, human. I wasn't afraid of people who weren't my stepdad, not even a big ugly guy like this one with the Civil War sideburns. The horn ripped a second time. Stopped in the road like a moron, I might have felt bad, but he mouthed swears at me in the rearview. His grill kissed my bumper, and I could feel the tremor of his engine. Maybe I didn't step on the gas because I wanted to provoke a reaction. My shrink liked to tell me I was combative. Whatever. If he stepped out of his rust monster, I'd make quick work of his knees with the tire iron I kept on the passenger floor. I made him go around me, smirking at his tobacco-spit frown as he passed. If I were dressed down he might have called me a bitch, but one look at me and he diverted eyes back to the road. If you stare at someone just the right way, they'll know they're in danger. Or maybe the wig just threw him off.

I remembered my client, Leland Mumm, was waiting for me. He didn't deserve someone to come late with shaky hands, whether those shakes came from arachnophobia or road rage. Not today.

IPF, or idiopathic pulmonary fibrosis, was killing Leland Mumm. Since his diagnosis three years ago, my client's lungs had stiffened with scar tissue. He described his breathing with two words: shredding lungs. Talking hurt, so he chose his words parsimoniously. For example, he would never have used the word "parsimoniously." Leland's lungs no longer transferred oxygen to his bloodstream, so the rest of his organs didn't get the oxygen they needed. Piece by piece, his insides were slowly suffocating.

Brutal way to go. Not Desdemona's gracious death in bush-league productions of Othello. From what Leland described, it was more like a pincushion bursting in the chest. Doctors weren't much help, because medicine didn't really understand the disease. With IPF, the agony is constant, and it can take five years to die.

In Leland's video interviews, he had trouble sitting up straight. He tipped to the side after a few minutes. Eventually we had to tape him in bed. Not the most flattering angle, but I adjusted the lighting to minimize the eye rings.

The video conveyed personal messages to friends and family. Last wishes. I burned DVDs to be mailed out when he passed, so he could explain why he was doing something most people would think was nuts, even selfish. Ten years ago, before I got started, clients might have sent their last messages by post. Some still wrote letters. I preferred video because it felt more intimate. In case cops in black riot gear rammed my door, the video also proved I was working with my client's consent.

When we first met, Leland could manage more words before his lungs pinched. He insisted we record a message to his wife, who had passed away a few years ago. In short bursts, he pieced a story together about when they first dated. The moment he realized he loved her. They were walking along the endless Berkeley Pier when a fisherman yanked a crab out of the Bay and it flew into her. Leland had known then he wanted to protect her. I'll admit, I admired the chivalry. When he got to the word "crab," he twisted in the sheets with a shock of pain.

I spoke to his pulmonologist by phone, but, paranoid about the legal fallout, she refused to meet me in person. Dr. Jocelyn Thibeault. She sounded austere, over-enunciating her English. I imagined her thin with telephone pole posture, probably in her fifties. She mailed Leland's medical records to a P.O. Box so I could peek at the X-rays. I'm no pulmonary specialist, but the doctor talked me through the radiograph, so I could see the mess of scar tissue on his lungs.

As with all clients, I met Leland roughly four weeks ago. A month before the *terminus*. That term feels cold to me, but I wasn't the one who coined it. I suppose you have to give some kind of name to an event that important. In any case, it's not a word I would ever use around Leland Mumm.

Leland wanted to die the first day I met him. He didn't want time to think it over, because he didn't want to lose his nerve. But I insisted on a waiting period to give my clients the chance to get cold feet. It was my own Brady Bill. Two other clients had changed their minds at their moments of truth. During the first meeting clients were eager. They thirsted for relief and could forget that they needed to put their affairs in order. The good-byes. The legal documents. Sometimes a final house cleaning. When we met, Leland didn't want me to leave. He pulled at my dress with a weak hand, imploring me to ease his pain. The best I could do was morphine.

In most cases, I'd meet the family, usually a spouse. Leland didn't have anyone he wanted me to meet. I didn't push him. A typical client would introduce me to his doctor, but because of her qualms, Her Majesty Dr. Thibeault refused to be in the same room as the executioner. So it was just Leland and me.

Leland was young for a client—only fifty-two, according to his records. He had a long build, and I suspected he'd had more meat on him before the disease. IPF had eaten away at the muscle, especially in his arms and legs.

Over the past month, I visited his hillside ranch house in Clayton once a week. I'd gotten to know the ochre peels of the bathroom wallpaper, the bend where the wood veneer had pulled away from the wall. This was the house where Leland grew up, and it looked like it hadn't changed much. Leland didn't open windows either, turning the house into a gardener's hotbed. Stale sweat and urine fermented the air.

While I helped with the good-byes and the legal documents, we chatted. Leland admitted he didn't have many visitors, and he seemed happy to hear another voice in his home. Because his condition ruined his lungs, he wanted me to do most of the talking. He asked a lot of questions. This was natural. People are curious. People are especially curious about the woman who's going to kill them. I shared anecdotes about myself, but never real facts. For my own safety, I didn't use my real name. My work required anonymity. My parents also raised me with an audacious sense of theatricality. If I were honest with myself, I also enjoyed having a stage persona.

Kali. That's the name I used with clients.

Kali is the four-armed Hindu goddess of death. She has been appropriated by hipster flakes as a symbol of feminine power. Maybe that's fair too. But make no mistake, Kali is a destructress. In one of her hands she holds a severed head.

I know, I know, so fucking dramatic. I'll admit to a little cultural appropriation for choosing a name like that. I don't know squat about Hindu culture. I don't even practice yoga. Since I was so gung ho about picking the name of a goddess, I could have found something more fitting. The best match might have been Ixtab, the Mayan goddess of suicide, also known as Rope Woman; but really, who was going to pronounce that? I almost chose Kalma, a Finnish goddess of death and decay, whose name meant, "the stench of corpses." But way too gruesome, right? I wanted to comfort my clients. Kali sounded like a normal name. I needed a fake identity, but I didn't want to be flippant about my work.

Because of his staccato breathing, Leland sometimes needed two breaths to cough out my name. "Ka-li." He pronounced it the way people pronounce "Cali" instead of saying "California." Some clients pronounced it "Kay-lee." It's actually "Kah-lee," but I never corrected anyone. It was a fake name, so what did it matter? I wasn't going to be the snooty five-star waiter who tells patrons it's pronounced *fi-LAY* instead of *fillettes*.

Leland was slow with words, but that didn't mean he was speechless. To imagine the way he talked, you'd have to insert ellipses every two or three words, and not where you'd want to put them. On our last visit, he asked with effort, "What does your dad think of all this?"

This edged against my boundaries, but I indulged the question. "He died." *Dad, not stepdad.*

"Sorry."

"Me too. He was a good dad."

"Did you help him pass?"

"Not unless I talked him to death."

"What was his name?" We both knew this was forbidden territory, but he couldn't help himself.

"Mr. Kali."

He smiled. We were just playing.

Slowly, I found out more about my client. A geologist, Leland spent most of his career working for mining companies. The hardest stint he'd ever pulled was a gold mine up in Canada, within a hundred miles of the Arctic Circle. As a sci-fi geek, he called it Ice Planet Hoth. In the summer he couldn't sleep. In the winter he drank too much and got belligerent. He showed me a scar on his stomach from where a feverish colleague stabbed him after twenty days without sun. It's not unreasonable to guess that he'd gotten lung disease after years of particulate pollution. Then again, he'd been a smoker for decades. After his diagnosis, the company gave him a settlement. Not fat enough to live like a rap mogul, but enough to keep the house and feed himself.

I was getting close to Leland's, curving through the octopus-branched oaks in the Mount Diablo foothills. Parched grass the color of camel fur scrambled up the slow grade where the hiking trails picked up. The neighborhood, if you could call it a neighborhood, was a sparse network of small homes buffered by a half mile of wild land. Leland told me wild boar roamed back here. That might have been horseshit, but I believed it.

Leland lived in a tumbledown single-story home with loose brown shingles. The roof slouched, and the sun and rain had wrung out the sides like driftwood. It had the sort of beat-up charm that might attract attention from budding photographers and painters. I thought scientists made a lot of money, but not him. Perhaps he spent it on something else.

I parked alongside his cream sedan, a Chevrolet Monte Carlo from the eighties, which, like the house, must have been perfect three decades ago. Like one of those old refrigerators that kids locked themselves in. *A classic.* Now the mountain's clay dust streaked the tires and the trunk didn't close all the way.

The neighborhood had banished noisemaking, unless you counted hawk screeches. So Leland probably heard my engine. He would be expecting me, but I stayed in the car a moment longer to collect myself. This was all part of the preparation. After five years and twenty-seven clients, my nerves still rattled before the final meeting. This was more stressful than my paramedic work. When I charged into buildings in my other job, there was at least a chance I might save someone.

My ritual was similar before every terminus. I used my rental car as a dressing room—a green room, if you will. Any driver who's spewed hellfire at another motorist can tell you cars offer the delusion of privacy. So in my car I soothed myself, pretending no one was watching. My particular mode of relaxation began by flexing my body. I mean toes to top—every muscle. It sounds stupid, but it works. Flex and release. Flex and release. Loosens up the whole body. Prior to something this important, it also reminded me I was strong. Everyone has a point of pride, and mine was muscles. Mine weren't so big that they were scary, but notable for a girl.

I adjusted a purple wig so the bangs paralleled my eyebrows and painted lavender liner on my eyelids. My lips darkened to burnt wood. The last patches of makeup came from two dainty ziplock packets in my purse. If it weren't for the gray coloring, the packets might have looked like flour or cocaine. They were tiny ounces of ash, two bags worth. I dipped a pinky in each, and applied a smidge to each side of my neck. Nothing to alter the overall look of my costume—the smears of ash were added for my own benefit and undetectable to my clients.

This particular outfit matched Leland's tastes, but I always dressed loud for this work. An old boyfriend once said I had a kitten face. Another boy said my face was too soft to be on a body like mine. I took this to mean that people thought my features looked infantile, or at the very least juvenile, and I didn't want my clients feeling like some toddler was steering them into the afterlife. The makeup matured me, sharpening my features, so I looked fierce, even lethal. Like a scimitar-wielding death goddess. When I looked in the mirror, the severity of my face now fit the character I adopted for this work. Kali stared sharply back at me.

Rental cars have such sweet air conditioning, and as soon as I stepped outside I started to sweat. Sun scorched the driveway here on the ass-side of the mountain. The wet warmth of the morning foretold a muggy afternoon. I dabbed my forehead with a tissue. I didn't get two steps out of the car when I saw the black spider running across the walkway. Jesus, they moved fast. And this was a big one, the size of a goldfinch. But being Kali charged me with courage, and I thrummed with epinephrine. Without hesitation, I brought my heel down and crunched it like an ice cream cone, scraping my sole off on the pavement.

When I entered, the fetor almost pillowed me. Leland didn't

smell like other clients. Most smelled like they were dying, but this was worse than death. The air rotted like a summer dumpster. I stifled an involuntary gag, nothing Leland could have seen. According to Dr. Thibeault, a nurse cleaned him every few days, but it didn't help with the fumes. This suffering man managed to emit a decay that seemed inhuman.

With a compact layout, the main living area was open with oak floors and a window the expanse of a wall. Because the building squatted on the slope of Mount Diablo, the view faced away from the summit toward the minor rolling hills, without any homes to interrupt the scenery. Architects built-in custom cabinets, originally intended for dishware were now taken up by clothing and medical supplies. Outlined by sunlight, Leland lay in bed where I'd left him. Three weeks ago we'd moved the mattress to the living room because it gave him a better view. Now he swaddled himself in white sheets, his head rolled to the side that offered him sun and hills. He reminded me of Winslow Homer's *The Gulf Stream*, the black sailor on the brink of dehydration among the sharks.

I eased the door shut, but I still woke him.

"Kali." Leland's voice trailed by the end of my name. With effort he lifted his arm to wave.

"I'm here." I went to his bed and kissed him on the forehead. He tasted briny.

Leland was a dark man with a gaunt face and high cheekbones. If I were to guess, I'd say his lineage was Ethiopian or Somali. A descendant of African runway models. I'm tall for a woman, but he had several inches on me. Maybe six two. It was hard to tell since I never saw him standing. Leland Mumm was bedridden by the time I met him. He shuffled to the bathroom and back, but never during my visits. The way he looked now, he seemed like he'd collapse if he tried to stand. His bones stuck out all over. He didn't keep photos of himself around, so I couldn't tell how much body mass he might have lost. At this point, he couldn't have weighed much more than me.

I rumbled a chair across the floor and sat beside the bed, covering his hand with mine. "You've got spiders outside."

"I know," he rasped. "They're everywhere."

"If it makes you feel any better, you have one less."

He laughed faintly. "Big or small?"

"The size of a volleyball."

"And you survived."

"Barely."

Leland's wide smile reminded me of Steven Tyler. I've heard that teeth are the bellwethers of someone's overall health, but that's a load of crap. Leland Mumm was about to die, and his enamel gleamed. Not a filling in there.

He complimented my clothes. "Nice getup."

Death should feel special, so I always dressed for my final meetings. What, was I going to waltz in with mustard-stained sweats? What I wore completely depended on the person. For Leland I wore a form-fitting white cocktail dress with purple piping to match the wig and the eyeliner. As a self-proclaimed sci-fi geek, Leland wanted me to dress like the kind of expo booth hottie you'd find at Comic-Con. Back when he could walk, he apparently made annual pilgrimages so he could meet Stan Lee. Clients have asked for weirder outfits—one wanted a nun habit, and one wanted me in scrubs so I would seem more like a medical professional.

"That wig. Like the Jetsons." Leland's laugh hacked up something. Weak as he was, he still ogled my legs. He didn't keep photos of his wife out, so I couldn't tell if I was even his type. But I didn't mind. If I were in his boat, I'd want something decent to look at on my last day.

"You requested it."

"You look good. Real good," he wheezed and squeezed my hand. "Gloves to match."

Purple satin opera gloves stretched from my fingers to elbows. "As good as latex. I can still handle the delicate stuff."

"Gloves, like a criminal," Leland mused. "You feel like a criminal?"

A client had never asked me anything like this, and Leland was usually so playful I would have shrugged it off, but there was something abrasive in his tone. Something in the way he shifted his look from my left eye to my right, possibly trying to detect some guilt in my reaction. I had to catch myself so I didn't rebuke him. There was that combative streak the doctors always complained about. Like a jack-in-the-box, it sprang out so fast, and took so much more effort to push back down. "So long as there are laws, I'll feel like a criminal breaking them. But I don't feel like it's wrong." I stripped off the gloves. "We don't need these." With bare hands I touched his hair as if primping a floral bouquet.

He wore oversize flannel pajamas with trains on them. Such a sweet nerd of a man.

"You hot in these?"

"I get cold." He drew his blankets closer to his body, withdrawing his arm under the covers like an eel back into its crevice. He shut his eyes, and I noted the slight tremor of his lids before he opened them and nodded to the nightstand. "It's all there."

A stack of documents fanned across the small table. He'd also been reading Dr. Jeffrey Holt's *The Peaceful End*, marked toward the back with a green plastic book clip shaped like a tongue. Most of my clients had read it, and all of them had heard of it. A handbook for people who want to take control over their own deaths, it covers everything anyone needs to know about assisted suicide and provides a selection of methods. A popular option described is the bag-and-helium method. Basically, a turkey-sized oven bag hooks up to the same kind of tank used to inflate balloons. Many have tried to convince me how quick and painless it is, but I've never met someone who really wants to die with a bag over his head. But the book is important in many ways, and Leland Mumm followed many of its recommendations, which included preparing the materials that now lay on his nightstand. In addition to the DVDs, these included a living will and durable power of attorney document. Finally, a sheet of paper with thick red letters: DNR. *Do not resuscitate.* I would leave this on Leland's chest when I left, in case anyone came afterward and thought to revive him.

I opened one fat envelope with my name on it. Leland had given me a quarter-inch of cash. As I thumbed through it, he noted my confusion. "That's for you."

I reminded him, "I don't take money."

"It's a donation."

"Someone else can have it."

"Who else?" He spaced out, perhaps remembering his wife.

This wasn't the first time someone tried to pay me. Some people weren't comfortable receiving anything unless they gave something in return. "Thank you." I slid the envelope into my satchel. After this was over, I'd put it back. I wouldn't take the money, but I wouldn't insult him by refusing it either.

"How are you feeling?"

"How do you think?" The playful tone ebbed out of his voice. "God awful."

He seemed afraid, and I pressed my fingers into his palm.

"You're strong," he remarked. Then with several breath breaks, he asked, "Can we please do this? The wait is killing me."

"You're ready?"

He answered without hesitation. "I was ready weeks ago."

I unlatched my leather satchel and assembled my equipment. This part was the hardest for me, and I found it difficult to keep from tearing up. Death is sad. Every time. Not even the process of death so much as the frailty that leads to it, the helplessness. It always got to me. Leland Mumm also felt different than other clients, and I'm not just saying that in hindsight. My fellow paramedics—the ones who were parents—were the ones shell-shocked when they saw kids get hurt. Similarly, I thought that since Leland Mumm was roughly the same age my dad would have been, this hit close to home. But Leland didn't really remind me of my dad. He just didn't have anyone. Without family and friends to surround him during his quietus, the bleakness of his solitude ate at me.

I wish I'd learned to ape the poker faces I saw on other

paramedics and docs, but I never mastered detachment. As I prepped the needle, my stomach churned. It always felt like this, and I always considered it a weakness. No one wanted to see his personal Hindu goddess get all blubbery. To stop my eyes from watering, I practiced a look that made it seem like I was concentrating on my job with laser precision.

"Different kind of needle."

"It's called a butterfly syringe." Also known as a winged infusion set, this was a tool of the trade. Kevorkian himself used these. Most of my clients were on the older side, and the needle was designed to ease into smaller and more brittle veins.

"Walk me through it again," he said. Under the covers, he wrapped his arms tightly around his trunk, embracing himself. Many clients liked to talk through our final meeting so they could diffuse the fear.

"The first dose puts you to sleep. The second will turn off the lights."

"How many people have you helped?" He asked.

His tone shifted again, and now he sounded suspicious. It triggered my fiery impulses, sending a hot swell through my blood, and requiring a deep breath to calm down again. "Enough to know what I'm doing." The answer was twenty-seven.

"You'll find the vein all right? You're not going to play darts with my arm?"

"You shouldn't feel more than a pinch." I was a trained paramedic, and kept up my accuracy by sticking needles into oranges at home.

He breathed louder, faster. "I'm scared."

"I know. You know you're in control."

"I know that." He seemed certain on this point.

"Are you sure you want this?"

He nodded, maybe too eagerly. "Badly."

"I can give you a sedative if you want."

"I don't want more needles."

I shook an orange pill bottle from my satchel. "Diazepam. Valium. It can take the edge off."

His eyes danced around the room while he considered it. "How long?"

"You'd feel it in under a half hour."

"How long after you stick me?"

"After I give you the first injection, you should fall asleep in under a minute."

"Stick with plan A." I stroked his arm. An invisible layer of semidry sweat had greased his skin. He tried to smile, but his mouth just twitched. He ran his tongue between his lips and teeth to try and moisten his mouth.

I readied the needle at his arm and tried to find a vein. He was dehydrated, so I had to tap a few times. "Do you want to close your eyes for the pinch?"

"Give me one more moment," he implored.

"All the time you want."

"I'd like to pray." Leland had never brought up religion, and this wasn't my area of expertise, but other clients had asked. He held my hand to his chest, and his ribs quaked with a violent heartbeat. "Pray with me."

"Of course."

We closed our eyes.

Lost in a meditative moment, I almost ignored the sensation of something hard brushing against my wrist. Hard, like a bracelet. Cold metal pressed into my skin, first lightly and then sharply. Then I heard the click. Eyes open, I saw a gleam of silver steel clasp around my right wrist. A chrome chain draped from the cuff in a wide arc to a thick teak bedpost topped with a carved pinecone. Leland Mumm had chained my arm to the bed frame.

When he spoke, his voice was clear and resonant. "Kali, I'm with the police."

Trigger temper. I latched onto Leland's neck with one hand. My volatile impulses set loose, I tried to crush his windpipe. I'd never attempted to hurt someone like this, but I dug my knuckles deep into his neck. To protect himself, he hunched his shoulders and stiffened his tendons into wires. His muscles flexed with a shocking power. This man was suddenly vital and dangerous. Leaning over him, I bore my weight down on his body. When my thumb wormed into the ribbed hose of his trachea, he gagged. His hands clawed at my arms, but in my furious blackout I kept my arms stiff as dowels. My palm clamped down over his arteries, and the way his eyelids flickered, I could tell he was losing oxygen fast. A few more seconds, he might have blacked out. I might have killed him.

Something fast flew into my face, like a kamikaze bird smacking a window. His fist hammered my left cheekbone, and my head snapped to the side. The impact shook me loose. My fingers lost their grip. Slackening with the force of the punch, I slid off the mattress. When my skull struck the floor, needles burst through my brain before the pitch darkness enveloped me.

CHAPTER 2

"You went rabid on me," he said, delighting in my ridicule. There were no ellipses between the words now.

Leland only had a few seconds after he knocked me down, but he made use of them. He flopped me onto the bed and kicked my leather satchel across the room. Then he patted me down for weapons, even though the most dangerous thing on me was the syringe. He rolled that across the floor, too.

Our positions reversed: I lay on the death-stink covers, tethered like a sacrificial goat. The mattress was still warm from his body heat. Leland was on his feet, looking down at me. *Miracle recovery*. His locomotive pajamas sagged at the crotch.

With my left arm pulled across my body, I yanked the chrome chain taut with the hope that it might decapitate the carved pinecone atop the bedpost. Leland kept his distance, which was a smart move. As soon as my head cleared, I kicked like crazy. When I couldn't reach him with my boots, I grabbed what I could with my free hand and chucked it at him, including his coffee-stained copy of *The Peaceful End*. The green plastic book clip fell out and into the covers, and the book only flapped a few feet. Envelopes whirled like Frisbees, but few hit him, and nothing hurt him.

Leland gave me the same smirk as when he'd ask, "When are you going to tell me your real name?" But he'd mutated into a different man, fast and formidable.

A residual ache swelled under my left eye, and Leland appeared blurry as he hovered over me. I savagely tore at my handcuffs. As a firefighter, I should have known this wouldn't have gotten me anywhere, but the pain and panic prevented rational thought.

It's not that I'd never been punched. On plenty of calls, an addict half out of her senses could crazy it up and clobber me when I didn't expect it. It wasn't ever pleasant, but the shock of being punched was worse than the pain itself. Years of sparring taught me how to take a shot, and how to hit back. Leland Mumm hit hard, but he wasn't Wladimir Klitschko. Just a tad stronger than my stepdad. He'd caught me off guard and landed a lucky blow. If I'd been ready for it, he wouldn't have pushed me off my feet.

He seemed to marvel at my flushed face and gurgle of obscenities. The past several moments had changed me too. My legs thrashed whip-wild, and my growls and swears sounded feral.

The chain held. After a few minutes, my wrist burned and my lungs heaved. My skin pinked around a thread of crimson where the cuff sliced a faint incision line. I wasn't about to break the bed frame. Not teak. The wood was too dense to crack the bedpost and too heavy for me to upturn the whole thing and whack apart the joints.

I split my attention between my shackles and Leland. I was still finding new pain from the punch, shooting down through my jaw now, and found it impossible to concentrate on any singular thing. I stared at Leland's face above me, trying to focus on the tip of his nose with my foggy eye. Leland seemed taller now, or maybe that illusion was created from him on his feet and me on the mattress. When he sneered, all those healthy teeth reminded me what a goddamned sucker I'd been. I should have known something was up when I saw those pearlies. What I wouldn't have given to chip a few with a boot heel.

"Who are you?" I ran a finger over the handcuff keyhole, as good as spinning a safe dial without the combination.

I kept expecting Leland to climb on top of me, but he hadn't moved since he shackled me. "I told you. Cop," he said with no frailty in his voice.

"No, you're not. No fucking cop would chain me to a bed. Punch me in the face."

"Sorry you think that. Because that's exactly what a cop would do."

Blood warmed the plumping welt under my eye. Where the cheek split, a trickle ran down my face and tickled the skin over where it hurt. "Fucker—I'm bleeding!"

"Believe what you want, but you're good and busted."

"Bullshit. What about Miranda?"

"Keep your mouth shut if you want. Call a lawyer when you can. That about cover it?"

I rattled my handcuffs, but if I fought anymore, I was going to spring a vein. Instead, I looked for weapons. I'd thrown all the loose stuff at Leland, leaving nothing on the nightstand. Pivoting off the mattress and stretching as far as the chain would allow, I stood on the floor and mule-kicked the nightstand at him. The flimsy table was light enough to sail at him, but he sidestepped it like fucking Fred Astaire. When it splintered on the wall behind him, he seemed amused. I went back to fidgeting with the lock, desperate enough to try working my pinky nail into the keyhole.

"It's not going to work," he said.

Handcuffs were easy. All I needed was a paper clip to spring it. But I didn't have a paper clip. As Leland predicted, my pinky nail didn't fit. All my tools were in my cowhide satchel, and that satchel sat by Leland's ankle. Frustrated, I grasped the chain with both hands and tug-o-warred with the bedpost, but only succeeded in tearing the skin on my palms.

"You're not going to pull the chain apart. You're going to hurt yourself."

The friction of steel against flesh dug down to the bone, and that hairline incision in my wrist began leaking rivulets of blood. The pain was enough for me to give it a rest.

The loss of control overwhelmed me. I couldn't control my own body, not with my heart shuddering and my lungs on fire. I couldn't remember breathing this hard, not even during the physical aptitude test for the fire department, and for that I had to sprint up and down six flights of stairs with fifty pounds of gear. Worse yet, I couldn't control the man in the room. Leland was out of my reach and unpredictable. If I expected him to zig, he might zag.

He spoke like a toastmaster. "We're going to have a long talk, but there's something I've really got to do first." He unbuttoned his flannel pajama top, button by yellow button. When I saw his bare stomach, I wrenched the chain again until the pain shooting up my arm made my shoulder spasm.

He bunched the flannel and absently tossed it against the wall. I didn't want to look at him, but I felt like I needed to monitor Leland in case he came at me. I imagined him on top of me, his hot mothball breath steaming up my nostrils. The baggy clothes had hidden his musculature. Leland Mumm was thin but tight, a welterweight. *Sneaky mofo.*

"Kali. You killed nine people." Again, it was twenty-seven. He'd counted wrong. "Did you expect this would have a happy ending?"

I writhed against my clasp. Smears of my blood rouged the sheets.

"Jesus Christ, calm down!" In the same breath, he pulled his pajama bottoms over his hips, and they dropped to his ankles. "You can't imagine how good it feels to take these off." He wore stained white briefs. In a moment he'd be naked. "I'm sorry to be so open about this, but we're on intimate terms by now, aren't we?" I dry heaved. He snapped. "For Christ's sake, get a hold of yourself. It's going to be a long day for you."

I waited for him to charge at me. My mind raced, fishing for defensive options. He was naked, I reminded myself, and I was clothed. I could squat 260 pounds. His nuts were right there at the level of the mattress. If he ran straight at me, I might crack his pelvis. I drew my knee to my chest, readying my left leg, the strong one, for a kick.

But Leland turned and walked through the bathroom door.

A few seconds later, the shower ran.

"I hope you don't mind," he called through the open door. "I have to get clean. You have no idea what it takes to stink like you're dying." His voice sounded like it came through a soup can. "I figured you'd have been around death enough to smell it on people. That means I haven't showered for a week. I'll be honest, that was tough. You ever been that long without a shower?"

Now that he was out of the room, I fished around the sheets, in case I could find a stray object under the covers narrow enough to stand in for a paper clip. *Nothing.* The entire house had been staged, and since no one really lived there, no one would have carelessly discarded items during day-to-day routines. Leland had only packed in enough props to make the place believable. I'd knocked a pill bottle off the nightstand. It was close enough that I could snare it with a boot, but when I twisted off the lid, the bottle spilled out breath mints.

He repeated himself. "Kali, have you ever been that long without a shower?" Presumably, he was checking to make sure I hadn't popped out of my cuffs.

"Yes," I spat. I felt between the mattresses for a trace of something, maybe a safety pin. *Nothing.*

"You know what the secret is to smelling like death?" He paused for effect. "FlyNap! You ever heard of it?"

This time I didn't wait for him to ask again. Maybe if I kept our banter going, we'd keep things congenial. "Fuck no." Maybe not that congenial.

He rinsed out his mouth in the shower cascade and coughed the backwash into the tub. Revolting. When someone is repulsed by the sound of body noises like eating, there's a name for that. *Misophonia.* Mine flared up listening to the swish of his saliva while he hawked up the shower water.

Soon enough the pipes whined and the water stopped. The curtain ripped back. Leland appeared in the doorway, dripping with a terrycloth towel wrapped around his waist. "FlyNap!" He sounded like a kid excited by something he learned in class. "It's an anesthetic they use to put drosophila to sleep—fruit flies."

I positioned myself back on the bed so I could kick easily. "I know what drosophilas are."

"Of course you do," he said dismissively. "I guess geneticists use the stuff to put flies to sleep, so they can count out which ones have red eyes, or some nonsense like that. It has the same compounds you find in rotting meat. So after a week of not showering, the added element you're smelling is a few drops of…"

"FlyNap. I get it."

"You know what you get? A perfect death cologne. I was worried you couldn't be fooled, but I'm very happy you were." He disappeared from the doorway. "You have no idea how bad it was. I mean, you only had to be around that smell for a couple hours tops. I had to live with it for weeks. A few days ago, I had to run a menthol stick under my nose just to get some relief."

The master of the quick change came out in charcoal slacks and a T-shirt. Over the tee he buttoned up a blue Oxford, like he was getting ready for a business meeting. "You ever heard of Richard Angelo?"

"Is that the inventor of FlyNap?"

He scoured my face for signs of sarcasm. "He was a nurse. I'm sorry, let me restate that. He was a murderer. He killed ten patients using pancuronium bromide, a muscle relaxant."

"Never heard of him."

"How about Efren Saldivar? Called him 'The Angel of Death.' Respiratory therapist, probably killed more than a hundred patients. Drug of choice? Pancuronium."

"I don't know who those people are. And I'm not one of them."

"Pancuronium's a funny drug. They use it in executions. You probably know that."

I did. It was one of three drugs. Sodium thiopental to induce coma. Pancuronium bromide to shut down respiratory systems. An optional third would be potassium chloride to stop the heart. But what he didn't say was that they used the same cocktail without the potassium chloride in the Netherlands, where they had done the greatest work around euthanasia to date.

"Nine other people in Northern California dead with 'DNR' cards on them. Pancuronium in the blood." He snatched the syringe from the floor and flicked the barrel. "And I bet you I'd find it in here too." He studied me, maybe waiting for a change in my mood, an "I gotta come clean" moment.

My mood did change. I grew more afraid of him because the danger he represented was turning from a physical threat to something much worse. My diaphragm trembled as I forgot how to breathe.

"That's why this is happening to you."

He grabbed my satchel off the floor. Seated in the chair by the bed—now dragged outside my kicking radius—Leland dumped out its contents. "Let's see what we have."

A different kind of panic crept into me. This guy might really be a policeman. If he was telling the truth, he was going to arrest me. We'd mentioned Miranda—maybe he had already arrested me. I thought about having all my dark secrets exposed for my shame and others' judgment. All the infinite possibilities of my life whittled down to captivity. Beyond butterflies now, I really thought I might puke. This man had tricked me; and above everything else, I felt indignant that all of this had come about because I'd been the rube in an elaborate prank.

I talked so I wouldn't hurl. "You're not even sick, are you?"

Leland picked through my purse litter without looking up. "'Fraid not."

"You look sick."

"Just skinny. Always was."

"You should get yourself checked. I've seen a lot of sick people, and you look sick."

"In the pink. Just had my annual physical. I have a quick metabolism." He found my backup syringe and squinted into the empty barrel.

"You had medical records. X-rays."

"Borrowed from a hospital."

I remembered the phantom phone physician. "Dr. Thibeault. Who's she?"

"My partner." He unscrewed my eyeliner and sniffed the brush.

"Where is she now?"

Maybe he would have answered, but he jubilated in something he snatched off the floor. "Yahtzee!" He held up my driver's license, eyeballing the photo and comparing it to the purple-wigged gal on the bed. *Crap.* I felt my wig. In the scuffle it had been pulled off kilter, and some of my own plain caramel-colored hair showed through.

Leland's joy didn't linger. Not when he read the name on the license. "Martha Stewart."

This should go without saying, but the license was phony. I sassed, "I have to explain it a lot, but it's what my parents wanted."

Sunlight glinted off the lamination as he scanned for the golden seal of California. "You actually get by with this?"

"I rented a car with it."

"People are morons." Now he rolled my lipstick between his fingers, uncapped it and twisted the charcoal tip out of the tube. "You're smart, I'll give you that. Fake license. Rental car."

On this point, I felt victorious. Anything with my real name on it was back in my apartment. "Sorry to disappoint."

Examining my ID again, he mused at my photo. "You have a great smile. When you do smile, that is."

I didn't want this man judging my appearance, for better or worse. Plus, he was patronizing me. I looked goofy and toothy in that photo, surprised at my own happiness as if the prom king had just asked me onto the dance floor. I have pale and pinkish skin, but I'd been out in some sun back then. The sun brought out my nose freckles, and my teeth stood out like marshmallows in cocoa.

He found cash in my purse, and not just what he tried to give me as a donation. "You just carry cash? No credit cards? What happens if you run out of gas?"

"I plan ahead." More than he knew. In addition to the purse money, I toted a hundred-dollar fold in my underwear.

"Kali, Kali, Kali." He said my name like it was a dessert he was about to gorge. "Why don't you tell me who you are?"

I tried to confirm for myself that he was a police detective. "Where is your partner?"

"Somewhere busting some other jackass," he said halfheartedly. "You're not going to give me your name?"

"What do you think?"

"Worth asking, though." He rustled a packet of travel tissues decorated with illustrations of She-Hulk. To himself, he noted, "Cartoon superheroes. Interesting." Then to me: "We're going to be at this a while, huh?"

"Looks like it."

Leland poked through the items on the floor with a pen and found my car keys. He dangled them in front of his nose as if trying to spy a wasp in amber. "Now we're getting somewhere. Don't go anywhere."

He bounded off the chair and walked out the front door, leaving me alone. The door gaped.

As soon as he was out of sight, I was back at my handcuffs like I was buried alive and tunneling my way out. I rolled out of bed as far as the chain would allow and fished under the pillows and sheets to find something that could pick a lock. Nothing bigger than a sandy breadcrumb ran between my fingers.

A moment later, my rental car honked as he tested the locks. Hopefully he'd comb through it a while. Nothing of mine was in there.

I thought about screaming for help, but the first person on the scene would be Leland Mumm. If I made enough noise, maybe a distant neighbor would phone in a disturbance. That just meant more cops would show up. I remembered that Leland never showed me a badge. If he wasn't a detective, then I'd be inviting law enforcement into a situation, putting myself in serious legal jeopardy. Then again, if Leland wasn't with the police, he might do much worse if no one came. I told myself that if he wanted to rape or kill me, he might have gotten started by now—but I wasn't sure.

My fingers poked something sharp and thin by a leg of the bed frame. A toothpick? A paper clip? Whatever it was, it was a *prize*. I snatched it. It was the green plastic book clip he'd used for *The Peaceful End*. I pinched it gently, and then snapped off the delicate loop around the outside. The fragment gave me a piece of curved plastic that fit into the keyhole. I worked the green plastic shard around the hole, but popping the lock was harder than when I'd practiced. My hands quivered. Leland would return any moment. Every few seconds, I snapped my head over my shoulder to check the front door.

While my right hand maneuvered the plastic, my left hand shivered in the manacle, raw and slowly swelling. The lock shivered with it. Time after time, the plastic slipped around the keyway.

"Now we're getting somewhere." Leland spoke two seconds before he came back through the door, allowing me to palm the plastic and pounce back on the mattress, as if I'd lounged the whole time he was raccooning through my car. "I saw the remnants of that tarantula on the walk. You really don't like spiders, do you?" I said nothing. There were plenty of those crawlies around there, and just to fuck with me he might pluck another from his lawn and let it scrabble around under the sheets. "I get it. They're creepy. Good to know, though." He tapped his temple. "I'll file that little factoid away in the safe deposit."

Leland slid a waiter's mini spiral notebook out of his pocket and scribbled. "You removed the plates. Very smart." I rented the most generic car I could; in this case, a silver hatchback. Replaced the plates with a generic dealership placard, so it looked like I'd just bought the thing. "Not as smart as you could be, though. Know what you missed? The VIN." The triumphant bastard sang to me: "The...fucking...VIN."

I didn't own a car. Hence, I didn't know what a *vin* was. *The Vincent?* Leland noticed. "VIN. Vehicle identification number. Right in your glove compartment." The VIN. The fucking VIN. "You know who they tracked down using the VIN?" No guesses from me. "Timothy McVeigh."

The way my left hand stretched over my forehead, I might have been swooning on a fainting sofa. This provided just enough of a blind spot for me to work the lock with my right hand. Clumsy so far, I kept missing the keyhole. My fingers started cramping.

Leland opened a cabinet and produced a laptop. When he sauntered back to the chair, he ignored me while he unfolded it and clacked at the keyboard. I fidgeted with my lock. We could have been miserably married for all the attention we paid one another.

"Eureka," he said dryly to himself. "Got the rental agency." Detective or not, he had access to some kind of restricted information.

The plastic pin snapped. Leland lifted his head and combed over me with his eyes, trying to identify the source of the sound. Blood flushed my face, and my chest rose and fell. After the scan, Leland looked back down at his screen, and I felt between my fingers. Half my plastic needle had dropped behind my pillow, and I choked up on the remaining splinter and found the keyhole again.

Leland typed a number on his cell phone and raised a polite "one sec" index finger. To someone on the other end, he said, "Got something." He read the name and address of the rental agency. "Used a fake name. Draw a five-mile radius around the rental place and check for gyms. She has muscles." He studied my shoulders and legs from across the room. Coming from my captor, the comments about my body again made me uneasy. "Trains with weights. She looks broke, so start with cheapo gyms and mom-and-pop joints. I'll send you a headshot." He hung up, and then angled his camera phone over me. "Cheese." *Flash.* My scowl shot out into the ether.

As he messaged my photo, I felt something magical at my fingertips.

The point of my plastic pick found its pressure point. The cuff unclasped from around my wrist.

Open a rabbit cage and the bunny won't rocket out. Similarly, I stalled to consider my options. Leland still had my car keys. Sprinting to my car wouldn't get me anywhere. If I ran for it, I'd tumble down the grade in clunky heels. The neighbors, if I reached them, might not be home. If they were, they might believe him over the raggedy tower in the white and purple cocktail dress. They might even call the police, and I'd be back to square one.

Another option would be to physically subdue Leland Mumm

and take my keys back. He was strong, but I hadn't gotten the chance to properly fight him.

Right after Christmas last year, the firehouse got a call on Jerrold Avenue in Hunter's Point. Gunshot through the thigh. A massive 300-pounder had just got out of prison and didn't want to go back. Wrestling him down to the stretcher was Herculean, even with a partner. He thrashed around, and between the latex gloves and the blood, our hands were slippery. That guy was like a wet bar of soap, and strong. But when he bashed me in the forehead, I caved in his nose with an elbow and he went limp. If I could immobilize that monster, I could handle the bean pole.

Leland passed on instructions through the phone with his back to me in the bathroom doorway. When I stood, my legs creaked from lying down for so long. I stretched out my fingers to test their strength and rotated my swollen wrist. Stalking toward him, I stayed quiet as a ghost, even in the boots. I snatched a syringe off the floor. Not the winged infusion set I was going to use, but the backup hypodermic, dart-shaped with a two-inch cannula. Extending the plunger with a thumb, I siphoned air into the barrel. I had no idea if an air bubble would actually kill him. The air bubble heart attack was a kind of urban legend, and I'd never tested it. I didn't like the idea of having to stab someone, much less kill him, but I would today. Kali might have come there to dispatch Leland Mumm, but I shouldn't have to explain that this kind of death was a different breed of chinchilla.

I skulked toward the bathroom door, lifting my feet lightly and rolling my soles on the ground. My ribs shook from my heart throbbing. I should have just run for it, but I needed to destroy this man if I wanted to escape. He wasn't ready for me, lollygagging in that doorway on his cell. And as I approached him, I fumed with anger. My face felt hot. I wanted to hurt him.

Leland thanked the person on the other end and disconnected. After a few seconds of heavy silence, he spun, noticing the silence in the room. We stood face-to-face.

"Son of a bitch!"

I lunged with the syringe, but not fast enough. That wiry prick had some fast-twitch muscles, and he dodged me. Maybe I was too hesitant and didn't thrust deep enough to be lethal. Still, I got him the second time. The tip punctured his stomach, but only far enough to break skin, just to the side of the scar he'd told me came from his Arctic knife wound. Someone had taught Leland what to do during a knife attack. Moving with a fluidity that came from trained repetition, he clawed my forearm and twisted me counterclockwise. The hypodermic rattled on the floor. Twist an arm the right way, and the attacker can be on his knees in seconds. A potential game ender. But someone had taught me this move and how to defend against it. I jabbed my free thumb into his neck, and we broke apart, stumbling farther into the bathroom. He tried to say something, but only gargled.

Elbows are a girl's best friend, because the whole body goes into every blow. When Leland covered his throat, his face opened up as a target, and my elbow caught him on the cheek. He reeled back into the shower, cracked the tiles and smeared a little blood on the ceramic. I landed a couple more heavy elbows to his head. When he tried to prop himself up on the tiles, he lost his footing. Backing into the shower stall, his leather sole slipped on the porcelain and Leland collapsed, knees over the tub rim, feet in the air.

I dropped to my knees and used my fists. When Leland threw up his forearms to protect his ears, I got inside and belted his solar plexus. He wheezed, but I didn't debilitate him. An hour ago this guy's body seemed like it could snap like a biscuit, but now his arms rigidly braced over his face. I always knew I was winning in a scrap when my opponent's arms started to get lazy. This guy was a rock. I pounded harder because I could feel how his muscles coiled. Like Ali against the ropes when Foreman was laying into him, he took the punishment and waited for his chance to spring back when I stopped. A disorienting high surged through me, and I stopped thinking about where to place my punches and started whaling on him. Trying to get to his face, most of my punches landed on his arms.

I should have used my legs. Such a dummy, getting down on the floor with him. With legs hanging over the sides of the tub, I could have driven a heel into his shins. Knocked out the knees. It would have been so easy. But I got carried away, fueled by a numbing heat, which made me forget the pain in my right wrist as I brought down both fists with equal abandon. I kept battering, and he just waited until I punched myself out.

The moment I gasped for breath, Leland came alive. One of his hands dropped. He pulled something out of his pocket roughly the size of a small vibrator, not much larger than a lipstick tube. I owned one of these in pink and kept it in my nightstand drawer. In the moment, I thought Leland Mumm might be attacking me with sex toy. He snaked it under my arm, then sprayed me in the face. A moment later, the most intense pain of my life burned my eyes blind.

Pepper spray doesn't necessarily paralyze the victim. On the contrary. With my sockets searing, I went wild. My arms and legs swung like medieval flails. Unsure of where to aim, I flagellated my limbs in all directions. Guttural screams punctuated the movements. Instead of disabling me, the pain only stirred me up. I kicked a dent in the plaster and bashed the sink out of the wall, so it sagged on the pipes. Somewhere in the maelstrom, a distinctive crunch told me I'd crushed the hypodermic under my heel.

Leland had the advantage, and he found a way to evade my punches and kicks. I felt his body maneuver around me, and his arm slithered around my neck from behind. He threw a sleeper hold on me and dragged me back to the bed, my heels sliding on the floor. I thrashed my legs and toppled the bedside chair, but that didn't help me. The handcuff found its way back around my wrist. It hurt more this time when the steel cut against my bones. I scratched some skin with my free hand, but it didn't stop Leland. Seconds later a cuff closed over the other wrist. I lay flat on the mattress again, now with both of my wrists lashed to the bedposts. All I could do was scream in protest.

Sometime between a half hour and an hour later, my eyes registered blurs, the most prominent being a smear shaped like

Leland's face. Hovering over the headboard, my legs couldn't get him. Then he started with the water. He poured water over my eyes and dabbed them with a towel. I thought the prick was waterboarding me and bucked as much as the chains would allow.

"Hold still," he said. "This will make the pain go away faster."

One might think that this kind of pain would limit my ability to speak, but despite the panic, I was able to curse just fine. Someone walking through the front door might have thought they stumbled across an exorcism.

Diligently, Leland Mumm poured the water over me, talking me through it as he went. "I know, it's the worst. I've gotten sprayed three times. Once I nailed myself while making an arrest. I was just starting out. I pointed the thing the wrong way and blasted myself in the face. Can you believe that?" Initially, the water made the pain even worse, like vinegar in a wound, and I writhed in response. "Second time, we were in the same kind of situation, trying to hold down a guy hopped up on PCP, back when PCP was still a thing. My own partner missed the guy and got me." He softened. "Open your eyes to let the water in."

I shook my face and moved every part of my body that I could. The bed bounced on its teak frame.

He waited for me to calm down, and then went on. "Third time was plain trickery. I washed out the canister, and the steam carried some of the vapors into my face. It got in deeper, the way the cold can creep in under your clothes."

I fought the towel, but he found a way to dab my face.

"Kali, hold still. Open your eyes to let the water in." More water drizzled over my face. Some snorted up my nose. "Have you ever taken chemistry class?" He asked.

I responded by howling into his face like a crazy person.

Without raising his voice, he said, "I know you can hear me, and I know you can respond. Have you ever taken a chemistry class? Kali." He stressed *Kali*.

I articulated for the first time since he sprayed me, and my voice croaked from all the screaming. "Yes. I've taken a chemistry class."

"Remember the water fountain? The one you use to flush out your eyes? That's what this is like. I'm flushing out your eyes. You need to open them. It will make the pain go away faster. I promise." Opening my eyes was a challenge, but I did it. The water eventually helped. Eventually, the piercing sting faded to a dull soreness, no more painful than dry eyes after an all-nighter. The skin around them smarted like a mild sunburn.

He picked the chair off the floor and returned to his seat. "You're a dangerous woman, no doubt about it." I squinted, and some of the excess water and tears drained out. Slowly, he came into focus.

"Stops you in your tracks, doesn't it? Nice belly ring, by the way." My dress had torn, and my navel was exposed.

He laughed heartily and patted down his body, especially a few inches left of his navel, where I'd stuck him with the needle. "You almost gave me my own belly button piercing." Now that our tussle was over, he seemed gleeful. "You got me good. I have to hand it to you. *Jesus!*" He prodded around his ribcage where I'd landed some of my deepest punches. "Do you realize how phenomenally *fucked* you are right now? You just assaulted an officer."

"Show me your badge."

"Fair enough." He opened a closet door and found a suit jacket that matched his trousers. From the inside pocket, he pulled out a gold shield and flopped it close to my face. In the time afforded me, I could read the words "Alameda County," and the number "5417." It looked real enough. The moisture drained from my tongue.

"You've never been arrested, have you? Probably never been stopped." I didn't reply, but he guessed the answer. "Lucky duck. Don't worry, I'll guide you through every step of the way."

Having just traded blows, I was less afraid of him. "If this is an arrest, why am I still here?"

"Technically, I haven't arrested you yet. I'm detaining you right now." He retrieved the copy of *The Peaceful End* and thumbed through it in his chair. He breathed deeply as he settled into his seat and cracked the cover. "I'm not sure what to do with you yet."

CPSIA information can be obtained
at www.ICGtesting.com
Printed in the USA
BVOW11s1705120816
458513BV00004B/5/P